"Then take off your coat and avoid hypothermia."

Her bottom lip jutted out. "You first."

He shrugged out of his parka and hung it on a hook by the door, raising one eyebrow as he did so.

She took another long drink then tugged her coat off and hung it next to his. Melting snow dripped onto the floorboards beneath it. Stubborn woman.

"Your lovely flannel shirt is also soaked," he said.

"Yeah, like I'm falling for that."

"Don't flatter yourself. I've seen lumberjacks make flannel sexier than you do."

He didn't know why he was goading her, but he felt on edge… wet, chilled and restless.

"Like you could resist me if I were standing naked in front of you," she said.

She paused, as if she weren't sure how those words came to be floating in the air between them. But there they were, raining down over him like hot sparks. Heat flooded through him, and he could feel his blood pumping. He watched her, the air crackling with awareness. The fire in the stove popped and something tumbled inside. His heart thudded in his chest at the word 'naked.'

"Try me," he finally said.

When finding Mrs. Right goes, oh, so wrong…

All or Nothing

Cheri Allan

~ Book Three ~
A Betting on Romance Novel

Five Oaks Books

All or Nothing

Editing by Orchard Edits
Cover Image Credits:
Logo image © Elena Elisseeva | Dreamstime.com
Candy hearts © Gail Tanski | Dreamstime.com
Candy heart & ring © Studioportosabbia | Dreamstime.com
Corgi puppy © Stephanie Swartz

Publishing History
First Five Oaks Books Edition, 2015
Print ISBN: 978-0-9904815-5-3
Digital ISBN: 978-0-9904815-4-6

Published in the United States of America

Acknowledgements

Thanks to Becka and Connie for suggesting the perfect housewarming presents for my bachelor; to my techie son for helping my techie hero speak the language (all errors are wholly mine); to Mr. Lucas for imagining an epic story that has inspired both real and fictional men and women; and to reality TV hosts everywhere. You have entertained me more than you can ever know.

~ Cheri

Other Titles by Cheri Allan

Luck of the Draw

Stacking the Deck

For my mom,

Because we both like strong heroines who speak their mind. But mostly, because she taught me what it means to be brave.

CHAPTER ONE

THERE ARE FEW THINGS that make a single man more uncomfortable than sitting across from a visibly pregnant woman.

Ian McIntyre pondered the irony of this as his gaze bounced off Valerie's gently rounded belly. She picked up her Styrofoam cup and frowned at him. "Don't give me that look. It's decaf."

His lawyer seemed unfazed by the exchange and continued to drone on about escrows and title fees. He shuffled another paper to the top of the pile and pointed to where Ian should sign. Then he and the seller's attorney stood and shook hands, collected their papers and said their goodbyes, and Ian was left staring at the empty surface of the weathered old table in front of him.

Valerie pushed back her chair and stood up. "Congratulations. This is usually when I hand over the keys and say enjoy your new home."

Ian shrugged, feeling the need to stretch his legs despite the fact that the closing had taken less than twenty minutes. Rather anticlimactic actually. "Guess that'll have to wait."

He pushed back his own heavy wooden chair and thought how ironic it was that an occasion he thought would feel, for lack of a better word, *monumental* would end up taking place in such a nondescript setting.

"When do you start work?" Valerie asked, zipping her briefcase.

He shrugged again. "Jim didn't say. Soon."

She paused and leaned forward. "You're supposed to be happy. You just closed on a property we've been trying to get for eight years. I think this calls for a celebration."

"Thanks, but I'm good."

"Not even coffee? Oh, that's right. You don't drink coffee." She hitched her briefcase strap over her shoulder and smoothed her shirt over her belly. "Neither do I. Much. I've definitely cut back." A wistful smile passed over her features, and for some reason it made Ian's chest tighten. "Well. It's been a pleasure."

"Same here," he said. "Thanks so much. I know it wasn't easy convincing them to sell."

Her lips tilted. "You made a pretty persuasive argument in the end."

He wasn't sure whether she was referring to his tragic backstory (as Val had taken to calling it over the years) or the money he'd thrown at it. No doubt it was the money.

And he had plenty of that.

He stepped into the bright summer sunshine outside the courthouse and looked up and down Sugar Falls' main street at a loss for what to do next. It felt a bit surreal to be standing here on a balmy New Hampshire weekday, the cars buzzing by, a few people walking up to Lucky's for a sandwich or into one of the shops in the old mill buildings as if it were any other day of the week. Which, of course, it was. The fountain his younger brother, Carter, had helped rebuild earlier that summer burbled down by the common, and a handful of young mothers with strollers and toddlers dipped their hands in to stay cool.

Ian smiled noncommittally as a group of men in dress shirts and ties, sleeves rolled up to beat the heat, hurried by him. He wondered what life would be like if he had to punch a clock. He pulled his car keys out of his cargo shorts.

Warm air swirled around him as he drove away from the center of town, toward the rolling hills beyond. The drive was pleasant enough, gently winding, picturesque, hints of Miller Brook popping occasionally into view before he turned off to head up Blackberry Hill. The thick canopy of trees overhead finally parted to reveal the Russell's sprawling farm on the right.

And Ian's new property on the left.

He pulled into the gravel drive, cut the engine, and stared through the windshield. He hadn't actually been to the property in years.

The woods he remembered playing in as a young boy stretched out to his right, behind a rambling stone wall, deep and dark and mysterious. The farm's fields crept up on the left. And the spot where his childhood home once stood was marked with nothing more than a thicket of blackberry bushes and a handful of young poplars.

Ian pushed the car door open and got out. He squinted against the sun as he looked down over the fields, sweat sticking his T-shirt to his chest. He remembered what those fields had looked like on cold fall mornings, the frost heavy on the long, bent grasses, the geese honking to one another as they congregated there, one of their many stops on their way south for the winter.

He knew there was a small seasonal stream that wound through the back woods toward town again. He used to play 'spy' out there with his younger brother, Carter, writing secret messages on the inside of flaps of bark on the white birches and ambushing each other with foam darts.

He turned toward the road. More memories flooded him. Walking home with fresh eggs from the Russell's farm. His dad untying the Christmas tree from the roof of the car. His mom walking toward him, looking so pretty and happy, holding his new little sister in her arms...

It felt odd to stand here after all these years knowing there was a big blank space of time in between the *then* and the *now,* with no more memories, his mother and father and the home he thought would be there forever... gone.

It annoyed him that the property looked so neglected. Once the remains of the house fire had been cleared, the recession had hit. The new owners hadn't been able to build as they'd hoped, and the property had languished.

Then his little brother had gotten engaged, and Ian figured he ought to do something with his life. He'd had his real estate agent, Valerie, approach the owners with a new offer. One they couldn't refuse.

He didn't have a wife, a family, a home or even a dog, but he had more money than he knew what to do with.

And now he had a patch of dirt.

"I thought I might find you here."

Ian started and turned. "Grams! What are you doing here?"

"Just visiting across the way. Hank Russell isn't feeling well. I brought him muffins."

"Plus you were spying on me."

"That, too." She walked carefully over the uneven ground toward him and held out a paper bag. "Muffin?"

"No, thanks."

She pursed her lips. "You don't eat right, Ian. That's not healthy."

"I eat when I get hungry."

"When you remember to come up for air."

He sighed and reached out a hand. Okay, they *did* smell good. "Fine." He opened the bag and pulled out a muffin kept warm by the heat of the day. Blueberry. Grams' specialty. He sank his teeth into one.

"You know, if you got married, you wouldn't have to wait for me to make you muffins."

"Very subtle, Grams. And also very 1950's of you."

She shrugged, undeterred, and rested against the bumper of his car. She pulled a water bottle from her fanny pack. "I'm a product of my

3

generation. What can I say?" She unscrewed the cap and held the bottle out to him. "Are you sure you want to go through with this?"

"My accountant says I need to stop paying rent so I can get a tax write-off for a home office." He glanced at her. "Don't say it."

"I'm being very quiet."

"I can hear you thinking. You're thinking I'm building this house so I can fill it with a wife and family and get back the life I lost when I was eight—and that's pathetic and probably requires psychiatric evaluation."

"You heard that?"

He took the bottle and guzzled. It *was* hot out. "Did it occur to you that, perhaps, I have a fondness for the old architecture? That I feel this site is *made* for the classic New England farmhouse with neoclassical details like layered entablature, elaborate cornice returns, and a deep, inviting porch no one has the money or patience to build anymore?"

"You've been talking to James again, I see."

He finished off the muffin in his hand and fished in the bag for another. "Yes. But he has a point. I'm thirty-four years old, Grams. I've got the means to rebuild an historic structure *and* help out my cousin. Give him a project he's excited to work on. It's a no-brainer and no more complicated than that."

She seemed to ponder this a moment. "Do you not *like* women, Ian?"

Ian choked on his muffin and took a long drink of water. "Excuse me? Yes, I like women!"

She shrugged. "It's okay to tell me. I'm not as old school as everyone thinks."

"I. Like. Women." He stuffed the rest of the muffin in the bag. "It's hot. I'm going home."

Grams trailed after him. "You just don't get out much unless it's alone on one of your hikes. It gets people wondering."

Ian stopped. He knew she wouldn't quit. She was like that. "Grams, it's a small town. Everybody knows the millionaire geek who created Treasure Trakker and lost his parents in a tragic fire. *Everybody*. I've been set up with or conveniently tripped over every available woman my age with a pulse and a smile in five counties—and nothing has worked out. They either wear more flannel than I do, or they can't *wait* to ditch backwoods New Hampshire and never look back. And don't get me started on the women who only see dollar signs and high heels in their future. They don't seem to grasp that the whole *point* of Treasure Trakker is to get people outside and active…"

"Maybe you need to stretch beyond the local pond of fish. If you dated equally successful women…"

He was just about to ask where he was supposed to find these equally successful women when Grams thumped him on the back with her palm as if he were choking.

"I've got it! Don't you worry. I know *just* the person to set you up. She has a 100% success rate!"

"Fantastic." Ian opened the door of his car. "Thanks for the muffins. You let me know when you've found Cinderella."

Grams shut the door on him before he could get in. "It wouldn't hurt for you to listen when I'm speaking. I'm not talking about *my* success rate, although that's none too shabby either."

Ian rolled his eyes which earned him a glare. "You have a success rate of two. *Two* couples, Grams. And while you were around to witness these romances, I hardly think you were instrumental—"

"How incredibly little you know me," she *tsk tsked*. "How would you like to date twenty women from around the country who are beautiful, talented *and* successful?"

"Is this a trick question?"

"You, Ian, could be the next bachelor on the reality show *Happily Ever After!*"

Good thing he wasn't eating still or he would have spewed muffin all over his grandmother. *"What?"*

"It's perfect. The show's host, Marcia Powers, is a matchmaking guru. She'll go through her database of applicants to find the most compatible women to introduce you to, and then all *you* have to do is go on the show and get to know them!"

"Are you freaking kidding me?"

"Watch your language, young man, and, no, I'm not." She opened his car door and set the paper bag with the remaining muffins on his dashboard. "I'll e-mail her when I get home."

"I regret ever showing you how to use a computer."

"You'll thank me in the end."

"I won't, because I will never. *Ever*. Agree. To do this."

CHAPTER TWO

─────────────

Six months later…

"I CANNOT BELIEVE I ever agreed to do this."

"Well get over it, because you signed on the dotted line three months ago, and I don't remember anyone putting a gun to your head." Marcia stabbed the air in front of him with the point of her pen.

"Have you met my grandmother?" Ian asked.

"Little woman? Makes killer blueberry muffins?" Ian nodded. "Yes. Tell her to stop bringing them to the set. My ass has ballooned two sizes since I arrived here. Speaking of my ass, it is on the line big time unless I get you to choose a wife by the time the show airs."

"It's not that simple."

"Of course, it's that simple! You either pick super-model millionaire number *one* or super-model millionaire number *two!"*

"They have names."

Marcia rolled her eyes, her smoky eye makeup and glossy black hair stark contrasts to her vampire-like complexion. "Remind me again? They really do all look alike to me…"

"Look, I did the show. It didn't work. I'm *sorry* but I don't see what can be done. None of them were right for me."

"How can that possibly be? They are *exactly* what you asked for! Gorgeous, beauty queen, all-American good looks, nurturing personalities, good cooks… Hell in a hand-basket— that Hannah? Hailey?"

"Helen."

"Helen is a baker! A *baker*, Ian. Miss Alabama runner-up and a freaking *baker*. God, now you've got me saying it. She volunteers in a community garden and holds cooking classes for kids in the local homeless shelter! I cannot *make* this stuff up!"

"Would you please stop yelling?"

"I am not yelling! You'd *know* it if I were yelling!"

Nick pulled his head from behind the camera. "This is her indoor voice," he agreed.

Marcia whirled. "See? My indoor voice! Now sit down in that chair so we can get this interview finished!"

Ian sat, not because he wanted to, but because a teensy tiny part of him was genuinely scared of Marcia. Or, perhaps it was the way she could turn on a dime from charming to cutting, making her crew scatter with a single look as if they were oil floating on water and she was a single drop of dish soap.

Marcia flung herself into the chair opposite Ian, straightened her v-neck to showcase her boobs and closed her eyes for one deep, centering breath. She opened them. "So, Ian…" she said soothingly, flashing a concerned, empathetic glance at the camera, "I sense you're at a crossroads…"

"Yes, Marcia. You're right." He heaved a sigh. He knew his part by now. "I think I may be gay."

"*Cut!*" she bellowed before ejecting herself from her floral wing chair. "That's it! That is *it!* We're done!"

"Thank God," Ian murmured.

Marcia stabbed a perfectly manicured nail at him. "Not *you.* Everyone else. No, I will not bleed money through the nose on stage hands and handlers and craft services while you take your own sweet time cooperating! No. From now on, it's me, Nick and you—*like glue*—until we have our happily ever after. *Got it?"*

Ian gritted his teeth.

"I'll take that as a 'yes.' You! Bad dye-job! Yes, you! Get me another energy shot before you leave. And some Chai tea. And one of those goddamned blueberry muffins… And somebody tell that hot landscaper guy out front to put a shirt on. He's distracting."

"That's my little brother," Ian ground out.

"Is he single?"

"*No.*"

She shrugged. "Pity."

Marcia flung her hair over her shoulder and stepped around the dozen pizza boxes stacked next to the kitchen island. She turned back toward the faux backdrop and floral wing chairs the crew had erected in Ian's new living room. It hadn't been hard, because he lacked actual furniture of his own. "*Wait.* I'm having a vision," she said suddenly. "I think we need to step back and rethink how we're going about this." She gestured toward Ian. "This is good what you're doing, this wishy-washy attitude, because it's the classic get-what-you-asked-for cold feet. I see it a lot. My viewers have seen it a lot. What we need to do is paint you in a sympathetic light. *Hmm.*" She gestured widely with her hands as if displaying a marquee, "*The Reluctant Bachelor.*"

She stepped back and knocked over a to-go cup of coffee someone had left on the floor. "Oops. Somebody clean…" but the crew had already left for fear of being bellowed at again. "Well, anyway, I'm thinking we need to shoot you at home. Here. In your natural element, as it were." Her arm swept broadly again and she glanced over her shoulder. "After we get somebody to clean it up and stage it so it *looks* like a home, that is… but *then* we change the script from our usual format to: 'Life doesn't go as planned' sort of crap. How sometimes tragedy interferes… *Yadda yadda.* We'll get photos of the fire from the local newspaper. Some shots of the new house… I'm thinking a hand-held camera for this, Nick. Something that feels more intimate and dynamic. Like a documentary feel. What do you think?"

"I think——" Ian began.

"Not *you.*" She turned to Nick.

Nick raised one shoulder. He hadn't stopped filming her. "I think you're beautiful when you're on a roll."

Marcia's pale complexion tinged pink. "Stop," she said coyly. "No, seriously, stop. Why are you still filming?"

"You never know what gems you might find in the editing room."

Marcia opened her mouth but then paused. "Omigod. You are genius. Pure and utter genius on a *stick!*" She turned to Ian and poked a finger at him. "We're not done. Go see if your brother wants a drink of water so he can put his shirt back on. How is it so hot for November in New Hampshire? Who says there's no global warming?"

"It got down to nineteen degrees last night," said Ian. "It's not unusual to go from sixty to snowing this time of year."

"Well *I'm* hot." And with that she marched toward the front door, her pumps clacking like gunshots on the hardwood floor.

Ian stepped off the raised dais where they'd been filming. "She seems to have mellowed some since she left L.A."

Nick rolled his shoulders. He was tall and lanky and had a penchant for plaid flannel shirts. "Don't mock her. She's got a tough job."

Ian didn't bother to comment. Everyone could see Nick and Marcia had some bizarre and twisted dynamic going on. Everyone except Nick and Marcia.

He ran a hand through his hair—now that there wasn't a handler and a makeup person hovering near with a comb and hair gel ready to pounce errant strands back into place. He walked to the kitchen and pulled open a cupboard door to get a cup for water. Empty. He turned on the faucet and stuck his head under to drink straight from the tap.

"Remind me to find your cups."

Ian swiped his mouth with the back of his hand. "Hi, Grams."

"Your brother is almost done with the front walk. Looks beautiful! And thankfully this warm spell we're having kept the ground workable." Grams rummaged in his cupboards. "Have you unpacked *nothing?*"

"I just got back from filming a couple days ago, Grams. There hasn't been time. And they're still doing... stuff."

She stopped rummaging and gathered used to-go cups off the counter and swept them into a nearby pizza box. "Well? Who did you pick? What's she like?"

"You need to stop asking me. You know I can't say."

"Oh, come on! Just a hint? I promise I won't tell!"

"No can do."

"Oh, pooh. You're no fun! Well, I can't wait to see who it is." She swept by him with a bottle of water she'd taken from the fridge and headed toward the front door."

"Neither can I," he muttered.

Marcia strode back in from outside. "...it looks like the base camp for some Outward Bound trip! What's with all the camping gear? Not to mention that basement room with the toys. What grown man owns action figures?" She shuddered. "Okay, punch list: I need home decorations out front. Nothing cheesy. No scarecrows! Think wreaths of fall leaves and pumpkins, Martha Stewart crap, that sort of thing. And this..." she swept her arm toward the living room. "*This* needs to look like a home. A *man's* home. Can we do that? *Please?*"

Marcia's personal assistant, Ivy, stood in the doorway. "You want everyone back? They've left for the hotel." Ivy pulled out her cell phone.

Marcia clamped her hand on the phone to stop her. "Wait. Let me think. *Aargh!* Christian is going to have my head if I keep hemorrhaging money without anything to show for it. I can't keep the whole crew indefinitely. It was a long shot bringing them out here to begin with. No, don't call them all back. We'll skeleton crew from here on out." She looked around. "Ugh. But at a minimum, I *need* this house cleaned top to bottom. And furniture. Who doesn't own furniture?"

"Excuse me? Marcia? I may be able to help you out."

Ian watched in horror as Marcia turned toward his grandmother. Nothing good could come from the two of them talking.

"Grams, right? You're killing me with the muffins. To. Die. For."

"It's the cinnamon. Just a touch. And I use maple syrup as a sweetener." Grams stepped over some power cords. "I know a couple gals who could help you here, and they're local, so you won't have to pay for hotels. One of them is Ian's future sister-in-law. The other is—"

Marcia rolled her eyes. "Oh my God, you people are like hillbillies. Is there no one in this town you're not somehow related to? Fine. I'm desperate. Give Ivy a phone number, and we'll be in touch."

CHAPTER THREE

SHE'D KILL HIM. She'd gut him with this little plastic swizzle stir stick from her coffee and be *thrilled* at how long and tortuous and difficult the task would be, because he deserved to suffer for putting her through this.

"I know you're probably disappointed…" *Oh my God.* The idiot was rambling on, trying to make this somehow right when all she could do is refrain from seeing everything within reach as a murder weapon. The swizzle stick. Her paper placemat. *The sugar pourer.* It was a damned good thing he hadn't shared this news at the garage, or she would have been flush with sharp points and blunt instruments!

"Disappointed," Bailey spit out, her hands shaking from adrenaline, "doesn't even come *close* to describing what I'm feeling right now. How could you do this to me?"

She was going to be sick. She was going to kill this idiot and then she was going to vomit all over his dead corpse. The pie she'd just eaten roiled in her gut as her mind rifled through scenarios of how she could publicly gut Sully right here in the booth of her father's restaurant and still get away with the crime.

"It's early yet. I knew I had to tell you sooner than later so you'd have a chance to make it all work by the closing."

"*How?* How am I supposed to come up with twenty grand in less than a month? Do you know how long it took me to save my half? Do you know how many *years* I've put up with that jackass of an old fart making snarky comments about my ass just so I could get to this point?" She could hear her voice clogging with emotion, could feel the tears threatening hotly behind her lids, and it only made her angrier. "How can you sit there and eat pie—*pie I'm paying for!*—and tell me it'll work out? We don't live in a land of sunshine and unicorn farts, Sully! You've just screwed me. Why couldn't you have come to this revelation last week before we signed the purchase and sale agreement? Huh? *Huh?*"

He ran a hand through his thinning hair. He heaved a sigh. "Frankie wants to go to college, Bails. Nobody ever went to college in our family."

"Then why in hell should they start now? Sully, this is our future you're throwing away. On what? *Frankie?* Seriously? A 17 year-old that doesn't even know how to make the soda machine spit out free drinks? We had a deal. We're partners! I'm screwed if you bail on me now! Hell, I'll probably lose the down payment. *Shit!"* She stabbed the air in front of him with her fork. "You are paying me back if I lose that money, Sully. Do you hear me? You are paying me back!"

Sully dropped a couple bills on the table—as if paying for the damned pie and coffee made up for ditching her at the eleventh hour—and stood up. "I can see you're angry."

Bailey squiggled from the booth and stood to her full five feet three inches. "Angry doesn't even come *close*," she growled.

"I'm sorry."

She watched him go, his dirty, oil-stained workpants sitting low under his beer belly as he shrugged into the canvas jacket of the enemy: Willard's Auto.

It killed her that after all the years slaving away under that smarmy Willard, doing crap timing belt and exhaust repairs while Willard took all the easy, high-profit work like brake jobs and tire rotations. And she was *this close* to buying a shop of her own. *This close* to finally—*finally!*—being her own boss, and it was slipping away like water through her fingers.

She wanted to cry. She wanted to scream. She wanted to rip the damned Willard's Auto patch off Sully's grease-smeared jacket and shove it down his traitorous throat.

"I'll see you 'round," he said, avoiding her eyes.

She choked over the anger and swallowed hard. *"Go to hell."*

The bells over the door of Lucky's jangled as he walked out, taking with him Bailey's last hope of making a new future for herself.

"Oh, honey, you'll figure something out."

"Not now, Wanda," Bailey muttered. She snatched a bar towel off the back shelf and swiped her face with it. "I think I'm gonna hurl."

Wanda swept the table clear of pie plates and coffee cups and nodded in understanding. She'd once been the 'other woman'—the one Bailey's father had finally knocked up and left Bailey's mother for when Bailey was six. But Bailey didn't blame Wanda. She'd had that asshole beating up on her, the guy that would have gone to prison but wound up getting splattered all over lower Main Street and the front of the newspaper after the police stand-off outside that donut shop. No, Wanda had had some tough breaks, and she was good about giving Bailey free pie and coffee. Wanda liked to feed people, so Bailey forgave her for screwing around with and stealing her father who, quite frankly, if he were that easily stolen wasn't worth keeping anyway.

Bailey had long since ceased to be amazed by the number of times her father could build a woman up, just to let her down. Maybe that's what made her so mad about Sully. She should have known better.

She should have only ever relied on herself.

Bailey pushed through the door to Main Street trying to will away the red haze so she could *think* what to do next. Her stomach rolled again.

Shit. Shit, shit, shit, shit, *shit!* What was she going to do now?

She sucked in a ragged breath and blinked at the crisp, November sunshine. Damn.

Someone walked by and said hello, and she waved and pretended her world wasn't falling apart in shattered pieces all around her. She felt like a fish in a fishbowl with curious faces staring in at her wondering when she was going to go belly-up. She sniffed, swiped her face with her arm and then shoved her hands in her jeans pockets. She headed for her car.

The traffic on Main Street hummed behind her. She heard the occasional car door slamming. The too-loud music from some teen's souped-up pickup.

All of it blurred together in the background as her blood roared in her ears. *I'll see you 'round.*

She tried to separate the words from the burning in her lungs, but she couldn't. Sully wouldn't know that was the very worst thing he could have said to her.

He couldn't have known that those were the last words her dad had said all those years ago—right before he'd picked up his suitcase and walked out of their home to be with his new wife and baby.

The roaring grew louder and her vision dimmed. She stumbled to the edge of the gravel employee lot, gripping the rear bumper of Wanda's Taurus and threw up all over the dried remains of golden rod growing there, hot tears burning the backs of her eyes.

Oh God. Oh God. Oh God…

Her life was spinning out of control… again. Just when everything seemed right. Out of nowhere, *this happens.*

SHE COULDN'T SAY HOW long she knelt there, at the edge of the parking lot, the gravel digging into her knees through the fabric of her jeans. Then she heard the sound of voices and realized the crew from the machine shop were probably headed out for their afternoon smoke break. What a pathetic picture she'd make.

She spit, took a shuddering breath and fumbled for the tin of breath mints in her coat pocket before pulling herself upright. She had to pull it together.

She nodded to the guys, popped a breath mint in her mouth, and walked to her car.

The trees on either side of the road were now bare of leaves, letting the pale blue sky filter through their branches. The air was unseasonably warm, and she rolled down the windows to let the fresh air clear her head. She drove half-way up Blackberry Hill before she pulled off by the side of the road. Her hands still shook on the steering wheel.

She grabbed a water bottle from the back seat and went to the edge of the woods to rinse her mouth again and then took a long, cool drink. She needed to think. Liz would know what to do. She'd call her.

Bailey pulled her cell out of her pocket and dialed her best friend's number. It still seemed unreal that Liz was back in Sugar Falls after all these years. And getting married.

Meanwhile, it felt like her own life had just spun out of control, crashed through a guardrail, careened down a snowy embankment and landed on its roof.

At least she had cell service here.

"Hello!"

"Hey, it's me." Bailey cleared her throat. "Life sucks and I'm screwed. What's new with you?"

Liz chuckled. "Well, I'm engaged to Mr. Wonderful, planning my dream wedding, and I have a job for us! Wait. What did you just say?"

"Nothing. Nevermind. Go back to dreaming about your hunky hubby-to-be. So, um, what kind of job? Does it pay well?"

"I don't know what the going rate is. What's good pay for cleaning a house and styling it to look like a cozy home?"

"Twenty grand, give or take."

"Um. Not that much."

Figures.

"Bailey? What's going on?"

"Nothing I want to get into right now. Tell me about the job. I could use a distraction."

"Oh, thank you! I tell you, I'm swamped with wedding planning. We've got to nail down the menu, I'm up to my eyeballs making centerpieces, and the fitting is next week. Don't forget."

"It'll be the highlight of my week to try on a frilly dress for you."

"Wait until you see it in person. You'll love it! Ooh, but right now I need you to pop over to Carter's brother's new house and sparkle it up so I can stage it. Their grandmother just called me. I guess they need the place transformed into a home ASAP, and they're working on a skeleton crew from L.A., so who do you think they called to do the work?"

"I'm guessing nepotism is alive and well?"

"Yes it is, and I'm not afraid to take advantage of that fact. *My* staging job Bailey, *my design ideas,* will appear on national television! How cool is that? But before I go in to work my magic, I hear it needs some clean-up first, so that's where you come in."

"Perfect."

"I'll split the money with you." Liz quoted a number. It was not disappointing when one was looking at a gaping maw of a down payment to come up with in less than thirty days.

"When do they want me there?"

"Thirty minutes ago."

"I'm headed there now." Time enough to panic later.

CHAPTER FOUR

IAN RUBBED HIS NECK and stretched, glad to be back in the saddle, not that he'd ridden a horse a day in his life. He glanced around at his new "office" feeling happy he'd gotten the space set up again at least. Most people wouldn't build a new home and then move into the basement, but it was quiet and dark down here so there was no glare on his monitors, and he could set up his equipment and disappear into a familiar world for a while. Plus, Marcia had vetoed him spreading his "nerd crap" all over the upstairs until after filming was complete.

It had been two hours of complete bliss. Ever since he'd arrived back in New Hampshire three days ago, his new home had been a construction zone of set prep and crew members parading through.

This was probably the first time he'd been in the house alone.

He thought about his old apartment near downtown Sugar Falls. It had been in one of the old mill buildings, small but quirky, with industrial-age charm, a view of the Connecticut River and within walking distance of most anything he'd ever wanted. Simple.

He chuckled wryly to himself.

He'd left 'simple' six months ago. He knew he should feel grateful for the great job his cousin, Jim, had done in building the new house in such a short timeframe. Jim had expertly overseen the dozens of electricians, insulators, plumbers, roofers, sheetrockers, and painters, and now there were only a handful of punch-list items still to check off. The house was so new you could still smell the faint odor of fresh paint. And yet, it didn't feel like a home.

If you asked Grams, she'd insist it needed a woman's touch.

He grimaced a bit thinking of all the women he'd met on the show, women who assured him they wanted nothing more than to move to rural New Hampshire and settle down with him to make a home. He hated to admit how creepy he'd found it how desperate these women were to throw themselves at him, a complete stranger. Were their lives so empty they'd do anything to escape?

They hadn't all been like that, of course. Some had hung back a bit. Some, like Leah, had been more shy. One or two had been more of the shots and funnels crowd. Then there was the one he was convinced Marcia had thrown in because she was so nutso she threw all the others into a positive light.

All he remembered of that first week was a blur of women with tight clothes and tighter smiles all vying for one-on-one time to talk to him *meaningfully* about life and marriage and babies, alternating with ridiculously contrived group outings to public places where the noise of the show's crew and gawking fans and female chatter was enough to make him regret ever agreeing to give it a shot.

And why had he? Why had he agreed to put himself out there and make a spectacle of himself? Was *he* that desperate? That lonely?

He breathed out, slowly and deliberately, letting the air out silently. Maybe. Shit, *yes.* But traveling to the land of many boob-jobs, parading himself on national television and forcing himself to smile through all of Marcia's ridiculous 'challenges' hadn't made it any better either. In the end it had only made it abundantly clear he didn't have a clue what in hell he wanted.

But months ago, when Grams had first heard back from the show, when he'd stood on his new land and looked down toward the town of Sugar Falls in the distance, he'd convinced himself *this* is what he needed. He'd convinced himself he wanted a home, a wife, a mother for his future family. He was nearly thirty-five. Older than his little brother—the college drop-out whom no one ever thought would make anything of himself—and even Carter was getting married in a month. Grace, his little sister, was sensitive and free-spirited and yet even she was settling down, working to create a business for herself. Settled in her life. They were happy and whole.

What was he?

He was a video game developer who liked to hike and didn't know what the next step in life was. How could he, in good conscience, ask someone to share a future he couldn't even picture himself? It wasn't as if he hadn't tried to make it work. He'd listened and chatted and winnowed his choices until he'd narrowed it down to two.

Oh, sure, his family had liked both final girls. They'd fallen all over themselves to welcome each woman with open arms and relieved smiles, as if they'd somehow worried that Ian, who holed up in his apartment with his computers for company, would turn out to be the lonely bachelor uncle.

And despite an underlying uncertainty, as the season played out, he'd honestly enjoyed his time with each woman. When he and Mary Beth had been dropped in the middle of the desert and told to hike to safety, she'd been a trooper—even when the rattlesnake had cuddled up to her during the night. And Helen? He'd been overwhelmed with being given a dozen preschoolers to take on tour through Manhattan culminating in a pizza party at an arcade, but she'd been amazing at it, linking the kids together like a 'dragon' and slithering through the crowds of people. His heart had been hammering in his chest, but she'd made staying together fun and she even remembered to special-order gluten-free pizza for the girl with allergies.

Ian scrubbed his face again. He knew he was hiding, knew that as much as he wanted to wash his hands of the whole disaster that the *Happily Ever After* show had become, he needed to see it through. He owed it to the women who came on the show to meet him hoping he'd make them magically happy.

Plus, he'd signed that damned contract.

He leaned over and grabbed his hiking shoes from under his desk. He'd grab a water and get some fresh air. One step at a time. He couldn't ask any more of himself. Marcia couldn't ask any more of him. He couldn't *make* himself fall in love.

Hell, maybe Marcia was right. Maybe he had cold feet and was worried about making a mistake. He *cared* about both women. He cared so much, in fact, he didn't want to hurt them by taking things further until he was absolutely sure it was the right choice.

HE PADDED UP THE STAIRS, walking through the living room. Man, this house had a lot of windows. Had the original? He didn't remember feeling this exposed as a kid. Granted, it wasn't an exact replica of his childhood home; it was more evocative. He'd given his cousin, Jim, free reign to update for modern living while retaining the character and general layout of the original.

Still, it felt new. Foreign. Which shouldn't surprise him, but it did. Maybe once he got back to work his life would feel normal again. Whatever normal was.

Ian waved to his younger brother through the front window as Carter threw the last of his tools into his pick-up. Carter made a twirling motion near his ear and pointed toward Marcia who was still on the front lawn huddled with Nick and Ivy. She turned and gestured toward the house and caught Ian watching. She scowled. Ian backed out of view.

Cripes. He should probably get used to that look of disappointment. In six weeks, they'd start airing his season, and soon enough he would be forever known for delivering the least romantic line in history. Not once. *Twice.*

I just don't see myself running into a burning building for you.

He retreated down the hallway. So now he was hiding. From his friends. His family. Hiding in his own laundry room—the only room in the house without windows—with three months of dirty laundry and...

"Who the hell are you?"

Ian stared at the unknown woman as she raised one perfectly arched eyebrow at him. "I'm your cleaning lady," she said.

"I don't have a cleaning lady."

"You do now. Your grandmother sent me over. My mother does her hair. Name's Bailey." She didn't offer her hand. Just as well. He didn't want it, especially seeing as she was wearing gloves that looked like they belonged to a hazmat crew.

Christ. He didn't need a cleaning lady. He certainly didn't need some stranger with sloppy, stubby blonde ponytails and a T-shirt with cartoon dogs promoting a local microbrewery (no matter how good their stout winter lager might be) picking through his dirty laundry. He'd clean it himself, thank you very much. "Ms. Bailey, I've got this covered. Go home."

"No."

"I beg your pardon?"

"Do you know what I had to go through to get in here? I've had gynecological exams that were less invasive. If I don't come out smelling like window cleaner and carrying a bag of trash, those guys having a tailgate party out on the road are going to paste my face on every tabloid as one of your reality show wannabes. No way. No thank you." She arched that brow again and looked around the small room. "I hope you have a boatload of laundry detergent. We're gonna need it."

"What?" What guys?

"Soap. For cleaning." She drew the last word out long and slow as if she were speaking to a non-native speaker with a brain injury.

His stared at the stubborn set of her jaw for all of three seconds and shrugged. She'd grow tired of this game soon enough. "Fine. Snoop around. But I've lived in hotel rooms longer than this house. You won't find anything."

"God, I hope not." She proceeded to pick a pair of boxers from the floor and throw them with ill-concealed disgust into a growing pile in the corner. "Are you just going to stand there and stare at me all afternoon? If so, they're going to have to pay me extra."

He blinked. What was there to stare at aside from those godawful rubber gloves that made her look like she was prepping to clean a crime scene? "I'm not paying you anything."

She paused long enough to roll her eyes. They were bright blue, slightly slanted and flashed at him. She looked like an annoyed elf. A really hot elf that didn't give a shit what he thought about her. Shit. He *was* staring. "Not you. *The network*," she enunciated slowly. "You know, the one you screwed over by proving once and for all that nobody finds love on a reality matchmaking show? Oh my God, what is *on* this?" She held a shirt at arm's length toward him.

He focused on the shirt. "Chocolate."

"Are you sure?" Her nose wrinkled. "It looks like... something else."

"It's chocolate. They had a fondue fountain thing on one of the group dates. It got a little crazy that night."

"And nobody thought to wash it? Or throw it out?"

"I have fond memories of that shirt."

She tossed it into the laundry sink. "Yeah, of going bare-chested on national television, no doubt. Good times. Good times." She poured from the jug of detergent into the washer, loaded an armful of clothes and started pressing buttons. Good thing she knew how it worked, because he hadn't a clue. "Okay, Lover Boy, where are your trash bags? And by the way, Bailey is my first name, not my last."

As if it mattered to him. "Who says I didn't find love?"

Her eyes scanned him dismissively from his hair to his toes. "Just a hunch."

"You can tell this just by *looking* at me?"

She sighed. "Converse sneakers. No socks. Cargo shorts. A T-shirt so faded it looks like you've had it since high school. And you need a haircut."

"Oh my God. The inhumanity of it. How can you stand to look upon me?"

"You're a Peter Pan. You dress like a child, play video games for a living and save chocolate-soaked shirts. Trust me, I know your type. You'll never grow up."

"Says Tinker Bell."

"Don't call me that."

"Oh, I see. You can call me names, but I can't give you my first impression? Who's acting childish now?"

He stared at her, feeling, yes, slightly victorious and a little turned on.

Her lips compressed. They were lush and lightly pink. She didn't wear lipstick.

"I swear I'll charge extra if you insist on watching me," she said.

He took a step back, mentally shaking himself. "Don't flatter yourself. I've got better things to do." He didn't know what, but he'd think of something.

She spoke again. Her back to him. "Liz will be over later to start moving out that fake living room, so don't disappear. Oh, and if I were you, I wouldn't go walking around naked in front of your windows, I wasn't kidding about the paparazzi."

"I do not intend to—" He stepped into the hallway and peered out a window. A couple of vehicles he'd never seen before were parked on the road even though Marcia and her crew were now gone. "Are you freaking kidding me?"

"Nope. And at least one of them has a super long lens."

"Un-fucking-believable." Ian wasn't prone to swearing, but this was too much. He had to ask Liz about getting shades installed. He felt like a fish in a fishbowl.

"Oh, boo-hoo. You signed up for this. The show paid you a pretty penny from the looks of it, so I don't know what you're complaining about."

He poked his head around the laundry room door again. "Are you always this opinionated?"

She shrugged. "Yes."

"Well, keep your opinions to yourself while you're here if you don't mind. I'm getting socks." He had no idea why he'd just announced that.

He shook his head and walked away. He got as far as the bedroom before he realized he still hadn't gotten his water. He stood in the open door of his bedroom, listening to the sounds of indistinct muttering and water running.

Since the show began, he had become oddly accustomed to strangers occupying his personal space...camera men, set designers...hair and makeup people. But nothing about this woman felt customary. She felt... It felt...

He strode back to the laundry room, refusing to put a name on how he felt—or to allow this woman to come between him and the refrigerator when he wanted a damned bottle of water.

21

"Would you stop that?" he said.

"I'm almost done."

"I've changed my mind. I want you out."

She tossed a crumpled T-shirt onto a pile. "That Marcia chick warned me you'd be touchy."

"I'm touchy? *I'm* touchy?"

"Yes. Too many hot women to choose from? Oh, the trials…" She peered at a stain on another shirt and threw it in the laundry sink.

Ian's jaw gaped. "Excuse me? Let's back up the train, shall we? I'm not in *your* house rifling through *your* laundry pile and making sarcastic comments about *your* life. I can't believe a pipsqueak like you has the nerve to call me touchy." He took a step back, surprised by his own outburst. Something about the woman made him feel unsettled.

"Did you just call me a pipsqueak?"

He leaned against the door jamb and fought a smile. "It can't be the first time."

She slammed a pair of pants onto a pile. "How *dare* you?" she breathed as she struggled to step over the mound of laundry and stumbled toward him, stripping off her rubber gloves. "I do *not* need this grief!"

He stepped aside to let her by. "You're leaving? I'm crushed."

She pushed past him into the hall. "I may be small, but I am *not* to be underestimated."

"What are you going to do? Kick my shins?"

She turned, her eyes flashing, as if she were considering it. "How about I tell those guys at the end of your driveway I saw you naked, and I'd be surprised if you found a woman willing to take a guy who had such a *teeny, tiny*—"

"*Whoa!*" Ian took two long strides and blocked her path to the front door. "Really? We're going there? Who the hell are you and why did my grandmother send over a rabid chipmunk to clean my house?"

He could have predicted this. She kicked him in the shin.

"Ow. *Ow!* Stop that!" he held his hands on her shoulders as she tried to kick him again as if they were six year-olds on the playground. For some reason he found it amusing. And arousing. Lord help him. "Stop! We are adults!"

"If I'm a rabid chipmunk then you're a pig!"

"Am I being punked?" Ian tried to peer out the front door's sidelight while still holding the crazed, spastic, much-stronger-than-she-looked woman at arm's length. "Could you *please* settle down? I'm sorry about the chipmunk crack. I admit that was out of line."

22

She glared at him. "I'm *only* doing this for the money," she said, her breath coming quickly.

He eyed her warily. "And this is supposed to be reassuring how?"

She heaved a sigh and stilled. "You can let me go now."

"No. Not until you answer some questions and we set some ground rules. Rule number one: no kicking. Or spreading of false rumors. One is dishonest, and the other hurts like hell."

She rolled her eyes. "Fine. Like you're never dishonest? Like you were perfectly honest with all those desperate women on the show? Right."

Ian thought about his least romantic line. No, lying to women was probably not his issue.

"Rule number two: we cut the insults. I'll stop referring to your height disability, and you stop making unflattering assumptions about my character... and anatomy."

She gave him a mutinous look. "Fine."

"And last... far be it for me to poke the bear, but are you always this easily provoked?"

"Only on days when my *ex*-partner leaves me high and dry and tells me he's still sleeping with the enemy!"

He wanted to let the comment go; he intended to let it go; he *should* let it go. Instead, he said, "Ah. So your boyfriend cheated on you?" Okay. Yeah. He was annoyed, but he wasn't completely cut off from his sensitive side.

She frowned. "No. My would-be business partner just backed out three days *after* we signed a P&S agreement on a new garage, which means *I* have to come up with *his* share of the down payment or we... damn it... *I*... won't qualify for a loan!"

"A garage?"

"Yes. A garage. Not that it's any of your business."

He raised an eyebrow. "You brought it up."

"Yeah, well it just happened two hours ago. Seems he thinks he'll need the money to pay for his kid's college. Hello? I've seen Frankie. He'd be lucky to graduate summer camp."

"Tough break. Maybe you'd like to come back another time when you're feeling more yourself." Like never.

She huffed out a breath and rolled her shoulders. "No. I'm good. I just need to work off the frustration. Point me toward the trash bags. And do you have any chocolate? I ate my last Snickers wading through all the paperwork that Marcia lady gave me to sign. Good God. I think I sold her my soul."

Ian frowned. "You probably did. Did you read it?"

"Most of it. My eyes were glazing over near the end. It's just boilerplate stuff anyway. They'll send the secret service after me if I take pictures of you or the staff or the set or talk about you or the show or the network with any of my friends, my family, my dentist or space aliens. I cannot mention you or the show or the network or anything I've seen or heard or thought I've seen or heard in any format—digital or print or as-yet-to-be-invented—to my friends, my family, casual acquaintances or on social media, blah, blah, blah…" She made a dismissive gesture with her hand and wandered toward the kitchen. "Do you have *any* food? Snacks? Coffee? I missed lunch."

He shook his head and brushed by her on the way to the fridge, pretending he wasn't hyperaware of her compact body in those worn-out jeans and that ridiculous T-shirt. She didn't even wear makeup. Maybe he was just shocked, because she was the first woman he'd seen in the past three months who didn't walk around dressed to kill 24/7. Hell, half the women on the show wore makeup *to bed*.

He opened the refrigerator door and grabbed a water bottle. "I have water and whatever craft services left in here before Marcia sent them all home. I'm going back to my office."

"Where are your trash bags?"

He shrugged. "You're clearly adept at scavenging. Knock yourself out."

BAILEY WATCHED HIM STRIDE away and disappear down the cellar stairs. She blew out a breath through her nose.

That went well.

But in her own defense, she'd had a pissy day. She deserved to have a bit of an airing of grievances. The shin-kicking may have been a teensy bit excessive, but there was nothing she could do about it now.

She yanked open the fridge and shoved some random, plastic-wrapped platters around. *There.* That looked good. She pulled out a pre-made sandwich of some sort, grabbed a bottle of water, and knocked the door closed with her elbow. Not seeing any napkins or clean surfaces, she shrugged, bit into her sandwich and hoisted herself onto the counter-top, adroitly catching her sandwich before it fell to the floor.

She chewed and pondered this new turn of events.

Con: Sully had sent her up the creek, and she was royally, completely pissed. See if she bought him a pound of his favorite salt water taffy for Christmas this year!

Pro: Liz had called her right before she'd left to do something angry and possibly illegal—like slash Sully's tires or write insults on his restored Camaro with a cutting torch—and offered her a job.

Con: The job had to be with Ian, Liz's future brother-in-law, stuck-up internet game developer and obvious womanizer. Who else would sign up for *Happily Ever After* but a horny guy that just wants to get laid?

Pro: Ian was smokin' hot.

No. Wait. That was a con. He'd insulted her. She didn't like him. Even if he did make her traitorous blood hum *zippity-doo-dah* through her veins standing there in an old T-shirt that was probably soft as butter and clung to his athletic, wiry build like a second skin. Not that she'd noticed or anything.

Damn.

She could *not* be turned on my Liz's future brother-in-law. That was just. *Ew.*

So not going to happen.

There was something obviously wrong with him if he looked *that* flippin' good and was *still* single. He was obviously an adolescent at heart—he made video games for crying out loud.

Still, she was annoyed with him, not *dead*. And Ian had that edgy, sinewy body type that was her all-time, major man weakness. Like a lust-filled Achilles heel. Damn him.

She wolfed down the rest of the sandwich, guzzled the water and launched herself off the counter. Better. If she didn't eat on a regular basis… as in throughout the day… she tended to get a bit impatient. (Some said cranky.) She shook off the lingering lustful thoughts for the man-geek who had disappeared to his basement lair and decided to get to work.

Bailey found a box of trash bags stuffed in a cupboard and proceeded to collect the worst of the debris and set it by the front door. She looked around for basic cleaning tools (e.g. a broom or dust pan) and found absolutely nothing. Huh. Usually the clients provided everything. Usually they had furniture.

Fine. She'd come back with her own cleaning supplies. While it was new, the house had the usual bits of random dust and such from construction as well as the mess and props left from the filming crew. Liz had implied that she'd want help with staging things once they started unpacking... not that any of this nickel and diming would give Bailey the twenty grand she needed to make up for Sully bailing on her.

Bailey stalked over to the basement stairs and pounded on the door. She didn't bother to wait for a reply. "I've done as much as I can for the moment. I'll have to come back, because I can't find a broom or vacuum or anything." She waited. Nothing. Not even a grunt.

She walked down the steps into the basement. It smelled of fresh-sawn lumber and new concrete. Ian was sitting at a long folding table set up with computer equipment with his back to her, a pair of headphones over his ears.

"Make sure to sign this version with at least a 512-bit hash and add a remotely fetched hash key... No, it's not overkill. If you leave it as 256-bits, anyone could hack in and do a redirect from the app." He blew out a frustrated breath. "Is Cam there? He knows what needs to happen. Fine. Have him call me."

He clicked some keys and muttered to himself. "Idiots. Are they asking for someone to inject a fake site?"

"Hi," she said.

"What the—? What is wrong with you?" he sputtered, yanking off his headphones. "You shouldn't sneak up on people like that."

"Don't you know you should never put your back to the door? It's bad Feng Shui."

He scowled, all dark brooding manly man. Good lord she needed to get out more. "What do you want?"

"I've bagged up the trash and am waiting on the laundry, but I can't find any cleaning supplies. Do you own a broom?"

He pointed to the far side of the basement which was stacked with boxes. "I did. It's probably somewhere over there."

Bailey picked up a large long box to move it.

"Hey, be careful with that!" Before she knew it, Ian had sprung from his seat and was carefully lifting the box from her hands.

"What's in that?"

"It's a collector's item. Very delicate."

"You've piqued my curiosity. Blow-up girlfriends usually don't break."

"Do I look like the kind of guy who needs a blow-up girlfriend?"

Okay, no. "What's in the box?"

"None of your business."

"It's my business if I have to clean it. Or unpack it to help Liz stage the house..."

"I'll unpack this one."

"You know my imagination is running wild here. It's an awfully long and lightweight box. Maybe it's—"

He heaved a sigh like he was reluctant to admit… "It's a lightsaber."

"A what?"

"It's a lightsaber," he said. "A collector's edition."

"Seriously?"

"I don't want to hear your snarky comments. I bought it years ago when I got my first royalties from Treasure Trakker. It was an impulse buy. Plus, I thought it looked cool."

"Can I see it?" Her pulse kicked up a notch.

"Why?"

"Because I don't believe you."

"I don't care what you believe."

"Anyone I know who owned a collector's edition lightsaber would *want* to show it off."

"You'll break it."

"I won't. I promise. Let me see it."

He frowned. "You're only pretending to be interested."

"I'm not. What color is it?"

He rolled his eyes and went to set it out of her reach. "Blue."

"Oh, so it's only a Force FX and not a limited edition replica hilt?"

He blinked at her. His head tilted. "You're telling me you've watched *Star Wars*? And *liked* it?"

"Is that so hard to believe? It's a good story. I wasn't a fan of the prequels, though. They were milking a stone with those."

He looked at her funny. "I agree."

"So, can I see it? How heavy is it? I've always wondered whether the hilt replicas really felt like the real deal in your hand. Are they heavy?"

"They're made from machined aluminum, brass and copper— depending on the episode—so, yeah, they weigh six or seven pounds versus the FX ones. Those only weigh about three pounds."

"Better for actual battles than those retractable kids' ones, I'll bet."

"They're a hundred and fifty bucks a piece! You don't have battles with them."

She reached for the box again on tiptoe. "So what *do* you do with them?"

"You look at them."

"Huh. That seems kind of boring."

"That's being an adult."

"Says the man with a lightsaber collection. Fine. I don't need to see it. It's only Luke's." She began pushing other boxes aside in search of something that might contain a broom.

"What's that supposed to mean? Luke's weapon is iconic."

She shrugged. "*Meh.* I'd rather have a blaster."

"That's just a glorified gun."

"It was good enough for Han Solo."

He rolled his eyes. "So that's where this is going? Every woman has the hots for Han. I suppose you wanted to be Princess Leia growing up."

She wrinkled her nose at him. So he was sexy but sexist. "No. I wanted to be Han. He was awesome."

"He was a smuggler. A criminal."

"That's just it. He wasn't accountable to anyone but himself. He was free."

"Free with a bounty on his head. Did you even *see* Episodes V and VI? Carbonite? Jabba the Hut?"

"There are always setbacks to being free."

"Like nearly being fed to the rancor. That thing would make quick work of you. You'd be nothing but a snack."

"I could take him," she said.

"You must have never watched it on the big screen then." He visibly shuddered. Probably for her benefit.

"Kind of hard to do that. It hasn't been in theaters in years. I've only seen it on a TV."

"You're missing out. The big screen is the only way to watch it. That's why I have a media room."

"Get out!" She slapped his bicep. It was pleasantly firm. Not that she noticed. "You have a media room?"

He shrugged. "It's not all set up yet, but I will. You can come see for yourself when I do."

She gave him a look. "Yeah, sure. So I can clean it with the broom you don't own? Thanks."

His gaze ran down her body from her old T-shirt to her grease-stained jeans. "I thought you were a mechanic."

Right. Not a woman he'd want to get cozy with in his 'I'm-so-rich-I-have-a-room-dedicated-to-movie-watching' room.

He couldn't have been more obvious about what he thought of her if he'd rented ad space on the Goodyear blimp. And just like that, she lost interest in his collection of Sci-Fi toys. And him. "I'm heading out. Tell Liz I'll catch her later. In the meantime, buy a broom."

"I'm not buying anything, because you have no reason to be back."

She swept by him with all the dignity she could muster. "Oh, I'll be back, all right. I need the money." She let her gaze slide over him. "And you obviously need the help."

CHAPTER FIVE

BAILEY TOSSED HER KEYS on the Formica-topped divider between the kitchen and living room that her mother insisted on referring to as the "island" and shrugged out of her jacket. "Mom? I'm home! I got the milk, but I couldn't find the cereal you like, so… where are you?"

"In my room."

Bailey started down the hall and tossed her jacket onto her bed. Her mom's door was ajar, so she nudged it open, "So, I picked up some—"

Her mother leapt from the full-length mirror and shrugged her robe onto her shoulder, belting it hurriedly. "What are you doing barging in like that?"

"The door was open."

"Can a woman not have her privacy?"

Bailey shrugged and hovered by the door. Her mom's face had flushed red and she was straightening the dozens of hair care products and cosmetics on her dressing table with shaking hands.

"What's wrong with you? And why are you not dressed? It's Wednesday. Shouldn't you be heading to Lucky's for Trivia Night?"

"I wasn't feeling well. I asked Meg to take my last blow-out and came home. I don't think I'll go."

"You're going to *miss* Trivia Night?"

Bailey wasn't sure what to make of this. Trivia Night was an institution at Lucky's, and her mother prided herself on finding the most obscure and entertaining questions to stump the crowd of regulars.

"Have you called Daniel to cancel? You know he always has Wanda prepare an extra-large batch of wings on Wednesdays. Can't you take an aspirin or something?"

"I said, I'm not feeling up to it. Someone else will have to fill in for me. Like you."

"What? No. You can't make me go down there." Bailey backed toward the door.

"Oh, stop. I've got all the questions prepared."

"You're not vomiting. Are you feverish?" Bailey pressed a hand to her mother's forehead. "It's cool. I think you'll be fine. It's only a couple of hours. You haven't missed a Wednesday in three years…since the time that woman lied about using color and you accidentally turned her hair orange the day before her wedding."

Her mother pushed Bailey's hand away and grabbed a stack of papers from her bed. "Here. I've printed out the questions. It's not rocket science. Wanda can give you pointers, but she's covering the deep fryer tonight on account of Skye's woman issues." She said this last bit on a sad, sympathetic note.

Skye's woman issues were, in fact, extremely heavy and painful periods, which, let's be honest, sucked. They were debilitating, sometimes dangerous, and seemed a cruel trick of fate for her younger half-sister who was as sweet as the desserts she made for the pub. But, when 'that time' hit, everyone pitched in and didn't mention it until Skye was back on her feet.

Her mother held the papers toward her. "Go on. It's the family business. For once, help your father out."

"I wish you wouldn't call him that."

"Why? He *is* your father."

"He was a sperm donor that knocked you up and left you."

"He was my husband, may I remind you. We had an amicable parting of ways, and he paid for me to go to beauty school."

"And that makes up for abandoning his wife and child?"

Her mother blew out a breath in exasperation. "He didn't abandon anyone, Bailey. We parted ways, because our lives were moving in different directions. I cannot believe we have to discuss this again. Now." Her mother's face wore a pained expression which made Bailey feel bad.

"I'm sorry. I've just had a sucky day. Sully bailed on me. So, I've got until the end of the month to figure out how I'm going to come up with the money for the down payment on the garage, or I'm screwed."

"How much do you need?"

Bailey told her. Her mother sat on the edge of the bed. "You could ask your fa—"

"*No.*"

"You'd refuse his help if it meant you would be able to start your own business? You'd be that stubborn?"

"In a word: yes. And you're assuming he'd have that sort of cash lying around waiting to invest in my future when he's never paid for anything else. Why would he start now?"

"Honey, I told him I didn't want child support."

"What? Why would you do that?"

"I wasn't sure you were his."

Bailey staggered a couple steps and found the little padded bench by the dressing table. She sank down onto it. She was nearly thirty years old and *this* is how her mother chooses to tell her she might or might not be an Adams? "What? You mean Daniel is *not* my father?"

"Well, yes, he is. Anyone with eyes can see the family resemblance now, but back then… well, I'm not proud of the fact, but the reason your father may have strayed was because I was… experimenting."

"Experimenting?"

"Sexually."

"Oh, dear God in heaven…"

"Now, it's not what you think."

"La la la la la!"

"I know to look at me now you wouldn't guess this, but I haven't always been this confident in myself. And I was not very experienced growing up. Your grandparents, God rest their souls, were quite strict. I was curious about things."

Bailey stared at her mother in horror. "Please. Don't. I beg of you."

"Why? It's perfectly natural to have urges in life. I've never questioned your comings and goings, have I? We're all human. And Danny was so good about letting me stretch my wings."

"Ew. Just… ew!"

"Naturally, I couldn't be hypocritical. If we were going to have an open marriage…"

"*Gah!*"

"…I needed to let him experiment as well."

Bailey struggled to stand up. "Give me the papers. I'll do it. Just… stop talking."

"Honey, you needed to know eventually. I can't have you going through life thinking your father isn't responsible. He's a good man, we just moved in different directions."

"Yeah. He'd already moved into Wanda's bed when you were pregnant with me, and then knocked up two other women for good measure!"

"In his defense, I didn't tell him right away. He did stick around until you were in kindergarten."

"*Gah!*" Bailey walked toward the door. Her mother trailed after her.

"You shouldn't suppress your sexuality, honey. It's not healthy."

Bailey stopped and spun toward her mother. "You know what's not healthy? The twisted, dysfunctional, distorted reality of our extended, inter-bred collection of DNA. How can I *possibly* have a healthy sexuality when I cannot even safely *date* in this town?"

Her mother blew a long breath through expertly-lined, red lips. "I'm sorry I ever suggested that dating service. But I don't understand why we can't put it behind us. It was a one-time fluke."

"Excuse me? I got matched with my own siblings three times. *Three times!* And once was Skye! My own sister!"

"You do have a semi-masculine name. It could go either way. And with your occupation…" Her mother made a helpless gesture with her hands. "Can we really blame them?"

Bailey blinked. "Really? We're going there? Now this is *my* fault? I'm not the one that named me after a bar drink!"

"I think it's a clever idea. All I'm saying is if you made an effort to be a bit more feminine from time to time…"

"I'm plenty feminine. I've got all the parts. They work. I don't need to wear makeup and do my hair. Guys still hit on me." Sometimes.

"You have such a nice complexion, though, and with the right eye makeup, your blue eyes would look…"

"…like someone else. I wouldn't look like me. Stop that. Don't touch my hair."

Her mother pursed her lips and dropped her hand. "There's nothing wrong with taking pride in your appearance. At least take out those ridiculous pigtails. They make you look twelve."

Bailey grabbed a down vest from the hook by the door and snatched up her car keys. She didn't bother to say goodbye.

She backed out of the driveway and gave her old Toyota slightly more gas than was necessary. The tires spit out gravel as she pulled out of Orchard Estates onto the main road.

Orchard Estates. Ugh. She hated that name. Why did they always give trailer parks ridiculously pretentious names? They were mobile homes. Own it. Stop trying to make a pig out of a purse or whatever that saying was.

Bailey ran a hand through her hair and realized she was still sporting the pigtails her mother had criticized. She was tempted to leave them— she only really wore them when working—but one of the elastics was painfully tugging a single hair, so she reached up and slid each band out and tossed them in the cup holder. She ran a hand through the strands in place of a brush and decided it would have to do. It wasn't as if she was going to Lucky's to impress anyone. It was a bar for Pete's sake.

And the sooner she got this over with the better. Blech. She hated being on display. Hated having all eyes on her.

An involuntary shiver slid over her. She reached over to turn on the heat and then realized she still hadn't replaced the blower fan. That'd have to wait until she had more than two cents to spare. And a place to do the work.

She pulled into Lucky's and drove up into the gravel lot where the employees parked. There was a light breeze that rustled the dry leaves of the oak trees lining the back lot. Despite the relative warmth of the day, snow wouldn't be long in coming. It *was* November.

She pushed open the back door.

"Ah! There's my Lucky Charm!"

Bailey cringed and shrugged out of her vest. "Daniel."

Her father wiped his hands on his apron and hurried forward. He was a small man with sandy-blonde hair and blue eyes, and he reminded her of that actor from the *Back to the Future* movies with his high energy and annoying, cheerful expression.

She went rigid when he hugged her, ruffling her hair as if she were a child. "Your momma told me you'd be filling in for her. Let's get you changed."

"What's wrong with what I'm wearing?" He pushed her back toward his office anyway.

"I'll find you a Lucky's shirt. Hold on. I've got a spare in here somewhere…"

He pulled open drawers and file cabinets and finally produced a bright green polo and thrust it toward her. "It might be a little big, but we've no time to find another. You're on in five minutes."

Bailey grabbed the shirt as he gave her his trademark wink and slammed the door behind him. She held the shirt up. It was badly wrinkled… and an XXL.

She threw her vest and long-sleeved flannel shirt on a chair and pulled the polo over her T-shirt. It reached to mid-thigh. She snatched up her print-outs and headed to the bar.

"Hi, Bailey! How you doin', sweetie?"

Bailey ducked under the bar and waved to Wanda with her sheaf of papers. "I've been better. You?"

"Can't complain!" That was Wanda's standard reply to any question. Bailey had never met anyone more optimistic. Or round. Wanda was a broad-faced, pillow of a woman with a penchant for hot pink lipstick, dark beer and taking charge.

"I'll complain for both of us." She turned and let out an audible groan. "Starting now."

"Hey, Bailey!"

"Frankie? What are you doing here? Are you even old enough to drink? Don't you have SATs or Driver's Ed to study for?"

"It's wings night," he said, "and Wanda said I don't have to be legal to sit at the bar. She just can't serve me." He reached for the beer of the customer next to him while the man's back was turned.

Bailey swatted his hand. "Stop that! Officer Dayton is in a booth in the corner. You'll get us all in trouble. On second thought. Go ahead. If you go to jail instead of college, maybe your dad will invest in the garage after all."

Frankie's pock-marked cheeks turned ruddy. "Hey, sorry about that. They did a planning for college night at school on Monday. I guess it got him to thinking."

Bailey wordlessly pulled a glass down from the rack and filled it with tonic water. She tossed a few limes into it and stabbed it with a straw. "Do you even want to go to college?"

Frankie shrugged which was worse than a no. She hated ambivalence. Who could afford to waffle about what they wanted in life? What did that get you? Nowhere. No. Bailey knew damn well what she wanted, and it was not to stand up in front of a crowded bar on wings and three-dollar draft night playing twenty questions with seventeen year-olds who didn't even know what they wanted to do when they grew up.

She spat a lime seed that had come up her straw into the bar sink and grabbed the papers. Wanda stuck two fingers in her mouth and whistled for quiet.

"Welcome, everybody! It's trivia time! Winner gets a 2-for-1 coupon for any entree including pub select items or one free appetizer!" Bailey rolled her eyes. "Are you ready? Let's play!"

"Hey, okay," said Bailey. It was dim behind the bar, and she had to hold the pages up toward her face to see them clearly. "First question. Category is…" she held the pages closer still, "Famous Landmarks."

"You're doing it wrong!" someone called out from a corner booth. "Where's Sandi?"

Bailey peered over her sheets into the corner of the bar. "She wasn't feeling well. I'm filling in."

A general groan of disappointment rippled through the pub.

"Can she do it tomorrow?" someone else asked. "I've got twenty bucks on Hank and Owen making it into the finals."

"Excuse me?"

Wanda leaned over and pointed to a large chalkboard hanging behind the bar with team names, dates and scores. "You *track* Trivia Night results?"

"Hell, yeah," said Frankie. "Of course, my money is on Team T-squared."

Bailey frowned. "You have no money. And who is T-squared?"

"Treasure Trakker, of course."

Bailey closed her eyes for a nanosecond to regain her composure. She knew that voice. She'd accused the owner of that voice of perverted intentions and small dimensions less than an hour ago.

Ian McIntyre shrugged out of his jacket and looped it over his shoulder, which should have looked gay as hell, but only drew attention to that blasted navy tee clinging to his chest and the fact that he'd changed into a pair of faded Levi's that hugged him like they'd been best buddies for years. Bailey's throat went dry. She took another swig of tonic.

"Wanda? The usual?" he said.

His voice rolled over Bailey in whiskey-soaked waves as Wanda pulled a draft of a dark microbrewery beer that was one of Bailey's personal favorites and handed it over. *Erg.* She hated that he had good taste in beers. Ian turned to walk away.

"Hey, Lover Boy. You forgot to pay for that."

He looked over his shoulder and cocked an eyebrow. "Wanda will put it on my tab."

"We don't run tabs here."

His lips twitched. "Shows what you know." He took a sip of his beer and held it aloft. "Hey, everyone, we've got a newbie tonight. So go easy on her, and I'll sweeten the pot. The winning team gets dinner for free tonight!"

"We're not going to…"

He turned and leveled a look at Bailey. "On me."

She straightened her papers and cleared her throat. "Okay, so let's start."

"You need to announce the categories!" someone called out.

"Okay. Categories. 'Famous Landmarks,' 'Not so Fast,' 'Take a Hike…'" She flipped the page over. "'Live Free or Die' and 'Oh, So Sweet.'" She glanced up.

Wanda leaned toward her on her way by with a platter of wings. "Last week's winning team gets to choose first category."

Bailey peered at the chart. "Hank and Owen! You get to choose your category."

"'Famous Landmarks!'"

"Okay. On what day did the Old Man of the Mountain fall?"

A roar of 'too easy' and 'rigged' went up from the crowd. A toddler in a corner booth started to tantrum and the bell over the door rang as more people pressed into the pub.

Hank scratched his chin and consulted with Owen over their table. "May 3, 2002."

"Wrong, the correct answer is—"

"No! Don't say! The other teams have a chance to steal!"

What the—? This was way more complicated than she'd envisioned. What happened to shouting out the answers to things?

"The year was 2003, I believe," said Ian.

"That is correct."

A roar of approval went up. Ian sipped his beer from his chair in the corner and smirked at Bailey. Or, at least, she thought he looked smirky. Cocky, for sure.

"T-squared gets to choose the next category!" someone yelled. There seemed to be a lot of yelling going on.

Ian licked his lips and set his glass down. "I'll take 'Not so Fast' for twenty points."

Frankie grabbed an order pad from behind the bar and nodded at Bailey. "Don't worry. I'll keep score for tonight."

She nodded in thanks. "All right. The question is: Which animal has the greatest recorded land speed?"

"That's easy. Cheetah."

"That is correct."

"'Not so Fast' for thirty points," said Frankie.

"For thirty points. Which animal is faster? A zebra or an ostrich?"

"Hmm," Ian said as if he actually knew the answer and was trying to compare the two. "That's a toughie. I think they're too close to call."

She glanced at her paper and grinned. "Which is it? Zebra or ostrich?"

He angled his head a bit and raised that eyebrow. Oh, she would so enjoy seeing him get this wrong. "Neither," he finally said.

"What?"

"They are the same."

Dammit! "That is correct."

"'Not so Fast' for forty points," said Frankie.

"Is the race between a greyhound and a domestic rabbit fair?" she read.

Ian's lips tilted. "Certainly not from the rabbit's perspective."

"Not so Fast' for fifty!" Frankie called out. He was clearly enjoying this.

Bailey looked down and couldn't hide a grin. She met Ian's gaze head on. "For fifty points: What is the maximum speed of a chicken?"

"Sprinting or sustained?"

She glanced at her papers and up again. "Quit stalling."

The tip of his tongue reached out to touch his upper lip for a fraction of a second, and it made Bailey want to fan herself. "Less than ten," he finally said.

"Be more specific," she said.

"More than five."

"Get ready to steal, other teams!" said Bailey.

Ian took a sip and set his glass down thoughtfully. "Nine."

"That… is correct."

A roar went through the bar with much clapping, whistling and chair rattling and Ian stood a moment to bow and nod his thanks as her half-brother, Jack, called out from the kitchen, "Speed round!"

By the end of the speed round, Bailey was out of breath and her head was spinning.

"Woohoo!" chorused the Hot Mommas as they ordered another round of celebratory margaritas. "Take *that* Hank!"

The bell over the door jingled again and Bailey glanced up to see her BFF Liz and fiancé, Carter, walk in. Liz wiggled through the crowd.

"Did we miss the speed round?" Bailey nodded. "Oh, fudge. That's my favorite part."

"You come to this every week?"

"Well, yeah. It's a riot. Meg and Belinda invited me a few months ago, and then Carter, Ian, and Grace suggested we make a team."

"You're on Ian's team? My God, it's like you've got a secret life. I can't believe you never told me."

Liz shrugged. "I was afraid you'd be mad I wasn't boycotting the bar on moral grounds."

"I am."

Liz watched her fiancé wind his way toward his brother. "See? This is why I kept it to myself. Oh, I hope we're not far behind. The Hot Mommas have been killing the speed rounds lately and Grace has a cold this week. The amount of Popular Culture trivia that woman knows is mind boggling."

"You've still got the Flip 'n Switch, The Mystery Points and the Bonus rounds coming," Frankie said before spinning back around toward the bar.

Bailey stared at him blankly. "The whats?"

"It's okay," he said. "Just follow my lead."

Liz disappeared into the throng, and Frankie explained the complicated mathematics of scoring the Mystery Points round.

"The computer ordering system keeps track of it all. All you have to do is… oh, nevermind." Frankie ducked under the bar and started pressing buttons on the cash register.

"Hey! You shouldn't be back here! I'm sure it's against the law or something."

Frankie rolled his eyes and kept pressing buttons. He jotted some numbers on an order pad and dove back under to take his seat again. "Go ahead now. I've got them. I'll calculate the multipliers based on qualifying activities. You know, team members plus drafts plus entrees ordered…"

Her head was spinning. "How did you learn to do that?"

He shrugged. "I've seen Sandi, I mean, your mom, do it enough times. Come on. We should keep going. If I'm not home by eight-thirty my dad freaks."

Things progressed smoothly from then on. The Hot Mommas came out ahead for the evening which was cause for a great chorus of cheers and celebratory glass clinking. Bailey sucked on her straw and was grateful it was all over.

And then a hunky nerd wove his way toward her.

Bailey lowered her straw and attempted a nonchalant air. "The Hot Mommas won fair and square, so don't bother trying to ask for a recount."

He shook his head and fished in his back pocket for his wallet. "Actually, I was coming up to pay their tab."

"Oh." Well, that was… nice of him.

"Hey, Frankie. Nice job tonight."

Frankie's ruddy face turned redder at the compliment. "Thanks."

Ian turned back to her. "Be sure to add a plate of potato skins on that for our score keeper. He's earned it." Ian tapped the counter and turned to Frankie. "Remember what I said the other night."

"I will."

"Good."

Bailey watched a smile transform Ian's features from sexy nerd to sex-God. Damn. She took his credit card, rang up the charge and slid the signed receipt into the drawer.

"Thanks for the help, Frankie," she said. "You're all right. Well, I'm off." She waved to Wanda and ducked under the bar to head down toward the back office. Ian followed.

She stopped in the hallway. "I'm sorry. This area is for employees only."

"Cut me a break, will you? Those photographers you pointed out earlier followed me here. The only reason they didn't come in is because Jeff Dayton is sitting in the window, and he's already spoken to them about boundaries."

"Fine," she harrumphed. She paused. "So what *did* you tell him the other night?"

"Who?"

"Frankie."

Ian shrugged. "I said, 'Just because something hasn't been done doesn't mean it can't be.'" She frowned. "He was telling me about some college fair they were holding at school and how there was no point in going, because nobody in the Sullivan family ever went to college and they got along all right."

Bailey's mouth fell open. "So *you* convinced Frankie to go to college? Great!"

"You have a problem with that?"

"Well, yes, when it directly impacts me. His father backed out of a business deal because of your interference. Thanks a bunch."

She put her hand on the door to Daniel's office, but Ian spun her around. "First of all, *that's* the Frankie you were referring to earlier? The one you said would be lucky to graduate summer camp?"

"How many Frankies do you think live in Sugar Falls? Yes, that's the Frankie."

"Why would you say that? The kid has a real knack for organization and numbers."

"You haven't watched him bum money off his dad every time he comes into the shop. The kid's a leech."

"A leech." His green eyes went dark, his expression stony. "That kid has a good shot of making something of himself if given half a chance. And you would take that away?"

"Go away." She pushed into Daniel's office and rummaged around in the dark for her bag. Darned if she'd go near that jerk to flick the light switch.

He flicked it for her. Flourescent bulbs flickered to life above them. "For your information, that 'leech' doesn't have a lot of advantages. You should see where he lives…"

"We're neighbors."

"You're…?"

"Yes, you pompous, know-it-all, son-of-a—" her sentence got cut off as she struggled to pull the damned XXL polo over her head. "What about *my* dreams and *my* future? Did you stop to think about that? Frankie has plenty of time to do whatever he's going to do, but I've been working ten long years to scrape together enough to buy my own shop. Ten *years*. That's a flippin' long time, buddy, and I finally—finally!—had enough saved and convinced Sully to go in with me *and* found a property that will work and you go and f—!" She choked on the last word, the curse getting tangled with hot emotion in her throat.

He had the nerve to chuckle. "That's an awful dirty word about to come out of your pretty little mouth."

"Awful and dirty would be an upgrade from what I've been through! You've ruined *everything* and all for a kid that doesn't even know what he wants. *Jesus!* What if somebody took away your dream? How would you feel?"

"I'm living my dream."

She tossed the polo onto a chair, grabbed her shirt and vest and stalked out the door. "Geez. Must suck to peak at thirty-five."

He pushed open the back door and held it for her. "I'm only thirty-four."

"Whatever," she said brushing past.

"And who says I've peaked? I have goals."

She stopped and looked at him dismissively as she stuffed her arms into her shirt and vest. "I'm sure."

"You know, you are incredibly condescending for a woman who wears pigtails and flannel."

"And you're incredibly arrogant for a man who still plays with action figures."

"Who says I have action figures?"

"I saw the box."

"Those are collectables."

"Which is only more pathetic."

He stood on a step below her, making them nearly eye level. "You think I'm pathetic?"

She chewed her lip, hating how his eyebrow arched like some pompous English lord from those historical romances her mom was always reading, which, okay, yes, she may have picked up from time to time when she was bored. Sue her.

Plus he had those slightly longer sideburns like grunge rockers and Regency-era rakes. She had an overwhelming urge to touch them with her fingertips.

"No. I don't think you're pathetic," she finally said. "I think you're annoying. Who knows the average speed of a chicken? That's just weird."

"Now I'm weird?"

"You have sideburns," she blurted. "Who has sideburns anymore?" She reached out and touched her fingertips to them as if to make a point. They were feathery soft. Damn.

"You don't like my sideburns?"

Her voice came out in a rasp. "I don't like what they represent."

"I can't wait to hear this."

"You think you're above convention. You think you can set your own rules. You think…"

"I'll tell you what I think," he said, leaning closer. "I think you talk too much. And I think you're mad at Sully and life and you're taking it out on me, because I'm a handy target. But most of all…" And then he gripped her face, leaned forward, and stopped, his lips a mere breath away from hers. "I think my sideburns turn you on."

"In your dreams," she sputtered. She could feel her face grow hot under his fingertips and moved to knock away his hands when a bright light flashed. Then another.

"What the—?" Ian spun around. "Hey! Cut that out!"

A strange voice called out, "Thank you, Mr. McIntyre! Have a great evening!"

"What? Did he just take a picture of us?" Bailey spun toward the parking lot, the wind whipping her hair into her eyes. "Hey! What do you think—?"

Ian blocked her view with his chest. "Shush! Don't give them anything to quote. Just get in your car and leave."

"Did you just 'shush' me?"

He rolled his eyes. "It's me they're interested in. Because of the show. If you're not seen with me they'll leave you alone."

"If you'd stop trying to back me into a corner, it would be easier to leave."

Ian stepped away. "I'm not trying anything."

"Sure you're not." Bailey stalked down the steps, perversely annoyed that he *wasn't* trying anything, but it wasn't like guys like Ian McIntyre *ever* noticed weird Bailey Adams anyway.

She stuffed her hands into her vest pockets and hurried to her car.

UGH. SHE NEEDED A PLAN B.

The problem was: there was no Plan B. There was never any thought of, "Well, if this doesn't pan out, I'll move to Vegas and become a midget stripper," type of thing. No, it was only ever: Save for years, scrape together a down payment, buy a shop and do it.

Quitting (getting fired) last April from Willard's Auto just accelerated the process. It had seemed an amazing stroke of luck when Sully had approached her about leaving Willard's at the same time Valerie had mentioned the empty tire place near downtown was for sale.

Maybe Valerie would have some ideas.

It made Bailey's stomach feel a bit like she'd eaten bad potato salad just thinking about asking Valerie for a favor, but if Liz could swallow her bias against Vampire Val and accept the woman as her sister-in-law (there was no predicting the quirks of fate, was there?) then Bailey could, too. Maybe.

Crap. Life sucked. It sucked so hard it was like trying to get a grape up through a straw. Liz had helped Bailey and Sully hammer out an agreement, map out a business plan and apply for the loan on the property. They'd signed the purchase and sale. They'd put down a damned deposit. Everything hinged on Sully being a 50% partner in this. *Everything*.

Bailey stood at the top of the narrow steps and fumbled the key into the lock. She watched as Mr. Henderson's cat, Fluffy, streaked by. She pushed the door open. The lights were off. Her stomach rumbled, but she didn't feel like eating. She felt tired. And edgy. She wished she had enough gas money to drive around for a while. She didn't want to be here, again, the same faded walls staring back at her while her body still hummed with some annoying *awareness* she felt every time she got near Ian McIntyre. Every time she was near him, she had the simultaneous urges to kiss him until they were both senseless and throttle him for unknowingly ruining her life.

She closed her eyes a moment as she toed off her sneakers, then hung her vest by the door and padded through the living room. Her mom's bedroom door was closed. Bailey flipped the light-switch on in her own room, closed the door and tossed her cell phone onto the twin bed.

The overhead light flickered, popped and went black.

Perfect.

Bailey pushed off the door by the light of the alarm clock, grabbed the laptop she'd inherited from her younger half-brother and sat on the bed.

If Liz weren't happily planning her dream wedding, Bailey would call her. That's what friends did. What could Liz do for her? What could *anyone* do? And it's not as if Bailey had a rich uncle who would die and leave her one-seventh of his estate (assuming no more half-siblings materialized and her slice of the pie shrank even further.) She had no living grandparents. Her mother was an only child. Her father, well, there was no point in going there.

Her shoulders lifted and fell a bit as if someone had asked whether she was okay, and she scooted up against the wall beside the bed. Just her and her mom.

The breath left her lungs in a long, shaky exhale. She was twenty-eight, patching together odd jobs, ditched by her business partner, lusting after a guy totally and by every measure imaginable out of her league—and still sleeping in the same bed she'd had since she was ten.

Suddenly the room felt very small and dark.

She opened the laptop and stared at the screen. Funny how the internet, so vast and interconnected, could still leave a person feeling invisible. No one knew she was here, looking out at them. Waiting.

She wiped a hand over her face and took another breath. Feeling sorry for herself wasn't changing anything. So what if she'd had a setback? She could claw her way out again.

She'd done it before. She could do it again. Just not tonight.

She opened a browser window and typed 'Ian McIntyre Treasure Trakker' in the search bar. Liz would thank her for doing due diligence on the family she was marrying into.

Bailey hit return.

She still remembered how Liz had breathlessly called her mere days after the big engagement/fountain christening with the news that Ian had told the happy couple he wanted to pay for the whole wedding. *Everything*. Bailey remembered saying something snarky about wishing she had a Fairy Godmother with chest hair. She regretted it now. As much as she wanted to resent all of Liz's good fortune, somehow it gave her hope that in a universe where Liz could get engaged to her high school crush that miracles could happen. Hell, maybe it wasn't too late for Bailey to grow breasts, win the lottery and bag a man whose first name she cared to remember after the fact.

She sighed and clicked on a random search result. *She-ite*. Seriously? The man was like tiramisu drenched in chocolate sauce and served on a slab of pecan pie. Which sounded awesome, by the way, but that was beside the point. She clicked on a photo gallery of images for Ian McIntyre. Ian in a suit—*hot dang*—at some business deal for *Treasure*

Trakker Survival in the Outback. Another with him hiking through lush green rainforest in cargo shorts and hiking boots looking all muscular and capable and, okay, we'll say it, *ripped.* Next he's smiling, his arm around some random woman who looks like she's been plucked out of a line-up of wannabes on spring break and has the hottest bod, the smallest bikini, and the biggest bongos in the wet T-shirt contest. Ah. Treasure Trakker in Paradise. Figures.

There were photos of Ian running cross country in high school… that was a thing? And of Ian's highly Photoshopped (had to be) promo pics of him for the *Happily Ever After* show with a diamond ring in a little velvet box that Bailey would bet her last chocolate bar was a prop for a movie set, because diamonds that large didn't exist in real life. The thing would be a nuisance getting snagged putting hands in pockets or running fingers through hair. It looked as practical as those freakishly long fingernails on that guy in the world records book. Hideous, really.

Bailey stared at Ian on her screen. Dark hair geek-a-liciously in need of a haircut, eyes serious with a faint, slightly 'wish I were somewhere else' look about them, lips quirked self-deprecatingly. Sideburns just a smidge Colin Firth meets grunge rocker…

Oh, double fudge brownies. Who was she kidding? Her life was tanking and he was *hot.*

CHAPTER SIX

"IVY, I NEED ADVIL." Marcia slid off her heels and let her feet sink into the soft pile of the carpet under her feet. Her bunions were killing her.

"I gave you my last one twenty minutes ago. I'll pick some up when we get dinner."

Marcia frowned. "Dinner sounds good. I think Thai food. Nick? What do you think of Thai food for tonight?"

Nick poked his head through the adjoining door of their rooms in the quaint bed and breakfast on the edge of town. The rest of the crew were in the chain hotel. God bless Ivy for considering her migraines. "I think you'll be lucky to find a decent Thai place in Sugar Falls. I've heard good things about a pub called Lucky's."

"Oof. Pub food sounds too heavy. I need something fresh."

"I'll find something, Marcia," said Ivy. "Why don't you order a spritzer and massage, and I'll pick something up."

"Perfect. And more Advil."

"Got it."

After Ivy left, Nick strolled in and sat on the Victorian sofa in the sitting area of Marcia's suite. "Nice digs you've got here."

"You know that massage joke is growing old."

"You started it."

"How was I to know they wouldn't offer standard spa services?"

Nick's lips twitched in that way that made Marcia's toes curl into the carpet beneath her feet. There was something about the man that got her sparks flying, so to speak, damned lazy, gorgeous mountain man. But he was brilliant with the camera and never shot her from her bad side, so she wasn't planning to give him up any time soon.

"Let's take a walk," he said, although his long arm remained stretched across the back of the couch like he was settling in for a while.

"My feet hurt."

"Wear comfortable shoes."

"I don't own comfortable shoes," she pouted.

"Go barefoot."

"It's November."

"Come on," he said, standing up. "There's something I want to show you."

Marcia hurriedly pushed her bare feet into the flip-flops she brought for hotel showering and followed him into the hall. "This better be good."

"Trust me."

"That's what my ex-husband said right before he cleared out our joint checking account."

Nick gave her a long look over his shoulder. "Do I look like your ex-husband?"

"Well, no…" In fact, her ex-husband had been short and swarthy, and a lawyer, the little weasel. Nothing like the lanky Norwegian backside strolling down the back stairs in front of her.

Nick stopped at the bottom of the steps by the back door. "Wait here."

"Why?"

"Because I don't want you to ruin the surprise."

He slipped through a door off the back hallway, and a moment or two later she heard him call out for her to 'open up.' She pushed the door open. Nick stood with two puppies squiggling in his arms.

"Puppies?"

"Adorable aren't they?"

"Who do they belong to?"

He shrugged. "The B&B owners said the mom is a stray that used their shed out back for delivering the pups. But she has no tags or chip, and no one has claimed her. They've kept her and the pups here in the mud room until they can figure out what to do with them all."

"Poor things. Why don't they bring her to a shelter?"

"They were going to, but they figured if she was happy here, maybe they'd keep the mom and find homes for the pups. Want one?"

"Are you kidding? I don't know the first thing about dogs."

Nick picked up a brown ball and held it out to her. It had a white streak down its face like a lightening blaze and big brown eyes. "Okay, yes, it's adorable."

"See? Women love dogs."

"What did you say?"

"Women love dogs?"

Marcia grabbed the pup and looked at it critically. "You're right. Oh my God, you're right! Brilliant! We'll just have Ian adopt one of these mutts so women will love him for his dog! It'll prove he doesn't have commitment issues if he can commit to a dog, right? This is perfect. I'll take this one. This is the cutest one, right?" She held it aloft for him to look at.

"You're making Ian adopt a puppy?"

"Isn't that why you brought me here?"

Nick shook his head. "Woman, you are a force of nature."

Marcia grinned. "Thank you. Tell these good people to put the dog on the bill. And no substitutes. This one's the most photogenic, I think."

Nick's eyes flickered with amusement. "Shall I order that massage now?"

Her toes curled in her flip-flops. "Don't be cheeky. But I will take a martini. And, please, make sure it's the good stuff. My head can't take that cheap vermouth they tried to pawn off on me last night."

"As you wish."

She pressed her lips together to keep from grinning. Damn it, it turned her on when he went all *Princess Bride* on her. The man knew it, too. She handed him back the puppy and let her hips swish as she walked back through the door.

CHAPTER SEVEN

IAN YAWNED AND TRAILED after his future sister-in-law as she walked through his empty house taking notes on a yellow legal pad. She was a business analyst turned part-time designer/home stager—and currently peppering him with questions he hadn't a clue how to answer. He regretted staying up so late working on the latest update to Treasure Trakker, but he'd had some ideas to work through, and it felt good to have something familiar to immerse himself in.

"So, aside from an old recliner, your bed, dresser, a desk and some old bookcases, you have no furniture to speak of."

"It was just me. What did I need?"

Liz smiled, a warm smile, and Ian was glad Carter had found someone who fit into the family so well. "Marcia told me I needed to make it look homey. You need to give me a little guidance. What style do you tend to prefer? Modern? Traditional?"

"Homey is good."

She bit her lip. "Um, can you be a little more specific?"

"Comfortable. Not too stuffy or floofy. Regular colors."

"Regular colors," she repeated, tapping her pen on her note pad. "Okay! I think we're good. Why don't I work up some ideas, pull together some suggestions for focal pieces and we'll flesh it out from there?"

"Sounds good," he said as enthusiastically as he could.

She let out a sigh and dropped the pad to her side. "You don't care what I do, do you?"

He shrugged. "Not really. Not to knock what you do, but I don't need a specially designed house. I'd be happy if it looked like it did growing up here. Just… normal."

She tapped the pen against her closed lips and looked around her as if picturing 'normal.' "All right," she finally said. "I have some ideas. Let me run with them a bit, and I'll check in with you later with some basic color choices."

"I like blue."

Her lips tilted as if he'd said something funny. "Blue. Got it."

She grabbed her tote bag and swung open the front door. "Oh my goodness! Bailey! Here, let me help with that."

Ian stifled a groan. He was so not ready to face that woman again.

A mop and broom clattered to the living room floor as Liz grabbed a box of cleaning supplies from 'that woman' who was busy dragging a vacuum cleaner through the door while balancing a to-go cup in her other hand. "Thanks."

Liz set the cleaning supplies on the kitchen island and turned to Ian. "So, once you've got the main rooms cleaned up, we can go over which ones need staging first. I'm guessing this room and maybe the bedroom?"

"The bedroom? Why does anyone need to see my bedroom?"

Liz shrugged. "Marcia told me to get all the primary rooms ready for filming ASAP. I'll ask her about the bedroom. Anyway," she turned back to Bailey, "after we get the filming equipment and mess from the crew taken out of here, we'll need to prep for decorating. At a minimum, I imagine Marcia wants you to remove all the construction stickers from the windows and give them a good cleaning inside and out, polish all the interior woodwork and floors and sweep the porch and walkways. And, once the furniture starts arriving, I'll need help getting everything put in place, installing window treatments and the like."

"Is she qualified to do that?" Ian asked with no small degree of alarm. Liz sounded like Bailey was going to be spending far too much time here.

"Marcia's assistant said we were in charge and to 'make it happen.' We're going to make it happen."

"You got a problem with my hanging your curtains?" Bailey asked.

"None whatsoever," he lied.

"Good."

"Good."

"Okay! I've got to run." And then Liz was gone and he was alone. With her.

"Got any razor blades?" Bailey said.

He blinked. "Excuse me?"

"Razor blades. To remove the stickers from the windows. Putty knife, maybe? Oh, never mind. I'll use a credit card if I have to."

"Can we declare a truce already?"

"Were we fighting?"

"It sure as hell feels like it. Geesh. What the hell did I ever do to you anyway? But breathe in your general direction and perhaps not value your lifelong dream to own a garage? I mean, what girl doesn't grow up dreaming of hydraulic lifts and grease guns?"

"See? This is why I don't like you. You're always making my life difficult. And you're mocking me."

He chuckled and ran a weary hand over his face. As two day's growth of whiskers nipped at his palm he tried to make a mental note to shave. Sometime. "I wasn't mocking you. Honestly. I find it… interesting is all. You have to admit you're a little unusual."

"Because I'm self-reliant? And I can change my own tires?"

"In a word: yes."

She started unpacking the box of cleaning supplies onto his kitchen counter. Window cleaner. Lemon oil. Disinfectant spray. "You think I'm not feminine because I fix cars for a living?"

"Now there you go again, putting words in my mouth. I never said anything about your femininity. It's a wonder you aren't crushed by that giant chip on your shoulder."

She took a long drink from her to-go cup, her blue eyes staring at him. "I'll start with the downstairs windows."

"Fine."

"Fine."

A knock on the door silenced any further discussion. No sooner had Ian cracked the door open than Marcia came waltzing in.

"I brought you a present," she said without preamble. She tugged at the end of a rope and then he saw it. A dog. She'd brought him a damned dog.

"What the hell is that?"

"Your new puppy!" she said. "Go ahead. Get to know each other."

He frowned. "I don't want a dog. They pee on things. And chew things up. I don't have time for a dog."

"Oh my God, he's *adorable!*" If he hadn't heard it with his own ears he wouldn't have believed it. Bailey squealed. Like a thirteen year-old girl at a Taylor Swift concert. She was now crouched on the floor in his front hallway with a ball of brown fur jumping all over her, and Marcia was giving him a look of satisfaction and triumph he did not the least understand.

"See. Women *love* puppies. Even… who is this person?"

Bailey stopped frolicking with the dog long enough to glare at Marcia. "Bailey. You hired me two days ago."

"Oh, right." She turned back to Ian. "I'm doing you a favor here."

"I fail to see how dumping some stray dog in my foyer is a favor."

"May we talk privately?" she asked, making a less than subtle gesture toward Bailey and the ball of fur.

Ian walked toward the laundry room in silence. It was the one room he knew didn't afford a fishbowl view of his life. He definitely needed to talk to Liz about getting some blinds up sooner than later.

"I'm going to be blunt with you," said Marcia, as if there was a time she wasn't. "You're going to be skewered and flambéd on the fire of public opinion if we don't spin your little episode of cold feet into something the female viewers will find palatable."

"It's not cold feet. Helen and Mary Beth were great women, but I just didn't see myself—"

"Aargh! Do not repeat that to me again! It's bullshit! Face it, you have commitment issues!"

"If you yell at me, there's no point in having stepped away for this conversation."

Marcia sucked in a sharp breath and spoke through her teeth. "I have given you the chance of a lifetime, Ian, because I believed in you, and you are hanging me out to dry. Those women were *exactly* what you asked for. They have both fallen for you." She gestured around her. "They will make this mausoleum you've built into a *home*. Why are you dragging your feet? I'll tell you why! Because you don't know what to do with yourself once I give you everything you've asked for. You're afraid to peak at thirty-four."

What the—? Why was everyone fixated on his age all of a sudden? "Nothing could be further from the truth."

"Don't try to pretend I've just fallen off the turnip truck. I've made hundreds of matches. I know cold feet when I see it. Well, I'm not having it, and that dog out there is your ticket out of this mess you've made."

"I fail to see—"

"Listen, bud, that damned mutt is adorable. You heard what's-her-name say so. And if you can't commit to the perfect women, that dog is going to win the hearts of my viewers so maybe—just maybe—they'll forgive you for bruising the hearts of Helen and the redhead… the second one."

"Mary Beth."

"Yeah. That dog is going to buy us both some time to fix this mess. And you are going to pretend it is your deepest boyhood fantasy to adopt a dog of your very own."

"I've never had a dog. I don't know anything about them. We only had a cat."

"What's there to know? You walk them, feed them and hire a trainer." She opened the door and marched back to the living room.

"Wait!" Ian quickly followed. "What's going to happen to this dog when the show is over?"

Marcia shrugged and looked at the puddle on the floor of the foyer. "That's the least of your worries."

She was gone by the time it registered what that puddle was.

BAILEY SCRUFFLED THE PUPPY'S fur and made little kissy noises which made him yip and leap at her face, which made her giggle and caused him to run around the yard and jump excitedly on his short little legs. Finally, he squatted again and she figured it was safe to take him indoors. She picked him up and carried him inside as Marcia waved goodbye.

"Watch your step," she warned as the dog licked her face. She hated to give up the warm little bundle, but he was making it difficult to speak.

"You let him pee on my floor," said Ian.

The puppy dashed around the empty living room, sniffing and running in circles. "It was an accident. He's little. Besides, I didn't know I was in charge."

Ian continued to stare at the puddle on the floor. "You're in charge of cleaning the house, so it's in your best interests to control that thing."

"That thing has a name," she said. The puppy tumbled up and sat at her feet. Well, half on her foot. He started chewing her shoelace.

"It has no name, because it's not staying." He ran a weary hand through his hair.

"You heard Marcia. I don't think you have a choice."

He glanced up. "You heard that?"

"Hard not to. Trouble in paradise?"

He shook his head and walked away from the puddle. "None of your business."

Bailey tugged her shoe out of the pup's mouth and trailed after Ian. "You're going to have to pay me extra to clean up dog poo."

Ian spun on his heel. "Really? Is money all you ever think about? I have a *dog* I didn't ask for nor wanted pissing on my brand new hardwood floors and you're worried about getting paid?"

"Yes."

"Fine. You want to get paid? I'll pay you a thousand bucks to make that thing—"

"Chewy."

"—go away."

"Really? Done."

He frowned. "I mean safely and humanely."

She grabbed the little ball of fluff that was currently attacking her other shoe. "You even have to say that?"

"You seem quite mercenary all of a sudden. One never knows."

"I don't harm innocent puppies. Not even for money."

"Good to know." He turned around again. "Did you happen to bring a mop?"

She ignored that and trailed after him. "Won't your producer lady be mad you've given it away?" she asked.

"I'm not giving it away. I'm selling it."

"You're a lousy businessman if your idea of selling is paying money to someone instead of taking it."

"You are accepting the dog plus a stipend for its care in exchange for making it presentable and available so Marcia never has to know I haven't kept it."

"Wait. I'm not just taking it?"

"Yes, you most definitely are. But then it needs to be trained and here when we need it for filming."

"You want me to train it?"

"I believe I said that."

"And you're only giving me a thousand bucks for that?"

His eyebrow arched. "You want more?"

"Well… it's rather open-ended for one thing. For how long? What sort of training?"

"Normal training. Don't you know anything about dogs?"

Well, no. Not that she'd admit that *now*. "Of course. Who doesn't? But, um, training takes a lot of work. I can't promise he'll be perfect by tomorrow, for instance. Plus, I have other commitments…" Like trying to figure out how to raise another twenty grand by the end of the month with a puppy chewing at her shoes.

"Fine. Double it. But at least train it to go outside, will you?"

"Can I get that in writing?"

He paused. "You don't trust me?"

"I'd prefer it in writing."

"I've signed too many contracts lately. You'll have to accept my word on it."

"Then I want half of it up front."

He stared at her for one long moment then turned. "Clean up the puddle, and I'll write you a check."

CHAPTER EIGHT

BAILEY FINISHED CLEANING the front hallway and then scooped up her newest charge. He licked her face. Surprisingly, she didn't mind.

By the time she'd returned to the kitchen, the check was waiting on the counter. Bailey stared at it. Then she read the memo line. Ian had written, '*Extortion Payment #1.*'

Ha ha.

Mercenary? How about practical? She wasn't going to let a little thing like ignorance get in the way of earning a cool grand or two.

Bailey spent the next few hours scraping and polishing windows—a whole hell of a lot of them and all their individual panes—then decided she needed to break for lunch. Ian obviously had a similar idea, because he was in the kitchen rummaging when she came to collect her purse.

"I'll be back in a bit," she announced, walking for the door.

"Haven't you forgotten something?"

She looked around. "Oh. Right. My cell phone. Thanks." She scooped her phone off the counter.

"I meant the dog."

She looked to where the puppy was curled up on a rag pile in a corner of the living room. "He's sleeping."

"He's also your responsibility."

She let out a huff. "Fine." She scooped up the little dog, gave Ian a dirty look for being an unfeeling, cold-hearted man in a hot-damn suit, and marched down the front walk toward her car.

"Hey, Miss, watchya got there?"

Bailey looked up and was met with the sound of cameras going off. "Seriously? Why are you taking my picture? I'm just the cleaning lady."

"What's that then?"

"A dog, you idiot."

"Whose is it?"

"Mi—Ian McIntyre's, of course."

"Why do you have it, then?"

Bailey looked at the pup in her arms. "I'm, uh, taking it to the vet for its shots." She yanked open the back door to her car.

"What's its name?" asked a second voice.

Bailey paused. Wait a minute. She *knew* that voice. She peered into the branches of the tree above her. "Dylan? What the hell are you doing up there?"

"Hanging out?"

"Get down from there you fool. Does your mother know where you are?"

Dylan was Bailey's half-brother once removed. Or something like that. Wanda's kid. It wasn't clear if he was Daniel's progeny, because Dylan was dark and broad like his mother and born after Daniel had moved on to greener pastures.

"Shouldn't you be in school?"

"Day off. Professional development day."

"You're making that up. There's no such thing."

"Am not. I figured I'd come down here and get a piece of the action."

"Why are you in the tree?"

"The guys wouldn't let me share their van. Say cheese." He held up his cell phone and took a picture.

Bailey frowned. "Get down from there. You look ridiculous. I'm getting some lunch."

"I thought you were taking the dog to the vet," one of the other guys said to her back.

She shot him a dirty look, set Chewy in the passenger seat, and drove off in a cloud of gravel dust.

Twenty minutes later she was thinking she should have demanded three grand for the dog.

She stared at the dizzying assortment of leashes and toys and flea treatments all temptingly displayed at doggie height in *A-paws!*, the town's boutique pet store. She never in a million years would have shopped there instead of the discount behemoth by the river, but her half-sister Skye's older sister had just opened the place, and Bailey figured she could use the business. The options were overwhelming.

"I need the works," she said. "Soup to nuts. But basic stuff. Nothing fancy."

"Will this be cash, credit or charge?"

"It's for Ian McIntyre's new dog…"

"Oh! I'll be happy to invoice it for you," she said.

Invoice? "That'd be perfect."

"You said you need the works?"

"That's right. Everything a new dog owner would need. And training manuals if you have them."

"We have a small selection of training books by the register. I can recommend a couple of our most popular."

"Perfect." Bailey held up a Swarovski crystal-encrusted collar. "Does this come in baby blue?"

"Let me look out back."

Bailey turned to Chewy and kissed his little snout. "You and I are going to have sooooo much fun here!"

"I'M BA-AACK!"

Ian groaned to himself and pushed away from the computer. Apparently there would be no end to today's interruptions. Most people thought he spent his days playing video games. The truth was, he *did* spend a fair amount of time creating add-ons and updates to keep the Treasure Trakker name alive in the marketplace and incorporating the latest product placement requests into the adventure. He also stared out the window. And hiked.

The game was a simple concept, really. He'd thought of it when he was nineteen and the geocaching craze was heating up. Wouldn't it be fun, he'd thought, to blend the adventure and imaginary world of a video game with the excitement of interacting with destinations in the real world? And, what if one were to capitalize the venture and sell the rights to be included in the game to companies looking to advertise? You could integrate the game with a code available to scan at checkout or on a receipt that would add virtual points or powers to your characters in the game.

There'd be no end to the adventure—or profit—once enough corporate sponsors were on board, and it was a win-win for gamers and corporations alike, because if the game were interesting enough, patrons would buy a cup of coffee or a shirt simply to advance to the next game level.

Since its initial development, Ian had pitched—and sold—*Treasure Trakker Paradise* based on a tropical vacation; *Treasure Trakker War of the Worlds*, a science fiction adventure; and *Treasure Trakker Survival in the Outback*. He was in talks with the higher-ups about a couple other spin-offs for younger gamers as well as a version designed to provide fundraising opportunities to non-profits.

It was a tricky balance of technology and marketing, and he was happy to leave the bulk of the day-to-day coding, sales and management to others. What he most loved was the freedom to disappear into his own imagination and march to his own drum.

The company to which he'd sold the idea took care of commercializing the game while Ian enjoyed the royalties and the opportunities to incorporate new sponsors into the gaming experience.

For that part, he usually took long hikes to clear his head and let his creativity work its magic. So far, his magic ensured he would never have to worry about money. And his accountant ensured he didn't have to think about it.

"I'm leaving Chewy in the laundry room while I work! Just so you know!"

Ian rolled his eyes. He wasn't going to get any more work done with her banging around upstairs, so he might as well take a break. "Long lunch break," he said meeting her at the top of the stairs.

"I had to pick up some supplies for your dog."

"*Your* dog."

"Whatever. The bill is coming to you."

"What? I'm not paying—"

"You didn't want to put anything in writing," she said, pulling a laundry basket in front of the laundry room doorway to block the dog's exit. Her jeans pulled tight across her rounded bottom. It was a surprisingly appealing view. "So I decided my own terms." She stood up and smiled at him.

"See if you get that second grand," he countered.

She shrugged. "See if I don't leave him here, then."

"I—what the hell is that?"

"It's his little doggie suit. I thought he might get cold."

"He looks ridiculous."

"It's a little sheep costume! All the Halloween costumes were 75% off, so I knew you wouldn't mind. Besides it goes with his collar."

"Is that *diamond-encrusted?*"

"Don't be silly. They're Swarovski crystals."

"It's purple."

"Oh, that's because they didn't have blue."

Ian shook his head and eyed the lambswool-lined dog bed, the ceramic dishes with… "Is that a *personalized* dog dish?"

"They do it while you wait! Can you imagine?"

"It says Chewy. I didn't agree to that name. And it's spelled wrong. It should have an 'i-e' not a 'y.'"

She started walking toward the living room. "No returns on personalized items, I'm afraid."

He trailed after her. "I'm not paying for that stuff. You've bought the whole store!"

"I'm supporting a local business. I thought you'd be happy."

"No. You thought you'd found a way to annoy me. Mission accomplished."

She picked up her rags and window cleaner. "I was getting needed supplies for your dog. The annoyance thing is just a perk."

"For the last time, it's *not* my dog!"

"That's not what your fans outside think."

Ian snuck a peek out the front window. "I can't imagine what they think they're going to see here. I'm alone in my own home. I've half a mind to play with their heads." He turned toward Bailey.

"What are you looking at me like that for?"

He stepped toward her until they were toe to toe. "You enjoy playing with people's heads…" He leaned closer, enjoying the way she didn't back down.

"Do I?" she said.

"Oh, yeah. I think it's your number-one favorite activity."

Her gaze dropped to his mouth. "What do you know about my number-one favorite activity?"

It shouldn't have, but, yes, his mind went *there.*

"Maybe you should fill me in?" he said.

She smirked, a slight twist of her lips, and he got a little jolt of heat in his gut. They were full, sensual lips, like that hot actress who tripped on the steps at the Oscars. He shouldn't have been, but he was getting very turned on by her lips and the way she always had a come-back. Every time.

"Wouldn't you like that?" she said.

Oh, yes. Yes, he would, as a matter of fact. And it occurred to him that he was turned on. By her. By her snarkiness. By the faint smattering of freckles across the bridge of her pert little nose.

By all rights, he should have found her lack of fashion sense and plain appearance—hell, the woman didn't even wear lip balm from the looks of it—decidedly un-arousing. And yet his jeans were growing tighter by the minute.

"Don't look now," she said, "but Marcia is here."

"What?" *Shit!*

"Ding dong!" Marcia said, waving to them through the window. Yes, he needed curtains. Bailey opened the door. "I'm checking in on our little addition to the family, plus I need to steal our bachelor for a bit. Nick says the lighting is perfect for your contemplative, self-reflective hike segment, and the weather forecast for the next couple of days is iffy."

"My what?" said Ian.

"Where you go for a hike and think about your future and how you can't wait to bring home a woman to share this big beautiful house and that adorable dog with."

"Good luck," muttered Bailey. "Ian doesn't do a lot of sharing."

"Excuse me?" he protested. "I can be extremely generous!"

Bailey rolled her eyes.

Marcia turned a speculative gaze toward them. "You. Snarky girl. You don't like Ian?"

"Not liking presumes I have any feelings whatsoever for him."

"Really. You're totally indifferent?" he said. All right. Yes. It stung a bit, dissing him in front of Marcia. It was one thing to do it in private.

"Completely," she said.

Marcia turned to him. "We won't have optimal lighting for long. Can you change into sexy hiking gear—you know, relaxed and outdoorsy but in a rugged way? Wear something simple and classic like a white tee and navy jacket. Khaki pants. But not dressy ones. Oh, never mind. I'll choose for you…" With that, she stalked down the hallway toward his bedroom.

Bailey gaped at Marcia's retreating backside. "You're just going to stand there and let her pick out your clothes like you were in preschool?"

Ian shrugged. "She'd only tell me to change if I chose the wrong outfit."

Bailey picked up her cleaning supplies again. "At least the men I date can dress themselves."

He didn't know he was doing it until he felt his fingers close around her arm and turn her toward him. "The men you date probably wear orange."

Her gaze dropped to his fingers on her arm. "What do you know about the men I date?"

"What do you know about me?" He slid his hand down to her wrist, his fingertips resting on the pulse there. It skittered rapidly beneath the pad of his thumb. Indifferent, huh?

She swallowed. "I know enough."

"Is that so? Do you know what I'm feeling now? I'll give you a hint. It's not indifference."

"Annoyance?"

A smile teased the corner of her lips. His pulse quickened. *"Uh-uh."*

"I couldn't begin to guess," she said.

Her lips parted slightly, her breath coming light and quick, and a surge of something primal coursed through him. "I'll give you a hint," he said. He tugged lightly on her wrist, bringing her closer, watching her eyes turn dark as he leaned in for a kiss.

"I can't find— oh, sorry. Does she have something in her eye?" Marcia's shoes clicked on the hardwood floor as she stood over them, her arms loaded with clothes. She was looking at them knowing full well the only thing in anyone's eye was misplaced lust.

"Yes," Bailey said, jumping back from him. "An eyelash, but it's gone now. Everything's fine. You can go, um, take a hike now."

Marcia's head tilted, her eyes narrowing at Bailey. "Absolutely. Time to take a hike."

"I TELL YOU, there's something going on with those two."

Nick didn't answer, so Marcia frowned at the sunset which, by any normal assessment, was glorious. Streaks of warm, honey-colored light filtered through the bare trees. Breathtaking. And damned cold. She shivered in her down jacket and accepted the thermos Nick wordlessly handed her.

Mmm. Irish coffee. Nick knew her well. She let the hot, liquor-laced beverage warm her belly. If she had her way, they'd be snug back at the inn by now, but since they'd dismissed Ian, Nick wanted to do his meditation.

She watched him stare into space, his camera, for once, away from his face, and shifted impatiently on the rock she was sitting on. The cold of it seeped through her jeans and long underwear. She stood up.

"What makes you think that?" he finally said, still not looking at her.

He had a way of doing that... being tuned in to everything while looking as if he was mentally elsewhere. It was probably why the contestants on the show felt so at ease with him. He didn't appear to be watching them, so they grew to believe their every movement and word was private. It was a gift.

Like right now, she knew Nick was paying attention, because the pulse in his neck was moving. It was very sexy, that pulse, and if her hands weren't so friggin' cold, she'd be tempted to reach out and touch it.

He turned to her, a lazy, smooth motion, and raised an eyebrow.

She took another slug of coffee. "There's an energy between them. I feel it." She frowned and stared at the orange sun as it sank lower still.

It'd be dark soon. "She isn't what he wants, but there's something going on. She fires him up."

The lazy expression in Nick's eyes moved to his wide, mobile mouth. "You always say the best matches start with a spark."

She waved a dismissive hand. "A sexy spark, not a spark of annoyance. I think he's testing me."

Nick reached down for his camera. Apparently they were done meditating. "I think it has nothing to do with you."

"He can't be turned on by that… I hesitate to say woman, because I don't even think she owns lipstick."

Nick slid a glance toward her perfectly applied makeup. She knew it was perfectly applied, because she'd worked as a makeup artist before she'd hit upon the matchmaking business. "Not every woman has the ability to make the most of her natural beauty," he said.

Marcia sucked in a swift lungful of cold air. Damn the man was good with a compliment. "Indeed." They continued back toward where they'd parked the rental car.

She stumbled, and he took her elbow briefly to help her regain her balance. Her pulse quickened. "I can't let him get sidetracked. If I don't deliver a satisfying season finale, I'm screwed." She glanced at him. "And so are you."

"I'm only screwed when I want to be."

An impish smile curved her lips. Nick only ever talked in double entendres when they were alone and in the dark. So, she made sure it happened as frequently as possible.

"Is that so? I make it a personal policy not to get screwed at all."

"To the disappointment of many."

"No, I prefer to do the…"

His eyes shifted toward her, and she could just make out the wicked gleam in his expression. "I dare you to finish that sentence." His voice was like gravel.

She stopped on the trail, awareness and cold air shivering over her. The wind picked up, tugging Nick's hair into his eyes, and for just a moment she wished she dared to finish the sentence, to finish what they kept starting but never seemed to carry beyond the innuendo and word play. Because, what then? What happened next? What if the sex was bad or the crew found out or, God forbid, she started to *need* him?

Hell, she needed him now, but that was professionally. He was insightful and damned good at his job. No, needing him emotionally, too, was giving him too much to take away from her. She pushed her palm against his chest, her breath light and shallow in her chest, and walked backwards for a few steps before turning away. "Screwing," she said over her shoulder.

He chuckled, a low rumble, knowing she'd backed down again. She could hear his boots on the trail. He clicked on a flashlight for them. "So, what are you going to do about it?"

She tilted the thermos up for another swig, thinking. "Ian is confused and unsure. I think he needs to see what his choices are. Then it'll become clear. We need to bring the final two back into the picture."

"Too many choices might confuse him more."

"You're right. We'll bring back the baker. Hope? Ellen?"

"Helen."

"That one. She's perfect. I don't care if the spoiler sites go haywire. Let them talk. In fact, I *want* them to talk about how perfect she is. Once Ian sees the two side by side, hears all the social media chatter about them, there'll be no comparison."

Nick's lips tilted in a way that made Marcia suspect he was laughing at her, but then he said, "I agree," so of course, he couldn't be.

CHAPTER NINE

"LYDIA, GET THE DOOR, will you? Kate, put that down. You shouldn't be carrying anything in your condition. It's bad for the baby." *Grams?* Ian stopped in the hallway and looked to Liz, his future sister-in-law, who'd stopped in again ostensibly to 'take some more measurements.'

"Do you think he'll think it's too pink?" That was Lydia.

"It's salmon. Salmon is a masculine color. June! Pick up your end a bit more!"

Ian peered through the window at the circus unfolding on his front walkway and flicked on the porch light. Liz offered up an encouraging smile and opened the door. "Good evening, ladies. Watch your step. Kate, let me get that!"

Kate rolled her eyes. "It's a lamp, Liz. I can carry a lamp."

Liz gave Kate a quick hug and grabbed the lamp anyway. "Humor me or my great aunt will smack me with it.

"Thank you, ladies," Liz said. "I appreciate your coming over on such short notice. Grams, let me help. Ian? Come grab the other end of this secretary for me?"

Ian nodded to the women congregating on his porch. It looked like they'd just performed a hit-and-run at a church tag sale. He grabbed one end of the little wooden desk. "What is all this?"

Liz picked up the other end of the desk and motioned with her chin to a spot beneath the main stairwell just off the foyer. "After you and I talked earlier, I called your Grams and asked if she could help me make your house homey—give it a bit of history to make it look like it's evolved over time. One of my design professors suggested it as a way to make a space appear more organic and personal instead of designed, so I told the ladies to surprise me with—"

"Surprise!" Lydia said, dancing around in front of him in her leopard-print, over-sized shirt. He tried not to flinch. Women over sixty should not dress as animals. "I brought over one of my best majolica pieces. Where would you like it?"

Buried in the back yard?

"For now," Liz said, taking it carefully from Lydia, "let's set it on the mantel. I'll move things around once I see what you all have brought me to work with."

"Please don't leave that on my mantel," Ian pleaded as Lydia walked away. "It looks like Elton John and Liberace had a love child."

Liz laughed and rested a hand on his arm. "Relax. I'm sure that's the worst of it. I'll find a nice dark corner for it."

"Thank you."

"Liz," Grams said. "Run out to my car and grab the box from the back seat. Kate keeps trying to help."

Kate rolled her eyes and set the throw pillow she had in her hands on the newel post. "I'll go sit down."

"Um," Ian said.

They all turned toward the living room. Kate stopped in the archway.

"You have no furniture." Claire stated the obvious.

"Not much, no," he said.

"Where do you want the lamp?" June asked.

"Anywhere?"

Liz huffed back into the house and set the box on the floor. "Just set everything in the corner, ladies, and I'll set things up when the furniture arrives."

Grams huffed and opened the lid of the box. "Well, it's a good thing we brought over our housewarming gifts. Heaven knows you're unlikely to throw a housewarming party."

"Housewarming gifts?" Ian asked. "You mean, you want me to keep all this? Even the, um, vase?"

"Absolutely, honey. I know you'll treasure it like I have," said Lydia.

"I'll do my best."

"I brought a lasagna," Grams said lifting a foil covered pan from the box. "And this." She handed over a round plastic container. "It's a pie keeper." He looked at her. "With a pie inside."

He smiled. "Awesome."

"And I brought a ham," said Claire. She thrust a wedge-shaped can of ham at his chest. "I know you bachelors don't always do your grocery shopping like you should. This sucker will keep indefinitely, so you can even save it for the holidays."

"I may do that," he said. He wasn't entirely sure he wanted food that was shelf-stable through the apocalypse. He set the pie and ham on the little secretary in the hall.

"I brought you a quilt I made," said June. The women all *ooh*ed and *ahh*ed over it. Ian nodded in what he hoped was an appreciative fashion. It looked... blue.

"Thank you. That's... I'm sure Liz will find the perfect place to display it."

"Oh, and here's a basket for overnight guests." Grams said, handing him a small wicker basket.

"She means lady friends," Lydia clarified. Ian fought a groan. Someone should tell that woman to ease up on the blue eye shadow.

"Um, thanks?" Ian said. He poked through the basket. It held a toothbrush, travel-sized toothpaste, lip balm, soap, a comb... He lifted the tissue paper then promptly shoved it back into place. Heat crept up his neck. *Great*. His grandmother was giving him condoms. Like *that* wasn't guaranteed to shrivel important pieces of equipment.

"Oh! And I got you a potpourri candle!" Lydia pulled a little ceramic thing out of her shoulder bag. It was white with tiny pink rosebuds on it, like something a little old lady with a lot of cats would own. "You just add the scented oil here and put the little tealight here."

She passed it to him with an inexplicable eyebrow wiggle and dug into her bag again. "I couldn't find any oils I thought you'd like at the gift shop, so I ordered some on-line... Lucky me, they arrived yesterday. Ah! Here they are. A whole assortment."

She thrust the package toward him. He turned it over in his palm. His face flamed.

French Kiss Edible Warming Massage Oils.

Oh, dear God in heaven.

"There's French Vanilla, Cherries Jubilee, Hot Cinnamon—"

"Yup! I see. Thanks so much." He stuffed the massage oils in the wicker basket next to the condoms.

"I thought they sounded delicious. Like a baker's kitchen!"

Yeah, so *not* the room he was thinking of.

"I can't tell you what a time I had choosing. There are so many choices. But then I searched for scented warming oils for men and voila! There they were! Isn't it cute how they covered the package with little kissy lips?"

"Adorable," he choked.

"What young man wants to smell boring lavender or honeysuckle, that's what I want to know, right?" She turned to the other women in the foyer who all seemed to be nodding in agreement. Yikes.

What he'd give for honeysuckle scented oil. God help him, even *that* sounded inappropriate right now.

Kate stepped around the ladies, a knowing but sympathetic look on her face. "One last gift and then we're out of your hair for the night. Promise."

He took the rectangular package from her and pulled off the wrapping paper. A picture frame. He flipped it over.

"Mom and Dad," he said.

"I found it in your grandmother's photo album and thought I'd make a copy for you. I know you don't have many mementos from back then, so I thought it might be nice to have this in your new house."

He stared at the picture of his parents. Mom steadied the Mrs. New Hampshire crown on her head as dad beamed with pride. They both appeared impossibly young. Both impossibly alive.

His throat tightened.

"I hope it's okay," Kate said.

He shook his head and looked up. "Better than okay. Very thoughtful. Thank you."

"You're welcome."

"Oh, my goodness. Is that the time?" Lydia said, her bracelets jingling as she looked at her watch. "I need to get my beauty rest. Grace is coming tomorrow to help me pull out the holiday inventory. We're getting an early start. Claire? You're my ride."

"I know. I know. Don't get all in a dither. I'm coming."

Kate leaned forward and kissed Ian on the cheek. "Congratulations on the new home. It's beautiful."

"Thanks to your husband."

Kate's eyes grew all soft and happy. "He's very talented, isn't he? This house was just what he needed to take the step into doing larger projects. He's already gotten a couple inquiries for work for next spring."

"That's fantastic."

Kate rubbed her rounded belly absently. "We can use the money, that's for sure. And he loved the chance to work on something start to finish."

Ian smiled for her benefit. "I'm glad it worked out so well."

They said their goodbyes.

He walked to the empty living room and set the picture of his parents on the mantel next to the ugly pink vase.

"I won't keep it there."

Ian turned. "Liz. I thought you'd gone, too."

"I almost got swept away, but, no, I just brought the empty box out for your grandmother." She frowned. "I'm almost done though. Sorry to intrude."

He shook his head. "No worries. I don't mind the company."

She smiled. He liked Liz. It rather shocked him that Carter had landed a woman that was attractive, incredibly competent and intelligent. And to think she'd grown up right here in Sugar Falls. How ironic that a nationally-famous matchmaker had scoured her database for the best matches for Ian... and he was still standing in an empty house.

He glanced up at his folks as they smiled at the camera.

"They look very happy together."

Ian nodded. "They were."

"It must have been noisy growing up here. Two boys and Grace as your sister..." She bit her lip. "I mean, in the other house. Before..."

He made himself smile. "It's okay. I know what you meant. And it was." He stared back at the picture. "Your future husband was something of a terror. Did he ever tell you about the time he shot a foam dart under the porch thinking it was the cat and got sprayed by a skunk?"

She glanced at him sidelong. "You had a cat? He never mentioned that."

"Yeah. Carter may not remember her well. She died when he was still young."

"What happened to her?"

"Just disappeared one night. Probably a fisher cat or coyote got her." He shrugged even though he'd spent weeks calling for her each day after school until his throat was sore.

"I'm sorry." The silence stretched out a bit awkwardly between them like so many gravestones. "It'll be a good house for a family," she said with false brightness.

"Yeah." He glanced around the empty room. "Now to find one to move in, right?"

"All in good time," she said. "You need a wife first."

He nodded and went to retrieve the lasagna from the foyer. "I figured you'd have one delivered with the furniture. No muss no fuss."

"A wife?"

He poked his head around the doorway. "You're not?"

"You McIntyres have a very odd sense of humor. Good thing you're so sweet."

"Sweet? You're killing me."

"And handsome," she smiled.

"I'll be sure to let Grace know you think she's handsome."

Liz laughed and gathered her notepad and pencil off the kitchen counter. "She knows. I have such a girl crush on her. I told her so at the retreat last weekend while we were doing each other's…" He held a hand up to forestall any further revelations. "…nails."

"I'm happy to let you use my cabin, but I do not need to know what goes on during your, um…"

"Wine and Women Weekends? Don't worry. I've been sworn to secrecy, but thanks for letting us use it again. With the wedding only weeks away, it's been a welcome retreat from wedding planning overload. I swear, I love your grandmother, but if she sends me one more Pinterest picture of a table setting or wedding favor idea… Whoever gave that woman an internet connection should have their head examined."

"That would be me."

"Oops. Sorry."

"S'okay."

She twisted her lips. "Please don't say anything to your grandmother. I know I should be happy for the input given that Bailey isn't exactly your typical maid of honor. Not what you'd call a girlie-girl. Talking about place settings and candle colors makes her eyes glaze over."

"How does she survive your Wine and Women Weekends?"

Liz waved her hand breezily. "She hasn't been. Too busy trying to get her business off the ground."

"I thought the maid of honor was supposed to help with all that girlie-girl stuff. What *does* she do?"

"Compliments my choices, of course."

He tried to picture Bailey dressed in a fussy bridesmaid's dress, her chin daring him to make some comment, her bow lips compressed into a scowl. Thinking of her lips made him think about almost kissing them. Then, thinking about kissing her and how much she'd hate a frilly dress had him imagining her tearing it off after the wedding, layers of silky fabric falling in pastel pools at her feet…

He stopped himself short with alarm.

Dear Lord. He was lusting after the maid of honor. Correction. He was lusting after *Bailey*—the small woman with sharp toes that could raid a refrigerator like a beaver buzz-sawing a tree.

He pretended to chuckle even though he'd forgotten what Liz had just said and peered out the window. "Looks like that iffy weather they predicted is moving in. Better get home so that brother of mine doesn't worry."

CHAPTER TEN

"STOP LICKING MY ANKLE. Stop! It tickles." Bailey wiggled her foot away from the puppy and tousled its fur. He twisted around to nip at her fingers and ended up chasing his stubby little tail. "You are a nut. Now be very quiet, because I'm going to get a drink for you."

Bailey picked up Chewy's water bowl and snuck from her bedroom.

"What are you doing home so early? I thought you said not to expect you for dinner."

Bailey started at her mother's voice and shoved the heavy ceramic dish behind her back. "Waiting on the furniture now," she said. "What are you doing home?"

Her mother turned away. "I gave my last client to Meg." Her long, strawberry blonde hair, a stunning shade only found on young toddlers and in hair salons, looked less inflated than usual. Her mother teased it absently with her fingers.

Bailey frowned. "That's the second time this week."

Sandi squared her shoulders and walked to the kitchen. "Anyway, now that you're home, shall we make dinner?"

"Sure." Bailey stuck the bowl back inside her bedroom and shut the door again. "Are you still feeling under the weather?"

Her mother pursed her lips and grimaced. "I've just got some things on my mind, that's all. Nothing for you to worry about."

Bailey snagged a banana from a bowl and peeled it. She slid onto one of the stools at the island while Sandi pulled a box of pasta from the cupboard along with cheese and milk from the fridge.

Oh, no. Comfort food. Her mother only succumbed to carbs when she was really sick.

"Mom? What's going on? You're scaring me." Her mother turned, her hands still clutching the box of macaroni, her eyes bright with unshed tears.

"I don't want to burden you, honey."

"Oh my God, what's wrong?" The banana stuck to the roof of her mouth and she gulped it down.

"Probably nothing."

"But definitely something. Mom, you can tell me."

Her mother mumbled something, but she couldn't hear. "What?"

"I found a lump," she said a little louder.

Bailey's skin grew cold, but she had to say the words anyway. "What do you mean?"

Her mother turned, a tear escaping and sliding down her perfectly made-up cheek. "A lump. Here." She pointed to her chest.

"What... what does the doctor say?"

Her mother swiped the tear from her face and leaned down to grab a pot. "Nothing. I haven't seen a doctor yet."

"But you will. You will, right?"

Her mother silently filled the pot at the sink.

"Mom? You'll have it checked out, right?"

"Of course," she finally said.

"And soon."

Her mother didn't reply.

"Mom, you'll get it checked soon, right? Then you'll know whether it's something to worry about."

"I'll get it checked out," she said.

"Soon."

Her mother turned on the burner letting the igniter tick, tick, tick, for a few seconds longer than usual before turning the knob to high. "Linda's sister had a lump."

"I remember that. But she's had chemo and they think they got it all. So, it's good to get it checked out so if... if you need to, you can get well."

"I don't feel sick."

"That's good! It's early, then."

Her mother looked up. "She lost all her hair."

"Linda? She never looked different."

"It was a wig. I dyed it to match her natural hair color before she started chemo."

"That's amazing! I never would have guessed."

"I could lose my hair, Bailey."

"It's better than the alternative."

Her mother looked down at her hair as it cascaded over her shoulder and rested against the spot she'd pointed out to Bailey. "I don't want to be bald," she whispered.

"You could make yourself a wig if that happens. Who would be better able to pull it off?"

"She made me shave her head," her mother said. She met Bailey's gaze. "When it started falling out in clumps, she asked me to shave it all off. Do you know how hard that was?"

"It's just hair, Mom. It grows back."

Her mom shook her head. "You don't understand how long it takes to grow hair this length. And the chemicals change things. It grows back different after chemo."

"Maybe this is the universe telling you not to worry about your hair for once and start worrying about your health. Who cares what your hair looks like?"

"How can you say that?"

"Mom, it's *just* hair."

"This," she said, grabbing a hunk of the long strands, "is my billboard. *This* is why people come to me. *Me!* They don't want to come to a fifty-year-old bald woman to get their hair done!"

"You're not fifty."

"Yet."

True. She wouldn't be fifty until March. That was next year.

"Is that what this is about? Your birthday?"

Her mother gave her a long look and then sniffed and shook her hair behind her shoulders. "I'm going to my room. Tell me when the water boils."

"Mom…"

"I would have hoped I'd get some support from my own child."

"You do have my support. I'll make the appointment with the doctor if you want."

"Don't bother. I'll take care of it. We both know you don't do hospitals."

Her mother stalked off toward her bedroom and slammed the door with a hollow rattle. She sneezed. She sneezed again. The door opened. She sneezed a third time. "Have you been hugging Sammy again?" she accused Bailey through watery eyes. Sammy was the black Lab that lived next door.

"No."

A-choo! "Are you sure?"

"Absolutely."

A-choo! "Because you know how allergic I am to dogs."

A—!

Yip!

Her mother looked up at her sharply. Bailey pretended to cough. "Must be something…" *Yip! Hack!* "…in the air," she said. "Why don't you just go lay down and I'll, um, open the windows."

"You have a dog in there, don't you?"

"No." *Yip!* "It's a puppy."

"Bailey!"

"I'm sorry! It's not mine. He's just little. I thought if I kept him in my room, he wouldn't bother you."

A-choo!

"I'll take him back now. I'm sorry."

Bailey opened the door and out tumbled a little ball of fur. She felt warm tickling licks on her bare feet. Then the ball of fur began to squat. "No! No, Chewy! Outside!"

She scooped the dribbling dog under her arm and rushed outside to set him on the dirt drive. He licked her toes again. "Good doggie," she said. But nothing felt good. Nothing at all.

HER MOTHER WAS IN HER room when Bailey returned to gather the dog supplies. She'd left Chewy in her car as she gathered his leash, toys, dog bed and food dish. Then she threw it all in the trunk and stuck the key in the ignition. The low gas light came on. She figured she had just enough fuel to make it out to Blackberry Hill and back. She could worry about where the cash for gas would come from tomorrow.

She turned on the fan for heat and the dashboard emitted an anemic whir. She turned the knob to 'off'. She'd have to replace that blower fan as soon as she closed on the garage.

The drive up through town and up Blackberry Hill was quiet. Too quiet. It gave her time to think.

She couldn't bring herself to say it yet, even in her own mind. She thought of the lump in her mother's breast, Linda's wig, her mother without hair. She could think of all those things, but still her mind wouldn't allow her to take that extra step to say the 'c' word.

But she knew it was there. The word was like a boogie man just out of sight. She could feel it waiting in the shadows for her to let her guard down and leap out. It made her chest tight and her eyes ache, and the more she fought to block the possibility from her thoughts, the more pressing they became.

She pulled under the oak tree beside the road outside Ian's house and cut the engine. Thankfully she was alone.

Alone… with a dog she couldn't keep, outside the house of a man who couldn't stand her, pretending she could put off buying gas for four weeks so she could save every penny she had to make the loan go through even though she was thousands of dollars away from having enough.

The hopelessness of it hit her like the tiny pellets hitting her windshield. She watched them slither down the glass. A shiver ran through her, and Chewy scrambled over the console to sit in her lap.

She leaned over to hug him, pressing her face against his silky body and watched a tear drop and disappear into his fur. Talk about pathetic. She was crying into her puppy. Except it wasn't even her puppy.

A bright light blinded her from the driver's window, and she looked up.

"Bailey? What the hell are you doing here?"

Bailey swiped her eyes and shoved the driver's side door open with more force than was strictly necessary. Ian jumped back, the flashlight beam wobbling around them like a search light.

"You have to take him back," she said.

"That's not our deal."

"I don't care about the deal. Deal's off."

"You can't just call it off like that."

She slammed the door shut with her foot and started down the driveway ahead of him. "I can and I am."

She got to the top of the porch steps and reached for the door when he spun her around. "You can't— Are you *crying?*"

Bailey sniffed and wiped her face on Chewy's fur. "Allergies. I'm allergic," she insisted.

"You're not allergic to that thing. You're crying."

"Am not." A tear slid down her cheek. Chewy licked it.

Ian sighed and reached around her to open the door. "Get inside. It's starting to sleet."

She turned on her heel and walked through the door. She refused to look at him as she kicked off her shoes. They made too loud a noise on the bare hardwood floors. And she'd just polished these floors earlier today.

He walked past her down the hall. "When you're ready to tell me why you're stalking me, I'll be in the kitchen."

"I'm not," she said, following him, "stalking you."

"What am I supposed to think? You appear out of the blue, park outside my house and sit there. You look like you've slept in your clothes." He sniffed, his nose wrinkling. "And you smell like pee."

"That would be my coat. I think Chewy piddled on it when he was in my room."

Ian raised an eyebrow. "Hardly seems a reason to cry."

"I'm not crying about— I'm not crying." She set Chewy on the floor and shrugged out of her jacket. Sniffed it. *Ugh.* She set it on a bar stool.

"So what are you *not* crying about?"

"You wouldn't understand."

He reached into the fridge and pulled out a jug of cider then pulled two mugs from the cupboard. "Try me." He filled the mugs and set them in the microwave.

Bailey tried to gather her thoughts and swallow the raw, empty feeling inside before he was done pressing buttons. The soft whir of the microwave filled the air. "Someone I care about may be... sick," she finally said.

Ian looked at her and for once she didn't feel as if he was looking for a way to torment her. "I'm sorry. How sick?"

"Not sure yet."

"So, there's a chance it's not as bad as you think?"

She nodded. She couldn't bring herself to reply.

The microwave beeped. Ian pulled the mugs out, stuck his finger in one, and handed the other to her. "It might be a little hot. Go easy."

She cradled the mug in her hands. It had the Treasure Trakker logo on it in bright colors. Ian was wearing a long-sleeved T-shirt that read 'Find your Fantasy' and 'Trakker in Paradise' down the sleeves with the front emblazoned with the Treasure Trakker logo. Everywhere she looked, there were reminders that this guy and his experience were as far removed from scraping together a whole and happy life as you could get. He'd made himself a millionaire by the time most people were only graduating college.

She sipped the cider. It burned her lip a little. She hastily pulled it away and blew on it.

"I told you not to drink it yet."

"I don't need you telling me what to do right now."

He chuckled a bit. "I'm not trying to tell you what to do. I'm trying to be nice."

"Well, cut it out. I don't expect you to be nice."

"I don't expect you to cry."

She ventured another sip. It was warm, sweet and tart in her mouth. "Surprise. I'm human."

He didn't reply. Instead, he looked around at his empty living room and gestured for her to follow him. "Come on. There's no comfortable place to sit in here."

"I'm not going to your bedroom, mister."

He paused without turning around. "I was suggesting we go downstairs. I've set up the media room. Sort of. You'll see."

BAILEY PADDED IN HER stocking feet behind him, her footsteps heavy on the stairs. He found it amusing someone so small could walk so heavily. Little puppy nails *tip-tapped* on the floor.

"You might as well bring Sir Pees-A-Lot. But keep an eye on him. It's carpeted down here."

She scooped the pup into her arms. "He just peed, but that's a very cute name. I may need to get a new dog dish for him."

"Don't even think it."

He rounded the corner from where he'd set up his temporary office and opened the door. Bailey peered in.

"This is it?"

"It's not finished. Now that they've got the carpeting on the walls and floor, I'm waiting for the seats to arrive."

"So the bean bag chairs aren't your final choice?"

"Do you want to sit or not?"

She nodded, set her mug on the floor, and settled into a bean bag with the dog.

"Do you have popcorn?"

"Two bucks a bowl."

"Never mind then."

She shifted around in the chair, the foam beads inside scrunching as she reached for her mug again.

He lowered himself into the neighboring chair. Strange that he once thought them comfortable. He felt gangly in it now.

"So, want to talk about it?"

She sipped her cider. "No."

"Excellent. Want to watch a movie?"

"Sure."

He lurched out of his bean bag with a vow to get leather recliners pronto, sifted through his box of Blu-ray DVDs, and turned on the projector. "Okay, don't go freaking out, but it's better with the lights off."

"Sure thing, Lover Boy. That's what they all say."

He flicked off the overhead lighting and the strip LEDs glowed against the edges of the room.

"Ooh!" she said.

"It is kind of cool."

"A thirteen-year-old's wet dream."

"Are you always this crass?" he asked, grateful for the low light. Thinking about it brought a flash of heat to his face... among other places.

"Sorry. I'll behave. Cool set-up. Can't wait for you to get real chairs."

"Already planning on being invited back?"

"Start the movie, Lover Boy, or I'll make you loan me the popcorn. I missed dinner." As if on cue, her stomach growled audibly.

"Oh, for Pete's sake. Why didn't you say something?"

She shrugged, and he automatically reached out to pull her out of the bean bag. Her palm was small and strong in his, and he frowned as he felt the calluses there. The women he'd known always had perfectly manicured, perfectly smooth hands. A jolt of awareness shot up his arm, and she yanked her hand away before he could run his thumb over her palm again. She looked at him oddly.

He picked up the dog and walked toward the stairs. "I'll take this guy out for a bathroom break, and you can rustle up some food."

"What do you want?" she asked.

He shrugged. "Surprise me." He stopped. "But don't poison me."

"So picky."

A few minutes later he slammed the front door shut and set the dog on the hallway floor. "Dang! It's cold out there. It's not sure whether it wants to rain or sleet." He swiped ice pellets out of his hair. "So, what are we having?"

Bailey stared at the open refrigerator. "Not sure. You don't have a lot."

"What are you talking about? Ivy bought bags of groceries."

"Fine. See for yourself."

He looked into the fridge. Bins of fresh vegetables, packages of meat, a dozen eggs, and milk stared back at him. "This is loaded with options. You could make omelets, a salad, burgers..."

"*I* could make? Don't you have any granola bars or sandwich makings?"

"Deli meats are full of nitrates."

"They also lay neat and tidy on bread. They're even bread shaped. That's how you know they go together."

"I didn't ask her for deli meats. There's chicken in there. How about that?"

"Sounds good! Okay, I'll wash the lettuce and you can cut up the chicken. We can have chef salads."

"You need to cook it."

She closed the fridge door and crossed her arms. "Okay. Let's get this out there now. I don't cook. No, correction. I *can't* cook."

"Nobody *can't* cook," he scoffed.

"If you can burn it or make it fall or otherwise turn it inedible and unrecognizable, I'm your gal. I repeat: I don't cook."

"That's ridiculous. What do you eat?"

"Stuff."

"Crap is more likely." He shook his head and brushed by her to wash his hands. "Well, now that we're here, *I'm* hungry. A chicken Caesar salad sounds good. I'll grill the chicken if you get the salad part ready. Can you handle that or is that too complicated?"

"If I don't have to cook it, I'm good."

He pulled the chicken out of the fridge and collected some seasonings from a drawer. "I thought you were a mechanic. Don't tell me you can weld but not cook."

"I'm actually an excellent welder. It's hard to forget you have a flaming torch in your hand."

"Indeed."

Half an hour later he tapped the rear patio door with his foot. "Damn, it's getting nasty out there. I nearly took a header on my way to the grill."

Bailey peered around him into the dark. "How nasty?"

"The sleet has turned to freezing rain."

She stared at him as if he'd told her she was being exiled to Siberia.

"Don't look at me. I didn't plan the weather. You can bunk here for the night if you want. It's not like I don't have the room."

"Bunk where?"

He thought about his bed… the only padded horizontal surface in the house aside from the bean bag chairs in the basement. "We'll figure it out. Come on, relax. We've got food, a movie, and a working furnace. I think you'll survive."

She took the platter of grilled chicken from his hands and let out a breath. "Fine."

"That's the spirit."

BAILEY BALANCED HER salad and cider on a cookie sheet and sank into her bean bag chair. The foam beads inside scrunched audibly like a giant whoopee cushion. Strangely, it didn't bother her. Instead, she felt young and carefree and relaxed in a way that made her perversely uncomfortable.

She should feel nervous or at least awkward being trapped in a house with a virtual stranger, but Ian didn't feel like a stranger. Not at all. He felt like the big brother she'd never grown up with, except she didn't feel brotherly feelings toward him. She shoved a forkful of lettuce into her mouth.

Not that she *had* feelings for him. She just didn't think of him as a brother. Or at all, of course. Definitely, she was not noticing his feet in navy socks poking out from the faded and frayed hem of his jeans. Jeans that fit him like a Levi's commercial.

Retreat! Retreat! Her mind screamed. *Back away from the attraction!*

She ventured a peek at Ian as he folded his body into the matching seat beside her. She swallowed. "You look ridiculous," she said.

He raised one eyebrow, his knees nearly in his chest, and shoved a bite of chicken into his mouth.

"Grown men do not belong in bean bags," she continued.

He swallowed. "I've had these since college."

She looked down at the fabric rising up on either side of her, an image of Ian as a hunky, rangy college student lounging atop them coming to mind. It made her hyper-aware of the fact that she was picturing his body. Naked, for some reason. "Ew," she said.

His fork clattered to his own cookie sheet tray. "If you find me and my home and my hospitality so unwelcome, feel free to walk home."

There. That was better. It made her uncomfortable to feel too relaxed and… happy… around Ian. She liked it better when his eyes flashed and the air crackled with energy around them.

The lights flickered.

"Did the lights just flicker?" she asked.

"I'm sure you just blinked."

The lights flickered again.

"Oh, crap, you're going to lose power," she said.

"Not necess—"

Before he'd even finished his sentence, the room went dark.

Bailey carefully set her fork on her cookie sheet, the silence stretching out between them. "I don't suppose you have a generator?"

"I don't even have a sofa, and you think I've got a generator?"

"How about a flashlight?"

There was silence from the other chair. The pitch black of the basement felt like it was closing in.

"Ian?"

"I'm thinking. Wait here. I don't want you spilling your cider on my brand new carpet."

She heard rustling as he maneuvered out of his chair, a thunk, a mumbled curse and then silence. Chewy licked her hand and she realized he'd probably been licking her chicken in the dark the little sneak. She held her tray above her head.

Moments later she heard a distinctive *swoosh-humm* sound.

"What the—?"

He swooshed a toy saber toward her. It flashed green and hummed again. He set it next to her bean bag. "Is green all right with you?"

"I like green."

"Fantastic."

A flash of blue lit the room and Ian sank into his seat again. "Well, I guess the movie is out of the question."

Bailey ate another bite of salad. "Mmm," she said in agreement. "*Mmm!* What did you put on this chicken? It's delicious!"

"Cajun seasoning. One of our sponsors is a high-end mail-order company for—"

"Never mind that. Oh my God, it's amazing!"

"Stop the presses. Was that a compliment?"

She shoved another bite of succulent chicken into her mouth and savored the subtle spices. "I can be nice. Now it's your turn. Compliment me on how well I rinsed the lettuce."

"I have yet to find a bit of sand," came his sarcastic reply.

"See? We can both be nice."

"Hey, I've been nice!"

"You were very grumpy that first day."

"You were a stranger in my home, and you were insulting me."

"You were pushing me, and I was already mad."

"I figured that out when you kicked me."

An image of Ian's stunned expression as her toe had made contact with his shin leapt to mind. She twitched her shoulders, remembering the warm pressure of his fingers there as he'd held her at bay. A shiver of something hot and not unpleasant washed over her. She stabbed another bite of chicken.

"That was probably over the line," she admitted.

"You think?"

"I complimented your chicken; don't push me."

She heard a low rumble of what might have been a chuckle in the dark. The sabers had powered off, so she nudged hers with her toe and it lit up again.

They ate in silence for a while.

"So, tell me. Have you always wanted to be an auto mechanic?" he asked.

She frowned and drank her cooling cider. "No. Not always."

Her voice sounded small in the dark room. She quietly let out a breath.

No, there'd been a time in a place far, far away from where she was now, that she'd stood on the verge of adolescence and pictured a different outcome for herself. She'd felt confident and charming, clever even. Her dress had flowed in silky waves to the ground, and she'd known that she was different from all the others—and she intended to show everyone what strength, femininity and confidence looked like.

"What changed?" he asked.

She set her fork on her tray with a clatter. "I grew up."

Instead of showing everyone how ridiculous they were, she'd stepped out onto that stage and... wavered.

The smile her mother had urged her to perfect, felt pasted on, and she could feel, even now, the urge to bolt course through her veins as it had so many years ago. The echo of someone snickering sounded in her memory, and the heavy, awful realization that she'd shown no one anything but how foolish she was, washed over her.

Later, when she turned sixteen, she *had* shown everyone what strength and femininity looked like. It looked like the girl you'd least expect to showing up for a vo-tech class and doing it with attitude, because *no one* would tell her she wasn't feminine enough or charming enough or stylish enough to *fix cars.*

And somewhere along the line she had realized she actually enjoyed it. Cars were puzzles you could wrench at, and curse at and it didn't matter whether you smiled or looked pretty doing it. You got the job done and you got paid and if you were lucky and smart enough and saved long enough, you could afford to be your own boss. You could finally make your own rules, snickerers be damned.

"It's an unusual occupation for a woman."

"I like being my own boss. Or, at least, I will." She grimaced. She had yet to admit to the bank and the seller that she didn't have all the money. Still hoping for a miracle, apparently.

"Something tells me you don't play well with others."

She turned to him. "Not true. I get along fine with people as long as they're honest with me."

"Ah. Honesty. That's what we're calling this… this porcupine impersonation you've been doing."

"I'm not always like this," she mumbled. She set her tray next to the bean bag and pulled a sleepy Chewy into her lap. "At least, not so much so."

He definitely chuckled that time, a low rumble that rolled over her. She smiled into the darkness.

"I've got nothing against your being a mechanic. It's a respectable trade. And I applaud your goal of owning your own business."

"Gee, thanks."

"I'm not thrilled you think I'm some sort of money tree you can exploit to reach your goals, but—"

"Now, wait a minute! I'm not exploiting anything. We have a deal."

"Uh-huh. Which is why you're now in my house, with the dog you're supposed to take care of, eating my food."

"Technically, I'm done with dinner. Which was delicious."

He laughed again. She liked it when he laughed. She stroked Chewy's soft fur. "I've never had a dog, you know."

"What?"

"Of my own. I *know* about dogs, of course. But they were always, um, neighbors' and friends' dogs. My mother is allergic."

"Are you sure you're qualified to train that thing?"

"More than you." Which wasn't saying much. "For instance, I know he needs to go to the vet for a check-up and shots, and you need to get him a dog license."

"You, no, *we* will do it. You'll end up ordering something ridiculous and expensive if I'm not there to watch you."

"What would I order at the vet's?"

"I don't know, but I'm sure you'd think of something." She heard a *humm* and saw a blue glow as he set his tray on the carpet next to his chair. "You're right. That was delicious. I'm a fantastic cook."

"Mmm. And humble."

"Some people would say that makes me a good catch."

He chuckled and stretched, the foam beads of his chair scrunching. Bailey tugged at her T-shirt that had shifted under her and wondered about the women who had gone on the *Happily Ever After* show with him.

No doubt they were taller. And charming. And good cooks.

She wondered which one he chose.

The dark room somehow made it okay to voice her thoughts. "Makes me wonder why you even need a wife."

"I don't *need* a wife."

"Then why'd you go on the show?"

He was quiet a moment. "Needing and wanting are two different things."

"So you *want* a wife?"

He shifted in his chair again. "It's time."

She snorted, an entirely unladylike sound. "What, are your eggs getting old?"

"If you must know, I'm the same age as my father when... when he died."

Chewy snored softly in her lap. "And he had a wife and three kids by then."

"Yes." His answer was clipped.

She bit her lip. "That's why you went on the show." Okay, that was... if not pathetic then at least sympathetic. For some reason it made her feel sorry for him... Mr. Richy-Rich Lover Boy.

She heard his heavy exhale. He didn't answer.

"Did you find her? Your future wife?" she asked.

"I can't talk about the show. With anyone."

Especially you. He didn't say that, but she thought it was implied.

"Aw, come on. Who am I going to tell?"

"I don't know. That kid who has been camped out in my tree for three days?"

"Dylan? He's my half-brother. He's mostly harmless."

"I'm surprised he's not out there now, but my guess is the paparazzi were all smart enough to check the weather forecast."

Bailey shifted and stretched, staring toward the ceiling. The carpeting on the walls muffled any sounds from outside making the room feel like a cocoon. "What do men want in a wife anyway? I mean, when you went on the show, what did you ask for? Is it like picking out a puppy? 'I'll take a spotted one that's not too big and follows simple commands?'"

"Give me some credit. I'm choosing a life partner not a pet."

"So how does it work, this spouse-shopping thing. Can you tell me that?"

"I'm not *buying* a wife."

"Semantics," she said with a wave of her hand.

He was quiet a moment. "I filled out a questionnaire and did a video interview for starters."

"Like how big is your bank balance and your winky?"

"Are you thirteen or what?"

"Oh, come on," she said. "If you didn't already know, those are the primary questions every woman asks herself before considering a guy."

"For marriage?"

"For dinner."

"Hmm. Should I take that as a compliment considering you've just eaten here?"

"This doesn't count. This is sheltering in place. It's a weather emergency."

"I see."

Bailey contemplated the size of his… bank account. Her face grew warm. "I'm just being honest. We women are very practical. There are some things that are non-starters."

"Like bank accounts and wankys."

"Winkys."

"Good God."

"So, fess up. What are your non-starters? What must the future Mrs. McIntyre possess? I'm curious. And we're not going anywhere."

"I don't know. She should be attractive, I guess."

"Obviously."

"And a good cook," he added. "Food is important. I like to cook."

No doubt rinsing a few leaves of lettuce didn't count as 'cooking' in his book.

"She should also be kind and nurturing," he concluded.

So, basically, *not* someone like Bailey.

"How did you sort through all the candidates?" she asked. "Sounds overwhelming."

She heard his sigh. "It is. Marcia helps out."

"The Nazi matchmaker?"

"She's not that bad. She has her systems and theories, but there's probably some validity to them." She must have made a dismissive sound, because he continued. "We fill out the questionnaire, sort of an on-line dating thing, and then we get matches from her database. She contacts the matches to find out who is interested and able to go on the show. After a couple weeks of getting to know the women and group outings, I narrow it down to women I think have real potential, and we engage in 'escalating intimacy' sessions."

"Ew. Sounds like porn."

"Far from it. They're scripted conversations based on Arthur Aron's experiment on strangers falling in love. A series of questions that encourage increasing levels of intimacy to accelerate what naturally happens when you meet someone knew. We don't even touch, but we are facing each other."

"Freaky."

"Freakishly effective. After the intimacy sessions, Marcia had me weed out a couple more, then I went on the 'challenge dates' where my date and I are thrown into high-stress situations to see if we grow together or apart."

"How romantic."

"Again. Effective. And good for ratings I'm told."

"What were some of the questions?"

"Mmm?"

"From the experiment. Give me some examples."

"I don't know. Like, 'Before you make a telephone call, do you rehearse what you plan to say?' and 'Describe your perfect day.' That sort of thing."

"Huh. I get more personal with the sandwich guy at the deli. And I'm still not inclined to date him."

"They get more probing. You'd have to do it to understand."

She thought about the questions a moment then turned toward him in the dark. "No," she said. "Riding up to the top of the mountain on a dirt bike during the summer and watching the sun set over the lake."

"You ride a dirt bike?"

"Used to. Sold it."

"Why?"

"Needed the cash."

He was silent a minute, and Bailey was about to get up when he spoke. "Yes, because I hate the fact that you can't see people's faces over the phone, and I don't like surprises. And my perfect day would be doing the Winter Wild and hiking up the mountain before the lifts open and watching the sun rise over the lake."

"No fair. You stole that from me. Think of another perfect day. The mountain thing is mine."

"Nuh-uh. You just reminded me of it. We're still whole seasons apart from one another."

"Fine. What else?"

"Name three things you and your partner have in common."

She bit her lip at the word 'partner.' For some reason it felt intimate. She went out on a limb and used him. "*Star Wars*. Fond memories of the mountain. We both eat."

He chuckled. "Fighting the process doesn't help."

"Maybe I'm not trying to fall in love with anyone."

"It's not about *trying* to fall in love, it's about being vulnerable. Open. Honest. Are you that afraid to admit we have anything in common?" he asked.

He shifted. She could hear his bean bag moving, a soft rustling sound, before he spoke again. "We both like to feel in control even if it comes off as opinionated or controlling. We both enjoy sparring in the dark. And we're both a little turned on by it."

"Speak for yourself," she said.

"Admit it," his voice was a low rumble in the dark. "You are."

"Fine. We don't always feel understood by people around us. We, um, sometimes pretend to have it all together when we don't, and... there is maybe something about challenging each other that's...."

He whispered, "That's what?"

"That's... invigorating."

"Invigorating, eh?"

No, she was not going down that road with him. The man was engaged right now to some other woman if Marcia's techniques had worked—and they always did—so it was time to shut this flirting-in-the-dark thing down.

She picked up the puppy and shifted to set him on the bean bag and stood up. "I should call my mother and let her know I'm all right."

He stood, too. "Of course."

He was close. She could feel the heat of his body, the scent of man and spice teasing her senses. She reached for her lightsaber so she could see. He must have had the same thought, because their heads collided in the dark.

"Ow!"

"Ouch!"

She rubbed her temple and reached out a hand to steady herself. It met with solid, warm body. Her fingertips skittered over fabric toward exposed skin. A neck. A cheek. Her fingers touched his hair as much holding him at bay as holding him still. "Are you hurt?"

"I'll live. You?" She felt his hands, warm and firm, shift over her head and in her hair.

"I'll live."

His hands didn't drop away. Instead, his palms lightly grazed her cheeks, his palms framing her face. One of his thumbs brushed over her skin. Her breath caught.

"You sure?" His voice was husky, a low gravelly sound, and her heartbeat skittered in her chest. Oh, dear God in heaven, she knew that tone of voice. Nothing made a woman turn to mush quite like a whiskey-rough voice in the dark.

"My forehead hurts a little," she admitted. Oh God, she was pathetic.

His thumb shifted higher, his voice closer. "I'm sorry about that."

She couldn't breathe. She stood in the dark, his hands cupping her face and waited. For what? What was he doing? What did she want him to do?

Hello? Kiss her! That's what she *wanted.* She wanted to kiss the man, Lord help her.

Her hands fell to his chest, palms flattened against the muscled wall in front of her. He was tall. She hadn't realized how tall until she was facing him in the dark, inhaling the scent of him. Sweet baby gherkins, he smelled good.

"Hopefully your forehead feels better than my mouth," he murmured. "You mashed my lip into my teeth."

She reached up with one hand and feather-touched his lip. "I'm sorry. Here?"

"*Mm-mmm,*" he said, and the next thing she knew, she felt the soft heat of his lips closing over her fingertip. Fire exploded inside her. Hot tamales, the man was sucking her finger!

She went rigid with shock as he slowly took her finger into his mouth and drew back again. Her heart hammered hard in her breast as all sorts of thoughts and sensations warred for prominence.

He pulled back fully, and she could feel his lips curve under the pad of her finger. She yanked it back in alarm.

"What are you doing?" she asked, her voice barely audible.

"I would think that would be obvious."

Yes, obviously confusing. Damn, what a player. What a sexy, hot, smokin' player!

Well, Bailey Adams wasn't one to be played. Bailey Adams took charge.

She grabbed his face, rose on tip-toe… and lip locked the man before he could try anything else.

A jolt of heat and pleasure surged through her as he smiled against her lips. She nipped his top lip until he opened them slightly then swept her tongue in. He tasted of cider and spice and forbidden fruit, and he groaned. His hand left her face, slid down her side, and pulled her toward him until—*hello!*—there were no secrets left between them.

After a few moments, she pulled back to catch a breath. "*Mmm.* I think it's time I check out your bank balance now."

"Imp," he growled, and he kissed her hard, grinding against her, his hands hot on her body.

Oh God! Oh God! Oh God!

How did this happen? She so had to tell Liz. Or not. Crap! How could she tell Liz she was snogging with her future brother-in-law?

Bailey pushed against him with her palms and ducked her head away so she could think which, frankly, was impossible when he was kissing her and running his hot hanky-panky hands all over her backside.

"Wait. I need to think," she said.

"More than one less than twenty," he said, his breath coming in soft bursts against her hair as he sought her lips again.

"What?"

"My net worth." He tilted her head back and claimed another fast, devastating kiss. "Or do we need a ruler?"

"No. No," she said, her mind focusing on his lower anatomy which was pressing against her through those damnable jeans. They were indecently aged like those commercials, as if the average person stayed the same size long enough to age jeans that perfectly. "We're good."

"Good," he said, and his hand swept down her back, cupping her rear and pulling her up against him. No, no ruler needed at all.

"Wait…" she said, his lips trailing hot and heavy down her throat. "I'm not sure about this. I mean, I have no problem making out with a guy who is smokin' hot." She pushed him back. "But this is wrong. Aren't you engaged?"

"You think I'm smokin' hot?"

"That wasn't the point I was trying to make."

He pulled back, too. Slightly. His hands still rested on her hips, imprinting them. "No. I know."

"Well? What do you have to say for yourself?" She couldn't fight him off forever. I mean, geez, she was only human.

He blew out a breath and ran a hand down his face.

"Oh my God. You *are* engaged." She tried to pull away more forcefully now, her ardor cooled like she'd taken the ice bucket challenge all over again.

"No! Don't—" His fingers tightened on her. "I'm not."

She stilled. "Are you sure?"

His tone was rueful. "I think I'd know."

"Oh." *Oh. Not* engaged.

His hands slid up to her waist, and he dropped his forehead to the top of her head. "I'm sorry," he said. "I don't know what's going on here. Shit! I didn't tell you what I just told you, got it? Marcia would have my head if she knew I was talking about the show." His hands suddenly dropped away as if he realized where and how he'd been holding her.

"We, ah, sure. It was nothing," she assured him.

"Nothing," he repeated.

"I mean, yes, *something*. But not anything that means anything. We're just two people for whom it has been a while... er... *I'm* a person for whom—"

"Two people," he corrected.

"Right—really?—okay, *two* people for whom it has been a while, and we got caught up in the moment. It was perfectly natural. It doesn't mean anything."

"No. It doesn't mean anything."

CHAPTER ELEVEN

IT HAD BEEN LESS THAN twelve hours since Bailey locked lips with Ian in his nerdy man-cave, and damned if she wasn't feeling twitchy all over just thinking about it. *Erg!* She needed to focus on figuring out how in hell she was going to raise the rest of the down payment by month's end, not moon over her best friend's future brother-in-law like some lovesick puppy. *Must. Focus.*

Bailey grabbed a wriggly Chewy and stepped out of her car. She waved to Dylan who appeared to be paying for a pizza at the end of Ian's driveway. At least he wasn't climbing trees since the freezing rain they'd had overnight.

As was typical this time of year, the temperatures had risen enough by morning that the freezing rain had turned to rain, and Bailey had snuck out without even saying goodbye. After their awkward clutch in the media room, Ian had offered his bed to crash on and magnanimously stated that he'd sleep on the bean bags, which was ridiculous given the fact that he'd look like a foot-long hotdog on a regular size bun. Bailey had insisted she would be fine, which turned out to be a lie, but when she'd woken to Chewy licking her face and taken him outside to pee, she'd realized it was safe to drive and had decided to get out while she could.

She blew on her to-go cup of mocha latte, her one splurge, and allowed herself to rethink her whole definition of nerds. Something here did not compute. Nerds were supposed to clean viruses off computers and other nerdy things—not walk around being all sexy and hot and *kissing her.*

The air was wet and raw, and she wouldn't be back staring at Ian's house except she had to figure out what to do with Chewy. Plus she'd promised Liz she'd help with the furniture placement, hanging of pictures and other stuff because, even though Liz wouldn't admit it, she was stressing about the wedding. Any normal woman would.

Chewy waddled along on his ridiculously frou-frou-y leash. It looked like something Paris Hilton would have on her dog, and would probably give a bigger dog a masculinity complex, but Chewy seemed indifferent, and it was satisfying to see Ian cringe every time she clipped it on the matching collar.

Liz met her at the door. "Thank goodness you're here! I've got furniture deliveries coming tomorrow, but I... what is that?"

"Ian's dog."

"Ian has a dog? Since when? And why do you have it?"

"Shared custody? Just kidding. I'm training it."

Liz's brow furrowed. "You don't know anything about dogs."

"Not true. Remember that black one that lives next door? I've petted him on numerous occasions. Plus the Titweiller's are having me walk Zack since a couple of weeks ago when she hurt her foot in that 5K."

Liz shut the door behind them. "I'm not even going to get into this. That Marcia lady has been all over my case to make this place a home ASAP, and I've got to run to Concord and find some decorations to dress it up on the outside, because she says the house looks 'too new.'" Liz rolled her eyes. "What I would have done to have *that* be the trouble with my parents' house."

Bailey sympathized to a point. Liz's parents had called her home to Sugar Falls last April to put their house on the market so they could live full-time in Florida. But, if they hadn't, Liz never would have gotten together again with Carter. And *both* houses were a heck of a lot better than living with an allergic mother in a double-wide trailer with a dog that couldn't seem to understand that her socks were not chew toys.

Bailey kicked off her sneakers on the front mat. "Where's Ian?"

"Downstairs, I think. What happened to your sock?"

Bailey glanced back at the hole in her brand new Smartwools. She'd be putting socks on Ian's bill, too. So what if she'd gotten these on super discount? Ian would be reimbursing her full price.

She found Ian at his 'desk.' "For a multi-millionaire, you'd think you'd invest in a decent home office."

He didn't even turn around in his chair. "Liz has promised me something when it's all done. In the meantime, Marcia wants my office to look like a den."

"Whatever. Here's Chewy. You have a two o'clock appointment for shots." She made to hand over the leash. Ian turned but did not reach for it.

"Aren't I paying you for this?" he said.

"You're paying me for training. This is veterinary care. It's not covered under our deal. Plus, I have other stuff to do."

"Like what? I heard you were fired from your last job."

"Technically, I quit preemptively, but that's irrelevant. I have a commitment."

"So what's so pressing you can't take the puff ball to the vet?"

"If you must know, I'm taking my mother to the doctor."

"Is she the one that might be sick?"

"Yes. I mean, no. It's just a routine visit." Nothing to stress about or obsess over. Women got mammograms all the time. "Anyway, I've got to drive her over to the Sugar Falls' Health Center, so…"

"Sure. Of course."

Bailey pulled back the leash. "Oh, no!"

"Now what? I said I'd do it."

"Chewy! He's been riding in my car for days! I can't give her a ride now. Her allergies will act up for sure! Skye was going to give her a ride, but she said her car's making some rattling noise she's worried about. It's probably nothing, but…"

"Doesn't your mother have a car?"

"Would I be stressing about this if she did? It died a few months back, and she didn't have the money to replace it right away. She usually rides with Wanda anyway. Maybe Dylan can…"

Ian stood up. "I can drive her."

"You?"

"Sure. It's only a mile or so from the vet's office. You bring Chewy in your car, I'll get your mother, and we'll meet over there. I'll get my keys."

"You don't have to—"

"Do anything I don't want to. I know. I'll follow you to your mother's."

Half an hour later the three of them stood on the sidewalk outside the health center.

Sandi turned to Ian. "Thank you for driving me."

"No problem, Mrs. Adams."

"I'd no idea you and Bailey were such good friends," she said somewhat accusingly before laying a perfectly manicured hand on Ian's arm. "Such a handsome taxi service."

Bailey cringed. "Mom, he's half your age."

Her mom turned to her with a quelling glance. "Wanda and Phil are perfectly happy, and *she's* sixteen years older. Some men like the life experience of a mature women."

"No one is accusing anyone of being mature," Ian said diplomatically. At least, Bailey thought he was being diplomatic. He might have just insulted both her and her mother.

"Well," her mother said, squaring her shoulders and taking a deep breath that highlighted her cleavage. She'd worn a rather revealing top for a blustery November day. "I guess it's time I head in."

Bailey reached over and squeezed her mom's arm. "It'll be okay," she said. "Knowing is better than not knowing."

"Is it?" her mom said, but then she turned and waved, and Bailey and Ian were left on the sidewalk.

"I suppose I'll ride over in your car." Ian looked at Bailey's car.

Bailey took a bolstering breath. He'd been nice enough to give her mom a ride, the least she could do is suck it up and take care of the vet visit. "I can do this myself," she said.

"No. He'll end up with gold crowns on his little puppy fangs or something. We'll both go."

Bailey shrugged as if it didn't matter and waited for Ian to fold himself into the passenger seat. They were at the vet's office in minutes.

Bailey hugged Chewy to her chest as Ian checked in with the receptionist. She swallowed and tried to breathe through her mouth so as to minimize the antiseptic, animal smell that wanted to suffocate her. Poor babies. So this is what fear smelled like. Antiseptic and pee.

"What's with the face?"

Ian was looking at her.

"I'm not making a face."

"You look like someone is going to give *you* a shot."

She felt the blood rush from her head at the word 'shot.' Chewy whimpered. She tried not to squash him.

"Mr. McIntyre? We're ready for you now."

The receptionist held open the door to an examining room, the shiny metal table looking like the perfect setting for an evil science experiment.

"You know," Bailey said, "it looks a little cramped in there. I'll wait out here. You can take him." She pushed Chewy at Ian's chest.

"Seriously? There's plenty of room."

Bailey shook her head and struggled to untangle the leash from her wrist, low-level panic shooting through her. "No. I'm good. You go ahead."

"What's gotten into you? You're acting weird."

"This is my normal self."

"Mr. McIntyre?" the vet called from the room.

"Just come on." Ian tugged at the leash which was somehow still caught in Bailey's sleeve, and she stumbled into the room after him.

"So who do we have here?" The vet, Dr. Killion, which sounded like an evil, animal-experimentation scientist name if ever there was one, grasped Chewy in her man-hands and set him on the examining table.

"Chewy," Ian muttered.

"Chewy," Dr. Killion repeated through sinister-white teeth. She bared them at Ian and Bailey then pulled out an oversized stethoscope and pressed it to Chewy's little chest.

"Eating, drinking and eliminating okay?"

Bailey resisted the urge to tug Chewy back from the doctor as she pried open his puppy mouth and wrenched on his little legs.

"All systems go," said Ian.

"Excellent. Well, I don't see anything alarming. She appears perfectly healthy, so we'll get her vaccinated and get you on your way."

"*He*," corrected Bailey.

"Pardon?"

"You said 'she.' Chewy is a 'he.'"

Dr. Killion flipped Chewy over. "No penis. And here's the… if she'd stop squirming… her…"

"Okay! Yup! We see!" Ian said, grinning somewhat maniacally.

"But what about this?" Bailey said, pointing to a little pointy nub covered with fur.

"That's a nipple."

"Are you sure?"

"Pretty sure, yes." Okay, that seemed a bit mocking.

"A nipple?" Bailey said.

"See here?" Dr. Killion held some fur aside further up. "Here's another nipple."

"Okay!" Ian said again. "He's a she. Got it."

"Of course. Could one of you hold her while I get her shots ready?"

Dr. Killion turned, stabbed a needle into a bottle of vaccine and said something.

Bailey was sure Dr. Killion was speaking, because her mouth moved, but then the doctor morphed oddly and listed to the side, and Bailey was sucked back into a tunnel, a roaring sound filling her ears. She reached out toward the table, but never felt it under her fingers.

The next thing she knew, Ian was leaning over her, his arms wrapped around her, one knee between her legs… and she was laying on a cold, hard, concrete floor and blinking up at him.

"What are you doing?" she asked. It seemed an appropriate question.

"She's okay," she heard him say.

"I'll take Chewy into the back and give you a moment then." That was Dr. Killion's voice.

"Thanks."

The door clicked shut, and Bailey put her hand to her head as a wave of something odd washed over her. "Did I just faint?"

"Like a tree in a forest. Good thing I saw it coming."

She struggled to sit up, and he rolled to the side. "I've never fainted before," she said. Okay, there was that *once…*

Ian winced and shifted to a sitting position. "Lucky me."

She glanced at him as he rubbed his kneecap. "Thank you."

He nodded. "Any idea what brought that on?"

"I'm not a fan of needles," she said in what could only be classified as the understatement of the millennium.

He glanced sidelong at her. "You could have said something."

"I didn't think it would be a big deal seeing as it wasn't *me.* Turns out, it was worse."

"No kidding."

"Is he okay? Chewy?"

"He—*she* is fine. Remind me not to bring you for her booster shots."

"There are *more?*"

"Yes. But they're *her* shots, not yours. You can relax."

"I can't believe he's a she."

"I can't believe you didn't know that."

She scowled and lurched to her feet. "You didn't either."

"I figured you'd looked."

"Puppies are squiggly. I saw a bump and that was that."

"It was a *nipple.* How can you not know the difference between a winky and a nipple?"

"You know you blush every time you say that word? It's just a part."

His eyebrows rose sharply. "I was protecting your sensibilities."

"I have no sensibilities."

"So I'm beginning to see. Come on, let's go check out." He rose to stand beside her and limped toward the door.

"Sorry about your knee. You're my hero."

He glanced down at her, his lips quirking up at the corner. "Don't mock me. I saved you from the E.R."

"And for that I'm truly thankful."

FOR ONCE IAN DIDN'T miss his old 1978 Catalina with the standard transmission. By the time he'd dropped Bailey's mother off and driven back to his own house, his knee was killing him. Bailey waited for him inside.

"You're still limping," she said.

"Brilliant observation."

"Here, sit on the stairs. I'll get ice."

"Better yet, I'll go lie down and you can get me lunch. I'm starved."

"Lunch?"

"I took a fall for you, Bailey. You owe me now."

She sighed. "Can we call a truce for a bit? I'm trying to be nice. There's no need to turn it ugly."

"My knee is swelling, it hurts like a son of a bitch, and I'm so hungry I'd eat your cooking. I don't care what you bring me, just throw something together and bring me a bag of frozen veggies for my knee. And Advil. I need Advil."

Bailey took his arm over her shoulders to help him down the hall which was a sweet gesture but totally ineffective. He found himself leaning closer just to catch a whiff of her lemony scent which caused her to stumble under his weight. He straightened and hobbled toward his room.

The front door slammed. "Yoo-hoo! How's our sexy bachelor today? I've got company!"

"Oh, shit," he mumbled. He glanced at Bailey. "A hundred bucks if you make her go away."

"You think I can be bought for so little?"

He raised an eyebrow.

"Deal," she said. "Can you make it the rest of the way?"

"Don't forget the Advil," he said.

Bailey shrugged out from under his arm and strode toward the front door. "Actually, Marcia, Ian's not feeling..."

"Ta-da!"

Marcia stood inside the door with Nick, Ivy, and a woman with the face of Jennifer Garner and the body of Sophia Vergera. The woman held a platter of cupcakes. Bailey took an instant dislike to her.

"Hello," Bailey said. She felt small next to this woman. And unkempt. She yanked the ponytail holder out of her hair and attempted to casually comb it out with her fingers. She extended her right hand.

The woman smiled charmingly and held the platter of cupcakes aloft as if to say, "So sorry, but I come bearing sweets, so my hands are full, and you still have a wad of your knotted hair tangled in your fingers, so I'll just hold these out of harm's way." Which, of course, she couldn't have seen, but Bailey dropped her hand and twitched her fingers next to her side to shake the tickling hair free.

"Where's Ian?" Marcia asked, clearly unhappy her grand entrance was for naught.

"He's, um, not feeling well."

The brunette with the cupcakes smiled confidently. "I know what will perk him up."

Bailey scowled. For some reason she didn't want this woman perking anything on Ian.

"He's throwing up," she lied. "You don't want to go in there."

"Oh, mother of dragon farts!" Marcia spat. "It's probably that norovirus that blasted handler had. Come on, Helen. We'll take you back to the inn and work on the profile segment there."

"Wait. I'll leave him a cupcake for when he feels like eating again. It'll lift his spirits."

Bailey blocked the hallway with her body. "I wouldn't do that if I were you. It's awful back there. Get out while you can."

"What are you doing here, then?" Marcia wanted to know.

"I'm taking care of Chewy. Ian's just too sick right now."

"I won't bother him," the Helen woman said. She slid past Bailey in a cloud of bright, citrusy fragrance and started down the hall as if she knew the location of his bedroom already.

"Um," Bailey said, "Why don't you set those in the kitchen? The whole tray might be overwhelming."

As Helen set the tray down in the kitchen, Bailey high-tailed it toward Ian's room. She burst in. "Gag!" she said. "Now!"

"What?"

"Just, make gagging noises! I'll explain later."

A soft knock sounded on the door, and Bailey grabbed a can of lemon polish and sprayed it around them in a cloud. "What the hell—?"

"Hello? May I come in?"

Ian's face went slack. "Helen?"

Gag, Bailey mouthed again. He coughed into his hand. It probably wasn't faked, because the lemon polish was a bit overwhelming.

"Oh, poor baby," Helen gushed. Bailey rolled her eyes.

Helen hurried over and laid a hand across Ian's forehead. "You don't feel hot, thank goodness. I heard you haven't felt yourself."

"No," Ian said, sinking to the mattress. "No, I haven't."

Helen smiled reassuringly and set the cupcake on Ian's dresser. "For you. Once you are feeling more yourself. I'd like to say I made them, but

I just arrived. There's a sweet little bakery in town reminds me of when I started out. We'll have to go there when you're feeling better."

Ian nodded. "Sure. That sounds great. I'm sorry about this." He gestured vaguely toward himself and his rumpled bed then winced.

"Oh, dear," Helen said, rushing to fluff his pillow. "I'm overtaxing you. I'll go." And yet she stood, hovering like some annoyingly sexy mother hen.

"That's probably for the best," Ian said with another wince. Bailey gave him a look, and he coughed into his hand.

"Thank goodness you have a friend here to help you. I don't believe I caught your name." Helen turned her sugar-sweet smile on Bailey.

"Bailey."

"Bailey? What a lovely name. I always wished I had a more unusual name," said the woman who was named after the *most beautiful woman on Earth.* "Do help yourself to a cupcake while you're here. They're quite good."

"I know. My sister made them."

"She's very talented," Helen cooed warmly.

"Yes, she is."

"All right," Helen said, brushing Ian's hair from his forehead with another concerned frown. "I'll let you rest. Take care." She turned. "Nice to meet you, Bailey."

"Um, you, too," Bailey muttered.

The door closed. Bailey turned to Ian with relief. "Thank God she's gone."

"She's not so bad."

"If you like the sweet, solicitous sort."

He chuckled then winced again. "Can you bring me that ice now?"

"Sure." She reached toward the dresser. "And leave the cupcake," he growled.

Bailey checked to be sure the coast was clear and gathered supplies from Ian's kitchen on a cookie sheet. Ten minutes later, she nudged open his bedroom door with her elbow and bobbled the tray. "What the—?"

"Does no one knock?" Ian muttered. He was stooped over next to his bed, wrestling with the cuff of his jeans.

"Flashing your tightie-whities now? Not cool." Bailey picked up a cupcake and took a giant bite.

"You can stand outside if you don't mind."

"I'm fine," she said, chewing. He sat onto the bed and winced again as he bent his leg to tug at his jeans. "You need help?" she asked around the cupcake.

He looked up through his lashes and Bailey gulped the rest in one swallow. "Sure," he said. "Seeing as you're standing there."

She brushed off her hands and knelt down to grab the cuff of his pants and pulled. The groan he emitted somewhat negated the steaminess of the moment. Somewhat.

He fell back onto the bed and she got a good look at his knee. "Not looking good there, Lover Boy."

"No shit." He waved toward his dresser. "Can you find me a pair of sweats?"

"Sure." Bailey tossed him the bag of frozen cauliflower and rummaged through his drawers for sweats. "So, this Helen, is she the one you picked? I thought you said you weren't engaged."

"I can't talk about it. I'm under contract."

She turned and handed him a pair of sweats. She rolled her eyes. "As if you need the money."

"It's not about that. I made a commitment." He shimmied the pants over his hips and lay back with a groan.

"Here's your Advil." She handed him the pills then plucked Chewy from the floor and plopped her on his chest.

"Hey!"

"Oh, stop grousing. Puppies make everyone feel better."

"Can I get a glass of water or something to take these?"

"I knew I forgot something. Just kidding!" She reached behind her and took the bottled water off the tray. "And, because I knew you were feeling lowly, I made my specialty."

"I can't wait."

"Sit up. Sit up." She held the tray above him until he'd scooted into a sitting position against the headboard then lowered the tray with great fanfare. "Behold, a Bailey Adams Classic."

"What the hell is this?"

"A taste sensation. Try it."

Ian picked up one of the two sandwich halves on the plate. "You're trying to poison me, aren't you?"

She grabbed the other half and bit into it. "Mmm. *So* good."

He peeled back the top slice of bread. "What the hell is this?"

"A peanut butter and Doritos sandwich."

Ian made a strangled noise of disbelief.

"Yes, I'll admit the wheat bread is kind of a first for me, but that's all that Ivy chick bought you, so I made do. Lucky for you, I had a bag of Doritos in my car."

"Lucky for me." He eyed the sandwich dubiously.

Bailey sank her teeth into another bite. She'd lightly toasted the bread before adding the peanut butter, so the peanut butter oozed, soft and fragrant, around the crunchy, spicy chips. Heaven.

Ian ventured a bite. His eyes widened.

"Told you," she said.

"This is pure genius," he breathed, loudly chewing.

"Thank you." She sucked in a bread crumb and choked a bit, grabbed his water and drank it. "Sorry. Went down the wrong way."

His gaze rested on the bottle between them. "You have no filters, you know that, don't you?"

"I think of filters as a haze of little white lies between people."

"Some might call them social graces, but let's not quibble."

"You're joking with me!" she said.

"You may take it that way."

"No, that's funny. You have a sense of humor when you're wounded."

"Did you find any fruit or vegetables to go with this?" he asked, taking another bite of sandwich.

"Apples, bananas, carrots, grapes and a red pepper."

"I'll take an apple."

"Good choice. I'll bring you another cupcake, too. That Helen chick left the tray in your kitchen."

Bailey closed the bedroom door on her way out. She chose a couple of apples from the crisper draw to wash at the kitchen sink.

"I heard Ian's not feeling well. I hope it's not that bug that's been going around." Liz stood in the living room holding a measuring tape across the window.

"Liz! I didn't know you were here."

"Just got here a few minutes ago. Ran into Marcia and her entourage in the driveway. They warned me to keep my distance from Ian. I didn't want to bother him, though, so I let myself in."

Liz scribbled something on her little yellow notepad and started laying the tape along the floor.

"He's actually not sick. I just told them that so they'd go away."

"Really? Why?"

"He's, um, injured. He didn't want to be bothered, so I told them he was sick."

"Yes, vomit usually tends to turn people away at the door. What happened?"

"What makes you think something happened?"

"Liz looked up from her measuring tape. "You said he was injured."

"Oh! Right. He, um, hurt his knee. Fell on it. It's all swollen."

Liz wrote something else on her notepad. "Well, I just wanted to double check a couple measurements before I bought the window treatments and area rugs. The furniture should arrive in a day or two. Thanks so much for helping me here. What with the wedding prep, I'm swamped, but I couldn't say no."

"No problem."

Bailey waited for Liz to finish jotting down another note. "Um, Liz? Before you go, I wondered if you had some time to go over some numbers with me for the new shop."

"Again? I thought that was settled? Isn't your closing the first of December?"

"Yeah. Not so much so."

Liz stood warily. "Uh-oh."

"Sully bailed on me."

"*What?* When? Why haven't you said anything?"

"A few days ago." Bailey blew the hair away from her eyes and rubbed her apple on her shirt to dry it. "A lot has been going on." Her mother. The dog. Ian the hottie who'd just flashed her his tightie-whities which she *could not* get out of her mind.

Liz checked her watch. She was the only person Bailey knew who owned one anymore. "I'm sorry. I'd say we should go talk now, but I'm meeting Carter at the inn to discuss the menu in half an hour."

"The menu? Your wedding is in six weeks!"

"I know. We're way behind. I'll call you? Set up a time to chat?"

Bailey nodded. "Sure." It wasn't as if the bleak picture of future failure was going to change in the next twenty-four hours. It had taken years of scraping together spare cash here and there, shopping at thrift stores and patching together cars meant for the junkyard so she could afford her half of the down payment on the garage to begin with.

How could she possibly make up Sully's half in less than a month?

She needed to win the lottery, sell a body part or renegotiate the terms. She might not be a math whiz, but even she knew the odds of winning the lottery weren't good, the odds of successfully selling a kidney were even less, and Valerie had only agreed to help Bailey as a favor to her sister-in-law and now that the pop-up timer on her pregnant belly had nearly popped, Bailey would be lucky the closing wouldn't happen at the hospital. There was no way Valerie would be in a state to help renegotiate the deal now. And, more importantly, there was only so long Bailey could get by without a steady job without using her own savings to live on.

Bailey waved Liz goodbye and brought the other apple to Ian.

She stood over him and took another bite, crunching loudly.

"Are you all set now? I should go," she said.

"Go? Who is going to take care of Chewy? I can barely walk."

"Oh, for God's sake, it's not so bad."

"Have you *seen* my knee?"

"Chewy will be fine. I've got another job to get to."

"Don't tell me. You're stealing money from someone else on the sly?"

"Ha. Ha. I'm dog walking, and then I have a cleaning job after that."

He chewed and swallowed. "Is this what you do? Patch together odd jobs? I thought you were a mechanic."

"I was. *Am*. But things have been a bit up in the air since last April when I had a falling out with the owner of the shop where I worked." She'd kneed him in the groin when he'd grabbed her ass one too many times, quit on the spot, and moved back in with her mother to make ends meet.

She'd been there ever since.

"It's November," Ian pointed out unhelpfully, "that's over six months."

"No shit, Sherlock. I'm working on it. Or, did you forget I'm trying to buy a shop of my own?"

"You'd think you would have figured that out sooner, that's all."

"Look, the garage wasn't on the market until a couple of months ago, and I had to talk Sully into going in on it with me. He still works for the enemy."

"How much do you need to make up his half?"

"Twenty grand, give or take."

"And you think you'll make that walking dogs and cleaning houses?"

"No! No, I don't! Thanks so much for pointing out the obvious. And even if I *do* somehow scrape together the money, the business plan we submitted has Sully pulling in his own share of work…"

"Have you talked to him about whether he'd still come work for you?"

"No. Not yet." Although that was a good idea.

"It seems to me…"

"It's none of your business."

"Right."

"I meant, it's nothing you need to worry about. It's my problem." Plus she'd been so mad at first, she hadn't thought beyond the first blinding panic that had washed over her.

"I wasn't offering to help."

"Gee, thanks."

"You seem as if you don't have a lot of direction in life, that's all."

"And you've got it all figured out?"

"This isn't about me."

"Good, because I don't think I need advice from a guy who doesn't know what it's like to struggle."

He frowned at her. "Who says I don't?"

"Oh, please. We both know we were born on opposite sides of the tracks. I grew up listening to drunks yelling at their wives and dogs at two a.m., a father who was more concerned about his own made-up medical issues than any of his kids, never knowing whether the cute guy at the pizza place I had a secret crush on was actually my half-brother or not, and you grew up on the lake... probably skiing and playing rugby and having family Thanksgivings that looked like somebody was filming a Butterball Turkey commercial."

Ian was silent. She'd nailed it on the last one, for sure. "I never played rugby."

"Whatever. The fact is: we have nothing in common."

Ian repositioned the frozen veggies on his knee. "So, *was* he your half-brother?"

She took another bite of apple. "No. He wasn't, but it didn't matter in the end. Turns out he's gay."

"Tough break."

Bailey shrugged. "Makes awesome pizza though." She reached over and nabbed a chip that had fallen out of Ian's sandwich and onto his plate. She really should go. The Titweillers were notoriously anal about punctuality.

"So, what's the plan? Can you get someone to loan you the money?"

"Take a loan out to get a loan? Not unless I can get it interest-free, and I don't see anyone lining up to gift me twenty grand."

"No one to ask? Grandparents? Your father?"

"Grandparents are all dead. My mother just gets by, and Daniel never paid a cent of child support, so I'm thinking it's unlikely he's going to hand over a check now."

"Have you asked?"

"I'd sooner gut myself with a plastic spatula."

"A simple 'no' would have sufficed."

Bailey gestured to his tray. "You done? I'll take it to the kitchen before I go."

He took his time swallowing and then glugged the water, his head tilted back and his throat working in a way that made Bailey forget about why she needed to be somewhere else. "When are you coming back?" he asked.

"Tomorrow? I'm not sure. Liz said the furniture would be coming in the next day or so and she'd need help arranging and unpacking..."

"Not tonight? I need you to train Chewy."

A bone-weary fatigue washed over her. She shut her eyes and picked up the tray. "We both know that's a joke."

"Not to me. Have you seen my knee? I don't care if you're the dog whisperer or not. I need someone to take her in and out and feed her. And if you can't do it at your place because of your mother's allergies, you'll have to come and do it here."

"I'm not cashing your check."

"That would be a mistake, because I intend for you to earn every last cent of it."

She met his gaze and something sparked there. Something she didn't understand but flashed brighter and more pure each time. "Fine. If that's what you want. I'll be back later."

His voice was at her back as she left. "Bring dinner!"

SHE WAS A CHARITY case now. The truth made her itch uncomfortably, or maybe that was fleas from Zack, the Burnese she'd walked this afternoon. As if anyone had ever heard of an all-organic, non-toxic, pesticide-free flea collar. There was a reason the tried and true chemicals worked. They killed things. Zack's owners, though, were rich as sin and the fact that the dog shed like nobody's business gave Bailey a twice weekly cleaning and dog grooming gig. Win-win.

She would have considered going into the pet-care business but Sandi's allergies, and the fact that she knew practically nothing about animal care, kind of squelched that as a possibility.

She stood in the shower and quickly rinsed off, pulling on a pair of old corduroy jeans and a soft, long-sleeved tee. She decided against pigtails, instead scrunching her hair into casual waves as it dried, before heading to Ian's again.

Ian. Ugh.

What a mess.

What was she doing with the guy? He had hot tamale Miss Southern Belle bringing him cupcakes on a literal freakin' platter. Sure, he'd denied being engaged, yet every time she brought up the outcome of the show, he got all cagey. What was that all about? If only she'd thought to get a look at whether that Helen chick had a rock on her hand. Bailey had been too mesmerized by the woman's perfectly presented boobs in that silky, white top. And Bailey wasn't even marginally a lesbian, so Lord knew Ian was probably transfixed like a mind-capture gun.

She had to stop thinking about Ian. It was more important to find the time to sit down with Liz and work the numbers again for the business. *Was* there a way to make the projections work without Sully in the picture? What if he weren't a co-owner being paid in equity but an employee? If she were to miraculously find the money for the loan, could she afford to keep him on as an employee? Would he agree? Or would she be stuck, God forbid, living with her mother forever?

Feeling markedly more depressed, Bailey got in her car and shivered her way into town and over to Ian's house. She could not fix that heating fan soon enough.

Kicking the car door closed, she grabbed the to-go bags from the back seat and came face to face with one of the paparazzi regulars.

"Whattya got there?"

"Food."

"You're here a lot. What's your relationship with the bachelor? Would you characterize yourself as close to him? Does his fiancée know how often you're here? We heard Ian has the stomach flu. Why would you be bringing him food?"

Bailey stopped and rounded on the guy. He was a bit paunchy or maybe that was the multiple layers of clothing he was wearing to keep warm. Her guess was these guys typically worked in warmer climes. "Look. I'm a family friend. Nothing more. The network is paying me to help out around the house and such while Ian—Mr. McIntyre—gets settled. And he said he was feeling better, so I offered to bring him food. There's nothing more sordid than that going on, so why don't you just go home?"

"Lady, I can make enough off of one good photo to sit pretty for weeks. Give me the money shot, and you've seen the last of me."

"Weeks? You're kidding me."

"Swear on my Nonna's grave."

Bailey gestured behind him. "What about those guys? Wouldn't you each need a money shot to leave?"

The guy turned. "*Eh.* Depends on whether the story is wrapped up or continuing."

"No deal then."

BAILEY UNCLIPPED CHEWY'S leash after taking her out for a potty break and let her scamper down the basement hall toward Ian's office. She heard Ian greet the puppy, his low voice rumbling nonsensical praise. She rounded the corner to find Chewy giddily panting from Ian's lap.

"You're the world's biggest softie," she said.

He nuzzled the top of the dog's head. "And she's the most adorable puppy ever."

Bailey reached out and ruffled Chewy's velvety ears. "Speaks the truth, he does," she said.

Ian rolled his eyes. "Speaks the truth, he does," he repeated. "Add more gravel to it, she must."

"It sounds like you're coughing up a loogey."

"Just the fact that you even have a word for that is both amazing and horrifying."

She stepped away, wandering really, because even though it was time to go—she'd taken care of the dog, picked up and swept the entry—she didn't want to leave. Sandi was at the pub tonight for Trivia Night, and Bailey didn't want to be alone.

Being alone led to thinking about life and cancer and failure and, frankly, it sucked.

She strolled over to the glass-fronted bookcase where Ian had his collections displayed. She reached out to touch the glass. "I can't believe what a geek you are."

"Says the woman doing a Yoda impersonation."

"That was in fun. This," she said, motioning to the enshrined memorabilia, "is taking things way too seriously."

On impulse she tried the latch. It opened.

"Don't go in there."

She swung the door open. "Relax. I'm just looking." She reached in and grasped a hilt. Ian was right. It *was* nicely balanced and felt *real* in her palm.

He leapt up from his chair, his injured knee only slowing him slightly as Chewy tumbled to the floor. "Hey! You look with your eyes not your hands."

She ignored him, replacing the hilt in exchange for a full-bladed version.

"Come on," he said. "Put it away. I'm trying to work down here."

She swung the blade toward him. "Do or do not. There is no try."

He put his hands on his hips. "Yoda wasn't trying to slice Luke's arm off when he said that."

"And Luke wasn't being a boring old computer geek. Come on. For making videos games for a living, you're a real stick in the mud. Or should I say, bog?"

"It was a swamp, and that's a low blow."

"Choose your weapon," she said.

"You'll scuff it."

She pointed the blade at the floor. "So? You can buy a new one."

She smacked him lightly on the arm. The blade whooshed and flashed. Ian backed away a step. She advanced, exhilaration passing through her.

Ian snaked out a hand and grabbed the other lightsaber from the bookcase and stuffed a blaster into the rear of his waistband of his jeans. "You'll regret this, Rebel Scum."

Bailey grinned and lunged, and Ian neatly deflected her blade. She swung again, and he raised his left arm behind him.

"What the hell kind of stance is that?" she asked swiping at him again. Chewy barked puppy barks at their feet.

He stabbed her right shoulder then danced away again. "I took fencing in college."

"Of course, you did." She swirled, crying out in a war cry then rolled away, springing to her feet again.

"What the hell was that?"

"Me outsmarting you," she said, swinging her blade and backing toward the door.

"Oh yeah?" He advanced again.

"Yeah," she said. Then she lunged, shrieked, and ran down the hallway and out the back door into the night.

The frozen grass crunched under her shoes, and the sky lit with a million stars overhead. Cold air rushed into her lungs, stealing her breath.

Ian charged after her, swinging his blade in wide, swooshing streaks of blue. Dang. Apparently, his knee wasn't slowing him down as much as she'd hoped.

Bailey dodged and crouched, smacking the side of Ian's knees before rolling away again.

"Where the hell did you learn that move?" Ian asked, laughing under his breath.

"I just made it up." He deflected two more strikes. "But I wouldn't recommend it. The ground out here is hard. And lumpy."

"Plus, this is where I bring Chewy out at night."

"What?" She lunged again. "Oh, that's just mean!"

He laughed and leapt away, swinging his blade and dancing around her as she swung with both hands on the hilt.

She panted, dodging his thrusts. Then she shut off her blade and ran into the dark. "Stealth mode!" she yelled.

He laughed. "It's hardly stealth mode when I can hear you running."

She ignored him, her blood pounding loudly in her ears, grinning like a fool, as she dove behind the shelter of a tree. She could hear Ian advancing, his breath coming in short bursts, his footfalls crunching over the frozen ground.

"Give up," he said. "You are beaten. I am too good."

"I have a secret weapon," she said as she quietly crouched down and set her lightsaber on the ground.

He stepped around the tree and the faint light from the back hallway of the house illuminated him like a moonbeam. As he came into view, she triggered the lights on her blade with her toe then leaped around the other side of the tree and grabbed the blaster from his waistband. She pointed it at his back.

"Gotchya," she breathed.

"A trick," he said, dropping his weapon and raising his hands in the air.

She laughed, victory coursing through her like a jolt of electricity. "I never said I played fair."

He spun in the dark and knocked the blaster out of her hand. It clattered to the ground somewhere in the shadows. "Neither did I," he said.

She laughed again, a bit nervously this time, and he paused.

"Do that again," he said.

"Do what?" She could hear his breath puffing into the night, feel the heat of him near her.

"Laugh."

She chuckled self-consciously. "Why?"

"Because I just realized you don't do it nearly enough. And I like it."

And before she could formulate a response, he leaned toward her and his lips descended to hers, and he kissed her in the cold and in the dark. But all she felt was heat, and all she saw was brightness, because, sweet Power of the Force, he was kissing her!

Then he pulled away again and murmured, "I like that, too."

She wanted to play it smooth and casual, as if guys like Ian kissed her in the dark after mock duels all the time. But all she felt was confused and flustered and worked up in ways she didn't know what to do with.

She blinked up at him, speechless, the taste of him still on her lips, and she panicked. Clearly, he was waiting for some reply, but the longer she waited without speaking the more she convinced herself that if he hadn't already gone back for more, he regretted kissing her to begin with... which was horrifying and humiliating and paralyzing...

So she nodded awkwardly and stepped away toward the house, Chewy yipping at her feet. "I should go," she said.

And even though he frowned a little, he let her.

CHAPTER TWELVE

BAILEY TAPPED HER pencil on the pad of paper in front of her. The page stared blankly back at her. Ideas. Ideas! Surely she could think of something to make it work? She'd finally run the numbers by Liz, quickly and over the phone, because she didn't want to burden her best friend during the happiest time of her life. And she didn't want to admit, even to Liz, that she'd somehow messed this up. She stared at the walls of her room feeling like a peon employee in a Dilbert cartoon, trapped in her cubicle. She had to get out. Had to *do* something.

"I'm heading out for a while," she called through the wall. Yes, it sucked knowing the walls were so thin she could have conversations through them.

"Wear a coat!" her mom called back.

Bailey snagged her down vest off the hook by the door, stuffed her car keys in the pocket and trotted down the steps of their double-wide. She stopped, her hand jiggling the keys in her pocket, a restless energy humming through her. She glanced over at her car and decided it didn't make sense to waste gas money on a restless brain, so she stuffed her hands in her vest pockets and set off toward the entrance of Orchard Estates.

Lenny Henderson grunted from his carport as she walked by, sorting through his precious recyclables as if New Hampshire had a deposit for empty cans or bottles. He spent even more time rearranging his collections now that his wife had gone into that home for Alzheimer's patients. Bailey waved and forced a smile. Yeah, life was sucky right now, but there was always suckier.

Lenny's fat cat, Fluffy, was struggling to climb up Mrs. Robinson's bird feeder to get at the squirrels gorging on sunflower seeds. Bailey wasn't sure who she was rooting for—the cat was so chubby it would be a major accomplishment to reach the squirrels—so she shooed them all until they scattered onto roofs and under cars.

Yup. Chasing the neighbor's cat was about as close as she'd ever gotten to training an animal. She ought to feel guilty over it, but she didn't. Ian was knee deep in extra cash from the looks of it, and they *did* have a deal. Was it her fault he was a poor judge of character?

SEVERAL DAYS HAD passed since the night Ian had gone a bit insane and not only pranced around his own backyard like a twelve year-old but given in to the temptation of kissing Bailey. Again.

She had, of course, freaked out about it which he didn't blame her. He wasn't in a position to start anything with anyone given his contract, and Marcia had told him up-front that no matter what happened between the time the show finished taping and the season aired, he needed to keep his hands to himself and keep out of the tabloids.

Seems there'd been some brouhaha last season with the final couple getting caught together which spoiled the surprise factor of the season and put Marcia in hot water with her higher-ups.

He grunted and heaved the sofa across the living room for the third time as Liz frowned at the layout. He and Carter waited to see if she approved this time.

He should cool it with Bailey, it was just… he had *fun* with her. And apparently fun included kissing her and turning that self-confident, slightly snarky expression she often wore into one of bewildered, wide-eyed heat.

He stifled a groan as Liz shook her head and asked them to move the sofa back again. He needed to stop thinking of Bailey and kissing and the word 'heat,' because he could hear the woman rattling around downstairs doing her dusting or vacuuming or what-not, and his brother kept giving him annoyingly knowing looks.

"Ian? Can I speak with you a moment. *Privately?*"

Bailey stood at the end of the hall and gestured toward him. She had an odd look on her face. He stumbled forward a few more feet and dropped his end of the leather sofa on the floor with a thud. His brother grunted and scowled.

"You've got another ten feet to go," Carter said.

"I'm taking a break. I'm tired of rearranging the same furniture. Why didn't we have the delivery guys put it where it was going to go to begin with?"

"Your producer wanted it arranged so the camera guy could get around easier, so pick up your end. We've still got a loveseat, a TV armoire and that marble coffee table to move."

Liz set her yellow notepad on the mantel. "I'll text Ivy and see how much space they need to film the foyer."

Carter dropped the other end of the sofa with a thunk.

"I'll be back in a minute," Ian promised. He met Bailey at the top of the basement stairs. "What's up?"

"Okay, you pervert," she hissed, "I expect a check for ten grand in my hand before I leave, or I'm telling the world about this!" She slammed a small black box with wires sticking out into his chest.

Oof. "What the hell?"

"That's what I'm thinking, you sleazeball! How dare you? No *wonder* you were all hot and heavy to get your hands on me the other night!"

"Would you keep your voice down? I thought that was a mutual thing we decided didn't mean anything." He nudged her onto the stairs and shut the door behind him so Liz and Carter wouldn't overhear. "Now what the hell are you talking about?"

"*This!*" she said shoving the plastic thing at his chest again. "And don't tell me you haven't seen it before, because we both know what this is! *You're spying on me!*"

"I'm what?"

She looked around her suspiciously. "You've got nanny cams all over, don't you? No *wonder* you're still single. You're a *freak!*"

"Wait a minute. Back up the train. Where did you find this?"

"As if you didn't know."

"Humor me," he ground out.

She continued down the stairs and pointed to the crown molding just inside the back door. "I was taking Chewy out for his business and something reflected the light, so I took a closer look and found *this* hidden up there. You've got them everywhere! You'd better not have one in your bathroom, or I'll sue you for…"

He held up a hand. "Did you say *everywhere?*"

"Yes, you creep."

"Bailey, these aren't mine. I swear to God, these are not mine. Show me the others. But do it discreetly."

"Why should I?"

He stepped toward her and muttered through his teeth. "Because I think we're *both* being spied on."

Her face went slack for a stunned moment before bright color flooded her cheeks. "Are you saying—? They can't *do* that!"

"Actually, technically, they probably can."

"That's an invasion of privacy! Are you going to put up with that? How dare they? This is your *home!*"

"I appreciate the indignation, but I signed up for a reality TV show. I don't have any privacy anymore. Technically we're still filming."

"But…"

"And that contract you signed probably allows them to film you as well."

"So you're saying we just have to *accept* this?"

"Did you cash their check?"

"Yes."

"Then, yes, you have to accept it."

She lifted her chin with a stubborn expression. "I may have to accept it, but I sure as hell don't have to play nice."

She had a mulish look that instantly made him uneasy. "What do you mean?"

"Just watch me. I intend to play with their heads. You with me?"

Bailey grabbed his hand and motioned for him to follow her into the media room. He had no idea what she planned, but her blue eyes flashed with mischief and he found himself curious what she'd do next.

She closed the media room door behind them and went on tip-toe. Her lips grazed his ear. "There's a nanny cam behind you up by the projector. So, I'm going to say something and then you kiss me like you've just returned from war. Got it?"

His eyes widened in surprise, but her hand was already sliding into the back of his hair. "*Ohh,* Ian," she said. "I'm having *such* a hard time pretending. When will you be free again?"

Good Lord. The woman had clearly never acted before in her life. "I don't know what to say," he said honestly.

She wiggled her eyebrows at him. "I *mean*, I know you feel you need to find some gorgeous, nurturing woman who dresses better than me and cooks you dinners, but even *you* have to admit the sex is so *hot* between us…"

He choked a little on his laughter. "It's like nothing I've ever experienced."

"You're telling me," she said, sidling up against him. She grabbed his ass and, yes, he had to admit it, he wasn't entirely indifferent.

"Things are different now," he said, grabbing her shoulders before she knocked him over. "I can't just walk away from the show. I have obligations."

"You may have obligations," she said in a voice that had gone all sultry and low, "but I have *needs.*"

"Needs?" he mouthed to her, incredulous. Really? She thought this was convincing?

"Yes, right now. I'm *so* hot for you, Ian. I think I might spontaneously combust!"

"Seriously?" he whispered. "You're terrible at this."

"Kiss me," she whispered back.

"What?"

"Kiss me," she demanded in her faux sultry voice again. "*Now.*"

He leaned forward, because he'd pull a muscle if he tried to fight the hand she had braced on the back of his skull, and pressed his lips to hers.

"Like you mean it," she mumbled against his mouth. "I know you can do it, Lover Boy."

Her eyes danced as she used the nickname she'd given him, and she squeezed his ass for good measure.

So he gave her what she asked for.

His left hand came up to cup her cheek, his right hand slid to her waist, and he grinned lightly before sliding his lips, oh, so slowly, against hers, a teasing, sweet caress. He pressed forward again, tasting the sweet softness of her lips, his tongue darting out lightly, teasing, tempting her to respond in kind. She moaned, a murmur really, and he deepened the kiss, without hurrying, as if he had all the time in the world to eke out all the pleasure he could from this one point of contact.

Her tongue darted out to tangle with his, and his right hand slid up, gliding over her breast, sliding back again, his thumb ever so lightly teasing the nipple through her shirt. Hell, she wanted a kiss? This is how he kissed, and her breast felt pretty damn good in his hand.

She went rigid for one startled moment, and then clutched him against her, working her mouth up to his ear. "Your hand is on my boob," she whispered. "What's that all about?"

He slid his lips in feathery kisses along her jaw, up toward her hairline. "Your hand is on my ass."

She nipped at his earlobe and squeezed her fingers tighter into the fabric of his jeans. "The camera can *see* my hand. My chest is blocked by your body. It's not doing anyone any good to grope my chest."

"I'm getting into my part," he murmured into her hair. "I thought you'd appreciate my acting skills."

"Your acting gets any better, we'll be making porn," she nearly hissed.

"You started it," he said, squeezing her through her bra. She had perfect sized breasts that fit his palm nicely. "Not that I'm complaining."

She stepped back and smacked him on the arm. *Hard.*

"Hey!"

"How dare you!" she said.

He gripped her shoulders and pulled her closer. "Are we still acting? Because I'm not sure where you're going with this."

"*This,*" she said, motioning between them, "isn't going anywhere until you straighten up. I need to know where I stand."

"I'm," he rubbed his shoulder. "I'll have to think on this, Bailey. You've put me in an awkward spot." As in he had *no* idea what was going on.

"What about the baby?" she wailed.

He choked. "What the—? *What* baby?"

Fake tears would have sprung to her eyes if she'd had any skill, as it was she faux hitched a breath and squinched her face up funny. "How can you say that? Why, Chewy, of course! You can't think you'll just pass her off to another woman as if... as if I'd never been in her life! We've *bonded!*"

"Don't you think this is going overboard?"

"Overboard? Now I'm too sensitive? I've been *very* understanding. I let you go off on this show to 'find yourself' and now what?"

"Perhaps we need some time apart," he ventured.

"*No.* I'm not letting you off that easy. We have to work together. We have to get along. If not for Chewy's sake than for our families."

"Families?"

"Well, Liz is *like* family to me. I'm her maid of honor, and you're Carter's best man. And you know what people say about *that*..."

"We shouldn't hook up in the coat closet at the reception?"

"I don't even know why I talk to you. You're not taking me seriously."

His lips twitched. "Sometimes that's hard to do."

"We'll finish this conversation later." And with that, she twirled on her heel and stomp-walked upstairs.

He chuckled to himself, turning away from the hidden camera.

Yes, it irked him that Marcia had gone so far as to bug his home, and, no, it didn't surprise him one bit. He'd lived in the fishbowl of reality TV for ten weeks already, so he *was* somewhat inured to the invasion of privacy; however, nothing in his contract said he had to behave himself.

CHAPTER THIRTEEN

BAILEY TOSSED A MINI tennis ball, and Chewy happily tumbled after it. She'd made herself scarce the last few days after the lip-lock down in the media room. She should feel ashamed about the whole thing, but mostly she felt confused. And turned on. The problem with Ian was he was so 'just so' about things, and then he went and fenced with lightsabers and hammed it up for the nanny cam, and all Bailey's preconceived notions of what Ian McIntyre was like came crashing down around her.

Having Ian turn out to be fun and down-to-earth and basically *nice* made it harder to feel okay about taking advantage of him. She'd yet to cash that blasted check. She told herself she was waiting until she needed it for closing on the garage, but deep down she knew she was waiting to feel as if she'd earned it.

Which is why she was here, the day before Thanksgiving, walking Chewy and playing fetch.

Right.

"I suppose you'll be doing a big Thanksgiving with your family," she said as he said goodbye to whomever he'd been talking to on the phone and pulled off his headset.

Ian shrugged. "Yeah. Grams and Aunt Joan always host a big shindig."

"Nice."

He nodded.

"You?" he asked.

Bailey wrestled the ball from Chewy and tossed it again. "Oh, we don't usually do a big thing for the holiday. It's low-key."

"No relatives?"

She shrugged. "I don't have any living grandparents, and my mom's an only child, so…"

"You should come join us. I'm sure Aunt Joan wouldn't mind one more guest."

"Thanks, but that's okay. I've got, um, stuff to do." She leapt to her feet and brushed off her jeans. "Well, you have a great holiday. I'll, um, see you."

"Sure."

She shut the door before he could say anything more.

THE NEXT DAY, Chewy sat on the seat beside him, too short to see over the dashboard. He'd tried to figure out the pet restraint thing Bailey had bought and finally gave up. He wrapped his coat around the pup who promptly crawled out of it while he drove down the hill and around the lake to his aunt and uncle's house.

He should think of it as *his* house, too, because for all intents and purposes it was where he'd grown up, at least after the fire, but it never quite felt like home. He'd woken up, night after night, in the basement rec room they'd hurriedly converted to a bedroom and stared at the ceiling above him wondering if he were dreaming and realizing, again, he wasn't.

More often than not, he'd quietly turned on the TV and watched it without sound, the flashes of blue and green and red glowing like a place far, far away. Far, far away from where he lay, alone and heartbroken with a family who loved him but with whom he always felt like an outsider. Jim, Rachel, Brad and Amy were Joan and Pop's real kids. He and Grace and Carter were the orphans.

He'd say the word to himself sometimes. *Orphan*. Rolling it over in his mind as if somehow that would change the reality of it. Part of him felt heroic and special to have the label. But mostly, it felt like a heaviness that sat on his chest in the dark, making it hard to breathe. Sometimes the weight of it was so heavy, he had to leap out of bed and move or feel that it might crush him.

And so he'd mimic the battles playing on the silent screen at the other end of the room, his toy lightsaber slashing through the air as he fought back the crushing darkness until he was too exhausted to fight any longer.

Chewy crawled across the console and pushed into his lap as Ian pulled into Joan and Pop's driveway and parked. It looked like most everyone had already arrived.

The air was crisp, the sun high as he grabbed Chewy's leash and bag of kibble and made his way to the kitchen door everyone used. His cousin, Jim, helped little Lily out of her car-seat while four year-old Liam slammed his door shut. Kate followed a bit more slowly, her round belly looking markedly large for a woman only five months along. But what did Ian know?

Ian waved and held the door as Liam shot past with a plate of cheese and crackers. Smart boy.

A chorus of 'Happy Thanksgiving!' met each new arrival and Ian spent the next half hour introducing everyone to Chewy, deflecting questions about his stint on *Happily Ever After* and defensively snacking.

Carter elbowed him in the side. "I've got some beef jerky hidden in my coat in the hall," he whispered.

Ian nodded. "I have dog kibble in my pockets. Just so you know it's not protein snacks."

Carter nodded. "Thanks for the warning."

They grinned and Carter moved away to snuggle his wife-to-be as his sister, Grace, tickled Liam. Aunt Joan shooed Grams out of the kitchen. Again.

Then Pops rang the cow bell, and they all glanced at each other before surging forward to snag their coveted seats like a competitive game of adult musical chairs. Ian, by some bad turn of fate, landed next to Aunt Joan, God help him.

"Let's say grace," she announced.

They all bowed their heads. "Dear Lord," she began, "we thank you for this beautiful day, for the love of family..." Ian watched as Carter squeezed Liz's hand on the tablecloth across from him. "...for the blessings of new beginnings..." Jim glanced at Kate as she laid a palm on her belly and smiled back at him. "...and for the bounty of your table..." They all eyed the mounded platters and bowls before them. "We pray for peace and love and harmony for all of your creation. Amen."

"Amen!" they all murmured and then Aunt Joan pulled the foil off the turkey like a magician's unveiling. It looked magnificent.

Everyone fell over themselves saying so.

"It's gorgeous!"

"Just like a magazine cover!"

"Look at the little radish flowers she made!"

"Smells fantastic!"

Pops pulled out his freshly sharpened carving knife and set to work.

"Oh, not too much for me," Kate said quickly. "The babies don't leave much room for food."

The table came to a standstill. "Babies?" Grams repeated.

Kate looked at Jim, smiled, then looked around the table. "Yes. We're having *twins!*"

They all erupted in excited chatter as Pops passed around plates of turkey. Everyone helped themselves to the beautifully seasoned potatoes with little green herb flakes, fragrant stuffing, glazed, roasted root vegetables and homemade cranberry sauce.

Ian had a sudden craving for a peanut butter and Doritos sandwich.

Amidst the quiet of industrious serving, Liz piped up. "Truly, Mrs. Pearson, it looks like you must have Martha Stewart hidden in the kitchen. Everything looks beautiful."

"Thank you, dear."

Ian accepted a bowl of something hot and whitish—probably onions?—and helped himself to a small spoonful before offering some to his aunt.

"Oh, no thank you, dear. I didn't make much of that. I'll save it for everyone else to enjoy." He nodded and set it down in the middle of the table.

"Well, go ahead, everyone!" his aunt said. "Dig in!"

Ian looked at his plate and wondered where to start.

"*Mmm!*" Liz said from across the table. "These rolls are so fragrant!"

Carter must have coached her. Anyone could take the rolls. He decided to dig into the whitish dish. The special one.

"Oh, *mmm*, that's unusual. What's in the stuffing this year?" Doug asked from Rachel's side.

His aunt preened next to him. "It's a secret ingredient. I'm trying a new recipe."

A few faces paled. New recipes were uncharted territory. Unlike the tried and true disasters of the past, anything could go wrong with a new recipe.

"The turkey is very flavorful," Jim offered. His wife nodded her agreement.

Ian intended to outdo them all. He brought the whitish blob to his mouth, met Carter's eyes as if to say, 'take care of my dog if I don't return from wherever this takes me' and closed his lips over it. He chewed. His eyes flew open.

Carter's shoulders shook with suppressed laughter.

Ian smiled around his mouthful and quirked an eyebrow as if to say, "Jokes on you, because this is actually edible."

Carter quickly took a forkful of the same dish, probably in hopes of being the first to compliment it. He shoved it in his mouth, and a moment later his eyes shot to Ian's as if to say, "You tricked me, you bastard."

Ian grabbed his water glass and washed down the horrendous glop without further chewing. "*Mmm*. Amazing, Aunt Joan. You've outdone yourself this year."

She smiled and patted his shoulder, and Ian quirked an eyebrow at Carter as he made a valiant effort to swallow his mouthful of gelatinous goo with a straight face. A look of panic slid across his features, and Ian detected a moment's gag reflex coming into play before Carter schooled himself, grabbed Liz's cider and gulped heartily.

His forehead looked a bit sweaty, and he'd gone a tad white around the mouth. "Incredible," Carter breathed. "I honestly don't know if I want to eat anything more after that. Nothing could compare." He smiled his charming Carter smile.

Damn. Carter was smooth.

Liam mumbled something under his breath to his mother who pulled a small insulated lunch sack from under his chair with a murmured apology about picky eaters; although, Ian noticed her sneaking bites of whatever she'd brought for him.

That was okay. Women and children were exempt. Thanksgiving was a man's battle.

Ian cut himself a forkful of turkey. Usually turkey was straightforward. He glanced at Pops and then shoved it in his mouth.

Pops' lips compressed with laughter.

"You did the turkey different this year," Ian managed after drinking his weight in water. He needed a refill. Grams, the sneak, had already jumped up from the table to get more pickles.

"Brining," his aunt said. "It's supposed to make it tender."

And salty, apparently. Very, *very* salty.

Grace grinned smugly from her end of the table. She was fast on her feet, that one, and usually tried to snag an end seat... the better to hide food in the napkin in your lap. Ian looked around. "Chewy?"

"She's here," Grace said.

"Don't feed her table scraps or you'll be taking her home tonight," he said.

Grace brought her hand up to her drink glass guiltily. "I wouldn't dream of it."

Much clinking of glasses and enthusiastic knife and fork cutting ensued, and after everyone had pushed their food around their plates for a while and rearranged them into compact piles of 'I'm too stuffed to eat another bite' artistry, Jim jumped up.

"I'll clear," he said.

"Oh, let me help," Carter said.

Aunt Joan smiled on their helpful faces as they nabbed the plates out from under the noses of their significant others whose expressions promised undying love and hot sex for their gallantry.

Aunt Joan grabbed the bowl of whitish glop and held it toward him. "Did you want more before they snatch it away? They're so helpful every Thanksgiving. After cooking for two days straight, I'm beat."

"You've outdone yourself yet again," Ian murmured as he stood to take his plate to the kitchen. No way in hell he was going to put himself in a position for seconds.

"It's the least I can do. Your Grams is always cooking. She deserves one day a year that she can put her feet up and not think about it."

Ian grabbed Pops' plate on his way by for which he earned an expression of undying gratitude. "And I can use one day a year of cleansing," Pops murmured in his ear as he passed over a thoroughly wadded napkin. Wow. The man was a master of sleight-of-hand.

Ian set the plates on the kitchen counter as Carter rummaged in the fridge, presumably for something edible.

"I wonder if it was onion," Ian mused as he scraped food into the trash.

Carter popped up from behind the fridge door with a spoonful of peanut butter in hand. "I think it might have been fish."

"Was that a cheese sauce?" Jim asked.

Carter stuffed the peanut butter in his mouth. "I was trying not to taste it too much. Oh God. This is heaven."

They chuckled in shared misery. Liz opened the kitchen door.

She sniffed the air then opened the oven door. They all groaned at the sight of two beautiful pies on the rack. "If I claim we're all too stuffed for dessert, can we clean up and go to Lucky's for pie and coffee? They're open today."

Carter pulled the peanut butter spoon out of his mouth. "There's a reason I'm marrying you. You are *genius*."

SHE COULD NEVER understand why people would book Thanksgiving dinner at an Irish pub, and yet Lucky's was mobbed every year by people who probably didn't have anywhere to go or didn't get along with their relatives. Every year her mother suckered her into helping so the regular staff could get the day off if they wanted. So here she was again, serving up platters of turkey and gravy (or pot roast and gravy for the untraditional folks) with sides of peas and carrots and mashed or roasted potatoes—basically a platter of protein and carbs with a side of pie. And plenty of Guinness, because from all appearances, that went particularly well with turkey dinners.

That and spiked eggnog.

Bailey pushed her way from the kitchen loaded with another tray of turkey dinners and pasted on what she hoped was a tip-worthy smile. The bells at the door rang again, and she glanced over long enough to cringe. Oh, sweet potato pie. It was Marcia and that Nick guy. And Wanda was seating them in Bailey's section. Bailey delivered the dinners, made sure everyone was up to date on their cranberry sauce and Guinness, and flipped her order pad to a fresh page.

"Happy Thanksgiving and welcome to Lucky's. Can I start you off with a pint of Guinness on tap or a mug of Irish eggnog this bonnie day?"

Marcia had her head bent over the specials menu which consisted of Holiday Meal #1 or Holiday Meal #2. "What the hell is Irish eggnog?"

"Eggnog with a bit of Bailey's and Irish whiskey blended in."

"Sounds good. I'll have that."

"And to eat?"

Marcia shrugged "Salad. Whatever. Really just the eggnog." She glanced up. "You! You sure do get around, don't you?"

"Apparently. And for you?" she said looking at Nick.

"Holiday Meal #2. And a Guinness."

"All right. That's Irish eggnog and house salad for you and a number two with Guinness for you. Do you want mashed or roasted potatoes?"

"Roasted."

"Excellent choice."

"What's wrong with the mashed?" Marcia wanted to know. She glanced at Nick. "I always wonder why wait staff feel compelled to compliment us on our choices."

Bailey broke her pencil on her order pad. "It beats telling our customers what we really think of their orders."

"Is that so? Do you have something to say about my choices?"

"Yeah. Ordering the Irish eggnog implies you don't care about calories or your arteries, so why not skip the salad which no one eats by choice anyway and get the wild Maine blueberry pie before they run out? It's Skye's specialty. Even better than the pumpkin pie if you ask me. "

"I see. Can I get that with a scoop of vanilla ice cream?"

"Now we're talking. I'll go put a slice aside for you both before we run out."

Bailey flipped her order pad shut as Wanda shuffled by with a tray of desserts. If she were completely honest, she didn't hate working Thanksgiving. Unlike the rest of the year, people expected to come and hang out for a while. With the drone of a football game on the corner TVs and the smells of turkey and pie and coffee in the air, she imagined it was what Thanksgiving was like for most normal people.

And with her mother, Daniel, her half-siblings and their mothers, it was as close as she would ever get to a boisterous family gathering.

Bailey pulled a pint of Guinness, sprinkled nutmeg on the eggnog and plated up Skye's blueberry pie with an extra-large scoop of vanilla bean for Marcia. The woman was on expense account, she could afford to tip well. Plus, she figured she owed Marcia something for the excuse to snog with Ian for the hidden cameras. She added a squirt of whipped cream for good measure and returned to the table.

"So, how come you two are still in town for the holiday? I would have thought you'd want to go home to be with family."

Marcia snorted which Bailey was pretty sure she never did on camera. "Are you kidding? Just so my mother can give me grief about how old my ovaries are while my brother's rug-rats start a food fight? I don't think so."

Nick sipped his beer. "Technically, I don't think it's a food fight if the perpetrators are only two."

"They were flinging food across the table at one another. It's bad manners. I'm telling you, twins are adorable in theory only. They feed off one another in unholy ways. Plus the four year-old is a crybaby."

"You ate his pie."

"How was I to know it was his?"

"It was labeled gluten-free."

"It said 'G.F.'" She shrugged and looked at Bailey. "I thought it meant 'Good Food.' Honestly, I don't see why I'm always the bad guy. Gary's wife is always making miniature this and fancy that. God. Just buy something at Whole Foods and call it a day, Martha. Nobody's keeping score."

Marcia dug her fork deep into her pie and took a bite. "What?"

"Except you," Nick murmured, his lips tilting at the corner. Bailey figured it was as close as Nick ever got to smiling.

"Your meal should be right up," she said to Nick.

"So tell me," Marcia said as she stabbed a blueberry with a fork tine, "how come you're not celebrating the holiday with the McIntyre clan?"

"I had to work."

"I would have thought that a good *friend* of the family would have managed to get an invitation to join them. I hear his aunt puts on quite the spread. I'll have to ask Helen what they ha—*Oh!*" Marcia slapped a hand to her mouth. "You didn't hear that from me!"

"Helen's spending Thanksgiving with Ian?"

Marcia took a sip of eggnog. "I know she was invited. Ian's grandmother is so welcoming. Well, you know how she is."

Marcia winked at Nick who took another sip of Guinness with a blank expression.

Bailey forced a smile. "Well, if you don't need anything more. I'll go check on that dinner."

She backed away and fled to the kitchen.

"Bails! Stir the gravy vat, would you? I've got to plate up more turkey platters." Jack, Bailey's half-brother, was working the kitchen alone today on account that Daniel had 'felt a dizzy spell coming on' about an hour into the dinner shift. Bailey stirred the gravy, the steam making the hair that had escaped her pigtails stick to her forehead. The bells at the door rang again.

Wanda walked into the kitchen and sank onto a stool to wait for her orders to be ready. "Oh God, my feet hurt something fierce. You're a smart girl for never wearing high heels, Bailey. Bunions are the Lord's own revenge against the vanity of youth. By the way, a new group came in. They're all yours."

"Thanks."

She swung the kitchen door open and nearly turned right around again. What the heck were *they* doing here?

Liz and Carter; Ian; their cousin, Jim, and his wife, Kate, along with their two kids; Ian's sister, Grace; his cousin, Rachel, and *her* husband Dave or Dan or Doug; and a couple more she couldn't name all poured through the door and clustered around the front register. She squared her shoulders and stepped forward. "Happy Thanksgiving and welcome to Lucky's. What can I do for you this bonnie day?" she recited. She hated that Daniel made her say that. It was an American holiday for crying out loud.

Liz pushed to the front. "Bailey! Hi! Happy Thanksgiving!"

"Hi. Um, what are you all doing here? I thought you were at Carter's aunt's house."

"Oh, somehow the oven got turned to self-clean and burned the pies." Liz shrugged. "So, we thought we'd come here for dessert."

"And football," Carter said around her shoulder. "Thank goodness it's still half-time. I don't think we missed anything."

Liz turned back. "Do you have a few tables near-ish the TVs so we could have dessert? And a couple extra slices to-go? Carter's aunt and uncle are watching Chewy."

"Um, sure. Give me a minute to clear. I just had a family leave."

"Thanks." Liz began to follow.

Bailey stopped. "What are you doing?"

"I was going to help clear tables."

"You're not supposed to do that. You're a customer."

Liz sighed. "Don't you deserve a Thanksgiving, too?"

"I get that later. After we close."

"Yeah. At eight o'clock you eat a slice of pie and go home and crash. That's not a holiday."

Bailey began stacking dirty plates. "It's my holiday."

"Join us," Liz said, picking up dirty dishes and setting them in the bus bin with the plates. "Daniel will let you eat a slice of pie with us, I'm sure."

"He went home. He's having an episode. But anyway, I've got other customers. I can't."

Bailey swiped off the table with a wet bar rag, dried it with a second and was still laying out placemats as Ian's family settled themselves at adjacent booths and tables.

Bailey gathered booster seats for the little ones and avoided Ian's pointed gaze as best she could. And then she had to take his order.

"I'd like a slice of blueberry pie and an explanation."

"We're out."

"Of explanations?"

"Of blueberry pie."

He handed her the menu. "Okay, raspberry."

"That's not on the menu."

"Okay, then an explanation: I thought you said you had plans for the holiday?"

"I did—*do*—as you clearly see. I'm working."

He frowned. "All day?"

"Only since noon."

"It's five o'clock."

"Would anyone like coffee, tea, or Irish eggnog with your desserts?" she asked.

Ian pushed his chair back, but Bailey ignored him and took drink orders then hurried off before he spoke again.

She had four turkey dinners to deliver to the corner booth with the divorcees, Nick and Marcia were probably due for a drink refill, and she had to clear Table 5.

She balanced the heavy plates two to an arm and hurried back through the crowded pub toward the divorcees. Her feet were tired, her back ached, and she was so hungry she was tempted to sneak a bite of somebody's pie.

The ladies all but cheered when they saw their food and eagerly reached to help unload the plates.

This, unfortunately, was a mistake.

The women reached for the plates closest to themselves and lifted. Before she could adjust for the change in balance, the near plates tilted backward under their own weight, the gravy soaked mashed potatoes sliding through the turkey and plowing over the sides of the plates... and down Bailey's front.

"Flaming banana sundaes!" she croaked as hot gooey gravy dripped from her shirt and splatted to the floor to join the turkey and potatoes already there. She held the empty plates away from her and stared in horror at herself and the floor.

"Oh, you poor thing!" The closest woman said as she leapt from the booth to mop at Bailey's chest with her napkin. "Carrying plates like that is a skill, isn't it?"

Bailey looked up at the woman, aghast. "I wouldn't have dumped them if you hadn't—"

"Ladies! Why don't we move you to our table? We're happy to take your booth after your waitress has a chance to clean up." Ian offered from behind her. "We haven't been served, so it's no trouble at all."

The women grabbed their drinks and stepped gingerly over the gravy splatter on the floor thanking Ian for his kindness and gentlemanly manners and shooting Bailey glances as if *she* were responsible for this ugly mess. Bailey passed over the two plates that were still edible and rushed back to the kitchen, fuming. "I need two more turkey platters, stat."

Jack eyed her through the pass-through. "I usually use the to-go containers when I want something for later."

"Can it. I'm in no mood. Oh God. It's seeping into my bra!"

Jack slid two more turkey dinners toward her and she rushed back to the women. "Here you are. Anything else you need?" Corrective lenses, perhaps, and a little less sangria?

"Honey, could you take a step back? You're dripping."

Bailey grimaced and backed up... and ran right into a hot body.

Ian leaned down toward her ear. "May I speak with you a moment?"

Bailey turned, uncaring of whether he got gravy smears on his jeans. "I'm a little busy here."

He had the nerve to chuckle under his breath. "I see that. I think I can help."

Bailey didn't answer but walked back through the 'employees only' area. "Wanda? Can you clean up the dining room by the back booth while I fix this?"

Wanda gasped. "What the hell happened to you?"

"The divorcees tried to help unload their food."

"When will they learn to wait? They did the same thing to Martha on wings night. She got hot sauce in her eye and…"

"Another time, Wanda."

Bailey pushed into the employee bathroom and started yanking paper towels out of the dispenser. "Son of a Fudgsicle," she muttered as she smeared gravy off her shirt and into the sink. Ian pushed open the door behind her.

"This is a private bathroom," she announced.

"I'm trying to help."

"Help? Ha! That's how I got into this mess."

She turned on the faucet and poured water onto another wad of paper towels and snuck a glance in the mirror over the sink.

"Whoa! What are you doing?" she said, whirling to face him.

Ian pulled his head through his T-shirt and stood bare-chested behind her. "I was going to give you my shirt. As you can see, I'm wearing layers. Unless you want to wear that extra polo that could pass for a dress again." He held out his T-shirt. Bailey tried not to fixate on his bare chest.

It was a nice chest as bare chests went. A light smattering of hair without being all Sasquatch, and his muscles in his shoulders and in that yummy front area were lean and sinewy without being bulky.

Yes, she was salivating, but she *was* hungry, and Ian *was* half naked in front of her.

If the room didn't smell like fake vanilla air freshener and turkey gravy, it might have been somewhat erotic.

She hurriedly wiped her hands clean and took the T-shirt. "Thanks."

His lips twisted in amusement. "You're welcome."

He stood there, staring at her and, frankly, her staring at him for a few moments longer than strictly necessary to transfer a T-shirt from one hand to another, long enough for Bailey to wonder if he expected her to pull her own shirt off in front of him and change while he was still in the room.

Long enough for her to consider doing just that.

Ian shrugged into the sleeves of his button down again and began buttoning it from the bottom up, which seemed bass-ackwards if you asked her, but it did have the benefit of leaving a drool-worthy view of his chest visible for sweet seconds longer…

"I'll see you out there," he said.

"Could you actually, um, do me a favor?"

He raised an eyebrow. She couldn't believe she was going for it, but blast it, he *was* a really smokin' specimen of male flesh, and she, well, she had no pride. Plus, she didn't want gravy in her hair.

"Could you, um, help me get my shirt off without getting gravy in my hair?"

He froze, letting the top three buttons flap open which was entirely distracting. And appreciated. "Do you want me to get Liz?"

"Oh. *Yeah*. That's probably a good plan."

"I'll be right back."

He shot out of the bathroom as if she'd lit his shirttails on fire, and Bailey slumped against the sink. *Aargh!* How embarrassing! She'd just asked the hunky guy she was working for to take her shirt off—and he *refused!* She wouldn't be able to show her face in public ever again.

"Bailey?" Liz knocked twice, and Bailey opened the door. "Good God, what a mess."

"Can you help me take off my shirt so I don't smear gravy in my hair?"

"Sure. Oh, yuck. Let me just roll it over the gravy and we'll work together."

They made quick work of the gravy-soaked shirt. Bailey pulled Ian's T-shirt over her head, trying not to visibly inhale while she did so. Oh sweet mercy, it smelled *really good.*

Liz had a knowing look on her face, but Bailey lifted her chin, grabbed the door, and mumbled something about needing to get back to her customers.

When she returned, Wanda had taken care of the divorcees, Nick and Marcia, and the young family at Table 3 whose turkey hadn't thawed in time for the big day. Bailey stood at the bar, unsure of what to do next. The McIntyre/Pearson clan laughed and chatted, one of the little ones animatedly recounting some story featuring someone's baby.

For some inexplicable reason, her right eye felt like the time she'd gotten cayenne pepper in it from the first and last time she'd helped Jack in the kitchen, and she couldn't blink fast enough to make the tears go away. She sniffed and grimaced and pretended to reroll napkins around the silverware in the bin which, let's be honest, no one *ever* felt the need to do and then—*gah!*—Ian was coming toward her again!

"What do you want?" she muttered trying to sound gruff and not sniffly.

"I was going to invite you to join us."

"I can't. I'm working." She refolded in earnest now.

"Looks like the dinner crowd is winding down, and Wanda said it wouldn't be a problem, that you deserved a break."

She looked up. "You already asked Wanda? Wasn't that a little heavy handed?"

His lips quirked at the corner a bit. "Would you join us if I told you it was Liz's idea?"

"Was it?"

His head shook infinitesimally. *No.*

She swallowed over the sudden lump in her throat that seemed to be working in concert with the cayenne-pepper eye. "I see." She glanced over again at the boisterous, happy family. "I don't want to intrude."

He reached across the bar and took the napkin roll out of her hand. "Stop being difficult. You know you want to, and I'm hungry for pie."

She was about to protest again, albeit feebly, when Wanda—the traitor—waltzed by with a tray full of pie slices. "Come on Bails. Have a seat. I put extra vanilla bean on yours just like you like it."

Ian quirked an eyebrow, and Bailey could do nothing but crawl under the bar again to join them.

She stuck a fork into her pie and her stomach rumbled. Liz laughed. "Haven't you fed the beast yet today?"

Bailey shook her head and stuffed her mouth with pie.

Ian leaned over. "*Have* you eaten today?"

"I am now," she said around the pie.

He rolled his eyes and motioned for Wanda. She scurried over so he could speak into her ear, then she smiled, patted him on the back and left again.

A couple minutes later she returned to the tables with platters of turkey and potatoes and pot roast... and a stack of plates.

"What's going on?" Bailey asked.

"Oh, thank God," Carter breathed as he nabbed an empty plate. "That was the worst Thanksgiving dinner ever, God bless her."

Ian's cousin, Rachel, grabbed a plate and passed one to her husband. "What was in the stuffing this year anyway? I couldn't figure it out. Those chewy things?"

"They might have been raisins," Liz said. "Or maybe fig pieces? I stopped chewing and just swallowed once I hit the slimy bits."

"I haven't dared eat stuffing since the oyster dressing food poisoning disaster," Carter said.

Everyone winced.

Carter turned toward Grace. "As I recall you were the only one to escape unscathed."

"The benefits of being a vegetarian," said Grace.

"Cheater."

Grace laughed. "Hey, someone had to drive you all to the E.R."

Rachel's husband helped himself to turkey and mashed potatoes. "God bless your mother, Rachel, for trying to go domestic one day a year to give your Grams the day off, but even *she* wasn't eating."

"I saw Grams sneak a roast beef sandwich when you guys were cleaning up," Grace added. "She had it hidden in the end table next to her recliner."

"The sneak," Carter said.

Bailey frowned. "*None* of you ate dinner?"

Ian shrugged and shoveled food onto his plate. "We never do. Grams is the real cook in the family, but every year my aunt gets it in her head she's going to give us all a special meal as her thanks to all of us. Ever since that skiing accident years ago when she broke her nose, she's lost her sense of smell."

"And taste," Carter added.

"So her cooking is abysmal."

"Don't forget potentially fatal." Carter said.

Everyone winced again.

"So before dinner we load up on nuts and cheese and crackers, do our best to selectively force down what we can of the main meal and then go home and raid our fridges."

Bailey snorted. "That's awful! Why don't you just tell her?"

They all looked at one another. "Because that's not what Thanksgiving is all about."

Ian set an empty plate in from of Bailey and held out the platter of turkey. She mumbled a thank you and helped herself to food. They laughed and passed food and poked fun at one another until little Lily belched like a sailor and her older brother snorted soda out his nose and Jim and Kate declared it their cue to head out with their brood. Rachel and Doug soon followed with their little one, and then Liz and Carter got a little hands-y and decided to excuse themselves as well.

Bailey pushed a roasted potato around on her plate and looked at the empty tables left behind—along with all the dirty dishes—and realized as much as she could pretend for a little while that she was a part of the celebration, the fact remained that she was working. And it was her job to clean up.

She stood and avoided Ian's gaze as she began to collect the dirty dishes.

"Sit down. I'm still eating," he said.

"These tables won't clear themselves," she said, continuing to collect plates.

Ian grabbed her waistband with one hand and gave it a tug until she tumbled into the seat beside him again. "I said, sit down. You've worked all day. Take a load off."

"It's my job, Ian. That's what working means."

He put the last bite of pie into his mouth and shoved the plate away. "I know what working means," he said. "*Mmm*. That was delicious."

She made as if to stand again, but he held her down with a strategically placed arm across her shoulders. "Relax. I'm trying to digest here. It's not peaceful to have you hovering over me clacking dishes together."

"But Marcia—"

"Left a while ago."

She gritted her teeth, determined to be annoyed with his arm on her person, except it felt warm. Good. She hadn't had enough boyfriends to know what this felt like, the casual weight of a man's arm across your shoulders. It was comfortably settling and brought her close enough to smell more of his woodsy scent.

"See? Isn't this nice? We can enjoy relaxing after a good meal. This is what Thanksgiving is all about."

"You just said it was about strategically pre-eating."

He chuckled, his chest vibrating against her side. "That, too."

"I really should get back to work. Wanda has already taken care of two of my tables.

Ian heaved a sigh and pushed his chair back. "All right. We can clear now."

Bailey grabbed the bus bin from a nearby cleaning station. "We?"

Ian started scraping food scraps into a serving bowl before stacking the plates. "Yeah. When you eat, don't you help each other clean up, too?"

She shrugged and set the dirty plates in the bus bin. "I wouldn't know. We don't do a formal dinner."

"You mean *this* was your Thanksgiving dinner?"

"Yeah."

"Then you can count yourself lucky you didn't have to play culinary Russian Roulette at Aunt Joan's."

"You're the lucky one. I'd do anything to have that kind of Thanksgiving."

"By risking food poisoning?"

"This isn't a joke," she said, wiping down the cleared tables with a damp rag.

"Bailey, I know it's not a joke, but you have to see that nobody's holiday is perfect."

She stopped and looked at him. "You don't get it. It's not about the food. It's about," she gestured to the empty seats, "*this*. Everybody. You don't know how good you have it."

"Oh, yeah?"

"Yeah." She picked up the full bus bin and stalked back toward the dishwasher. Wanda's nephew, Mark, waved back through the steam billowing from the pre-rinse station.

Ian blocked her return path, his arms folded across his chest. "Do you want to know the year Aunt Joan first hosted Thanksgiving?"

Bailey heaved a sigh. "I get the impression you intend to tell me."

"The year my parents died."

She'd been about to say something, but the words died on her tongue. She waited.

"Until then, my parents hosted every year. My mom was an incredible cook. *Incredible*. Nothing fancy, just good, honest food that made you cry when the dishes were empty.

"Aunt Joan knew that the bar was high, but she didn't want us kids to miss out on the big feast we were used to, so she announced it was her gift to us. *She* was cooking the meal that year.

"And it was terrible. Shockingly, horribly terrible. I remember staring at my plate full of food and missing my mother so damn much I almost cried right then and there in front of everybody."

"I'm sorry." She didn't have anything else to say.

"So I said I didn't feel well, and I hid in the breezeway until my Grams came and found me.

"She told me to suck it up and get back to the table, because Aunt Joan had cooked a special meal for all of us and we were damned well going to pretend to enjoy it."

"A warm fuzzy woman, your grandmother."

"Then she palmed me a peanut butter sandwich and told me I was a smart boy and to never arrive hungry to one of Aunt Joan's dinners ever again. You really want peanut butter and jelly for Thanksgiving?"

"Yes!" Bailey said. "*Yes!* That's exactly what I want. I *want* to pretend to enjoy an awful meal. I've never had that. You want to know what my holiday is usually like? I eat pie standing up in the back of this kitchen while my feet hurt pretending it's normal and okay to celebrate the holiday surrounded by my half-siblings and random women my father has slept with."

He waved his hand in the air. "So delay it a bit. You can celebrate the day after or with your mother in the morning before you open here."

She shook her head. "It's too hectic in the morning. And the one year my mom picked up take-out KFC for the two of us, it just seemed pathetic."

His lips hitched at the corner. "That is pathetic."

"Thanks."

"Why didn't you say something yesterday when I asked about your plans?"

"What was I going to say? My holiday always sucks?"

"No. Why didn't you say you didn't have a place to go?"

"Because I'm not a charity case. I *had* somewhere to go—here. And I'm not a fan of food poisoning."

His lips formed a smile. "No one is, believe me."

She stood there in the hall, the steam of the dishwasher at her back, the subtle murmurs of the pub further away, waiting for him to make his move.

"Ah, there's my Lucky Charm." Daniel swung open the door to his office. "You're a good lass working all day. Your dear mother has eased my aching back considerably. She has the fingers of an angel, that one."

Words *no* daughter in the history of mankind has ever wanted to hear. "That's, um, great. I thought you guys left hours ago."

Sandi appeared behind Daniel looking flushed. "Oh!" she said. "Is the dinner rush over?"

"Pretty much. I was going to go eat my pie."

"*Mmm.*" Sandi looked at Ian and Bailey and back again. "Why don't you take some to-go? You've been cooped up here all day. You two kids should get some fresh air."

"It's twenty degrees out, Mom."

"It'll feel good." Sandi winked maniacally.

"We're all looking forward to seeing your television debut, Ian," Daniel added. "Meet lots of lovely ladies, did you?"

Sandi swatted Daniel's arm so Bailey didn't have to.

"Um. Yes. They were very nice," Ian said.

"When do they start airing your season?" Sandi asked.

"First Monday in January."

Daniel looked at Sandi. "I should do a wings and drafts special on Mondays for the season. We'll make it the place to come watch!"

Sandi grinned like a fool. "You're such a brilliant businessman, Daniel."

Daniel turned to Ian. "Any chance we can get the man of the hour to come by from time to time to make things festive?"

"I'd be—" Ian began.

"Too busy," Bailey finished for him. "And I'm sure he'd have to check with the producers of the show before committing to anything."

"Well, sure. We'll keep it open. If you find the time, my boy, we'd love to have you. Hope you found your missus. If there's anything we Irish love, it's a good love story."

"What a bunch of blarney," Bailey murmured. Sandi gave her a dirty look.

"I should probably head out," Ian said.

"Have Bailey give you some pie to-go," Daniel said. "On us!"

Bailey practically pushed Ian back into the restaurant. "Like you'd pimp yourself out to my father all for a slice of free pie," she muttered.

Ian stopped, and Bailey accidentally bumped into him before correcting herself. "It's worth a shot," he said.

"What?"

"Just kidding. I need a few slices to-go for my Grams and aunt and uncle though."

"Anything else?"

"Yeah. Go home and shower," he said, grinning. "You smell like gravy."

CHAPTER FOURTEEN

"*NOW* ARE YOU GOING to tell me there's nothing going on?"

Marcia pressed the pause button on the DVD player and turned on Nick. Thank goodness she'd had the good sense to have Nick rig up those nanny cams and mini recorders at the house or she'd still be lulled into thinking Ian was playing by the rules.

"I never said there wasn't."

"Damn! I knew she'd be trouble. No woman who eschews mascara can be trusted. Thank God we've got Eileen here now."

"Helen."

"Yes, she'll show Ian the kind of woman he wants in his life long-term. The man has no idea who he's dealing with here."

Nick's lips tilted. "No idea."

"I can't believe he kissed her. Men are pigs. Except you. You're the exception."

"It takes two to tango."

She rolled her eyes. It wasn't a good look for her, but Nick had seen worse. "Sometimes it takes three plus a stripper."

"Your ex-husband was an idiot."

"Yes, yes, he was. But I married him, didn't I?"

She tapped a perfectly manicured nail against her lips. "Clearly, I've got to throw these two together more… challenge them… so he sees this cleaning woman isn't the future mother of his children. Good God, have you seen her manicure?"

"No."

"Exactly. Nothing. No polish, no buff. Nothing. Just," she shivered, "nails."

"Good God."

Marcia slanted him a look. "Don't mock me. She's not what he's looking for."

"How do you know?"

"It's my job to know. Their relationship isn't mature. They relate like, like siblings, always poking at each other. I guarantee that if they were challenged, they'd turn on each other. In fact," she turned to Nick cheerfully, "I don't know why I didn't think of it sooner. We simply challenge them... and when things start to fall apart, we'll send Helen in to close the deal."

"You seem pretty confident."

"I have every right to be. I have an unbroken track record. Those other matchmaking shows aren't trying to put people together, they're only out for the TV drama, but *I* deliver what people want: results. I weed out the drama queens and the fame whores. The only ones who survive my challenges are those that truly want a relationship and are willing to work for it. And it's basic human psychology when a couple finds itself in an 'us against the world' situation, they'll grow closer together."

"Or spontaneously implode."

"Yes, but that's where my talent for identifying good matches comes into play."

"And Ian is a sucker for a good manicure?"

"No. Ian is a sucker for a mother figure. Face it. Any man who lost his mother when he was a kid will seek a wife just like dear old mum. He never knew her as an adult, so he didn't have a chance to develop any angst. His case is cut and dried."

"If it's so cut and dried, why are we in Sugar Falls?"

Marcia blew out a breath. "He's out of sorts, because we pulled him out of his comfort zone. Now that he's home again, he'll see how smoothly Helen will fit into his life here. As soon as she gets back from Alabama." She rolled her eyes. "Southerners and their 'traditions.' She should have gone to Ian's for Thanksgiving. *That* would have clinched the deal. Whatever. We've got a wedding just a few weeks from now. That's ripe with opportunity to throw them together. There's still time. I'm thinking of an event where Helen will shine... and Bailey will show her true colors."

"You're the master."

She turned and gifted him a sly smile. "Yes. Yes, I am."

CHAPTER FIFTEEN

IAN STOOD BY THE window and stared out at the dying light, the sun low on the horizon, the fields gray and quiet. The sun set early this time of year. The December wind howled through the eaves, making him grateful he was warm and snug inside. Jim had set him up with triple-insulated windows and radiant heating in the floors. Ian didn't even have to wear slippers and wool socks like he used to when he was a kid.

Yet, he found he missed huddling around the heating vent for a blast of warm air. He missed a lot of things.

He scrubbed a hand over his face and turned away from the window. Strange how the same view he used to peer out at as a child, that felt so much like *home,* now seemed like a photograph he was viewing. It was as if he were detached from it now, seeing it from afar, the intervening years making him numb to the feel of it.

And he hated it.

He hated how the field and the windows—the whole damn house— were like a movie set recreated somewhere else to fool him. As if Hollywood had worked their magic and re-imagined every detail except for the life and the energy that had made it a home.

But, it wasn't a home, and that was the problem. It was a house. A house, yes, that looked very much like he remembered and sat in the same place. But the years had taken from it the essence that made it more. The years had stolen the two most important people from it, and now… now when he walked the halls and stared out the windows the missing… the emptiness… threatened to swallow him.

Oh God. He'd built his million-dollar home, and he *hated it.*

His low chuckle echoed in the quiet house. What a fool. He'd built a shrine to his dead parents and no amount of staging or the perfect wife would make it what it used to be: a whole family.

The only place he felt whole anymore, the only place he felt close to his mom and dad, was at the cabin. That, at least, was largely unchanged.

That still held relics of their shared past—an old two-man saw from his dad's dad, a crocheted afghan from his mother.

"Who am I kidding?" he mumbled aloud.

No one. That was the truth of the matter.

Hell, Bailey would probably say something supportive like, "Duh. We all knew it was stupid to build the house. You can't go back and who the hell wants to, anyway? You'd just have to go through your parents' death again. Time travel is for suckers."

Okay, so she wasn't *actually* in front of him telling him he was stupid and a sucker, but picturing her doing so made him chuckle again with humor this time.

Christmas was only a couple of weeks away now and the wedding just a week after that, but Ian found himself thinking less about either event and more about the woman who didn't fit into his life but whom he couldn't seem to let go of.

He'd found himself thinking about Bailey a lot since Thanksgiving— looking forward to her picking Chewy up for play dates with Zach the Bernese or leaving her candy wrappers and to-go cups in his kitchen trash as if she belonged in his life.

He wasn't sure why the sight of trash made him happy. Maybe it was simply because it was evidence he wasn't alone in this big house. Or maybe it was because he could picture her expression—bright, flashing blue eyes and sexy, pursed lips—as if she dared him to question her food choices.

She had no idea he'd stashed a bag of Doritos in the cupboard. Just for her.

CHAPTER SIXTEEN

BAILEY RUBBED HER hands together for warmth and glanced at the sky. Christmas had come and gone in the usual blur of tinsel and fruitcake. She'd pulled triple shifts serving at Lucky's and the many private holiday parties Daniel catered. Ian had been under some deadline to turn out a new update for his game, writing code or whatnot down in his dungeon basement 18-hours a day—alternately avoiding her and searing her with burning hot looks whenever she stopped by to play with Chewy or help Liz meet some new request from Marcia so the house could morph itself through a blurry succession of holidays for the cameras.

Now it was New Year's Eve. Her best friend was getting married the next day, she continued to have confusing and lustful thoughts about her pseudo employer/best friend's future brother-in-law, and she was pretty certain she'd made a mistake in wearing the thong the lady at the bridal shop insisted was the only undergarment she could possibly wear under the super-silky rehearsal dress Liz had talked her into. Still, it had been all she could manage to walk Zach, run home to shower and pack and figure out the logistics of musical car keys. She didn't want to worry about forgetting to wear the right underwear tonight.

Skye handed over the keys to her tiny compact. "Thanks for doing this."

Bailey pocketed the keys. "No problem. It feels good to fix something for a change rather than cleaning houses and waiting tables. You're sure you don't need it back until tomorrow?"

"No, I'm good. I'll catch a ride home with Wanda. You'll want to head out for the rehearsal dinner sooner than later. They're saying the snow's going to start any time now, and we'll get eight to ten inches by morning. Oh. Here. Take this. It's Turtle Cheesecake. As a thank you."

Bailey gripped the white box tightly. The wind was picking up, a few small flurries sifting down from the gray sky above. "If anyone had to inherit the cooking genes, I'm so glad it was you. You are awesome."

Skye lifted a delicate shoulder. "We all have our gifts. And right now, I'll appreciate you making that annoying rattle go away."

Bailey grinned. It was probably just a missing bolt on a heat shield. A ten-minute fix start to finish. She'd be done in plenty of time to beat the snow and get up to the inn before the rehearsal dinner.

She'd barely started the car and waved to Skye when her cell rang. "Hello?"

"Bailey, it's Valerie. Why haven't you returned any of my calls?"

"I've been busy." Plus, honestly, she'd been avoiding talking to Val ever since she'd had to back out of the deal on the garage. Val had talked to the owners about Sully bailing, and they'd let Bailey out of the contract and returned most of the earnest money. Still, it stung.

"Well, I wanted you to hear it from me and not someone else..." There was a pause on the other end. "The property is under agreement with another buyer now. I thought you'd want to know."

Bailey had expected this, but it still felt like somebody had just slugged her in the gut.

"Bailey? You there?"

Bailey shuddered out a breath. "Yeah."

"I'm sorry. I know you were hoping for it to work out somehow. We can keep looking. Look on the bright side. It'll give you a chance to save up a larger down payment."

"Right." Bailey bit back the tears. She didn't want Vampire Val to know she was crying. "Good point." Even though it had taken her a *decade* to save what she had.

She blinked and shook her head. *Damn.* She'd be *forty* by the time she could swing a garage on her own... and then everything would cost more anyway... She'd end up like her mom: working for someone else and never having enough to strike out on her own.

Oh God. She knew if she stayed on the line she would lose it. "Thanks for calling, Val. I've gotta go."

"Sure. Sure thing." The sympathy was worse than any jibe Val had ever thrown her way. "Uh, take care."

Bailey ended the call, threw her cell on the passenger seat and dropped her forehead to her hands as they gripped the steering wheel.

Well then. It was over. Really and truly over.

She sucked in a breath and raised her head, the disappointment so heavy it felt like sand sifting into her bones.

It wasn't as if she hadn't seen this coming. She'd already made the walk of shame to collect her earnest money check—or what was left of it after they'd taken a 'reasonable penalty amount' out of it. And, it wasn't as if she were *broke*. She had money. She'd simply been saving every last red cent—for years—for this one purpose which was now gone.

Phew. She blew out another breath, swiped her nose and eyes with her sleeve. "I don't suppose there's anything stopping me from replacing my blower fan anymore."

And then she laughed. Out loud. Because it felt anything but funny.

IT WAS NEARLY FIVE o'clock by the time she rolled into Sully's driveway. He lived in a small ranch-style house just outside Orchard Estates. The home had seen better days, but he had a good-sized garage out back and Sully had offered the use of it while he was away visiting his brother's family in Virginia, so Bailey wasn't going to complain.

She pulled the garage key out of her pocket as a few more flurries swirled around her, the air cold in her lungs. She didn't need Skye to give her a weather forecast to know it smelled like snow. She turned on the indoor lights and opened the overhead door to pull Skye's car inside, the sky heavy and gray in the fading light.

Good thing she'd thought to park her own car out back earlier. She didn't relish even the short walk over to her own house if it was going to be dark and blowing when she was done. Her fingers would be cold enough without heat in her car.

Bailey quickly closed the overhead and rubbed her hands together. She glanced around. Cripes. She'd only ever worked with Sully in Willard's garage. In his own space, Sully was a slob. Tools littered the workbench. Drawers on the rolling mechanic's chest were half open. An alternator sat like a disemboweled carcass on a back shelf. Maybe it was best things hadn't gone through for the partnership.

She found the hydraulic jack and popped it under the car and positioned the trouble light for easy access and flicked the switch. Nothing. Checking to see that it was indeed plugged in, she sighed and pulled her headlamp out of her pocket, grateful she'd thought to bring it. Lighting was always an issue when working on cars.

After hoisting the car, she looked around for jack stands and then saw them dangling from hooks in the ceiling—just out of reach. Fine. She'd do without. She shimmied under the car and carefully touched a gloved hand to the catalytic converter. You never touched a hot exhaust twice.

But, she hadn't driven far and it was cool enough that it was workable. She guessed the size of the bolt she'd need to reattach the heat shield, shimmied out, then shimmied her way back in.

Her fingers were cold and stiff, and she dropped the bolt twice and had to fish for it over her head on the gritty floor before she got it in the right hole. She quickly tightened it, gathered her wrenches and began to shimmy out again when she heard a *whoosh!* The car's underbelly rapidly descended toward her.

She had only a moment to instinctively put a hand in front of her face, desperately trying to remember what one was supposed to pray for in moments like this.

Then she was pinned.

She squeezed her eyes shut and her mind went blank for one stunned, horrified second, and she would have gasped except the edge of the car rested neatly across her chest, and she couldn't take a full breath for the life of her. She began to suck in shallow little breaths and then stopped breathing entirely for a moment for fear that that would lead to hyperventilating.

She had to take stock. She was alive, and if she could stay calm, she could still breathe. That roaring sound in her head was probably just adrenaline. She didn't have the breath to yell, but it wouldn't do any good even if she could, because no one was around to hear her.

Her cell phone rang from inside the car. She'd dropped it on the passenger seat after Valerie's call.

Oh, God. This was not good. Not good at all. Damn that Sully for having a crappy lift! Jesus. Damn and crappola! What was she going to do *now?*

She rubbed her temple with the hand that was already pinned conveniently near it, the garage eerily quiet.

She sucked in as deep a breath as she could and tried to squeeze out, but it was no use. For once in her life, she wished for even *smaller* breasts.

Think!

Okay. Liz wasn't expecting her at the inn until nearly eight, and she'd stashed her change of clothes in her car so she wouldn't have to waste time going home again, so even her mom wouldn't expect to see her until morning.

So, best case scenario, Liz would wait an hour to see if Bailey was held up by the weather, then she'd—hopefully—send out a search party. Which meant Bailey would be trapped under here for, oh, *four hours.* Worst case? They'd find her sometime tomorrow pinned under a clown car and dead of hypothermia. It was not the headline she'd pictured for herself.

She shivered, partly from fear and partly from the cold seeping up from the concrete floor through her jeans and flannel shirt because she'd tossed her jacket on the front seat, not wanting to snag it on Sully's dirty concrete floor. A pebble became a boulder under her elbow. She fought the urge to cry.

Her phone rang again from inside the car, and she wanted to laugh at the irony of it. But laughing required too much breath, and it hurt her chest anyway, so she bit her lip and tucked the fingers of her hand inside her waistband for warmth.

She sang little songs inside her head, tried to calculate the square roots of numbers, tried to remember what a square root *was*, and then recited the alphabet backwards to keep her mind off the fact that she was being crapped on by the universe. I mean, what the fruitcake? What had she done that she deserved to have the universe drop a miniature car on her like she was a character in *Cloudy with a Chance of Meatballs?* Which, by the way, would be awesome. She didn't understand, aside from the broccoli day, why storms of cheeseburgers would be such a terrible thing. A cheeseburger the size of your kitchen table? Come on! How cool would *that* be?

Her stomach growled and she groaned, because it reminded her that she was starving and Skye's turtle cheesecake was sitting about a foot above her face inside the back seat of the car. If she had a plasma torch, she could cut through the car and get it.

Of course, if she had a plasma cutter, she would also be able to reach her cell phone. But while she waited for help, she wouldn't starve.

Hmm. Yes, probably the hypothermia would get her before starvation…

She groaned again, which she discovered took less breath than yelling and was oddly therapeutic. She tried moaning, but the groans echoed interestingly off the undercarriage.

After groaning for a bit, her throat began to ache, and she lay still again. She wiggled her toes. Raised her knee. Lowered it again. Well, wasn't this just a crap-load of overcooked broccoli raining down?

The hinges on the door next to the overheads squeaked and Bailey held her breath to listen. Did the wind blow it open, or…?

"Bailey?" The door slammed shut.

Praise God! She was saved!

"Bailey? Bailey! Are you in here?" *Ian!* "I was at your mom's and she said you were here. If you don't get a move on, you'll be late. Christ, what are you doing here? Are you even dressed? Where are you?"

"I'm here."

"Where?"

"My thinking spot."

She heard footsteps walk past the other side of the car. "The bathroom?"

"No. *Here.* Under the car."

"Where? *Jesus.*" She heard urgent footsteps now as Ian moved closer, his breath heavy as he tried to work the jack.

"It's no use," she whispered. "The hydraulic..."

But then the car was miraculously rising above her, away from her, as if lifted by angels, and she could take a full breath again and it felt *so good.* She hurriedly shimmied along the cold, hard floor to safety as Ian's face came into view above her. Strangely, he did not look pleased to see her.

Ian let the car drop with a thud and stood over her, his breath coming fast. "Are you okay?"

"Yes, yes. I'm fine. Really. Just need a minute."

"I could kill you for that!"

"You just rescued me. That would be counterproductive," she said, rubbing her chest to ease the ache of having a toy car nearly crush her.

"Like I was going to have you die and the front page say 'Stupid Bailey Adams Killed in Freak Accident Because She Was Too Stupid to Use a Real Jack!'"

"It was a real jack, it was just faulty."

He put his head in his hands and started pacing.

"By the way," she said. "That was very manly of you, picking up the car like that."

He paused and looked at her, his eyes sparking. "It was a mini car. More of a golf cart."

"Still."

"Christ. We have to get to the rehearsal dinner. Liz wanted me to remind you to bring an overnight bag in case the weather turns bad later. She couldn't get a hold of you so she sent me to pick your things up. It's a good thing I did."

"That was very considerate of both of you." Bailey stood shakily and brushed the oily shop dust off her backside.

He blew out a long breath. "You okay? We should go. Liz and Carter wanted to have a drink and talk with us beforehand."

"About what?"

"I don't know," he blurted impatiently. "About their wedding tomorrow? You're her best friend and maid of honor. Shouldn't you know?"

"You and I both know that title's just for show. All I have to do is show up and compliment what a great job Liz has done on everything."

He opened the front door and slammed it closed again.

"What?" she asked.

"There's a news van outside."

"Why would you bring a news van here? We don't have time for that!"

He gave her a frustrated look. "I didn't bring anyone." He ran an agitated hand over his face. "Some local reporter wanted a quote for their annual *Ring in the New Year* romantic stories segment. Marcia put them up to it."

"What do they want with you?"

"Gee, let me think. I've been on a popular match-making reality show and have a brother getting married tomorrow. That might have something to do with it." He paced back toward her. "They always promise it'll take 'just a few minutes,' but then I'm stuck standing around for an hour freezing my butt off while they decide if they've got the right sound bite. *Shit!*"

He held up a hand. "My God. I'm still pumping with adrenaline." His eyes burned when he looked at her.

"Not now, Lover Boy. We'll take my car. It's parked out back. You hide in the back seat. I'll pretend you'll be coming out the front, and we'll ditch them. Let me just grab my cheesecake."

She retrieved her coat, phone and cheesecake from the car. "Let me just get changed!" she announced loudly through the front door of the garage. "And then you can use the bathroom to go number two!" Ian's eyebrows spiked to his hairline. "What? I'm buying us time," she whispered.

"By suggesting I've got a digestive issue? *Again?* Thanks?"

She grabbed his hand. "Come on. You're a basket case, you're liable to slug one of those guys if you go out pumped full of adrenaline like this. Just follow my lead."

Bailey went first, opening the back door of her Toyota and waving Ian in. She gave him the cheesecake, slammed the door shut, then walked back to the rear door of the garage. "Just let yourself out when you're done!" she called into the now empty garage. "I'll stop for some anti-diarrheal in town, so I'll meet you there!"

She grinned to herself as she slid the keys in the ignition and started the car.

"You wench," Ian breathed from the floor of her back seat. "I saved your hide and this is how you repay me?"

"*Shh*," she said. "Play your cards right, and I may share my cheesecake."

"Only you would *bring* food to a rehearsal dinner."

She shrugged and pulled onto the main road and waved at the news van as she drove down the street. She watched in the rearview mirror to be sure they weren't being followed, waited another few minutes then said over her shoulder, "I think you're safe to sit up now."

Ian crawled onto the back seat and stretched his neck. "Good. You don't have a very comfortable back seat."

"It's more comfortable than where I've been for the last hour." She blew on her fingertips as she drove, the snow swirling in the beam of the headlights. The overnight bag was a good idea. Good thing she'd already thought of it, as the snow was definitely accumulating.

Bailey pulled her cell phone out of her pocket and handed it to Ian. "Why don't you call Liz and Carter and let them know we're on our way before we lose reception?"

"Good plan."

A moment later, Ian handed the phone back. "Liz said to drive safely; it's snowing pretty heavily up at the inn. She said if we decide to turn back, they'll understand."

"No turning back now. She promised me a mimosa breakfast and morning massage. We're going. I can use all the creature comforts I can get. I think I bruised my entire ribcage."

"Speaking of comfort, can you turn on the heat?"

"No can do."

"Can we cut the passive-aggressive stuff? Even I can see you're freezing."

"Blower doesn't work."

"Seriously? I thought you were a mechanic, and yet you get trapped under a car and don't have a working heater during a New Hampshire winter?"

"First of all, I couldn't reach the jack stands, so that wasn't entirely my fault. And, secondly, I was waiting for income from my *new* shop before I spent money on a new fan, but then *somebody* screwed that up."

"So we're back to blaming me for all of this."

"No. We never stopped."

"You know what your problem is? You don't take personal responsibility for your actions."

"*Excuse me?*" She jerked as she said it and felt the car slide on the slick road. Ian didn't seem to notice.

"You heard me. You want to pass the blame. It's Willard's fault you had to quit your last real job. It's Sully's fault you got trapped tonight. It's *my* fault Sully bailed. Do you see a pattern here? Can you not see what might need to change?"

"Yes. I need to stop relying on men."

He snorted. An ugly noise she didn't find attractive at all. Also not attractive? Having him turn on her when she was uncomfortable and cranky and hungry. Plus, it was getting increasingly difficult to see out the windshield. She ran the windshield wipers. They skittered over chunks of ice.

"Hang tight. I need to scrape the windshield." She pulled over and got out to scrape at the ice build-up on the wipers and the windshield. She brushed wet snowflakes from the sleeve of her coat and hopped back in.

"Tell me again why we didn't take my car?" he asked from the back seat.

"As I recall, you were fleeing the mean old reporter who planned to ask why you weren't glowing with romantic love for the future Mrs. McIntyre."

He scowled at her in the rearview mirror as she pulled back onto the road. Her tires spun slightly then caught. The temperatures were hovering at freezing, which meant the snow was heavy and wet and packed dangerously on the road.

"Tell me you don't still have summer tires on this death trap."

"They're all-seasons."

"All-seasons? All-seasons are next to useless. You need studded snows."

"I need less chatter from the peanut gallery. I'm trying to concentrate here. The turn for the inn is easy to miss."

Fat flakes crashed against the windshield like a swirling vortex, the snow falling more heavily now that they'd entered the hills just outside of town. A mile or so back, there'd been tire tracks in the travel lane, but now the road lay like a white ribbon in front of them.

Bailey crested a small rise and felt the rear end of the car skid sideways. She eased off the gas and corrected slightly, the back end fishtailing behind her before she gained control again.

Ian swore. "This is ridiculous. You're going to kill us both. Let's go back and get my SUV."

"I have it under control, and we're more than half way there. The turn should be somewhere along here." She ran the windshield wipers again and strained to see in front of the car.

"We've got at least a few miles to go, and you can't even see out your windshield!"

Bailey braked, and the car slid to a stop. "You are welcome to walk."

"No, I think that's the turn up there."

She started the car moving again and peered to where he was pointing. "Are you sure? I thought it had a sign for the hiking trails right before it."

"No, I'm sure. Turn! You'll miss it!"

Bailey turned, the tires sliding on the wet snow until they gained traction. She ran the windshield wipers again and peered ahead. "This doesn't look right. There's supposed to be an old sugar shack on the left."

"You probably haven't gone far enough."

"Or we took a wrong turn."

Suddenly a blur of something dark cut across her vision and in the next moment, the car lurched forward with the horrible sound of metal grinding on metal.

"What the hell?" Ian unbuckled and leapt out of the back seat. His boots skidded on the ground. "You hit a gate!"

Bailey rolled down her window. "Told you we took a wrong turn."

Ian kicked the fender of her car. "Shit!"

"Hey! That's my car!" She swung open the driver's door.

He gestured to the front end. "Correction. *Was* your car."

She pushed him aside, wet snow sifting into the sides of her sneakers. "*Gah!* You! You did this!"

"*I* did this? *I* wasn't driving. If you'd had a working fan to defrost your windshield we might have been able to see where we were."

"Which is the middle of nowhere!" She stormed back to the driver's side and slumped back behind the wheel. "If you want a ride, I'd get in now."

"I don't think you're going anywhere."

"Just watch me."

"Bailey, something's leaking."

"Shit!" She leaped out and stared at the darkening spot in the snow. "I've probably punctured the radiator!" She pulled out her cell phone. Zero bars. "Double sh—!"

"Stop swearing. It's not helping."

"Oh, I'm sorry. I'm making your disaster unpleasant? Should I sing like Julie Andrews? What would you like *Edelweiss* cr *My Favorite Things?*"

Ian ignored her and pulled a flashlight from an inside pocket of his coat.

"You carry a flashlight?"

"You got a problem with that?"

"No. Flares would be nice. A space heater…"

"I have waterproof matches."

"You're a regular boy scout."

He walked away from the car toward the woods on the other side of the gate.

"Hey!" she called. "Shouldn't you be trying to go toward civilization so we can find a house and call a tow truck?"

"There are no houses here," he said. "We're in the middle of conservation land. It's over five hundred acres of undeveloped forest."

"Great. *Now* you're an expert on where we are?"

He blew out a breath, fat flakes sticking to his hair. "I should be. I own it."

"Of course you do."

Ian walked over to the sign board next to the gate and swiped at it with his arm to clear the snow away. The beam of his flashlight lit the trail marked there. "Look. We'll be fine. Grab your bag and follow me."

"I think I'll head back to the main road and take my chances flagging a plow truck."

He turned, snowflakes clinging to his eyelashes before melting against his cheek. "Suit yourself, but there's a hiker's cabin not far up this trail. It's no more than an eighth of a mile at most, and the inn is on the other side of the hill. We'll be able to hike there tomorrow in the daylight."

The snow in her sneakers melted through her socks, freezing her already cold feet. She pulled her hood over her head and grabbed her overnight bag. She'd leave her dress bag where it was. Something told her she didn't need it where they were headed. "Does this cabin have heat by any chance?"

"Once we start the woodstove."

She glanced back toward the road then toward the trail. "Fine."

In the end it was at most a few hundred yards. Far enough to feel as if they were on the brink of sure and certain disaster, their bodies left like human popsicles for the coyotes to feast upon, and near enough to make her wonder why she'd bothered arguing.

It didn't look like much, but she didn't care. Her feet were snowy blocks of ice, her fingers were numb and wet snow was melting through the hood of her jacket. Thank God she'd grabbed the cheesecake.

"It's *locked?*" Bailey stared in horror at the padlock on the door. They really were going to die out here.

The beam of the flashlight sliced away as Ian abandoned her in the dark. "Ian?"

"Relax! I'm getting the key. Oh, good, there's plenty of firewood under the side awning here."

"I suppose if you can't find the key, we can just torch the place with your matches."

"No need. I have the key." The beam of the flashlight skittered over the lock as Ian worked the key, and then the door swung open.

Bailey hurried inside. It was still and cold but at least her face wasn't getting pelted with tiny wet ice cubes. She looked around.

It was a single room with a bed against one wall, a potbelly woodstove, a couple mismatched chairs, a small table and a short counter with a small sink. A sink?

"Does this place have running water?" she asked hopefully.

"Only in the summer. The pipes would freeze out here in the winter. But, you'll be pleased to know there is an outhouse."

"Just so we're clear, there's nothing about that sentence that pleases me." She closed her eyes and groaned. "But can I borrow your flashlight?"

He chuckled and plucked an old-fashioned oil lamp off a hook on the wall and lit it with one of his precious matches. He handed her the lamp. "Just between you and me, this is less likely to get dropped into the abyss. There's a hook on the wall for the lamp. Outhouse is around back. Can't miss it."

"Terrific."

Bailey pulled her hood back over her head, grabbed the lamp and stepped back outside. The outhouse was where he said it would be and, lo' and behold, there was even toilet paper in a plastic bin. When she returned, a small flame flickered in the woodstove.

She shivered.

"Take off your shoes and socks."

"I'll think I'll wait for some heat to come out of that thing first."

He glanced up from where he crouched by the stove, feeding more pieces of kindling into the flame. "You'll be warmer if you take off your wet clothes."

"Oh, sure. I bet you say that to all the unsuspecting women you lure to your private little den of… of… what the hell is this place anyway?"

"My getaway spot."

"It's not particularly luxurious."

"Doesn't need to be." He walked over to the far side of the cabin and pulled open a hinged door in the floor.

"Oh God. Is that where you keep the dead bodies?"

"If by 'dead bodies' you mean alcohol, then yes." He looked up at her. "And if you play your cards right, I may even have a wine cooler or two down here from when my sister last came up with her girlfriends."

"I'd rather have a beer." He disappeared into the floor. Bailey peered over the edge. "So, what is down there?"

"A root cellar. Keeps things in storage without freezing. We've got some canned goods, a plastic bin with some odds and ends and, you're in luck," he came back up the steps, "alcohol."

He held up two choices, she selected a dark winter lager—one of her favorites—and went back to huddle in front of the stove. The flames were higher now and the illusion of heat made her feel a bit better; although, now that Ian had mentioned her feet, she was acutely aware of how they burned with cold. She eased off her sneakers and set them in front of the fire to dry.

"Socks, too. I promise it'll feel better."

He sat on the edge of the bed and pulled his own boots off. Of course *he'd* dressed for the weather. "I can give you a wool blanket to wrap yourself in if you want to hang up your coat."

"I'm fine." She huddled over the stove, the involuntary shiver which wracked her body proving her a liar.

"Anyone ever tell you you're too stubborn for your own good?"

"Anyone ever tell you you're too much of a know-it-all? Who has a flashlight randomly in their pocket?"

"Somebody who likes to be prepared?"

"Who has a cabin conveniently in the middle of nowhere? And what are the odds we'd get stuck here? Wait a minute. Did you *plan* this?"

"Oh, sure. I purposely stranded myself with a grumpy woman who's too foolish to take off wet clothes when I could be toasting my little brother at his rehearsal dinner at one of the finest restaurants in the area."

"I knew it!"

"Would you listen to yourself? Okay, maybe I thought this was the turn because it *did* look familiar, but I couldn't see particularly well out the windows of that rattle-trap you call a car, so this isn't my fault."

"Rattle-trap? That's my only transportation, and who is going to pay for the repairs? I can't even afford a tow truck."

Or, she *could* now that her life savings weren't going toward the garage. The realization brought depression crashing down on her like a car on a faulty lift. Oh, yeah. She'd already had that happen once tonight.

"Forget about the car. I'll buy you a new one if you'll stop talking about it."

She whirled on him then. "I don't want a new car! I want you to stop screwing up my life!"

"Did it ever occur to you that you might be screwing up *mine?*"

"My apologies. I've thrown a monkey wrench into the Golden Boy's fantasy world. What have *I* done?"

He rose from the bed and stood toe to toe with her. She had to raise her chin to look up at him. The pulse by his eyebrow thumped visibly. "You've turned my world upside down, that's what."

"Have I? Who knew I was so powerful?"

"Thanks to you, I have a dog named Chewy of all things, a fake romance with my cleaning lady and I'm stranded in a snow storm, because *you* had to get yourself stuck under a car."

"How inconvenient for you. May I remind you that the dog was definitely not my idea?"

"You named her."

"True." Bailey frowned. "What have you done with her? You haven't left her alone have you?"

"Of course not. Helen's watching her."

"What? You left her with that woman? What does she know about taking care of dogs?"

"More than either of us, I'd wager."

Ian's lips twitched up at the corners, and Bailey fought the answering pull within her. She could not agree with him. She could not, under any circumstances, soften toward this man.

Because if she did, then she'd be forced to admit she wasn't faking anything where he was concerned, and that scared the crap out of her.

"No one else could do it?" she said.

"Everyone else is at the rehearsal dinner. Face it. Chewy is fine. We're here for the night. Might as well make the best of it. In the daylight we'll hike over the hill to the inn."

Fine. Bailey held out her beer. "Got a bottle opener?"

IAN GRABBED THE bottle from her hand, pried the cap off with an

152

opener mounted on the wall behind the stove and handed it back.

"Thanks."

Her fingers brushed his knuckles. They were ice cold. He pulled the bottle from her hand again.

"Hey!"

"You get it back when you stop being so stubborn. Take off your coat. You're freezing."

"Shedding clothes seems counter-productive then."

"What are you afraid might happen?" he asked. "That I might get too excited by that oh-so-sexy flannel shirt, I won't be able to control myself?"

She grabbed her bottle back and took a hasty sip before setting it on the window sill. "I'm not afraid of anything."

"Then take off your coat and avoid hypothermia."

Her bottom lip jutted out. "You first."

He shrugged out of his parka and hung it on a hook by the door, raising one eyebrow as he did so.

She took another long drink then tugged her coat off and hung it next to his. Melting snow dripped onto the floorboards beneath it. Stubborn woman.

"Your lovely flannel shirt is also soaked," he said.

"Yeah, like I'm falling for that."

"Don't flatter yourself. I've seen lumberjacks make flannel sexier than you do."

He didn't know why he was goading her, but he felt on edge… wet, chilled and restless.

"Like you could resist me if I were standing naked in front of you," she said.

She paused, as if she weren't sure how those words came to be floating in the air between them. But there they were, raining down over him like hot sparks. Heat flooded through him, and he could feel his blood pumping. He watched her, the air crackling with awareness. The fire in the stove popped and something tumbled inside. His heart thudded in his chest at the word 'naked.'

"Try me," he finally said.

She stuffed a hand through her hair, slicking back the damp strands. Her hand shook.

"Or," he said, "Are you more afraid you couldn't resist *me?*"

"Right," she scoffed. "Like you're my type."

She turned her back, faking indifference, and took another long drink of her beer. But she wasn't indifferent. He could tell she was hyper-aware of him, because she jumped as he reached around her to pull the bottle out of her chilly fingers—before his hand would have even crossed her peripheral vision. He brought the bottle to his own mouth, and she turned to watch as he tipped it up, swallowing the cold liquid. Her eyes flickered down over his throat. He looked at her. "I think I am," he said.

She glanced away again, her tongue darting out to moisten her lips. "Go ahead, then. Get naked. See if I care."

"*Uh-uh.* Ladies first," he said.

A warm buzz slid down his throat along with the alcohol, settling in his gut, then sank lower still. He waited, anticipation kicking his pulse up another notch. He had no idea where this was going, but he liked the uncertainty. A lot.

They stood like that, facing each other, sizing one another up for untold minutes, and he was about to laugh it off.

But then she raised an eyebrow, her gaze fixed on his, and unbuttoned the top button of her shirt.

He swallowed involuntarily as her fingers fumbled with the second... then the third button. Damn. He hadn't anticipated how sexy this would actually be. Her lips moved slightly, a faint bit of saucy humor or bravado—he couldn't tell which—tugging at the edges. She slid out the last button and, gripping both edges, whipped the front of her shirt wide.

She wore a gray T-shirt underneath.

She laughed, a throaty sound as she dropped the shirt onto the edge of the bed. "Your turn," she said.

He froze for a moment, unsure of what he was expected to do. But then the part of his brain that recognized that he was standing in front of a hot woman taking her clothes off took over. He bent over, tugged off his sock, dangled it in the air like a stripper and dropped it next to her shirt.

Her lovely lips pursed in disapproval. "Socks don't count. That's cheating."

"My apologies. I didn't realize there were rules. Your turn."

They took turns taking off their socks, and then it was his turn again. "If anyone is cheating, it's you," he said. "I'm not wearing nearly as many layers." He pulled up the hem of his long-sleeved tee and pulled it over his head. Cold air hit his chest, tightening his skin.

Bailey's fingers gripped the edge of her T-shirt. She hesitated.

"Chickening out?" he asked.

"No. I'm just not wearing as many layers as you might think."

"What's that—?" but then she seemed to make a decision and yanked the tee over her head in one smooth motion, dropping it defiantly on the bed, and he didn't have to ask.

All or Nothing

No bra. She wore no bra at all.

He met her eyes. They were a bright, fiery blue, and she raised her chin.

"Viva la difference," he murmured.

"Your turn," she said.

His fingers fumbled a bit with the button on his waistband. What the hell was going on here? How did they go from getting out of wet parkas to getting naked? And yet even as the rational part of his brain pondered the turn of events, his hands didn't hesitate to slide his zipper down. He was a red-blooded male getting naked with a beautiful woman. This did not have to be thought through. He pushed his jeans to the floor and watched her reaction as he stepped out of them.

"No tightie-whities today?" she asked.

"I found my boxer briefs." Was he blushing? Damn. He was blushing.

"Lucky me."

"Quit stalling."

She slid her hands behind the button of her jeans and his mouth went dry as she wriggled her slim hips. Her jeans hit the floor, and she kicked them aside, revealing a sweet triangle of hot pink satin.

He swallowed. *Hard.*

They wore only their underwear now, and no amount of cold air could hide the fact that he currently sported a raging hard-on.

"Okay," she said, "your turn, Lover Boy."

He slid off his boxers. The skin on his back tightened with cold even as the fire warmed him from the front.

Bailey's gaze dropped to his erection.

"Indifferent, are we?" she said. Hot damn but he wanted to kiss that smirk right off her face.

"That's an automatic response to seeing a nearly naked woman. Don't take it personally. Your turn."

"No," she said. Her small breasts rose and fell with her breaths, and he could not look away from the tight rosy tips. Damn, he was dying here. He hadn't been this excited since he'd heard *Star Wars VII* was in pre-production.

"Let's up the ante," he heard her say. The blood was pounding in his ears, making it hard to hear her.

She whispered, "You do it."

His gaze dropped to the tiny triangle of fabric between her legs. The woman had him completely turned inside out. For God's sake, she wore flannel, no bra and the sexiest damn thong he'd ever seen. And if he wasn't mistaken, she was half-way to Brazil down there.

He choked. "Um. What?"

"Afraid you can't handle the temptation?" Her words were filled with false bravado. He could see the pulse at the base of her neck beating like a hummingbird's wings.

"I won't be the one to crack first, trust me," he said. It was a lie, of course. A one hundred percent bald-faced lie. He was hornier than the time his high school Spanish teacher made him dance the flamenco with Brittney Sanderson.

"Then do it." Bailey stood in front of him, her chin held high, her small, taut body rigid.

He dropped to his knees in front of her, gave her one last look up through his lashes, and leaned forward.

"What are you doing?" she squeaked, her hands sinking into his hair to hold his head back.

"Taking them off like you told me to." He planted his hands on her hips and found himself grinning up at her. "You didn't say I couldn't use my teeth."

"I didn't say you could, either." Her voice was barely a whisper, but as he leaned forward a second time, she didn't protest. Instead, her eyes widened further and her breathing hitched as he nipped at the edge of her thong and tugged, her scent and taste enveloping him.

He found it trickier than he'd anticipated, but after some effort, he managed to inch the thin ribbons that wrapped her hips far enough that they slid free and the scrap of material fell to the floor. He dropped his hands from her hips and stood up in front of her. She sucked in quick little breaths and watched him.

"There. Done." He reached around her, not quite touching, and picked up her bottle from the window sill. He finished its contents in a few long swallows. He could feel the shiver that ran over her skin as he brushed by her to set it down again.

"Now what?" she breathed.

He shrugged, the nonchalant gesture completely out of place considering his body was screaming for action. This was uncharted territory. "You tell me."

"So... we're just going to stand here naked and stare at each other?"

"Until you admit you're as turned on as I am, yes."

"You're turned on?"

He pointed down. "The flag is flying."

She grinned. "Hard to miss."

"You look flushed," he observed, his gaze settling on her breasts.

"The fire's warm."

"Mmm." He frowned and reached out to brush his thumb across the top of her ribcage just under her breast. "You have a mark." He glanced up. "Does it hurt?"

Her grin faltered. "Not too much."

Shit. What the hell was he doing? This woman had nearly been crushed by a car. She was probably still in shock from the ordeal. He shouldn't touch her like this, but now that he had, he couldn't move his hand away. He stroked the pad of his thumb across her skin again. She sucked in an unsteady breath.

"I'm glad you weren't seriously hurt," he found himself saying.

"Me, too," she whispered.

He turned away and grabbed a folded blanket from the end of the bed and brought it around her shoulders. "Your lips are turning blue," he said. "Not that it's not a good color on you."

She hugged the blanket tight around her and then got an odd look on her face before opening it again. "No sense leaving you out in the cold."

He swallowed, watching her. "You sure?"

She glanced down at him again. "Just admit I've won this round, but, yes, I'm freezing and you look… warm."

He grinned and stepped toward her. "Hot. Just say it. You think I look hot."

She laughed, her breasts brushing against his skin as they stepped toward one another. "How about, 'very warm'?"

He wrapped his arms around her, tugging her against him. Her body softened into his. It felt good. *Really* good. "Sizzling," he whispered into her hair.

He dipped his head down and kissed her softly on the lips, testing, tasting. But she pulled back, her eyes dark and uncertain, and buried her face in his chest.

He blew out a quiet breath. The fire crackled again, and he held her gently, rubbing his hands down her back until her shivering eased and her skin began to warm where they touched. She fit perfectly against him. Heat pumped through him.

He leaned back. "Better?"

"My toes are still cold."

He found her hand underneath the blanket and led them to the bed then pulled more blankets from a cupboard in the wall and laid them out, tucking Bailey underneath and crawling in beside her. There, by the time they found bare skin again, they'd be warm. "They'll warm up in a bit. We'll just lie here."

"Naked," she said, her lips curving a bit at the corners.

"It's working for me so far," he said. "Although," he shifted and tugged her more snugly against him despite the layers of blankets getting in the way, "a few adjustments." He pulled the covers over her shoulder.

"So we're just going to lay here by the fire, completely naked, while we ignore your obvious state of, er, patriotism and…"

And?

"Talk. We'll talk," he said. "Isn't that what you women like to do?" He could do this. He could hold a warm, naked woman in his arms and…

"Talk?" she said.

"Sure. I'll start. Your mother was very pleasant when I stopped by to find you this evening. Invited me in for coffee and everything."

"Oh God. She didn't."

"She did."

"I can't believe you went to my house."

"What? It's fine."

"Fine?"

"Okay, nice," he said.

"What's that supposed to mean?"

"Nothing." She gave him a look and he shrugged. "If you must know, I kind of pictured you living out of your car and taking showers in homes you clean, so it was a definite step up."

Her eyebrows shot to her hairline. "First of all: gee, thanks. Second of all: you wish. Like you could convince me to play along with one of your perverse sexual fantasies."

"Perverse sexual fantasies?"

"You know, all those bad porn flicks where the man just 'happens' upon the woman showering, so he can step in and—"

"Okay, first of all: *you* wish. And second of all: you watch porn?"

"Gross! No. Rarely. Okay, *once*." She fidgeted then smacked him in the shoulder with her palm. "Stop looking at me like that! I go all run at the mouth when you give me that look!"

He chuckled. "So I've noticed. Tell me about this porn problem you have…"

She rolled her eyes. "My half-brother and his friends were having a guys' night. I thought they were just watching baseball, so I went over for the taco dip and free beer. My mistake. End of story." He stared at her, silent. "What?"

"I'm giving you the look just in case that *isn't* the end of the story."

"That's not the look. It's more like this." She dipped her chin and wiggled her eyebrows.

He laughed. "I do not make that face."

"You so do. Every time you *think* you make that face."

"How do you know I'm thinking?"

"Touché."

"Ouch." He flattened his palm on his chest. "Okay," he said. "What am I thinking now?"

"You want my cheesecake?"

"Close." He looked at her mouth and back up at her eyes. "No, I'm thinking, 'I wonder if Bailey has condoms in her overnight bag?'"

He paused and watched her.

"What does that have to do with cheesecake?" she asked.

"Are you going to let me seduce you or not?" he asked with exasperation.

"Not if you muck it up. Cripes. Here, I'll be you." She reached up and smoothed her hand against his cheek, then pressed closer to brush her lips over his. "*Mmm*," she said against his mouth, "I wonder if you can guess what I'm thinking," she said, her voice attempting a male timbre.

"Tell me."

"I'm thinking it's a shame I didn't think to bring condoms when I stranded us in the middle of nowhere, but I'm going to make it up to you, Bailey, by showing you just how imaginative I can be."

She bit his lip lightly and pulled back with a mischievous grin.

"Are you done?" he asked, completely and utterly turned on now.

"Sure," she said.

He rolled her beneath him, and she gave a yelp of surprise. Then he kissed her, hotly and thoroughly, until the defiant look in her eyes turned to unfocused heat. He pulled back, his own breath ragged. "As I was saying, I wonder if Bailey has condoms in her overnight bag… because that'd mean she was thinking the same thing I was thinking when I put some in *mine*."

Her attention snapped to his. "You dirty boy scout," she whispered. "But bonus points for planning ahead."

"Keeping score are we?"

"Damn straight. And you're way ahead." She waggled her eyebrows. "I think I need to play some catch-up."

She ducked her head under the blanket. Her mouth met his abs, hot and moist, and he jumped in response. He could feel her lips grinning against his skin, and then he forgot to worry about anything as she slipped lower still.

THERE WAS NOT A LOT of thinking going on as Bailey pressed a trail of kisses down Ian's torso, and, frankly, that was probably for the best. Let's face it, it wasn't as if she often had the opportunity to kiss a man's abs—particularly ones as sculpted and fling-a-licious as Ian McIntyre's. *Hot tamales.* She was about to have sex!

"What are you doing?" he asked, his voice throaty and low. Bailey paused in her descent.

Doing? Wasn't it obvious? Okay, confession time, she didn't have a heck of a lot of experience in the whole seduction thing, but this was somewhat basic, wasn't it?

"Um," she mumbled against his skin. Oh lordy, he smelled *so good.* She wanted to lick him like a giant man-sicle from head to toe. The thought made her giggle against his belly.

"Something funny?" he asked, lifting the blankets to look at her.

She glanced up at his tousled dark hair and serious eyes and felt a rush of something warm and tingly down low.

She shook her head. "No."

"Then why were you laughing?" His eyebrows did that little vee thing that made him look all brooding romance novel hero. The warm tingle turned to a slow burn.

"I wasn't laughing."

"Okay. Good." He continued to watch her, and she sighed. "Great. Now I'm all self-conscious."

He flattened on the mattress. "No! Sorry. Go ahead. I never said anything and you never snorted."

She flipped the blanket from her head. "What? I didn't snort!"

He lifted his head. "You did, but I didn't hear. Carry on."

She pushed at his forehead with the heel of her hand. "Stop looking at me."

His chest rumbled with suppressed laughter. "I should have known sex with you would be a challenge. Will it help if I close my eyes?"

"And stop talking. You're making me nervous."

"I'm making you nervous? You're the unpredictable woman who has me at her mercy. If anyone should be nervous, it should be me."

"You're at my mercy?"

He opened one eye. "A little tip for you—any time you go below a guy's belly button, he's at your mercy."

"Really? I thought nowadays that was expected."

He opened his other eye. "Expected? More like, prayed for. That's usually a special request sort of thing."

She shimmied up his torso, her soft breasts pressing against his chest. "Let me get this straight...Your super-model women don't do things unless you make special requests?"

"I don't push for it, if that's what you're getting at."

"So what *do* they do?"

He closed his eyes. "Do we have to talk about this now?"

"I mean, do they just lie there? Do they do kinky *50 Shades* stuff? I want to know. It's been a little while since I last dated."

"No kidding. Here's another tip: less talking. More of that other stuff."

"So, no dirty talk?"

He sighed and propped himself on his elbows again. "What's going on with you? Five minutes ago you were all sexy seductress and now I feel like I'm in bed with a virgin."

She must have gone white, because his eyes got huge. "You're not, are you?"

"No! Of course not. Sheesh! I'm twenty-eight!"

He continued to look at her. She bit her lip. Crap. She was ruining things. She swallowed over the lump in her throat. "Fine. You may not believe this, but I'm not as experienced as you probably think I am."

His eyebrows did that vee thing again. "How inexperienced?"

She twisted her lips and twirled her fingertips around in his chest hair. "I've only had actual sex a few times."

"As in a few partners or actual acts of sex?"

She wanted to die. "The last one."

"Are you freakin' kidding me?" he said, nearly dumping her on the floor as he sat up.

"No. I'm not. Do you have a problem with that?"

"Why not? I mean, why haven't you?"

"There's nothing wrong with me! There just weren't that many opportunities, all right? It's a small town. I was always afraid I'd end up in bed with someone who'd later turn out to be my half-brother. Do you know how hard it is to date in a town not knowing who I'm related to?"

He seemed to settle down some. At least now he didn't look like he was going to bolt. "So, um, how'd you lose your virginity?"

"I visited Liz at college. Hunky frat guy. I was doing funnels. It's not a proud memory."

"Do you even remember his name?"

"Of course! David something-or-other-Schmidt. Quit looking at me like that! I'm sure you have the perfect loss-of-virginity story with rose petals and poetry and—"

"Jell-o shots in a hotel room after prom. My best friend's ex-girlfriend. Not a proud memory."

Huh, so they had drunken loss-of-virginity in common.

She picked at a lint ball on the blanket. "You're just saying that to make me feel better."

He chuckled, and his hand stroked her shoulder. "No. I'm not."

"What was her name?"

"Jenn something."

"Jenny Whitmeyer?"

"No. God, no. I forgot you'd assume it was someone local. No, she was from out of town."

They were quiet a moment and his hand stilled. "So, what's going on here? Why me? Why now?"

She shrugged her shoulder under the heat of his hand feeling suddenly, markedly exposed.

He tilted her chin up with his other hand and brushed the hair from her cheek. "No jokes. No laughing. No dares. Talk to me."

Her heart beat heavily in her chest and she fought to hold her gaze steady. He wanted the truth? Fine. She'd give him the truth. She sucked air into her lungs before she chickened out. "The truth is… I think you're hot. Smokin' hot. And even though I haven't done it much, I *like* sex, or at least the idea of it, and I figure the odds of falling into bed, naked, with a guy like you," she let her hand gesture toward all of him, "isn't going to happen all that often, so I might as well take advantage of it while I can."

He watched her, silently, for a few moments. "I see."

"Well?"

"Well, aside from the obvious performance anxiety this throws my way, thank you. I'm honored. But, and this is just total honesty now, if you dropped the defensive wall and wore a little less flannel, you'd have guys throwing themselves at your feet right and left. You know that, right?"

"Get out," she muttered.

"Seriously. And if you won't believe me, then just observe the fact that throughout this whole discussion, my, um—admiration—for you hasn't wavered."

Bailey snuck a glance down his torso and back up again. Nice.

He stroked her hair again, a tender gesture that had the breath hitching in her throat. "But I don't want to be another David something-or-other-Schmidt in your memory. If we're going to do this, we're doing it intentionally. We're not falling into bed because of a dare, or because we're naked… or because I happen to be drop-dead sexy."

162

She smacked him in the shoulder. "Get over yourself. Now you're getting cocky, because you know I don't have much to compare you to."

"I'm not cocky. I'm flattered. If we're being completely honest, I've wanted you since that first day you were touching my dirty underwear."

"Ew!"

"It's true." He frowned. "No woman has given me so much grief. It was refreshing. They're usually much more... solicitous."

"Not to point out the obvious, but you're rich, hot and kind of a sympathy magnet. Everybody knows about the McIntyre fire."

"Yeah, but you still treated me like I had to earn your respect."

"You do."

He grinned at her, his hand heavy and deliciously warm as he stroked it down her bare shoulder. "I know."

Her heart thumped in her chest, slow and hard as she looked at him. "Tell me something else about you."

He shrugged and blew out a breath. "There's nothing left to tell. I'm an open book. Like you said, everybody knows my story. Tragic fire killed my parents. I designed a viral video game that made me a millionaire, and now I'm settling down, because it's time. No secrets. No skeletons."

"Tell me about your *Star Wars* obsession."

"I don't have an obsession. It's an iconic—"

"Stop. You have action figures and collector's edition toys. It's an obsession. What's the deal?"

He shrugged again, his fingertips tracing small patterns on her shoulder. "Well?"

His fingers stilled. "I saw it the first time on the day of my parents' funeral."

"That's an odd choice for a funeral flick. Don't they usually do a slide show set to sappy music?"

"It was after the funeral. Everyone was gathered at my aunt and uncle's house. The usual food and family thing. I went down to the rec room to... to get away. That's when I watched it the first time. For an eight year-old boy who'd just lost his parents, it was easy to get sucked into the fantasy world. Much better than the real world at the time."

"I'll bet."

"So, that's it," he said. "What's your embarrassing secret?"

"That's hardly an embarrassing secret."

"What if I also told you that before I watched the movie, I also found my uncle's *Sports Illustrated* swimsuit magazines while I was down there... and I put them back to read his *Popular Science?*"

"Now that *is* embarrassing," she laughed. "Okay. Fine. When I was twelve I competed in the Sugar Falls Winter Carnival Snow Belle Pageant."

"You?"

"I wasn't my own person then. My mother did all the girls' hair and makeup and convinced me I was as good as anyone else who ever entered."

"I'm surprised you agreed to do it."

"I wouldn't have if it weren't for Ellen Lambert."

"The pediatric nurse who does that annual rubber duckie charity for the terminally-ill children?"

"Oh, don't make her sound so high and mighty. The woman was a cut-throat competitor when she was eleven. She pulled me aside in school and asked me if the rumors were true that I was competing for the Snow Belle Princess crown, and when I said I was thinking about it, she *laughed.*"

"The nerve."

"I was going to show her and all of them what I thought of their ridiculous pageant. So I went as..." her eyes met his briefly before skittering away as she mumbled the last words.

His eyebrows shot up. "You dressed as Princess Leia?"

"I was going to show them all how ridiculous their pageant was by dressing as the only princess I admired. Everybody else goes in cream-puff prom gowns they have to wad socks into the chests of to make fit, but I wasn't going to be like everybody else."

"I'm shocked Sandi agreed to this."

"She thought it was brilliant. She didn't know I wanted to show everyone how silly it all was. She got into it. She put temporary dye in my hair, gave me false eyelashes. She even sewed my dress. You know, the white one at the end of Episode IV?"

"I can picture it. I sense this story doesn't end well."

She lifted a shoulder and glanced away. Swallowed. "When I walked on stage, I didn't get applause like the other girls."

"What happened?"

"Everyone was just... silent. The whole opera house—completely silent. Nobody knew what to do. And I froze, because it wasn't until I was out there that I realized I *wanted* them to look at me and coo and clap like they were doing for everyone else. I wanted to be the princess, but as soon as I got out there I knew I'd ruined my chances, because I'd made fun of them all."

"What happened then?"

"Somebody snickered and then people started laughing. I didn't know what else to do, so I turned around and ran off the stage, tore the fake buns out of my hair and never looked back."

"Now that's a lie."

She looked at him. "You're looking back every day," he insisted. "Is this why you never dress up or do your hair or wear makeup? You're afraid the world will be silent?"

"Deep, Dr. Phil." But as the sarcastic comment tumbled from her lips, a single tear spilled onto her cheek.

Ian smiled and brought his hands together, softly clapping.

"Don't make fun of me," she sniffed.

"I'm not. I'm trying to tell you I think you're beautiful. Snarky and stubborn, but beautiful. I would have voted for you."

"Really?"

Several more tears followed, but he wiped them away with the pad of his thumb. "Yeah."

She smiled uncertainly as he leaned forward and brushed his lips against hers, soft and gentle. The he pulled her into a hug, tucking her head under his chin. "We don't have to do anything," he said, his voice resigned.

She felt her lip quiver. He was so *nice*. And rock-hard gorgeous. She could feel his erection pressing against her despite his words.

"Not a chance, Lover Boy." She planted a loud kiss on his mouth and smiled shakily. "Now that I've got you naked, I intend to flambé your banana."

"I'm sorry, I think we have to institute the no talking rule again. I don't even want to know what you mean by that."

"Just kiss me, then. Please?"

He grinned and rolled her to her back, sending warm happiness and sweet acceptance swirling into all the cold, uncertain recesses of her heart. "Sure thing, Leia."

CHAPTER SEVENTEEN

"GOOD MORNING."

Bailey rolled over and opened one eye. Ian was half-dressed, grinning... and eating her cheesecake.

"Hey!" she said, scrambling to sit up. "That's not yours!"

"I can't believe you wouldn't share with the man who gave you the best night of your life."

She pulled the blankets higher. My God. She'd slept naked? She never slept naked... and suddenly everything from the night before came crashing into her consciousness at once. She averted her gaze from his toned, muscular abs as a riot of conflicting thoughts and emotions crashed through her. Snark. She could do snark. "Don't flatter yourself."

His fork paused in midair. "You said so yourself."

"I was still seeing you through that post coital glow. It's like beer goggles. Give me my cheesecake."

He snagged another bite then handed the box over. She grabbed it with one hand, still clutching the blankets to her chest and fighting the urge to smooth her hair like a girlie-girl. Where did that urge even come from?

She bit her lip and wished she had a clue what proper protocol was for morning afters. Did she act all 'we should do that again'? Or was she supposed to get up and get dressed like she always woke up to eye candy eating cheesecake over her naked body? *Gah!* Damn that hairy-backed Derek for not only *not* giving her an orgasm like he'd promised but for not giving her a chance to practice her morning after skills. Idiot *would* have to have an allergic reaction to the stupid body spray she'd shelled out twelve bucks for...

"So..." she said, letting the word trail out. Ian would know how to handle this. He was the freakin' bachelor-du-jour, for Pete's sake.

He grinned lazily at her. "What?"

"What do you mean 'what'?"

"You said, 'so.' 'So' what?"

"Nothing." *Oh, come on! Help me out here!*

His eyebrows formed a vee. "What's wrong with you?"

She clutched the edge of the blanket, her fingers rigid and cold despite the bone-deep satisfied heat of the bed. "Nothing. Nothing's wrong. What's wrong with you?"

He swiped a hand over his face. *Oh sweet baby Jesus, that hand!* She'd never be able to look at his hands again without thinking about last night. Heat crept up her neck. Yes, okay. She was thinking about last night... and all the places his hands had been. *In detail.*

"You're really bad at this, aren't you?" he finally said, standing over her by the bed.

"Excuse me?"

"The morning after stuff. You look like a nun who's just woken up in a bordello. Just relax, will you? Don't freak out on me."

"I'm not freaking out." Okay. A little. "It's just hard to relax when I'm naked." She frowned. "I mean..."

But he chuckled and leaned in, pressing his lips to hers which only made her more nervous and self-conscious.

"You taste like cheesecake," she said when he finally pulled away again. "*My* cheesecake. You should ask permission before taking liberties."

One dark eyebrow went up. He lifted the blankets and silently slid in beside her, and then she became aware of a warm hand gliding over her skin under the covers as his eyes held hers. Nerve endings that usually required caffeine came alive under his touch. The corner of his mouth hitched up on one side. It should have made him appear cocky and self-assured, but it only served to make him look hopeful and endearing.

Dang. She was screwed. "What are you doing?" she asked.

"Wondering about you."

"With your hands?"

"It's how we men do our best thinking."

She frowned.

"I'm kidding," he said. His hand stilled. "Mostly."

She held her breath in her lungs, afraid to move, afraid to breathe morning breath on him. The cabin was quiet, the only sound the occasional crackle from the woodstove.

Ian let out a breath like a sigh and his hand left her side. "Come on. Much as I hate to say it, we should get going. The snow has stopped, so whenever you're ready, we can hike over to the inn and call a tow truck for your car."

Mention of the tow truck brought Bailey back to reality. Fudge brownies. Her car! *The wedding!*

She scrambled to sit up, modesty be damned. "What time is it?"

"About seven."

"*Seven?*" Crap. So much for mimosas and massages. "What are you standing around for? We've got to get over there." She hurried to pull yesterday's clothes back on.

"Relax. The wedding's not for hours yet."

She popped her head through her T-shirt and struggled to poke her arms through the inverted sleeves. "Would you quit saying that? There's no time to relax. I've got to get to civilization, get my ass over to the hair salon before my mother has a conniption, retrieve my dress from my car... and pretend we didn't do our best to put my record into the double digits last night."

He laughed. "For a woman who wears a thong, you're kind of uptight."

She glared at him through her hair. "I do not wear thongs. That was specifically a one-time thing for my rehearsal dinner dress. It was silk. And clingy." And nothing she'd ever wear now that she'd missed the rehearsal dinner.

She buttoned the last button on her flannel shirt and ran a hand through her hair. "Okay. Let's go."

He was watching her, an odd look on his face. "Right."

They tidied up, dampened down the stove and set out.

"MY FEET ARE FREEZING." Bailey slogged behind Ian on the trail. They'd been walking for several minutes and were, hopefully, nearing the rise Ian had promised was nearby. The air puffed out of her lungs in little clouds.

"Don't you own boots?" he asked.

"They're at the house."

"Well thank goodness you remembered your thong."

She ignored that and walked a few more feet. "So," she said, "we should get our stories straight."

She heard him chuckle. "No one cares what we were up to last night. It's their wedding day. They've got bigger things to worry about."

"I know, but just in case, let's not get all chatty about this. No one needs to know about this little indiscretion."

He paused and turned to her. "What do you mean, 'indiscretion'?"

"Hello? Last night? *Sheesh.* Do I have to spell it out?"

"I think you might."

"No one can know about last night, Ian! I know we're pretending to be into each other to annoy Marcia, but this," she made what she hoped was a descriptive gesture between them, "isn't something that leaves Snowy Acres here."

"I see."

"Don't give me that look. This can't be a surprise. You'll void your contract with the show if you end up starting something with me."

"What if I told you I don't care about the show?"

"What are you saying?"

Her feet were blocks of ice, but she didn't care. She was afraid to move. Afraid that if she distracted him he'd realize he was about to say something that might make her change her mind about everything.

His breath puffed into the space between them. "Nothing. Let's go. You're shivering again."

"No! I want to know what you were about to say."

He swiped a hand over his face, his whiskers morning-after sexy, and she bit her lip to keep from going on tip-toe and risking stubble burn on her cheeks.

As if reading her mind, he raised and pressed a warm palm to her cold cheek, then leaned in over the box of cheesecake and kissed her until her toes curled. He pulled back.

"You're right," he said. "No one should know about last night."

CHAPTER EIGHTEEN

"BAILEY! WHERE HAVE YOU BEEN?" Liz rushed forward, a vision in wedding morning style, wearing leggings, a cozy tunic sweater and chic, fuzzy boots. "I've been trying to call you all morning."

"All morning? It's barely 8:00 a.m."

"It's my *wedding* day, Bailey. I've been up since five. By the way, you missed morning yoga and massages. Hi, Ian."

Bailey dropped her bag by the check-in desk and refused to look over her shoulder at what she knew was a distractingly hunky guy hovering behind her.

Ian set his own bag next to Bailey's. "Sorry we missed the rehearsal dinner. I hope we didn't worry you too much."

Liz looked between them. "Bailey said you guys might not make it, but I assumed you would have stayed in town. What happened to you two?"

"Car trouble—"

"Wrong turn—" they said, speaking over one another.

"Ian told me to turn in the wrong place and—"

"Bailey drove into a security gate," he finished.

Liz's hand flew to her chest, soft-lavender manicure sparkling. "You stayed in your car all night?"

"No," said Ian. "Luckily we were near my cabin."

Liz's eyes shot to Bailey. "You stayed in Ian's cabin? The one with the root cellar?" *And one bed?* her expression seemed to say.

"You know about that?"

"Grace does a girls retreat there every so often." She looked at Ian and then back at Bailey, her eyes speaking volumes. "Well, that must have been cozy."

"We survived," Bailey said, looking hopefully around Liz for the innkeeper. She didn't feel up to playing twenty questions with Liz. "Can we talk after I've had a hot shower and a pot of coffee? And food? I mean, it's your wedding day! We need to get you ready!"

Liz waved away Bailey's concern. "I've got gobs of time. Let's get you settled. I'll have them send up a breakfast tray."

"I need to find the innkeeper."

"No worries," Liz said, pulling a key from her pocket. "I already checked you in when I saw you guys hiking over the hill."

Bailey swallowed and wondered whether Liz had seen Ian kiss her. Something in Liz's expression told her she had.

Liz turned to Ian. "Your room is near Carter's in the Sherwood Forest Wing. Go through the fireplace room, take a left and go long. You're in the Robinhood Room." Liz handed him the key.

Bailey raised an eyebrow. "Seriously?"

Liz grabbed Bailey's bag. "Don't laugh. We're in the Fairy Magic Wing. I've put you in the Flower Fairy Room."

"And where are you staying?"

Liz chuckled. "The Cinderella Suite, of course."

LIZ YANKED BAILEY into her suite and closed the door like a jailor. She turned, hands on hips. "Spill it. What happened with you two?"

Bailey shrugged out of her coat. "Nothing. What makes you think anything happened?"

"You have stubble burn on your cheek, and I just watched you two suck face on the hill. I hurried down to collect you before anybody else saw what neither of you seem able to hide."

"Do we have to talk about this now? It's your wedding day!"

"Yes, we have to talk now. I'm a total wreck. I need the distraction."

Bailey turned around. Liz was calm, cool and collected. "Liar. You've had this wedding planned since birth."

Liz didn't deny it. "What's in the box?"

"Turtle cheesecake. Skye gave it to me last night right before I got trapped under her car."

"What? You made out with Ian *and* got stuck under a car?"

Bailey shook her head and toed off her sneakers. "It's been an eventful night. But before anything else, I'm showering, because I cannot feel my toes."

"Fine. We'll talk after you shower. I'll call down for food."

Bailey grabbed her overnight bag and padded into the adjoining bath. "And coffee. Lots and lots of coffee."

When she emerged, scrubbed and dressed in sweats and feeling much warmer thanks to a fat terry robe, she found Liz sitting by the window drinking coffee. Bailey's stomach growled.

"There's bacon, a western omelet, French toast and the best home fries you've ever tasted. The room names here are hokey, but the food is fantastic."

"Then remind me again why my father is catering your reception?"

"Oh, it's just the innkeeper. She loves to cook but not for crowds. Any event over fifty people and you need a caterer. Carter didn't want anything too fussy anyway."

"You got that, then. I'll start with coffee." Bailey curled up in the chair opposite Liz and snitched a home fry while Liz poured her a mug.

"You're being markedly quiet."

"I'm tired," Bailey said.

"I'll bet."

"You're not going to leave this alone, are you? Even on your wedding day?"

Liz sipped her coffee. "I've got nothing better to do. Every time I try to step foot out of my room, Carter's grandmother yells at me for fear Carter might see me and jinx the wedding. Plus, I don't have to be at the hair salon until noon, so it's a day of rest and relaxation." She raised a silver dome. "Oh, try these little cinnamon walnut twists. To die for. Then you can tell me why you're fooling around with my fiancé's brother."

Bailey bit into a pastry and added a couple heaping teaspoons of sugar to her coffee. "You have to promise to tell no one. Even Carter."

"You know I can't do that. He's going to be my husband."

Bailey paused in the midst of blowing on her coffee and looked up. "It's all changing, isn't it? It didn't hit me until now, but when you get married, Carter will be your BFF. He'll be who you confide in."

"We'll always have girl secrets."

"Will we? Just the three of us? You just said you wouldn't keep a secret from him."

Liz set her mug down. "Bailey, what happened last night?"

"Don't freak out."

"Oh my God," Liz breathed. "You didn't just play a little footsie up there in that cabin. You—"

"Served up the whole enchilada."

"Holy crap. This is *huge!*"

"I know."

"Does he know?"

"Um. He was there, Liz."

"No. I mean, does he know how huge a deal this is for you?"

Bailey shoved the rest of the cinnamon twist into her mouth. "You don't have to make me sound like such a freak."

"Not a freak. Discerning. Was it good?"

"Which time?"

"*Ooooooh!* This *is* big!"

"Would you keep your voice down? This is big in that it's a big fat secret. We can't tell anyone. Especially Marcia."

"Oh my God. The show! Wait. Does this mean he didn't walk away with anyone? He's *not* engaged to that Helen woman?"

Bailey shrugged. "I don't know."

"*You don't know?*"

"Again. The voice. Where's that omelet?"

Liz pushed forward a silver dome, her brow knitted. "He wouldn't, you know. Ian wouldn't sleep with you if he'd chosen someone on the show. He's too nice a guy. Wow. This is the first time Marcia has failed. Grams is going to be so disappointed."

"Excuse me? What am I, chopped liver?"

"Well it's not like you and Ian are serious." Liz took a sip of coffee.

Bailey frowned and dug into the omelet. They weren't serious, were they? "It was just one night."

"Bailey, I love you like my sister, but Ian's a good guy. Don't mess around with him."

Bailey's throat felt tight as she looked across the table at the woman she thought would always be on her side. "Maybe you should be telling Ian not to mess around with me."

"See?" Liz reached across and gripped Bailey's hand. "It's already messy. I love you both, but if this is already causing upset, it's probably a bad idea."

"Like I said, it was a one-time thing, Liz. Don't get your panties in a bunch."

Liz tilted her head in that pompous way engaged people had when speaking to single people, like they wished they could only impart half their wisdom on love and happiness to the poor, miserable fool in front of them. "Maybe that's your answer. It's a one-time thing. I mean, they all suffered when they lost their parents, but maybe Ian, being the oldest, suffered the most. Maybe he went on the show because he believed it gave him the best shot at finding someone looking to build something long-term—a committed relationship, not a one-night shag."

"I see. So now I'm not commitment material." For some reason she'd lost her appetite. She swiped at her mouth with her napkin.

"I didn't say that. But to be honest, I guess I never pictured you, well, *with* someone."

"Gee thanks."

"I mean I know you *like* men, but you don't *like* them, you know?"

"I like men!"

"Fine. You don't trust them. And I get it! I get it. The whole Daniel thing. It's enough to make anyone guarded."

"Exactly."

"But Ian is a good guy... well-off... attractive... He deserves someone who wants to settle down. Your, um, issues make it hard for you to commit."

Bailey's fork clattered to the plate. "I see. Now I'm too screwed up to be good enough for him?"

"No. But do you even want a serious relationship right now?"

"I don't know what I want! We just had sex last night!"

"Volume," Liz whispered.

"But already I'm supposed to decide on a china pattern?" Bailey whispered back. "I don't recall you being all sure and committed after doing the deed with Carter. In fact, weren't you still engaged to someone else? Oh, I'm sorry. *Sort of* engaged."

Liz made a face. "No need to throw that back at me. I'm only saying if you're not ready to be in a committed relationship, don't get in the way of Ian finding someone to settle down with. He deserves to be happy."

"Don't I deserve to be happy?"

"Of course. That's not what I meant. You both deserve to be. But would you be happy together? What do you even have in common?"

Star Wars. Peanut butter and Doritos sandwiches. Chewy. "Last night was awesome."

"As Kate told me her Nana once said: there's more to a relationship than great sex."

"Then why is that where most relationships start?" Bailey drained her coffee and put a hand up to forestall further grilling. "Forget it. Thank you for your concern and all that, but Ian and I are adults. I don't plan on mucking up his future any more than I intend to let him muck up mine, so relax. It's your special day. We can slice and dice my love life at some later date, but I'd appreciate not thinking about this anymore right now."

Bailey glanced at the clock by the bed. "And if I don't get my butt down to the salon pronto, my mom will pitch a fit. She's beyond excited to do everyone's hair and makeup."

"Even yours?"

Bailey laughed without humor. "Especially mine."

CHAPTER NINETEEN

"BAILEY! PARK YOUR BUTT at that sink. You're late!"

Sandi stuck another foil thing in Liz's sister's hair and set a timer. "Now you hold on there, honey. Here's the new *People* magazine. I've flagged the good pages." She winked at Trish and marched over to Bailey.

"All right, you. Head under. I've got ideas, and I want time to do them."

"Don't get crazy on me, Mom. Just a trim."

"Fine. Mostly a trim. Then some fun stuff. But don't worry, it's all pre-approved by the bride herself. In fact, she gave me some ideas."

Bailey settled back in the chair. "If Liz says it's okay, then I'm sure it'll be fine."

An hour later Bailey stared at her reflection in the mirror. "Mom! You've made me blue! And purple! And, is that *pink?*"

"Oh, relax. It's only temporary color. It'll wash out in a day or two. A week at most."

"Mom! I look like a… like a…"

"You look awesome!" Liz cried from the door of the salon. She hurried over. "Oh, Bailey, it's gorgeous!"

"Get out. I look like a My Little Pony. She curled my hair…"

"And it's *perfect!* Oh, Sandi, this is exactly what I had in mind!"

Bailey turned back to the mirror. The reflected face didn't feel like her own. Her hair was close to its usual just-brushing-her-shoulders length, but today it fell in soft waves around her chin, and her mother had added thin strands of pale pastel color that caught the light when she moved. Tiny braids in a delicate diamond pattern swept away from each temple and disappeared behind her head with crystals sparkling here and there. And, somehow, she was going to have to preserve this entire effect for the next four hours?

"Hold your breath!" Sandi ordered, and then she fumigated Bailey with what seemed an entire can of hairspray. "Now, don't run away. We still have makeup. But first, let's get you going, Miss Bride-to-Be!"

Bailey leaned over toward Liz's chair hoping for a pocket of un-stiffened air to breathe. "This is payback for this morning."

"Not at all. It's whimsical and magical. Just wait until you see the decorations. It's like the *Nutcracker* meets *Frozen!*"

Bailey turned back to the mirror. "This is like the whole Winter Carnival fiasco all over again."

"Oh, pish posh. You looked adorable for that pageant. If you hadn't chickened out and nearly wretched in the orchestra pit, you would have been a contender." Sandi was lifting and dropping hunks of Liz's hair and making *mm-hmm* noises as if she hadn't just gutted her own daughter. "Excellent. Let's get you over to the wash station."

Bailey fumed in her chair and wished she cared about the magazines on the counter in front of her. Until she saw one with Ian on the cover. She grabbed it and stared in horror at the photo and caption.

"Two-Timing Bachelor in Hometown Love Nest?" Bailey squeaked. "Mom? Did you see this?"

Sandi shoved a curious Liz back down into the sink and squirted shampoo into her palm. "Came yesterday. Page thirty-two."

Bailey thumbed the pages like a woman possessed until she found the article. "Oh my God." The air stuck in her chest as if Sandi had sprayed her down twice. She skimmed the photos and captions. "*Fudge brownies!* How did they even get this?"

Liz fought off Sandi and sat up, sudsy water dripping down her face. "What is it?"

"Pictures. Of me and Ian." There they were at the vet. And again at his house as she turned at the door to remind him to buy trash bags. The way the photo was taken, though, it looked as if he was about to kiss her goodbye. "It says I've been spotted leaving at all hours, that we've adopted a dog together and that Marcia is livid Ian has played her for a fool! This is horrible!"

"The only thing horrible is the picture of you with those ridiculous pigtails. They make you look twelv—"

"*Mom!* So not the point! This… this was private. And how dare they say we're incompetent pet owners? She only got out once!"

"That's not the worst of it," muttered Sandi as she shoved Liz down to rinse. "Wait until you get to the—"

"I am *not* jealous of Helen! What source told them *that!*"

"An honest one."

Bailey looked down the bank of chairs to the last one. The occupant was getting a pedicure. Who the hell got pedicures in the winter? Marcia, that's who.

Bailey shot out of her chair and shook the magazine in Marcia's face. "Did you do this?"

Marcia shrugged. "It says an anonymous source."

"Ivy. I'll bet you made her do it. She's your minion. But, why?"

Marcia smiled smugly at her reflection in the mirror. "Ian needs to see how ridiculous this... relationship... with you is. Once the public expresses their outrage on social media, which they no doubt will, I have every confidence he'll see the path that's right for him."

Blind fury surged through her. "You had no right! You had no right to print private photos of us—of *me!*"

Marcia turned, her face perfectly composed. "I had every right. Feel free to look at your contract. Relax. You'll be compensated for your troubles."

"What do you mean by that?"

"I mean, you'll be paid. Also part of the contract."

"She doesn't need your dirty money!" Sandi called across the salon.

Bailey held up a hand. "How much?"

Marcia chuckled. "I like you. You're smarter than you look. Let's just say, a little bird told me you fell short on a loan recently. I think I can make up the difference."

"You're too late."

"There are always options. When one door closes and all that."

Dirty, traitorous hope surged to life inside her. Maybe Valerie could find another property, something she could afford on her own with just a bit more savings. "How much?"

"Enough. Trust me. But let's not talk business now. You have a wedding to prepare for." Marcia thanked the pedicurist and walked toward the front desk to peruse the display of hair products while her toes dried. Bailey followed.

Bailey eyed Marcia warily. "What's the catch?"

"There is no catch. In fact, I'm grateful to you. I think you'll make the show more interesting this season. We'll introduce you as the hometown girl from Ian's past, *yadda, yadda.* Viewers will adore the air of uncertainty, because, let's face it, the final choice is often *so* obvious." She leaned over conspiratorially. "But we know the truth."

"What truth?"

"Well, that the article and anything between you and Ian is childish fun. He's made his choice clear. Or hasn't he told you?"

"Told me what?"

Marcia's face went all fake concern. "That's he's bringing a date to the wedding."

"Who?"

"Helen, of course."

CHAPTER TWENTY

"YOU HAD NO RIGHT to do this. This is my brother's wedding!" Ian paced across his suite in the other direction.

Marcia had the nerve to roll her eyes. "I'd think you'd thank me. I'm saving you money. By discreetly filming and providing the cake, we can write our expenses here off to the network, and you don't have to pay for a fancy videographer. Your future sister-in-law thought it was a fabulous idea."

"She doesn't know you like I do. I'm fully capable of paying for the wedding."

"Oh, stop. Helen is only here to supervise the final display of the cake and…"

"Helen is here?"

"Of course. She designed the wedding cake, silly. Do you not talk to your brother?"

"I'm sure he has no idea who's making the damned cake and you know it."

"Well, once that's settled, she'll meet you in that little covered courtyard outside the conservatory so we can film you ushering her in. Ideally she'd be in the wedding party, but we can't fix that now…"

"I'm sorry? Now she's a *guest?*"

"She's more than a guest, Ian. She's your date."

"No."

"There isn't any reason to object."

"There is. It gives her the wrong impression. It implies to her and everyone else here that I see a future with her. Which I don't. This is a private event."

"May I remind you that your contract stipulates you are required to make public appearances at the show's discretion when and where we deem necessary up and through the final airing of the show? If you don't, you'll be in breach of contract. You'll not only forfeit the stipend you would have received but can also be sued for all expenses of production and any additional losses the show may feel were suffered as a result." She turned and smoothed her red knit dress. "In other words, even you, Mr. Hot Shot, would lose your shirt."

His stomach roiled, and it had nothing to do with the funky ham sandwich he'd wolfed down after arranging for Bailey's car to be towed. She wouldn't thank him for this, but he had it towed to her competition. Willard had promised an estimate by Monday.

Monday.

The day his season on *Happily Ever After* started airing.

Ian blew out a breath and wiped a weary hand down his face. What a stinking mess. "I fail to see how threatening me with a frivolous lawsuit fixes anything. I'm sorry things didn't work out like you hoped. I can't force myself to fall in love with someone. You can't either. Not your challenges nor—"

"This is what you don't seem to grasp. I don't *force* people to fall in love. I give them opportunities to challenge their feelings for one another in healthy ways so they move beyond the basic physical attraction. This is where the normal process of falling into deeper emotional commitment is accelerated. It's basic psychology."

"It's not working."

"The next step is to commit to the relationship. I need you exclusively invested in the process. You know what I always say: commit and love will follow. But no hanky-panky. That always muddies the waters." She walked to the door and turned. "But in your case. I may make an exception. If you feel it's time to play hide the salami with Helen, don't let my rules stop you." She had the audacity to *wink*.

"I'm not interested in sex with Helen."

"Oh, don't be ridiculous. Every heterosexual man on the planet is interested in having sex with Helen. Hell, *I'm* even a little turned on by her. Oh, don't give me that look. It was a joke. Sort of. Her calves are to die for."

"You may take your video, but I will tell you now that if your presence here in any way detracts from my family's enjoyment of my brother's wedding, I will write your home address into the Treasure Trakker game as a ten million point bonus location so every nerd in a two hundred mile radius lands on your doorstep to score extra lives."

"Very funny."

"Don't think I won't do it."

Marcia shook her head. "Oh, Ian. When will you realize you and I have the same end goal in sight? We both want you to find your happily-ever-after, and I mean that sincerely. You need to trust me on this. I've seen it play out dozens of times even before the show started. You're nervous, because you're afraid to love. I get it. You lost your parents at a tender age and you don't have a role model for what that happily-ever-after looks like. But, I'm here to tell you: Helen is your happily-ever-after. She and you are *perfect* for each other. She's the nurturing beauty queen you want and you're the quietly successful, beta male she wants."

"I'm sorry. Did you just say I was a *beta* male? As in a test version?"

Marcia had the audacity to chuckle. "Oh, honey. That's exactly why you are *perfect* for the former cheerleader who is all finished with dating the captain of the football team." She straightened his tie. "Now go enjoy yourself. It's your little brother's big day."

CHAPTER TWENTY-ONE

BAILEY SAT ON THE window seat and tried to breathe. Her dress had some sort of corset-y torture device built into the top that made her look like she actually had cleavage. But it pressed against the bruise from Skye's car and hurt like hell. Not that she'd say a word to Liz.

Liz, of course, looked like the quintessential blushing bride—if the bride wore a pale lavender wedding gown, purple highlights in her curling up-do and amethyst drop earrings.

Liz's mother and sister primped and fussed over microscopic mis-folds of Liz's veil and pieces of imaginary lint while Trish's youngest, Clara, toddled like a frilly pink marshmallow from one piece of furniture to the next.

A soft knock sounded, and Liz's father called through the door. "You almost ready, Chickie?"

A soft, watery smile fluttered across Liz's face, and her mother and sister bustled themselves out of the room in a flurry of air kisses and 'you're so beautifuls'.

Liz turned to Bailey and blew out a shaky breath. "Well, I guess this is it."

Bailey straightened from her seat. "The moment we've all been waiting for. You're finally marrying *Carter McIntyre.*"

Liz giggled like a sixteen-year-old. "I know!" But then her eyes grew bright. "I love him so much, Bailey. I feel like the luckiest woman in the world."

"Stop. You'll ruin Sandi's makeup job if you cry."

Liz dabbed lightly at the corners of her eyes with a tissue. "She did a beautiful job. I feel like a fairy princess. I was afraid she'd laugh and think my ideas were silly, but I feel beautiful."

"You *are* beautiful. And it's not the purple dress, either. You look so... *happy.*"

Liz clutched at Bailey's hand, the damp tissue trapped between them. "This is what I want for you. This is what *you* deserve, too. It'll come. I promise. You just have to let yourself be vulnerable. I know you put up the tough exterior for everyone else, but look at you! You look beautiful and magical today. Thank you for being willing to go along with me in this. We *both* look magical."

"At least you didn't ask me to wear my hair in Princess Leia buns."

"I'd never do that."

"I know."

Bailey swallowed hard and sniffed. Must be something musty in the room. "Shouldn't we get this show on the road?"

In the hall, Liz met her dad, and Bailey watched as he hugged her close and wordlessly lifted the veil into place.

Her chest felt tight and achy, and she knew it had nothing to do with dropping a car onto it and everything to do with knowing that she'd never have a moment like that for herself. She'd never stand in a stunning gown, about to meet the man of her dreams with a doting father smiling through his own tears as he walked her toward her future husband.

She swallowed again and turned away. Today was Liz's day, and Bailey intended to do everything in her power to ensure it was perfect.

Her hand brushed the silky fabric of her gown, and she let herself slow down for a moment to enjoy how it felt to be in something other than a pair of jeans and a flannel shirt. Different. Nice. The fabric fell in light waves. As she walked, it billowed around her legs, swirling noiselessly. It was the palest ice blue color she'd ever seen, with gathered straps and dyed-to-match Alencon lace and tiny seed pearls decorating the bodice (which she only knew because Liz had gone on and on about those details when she'd dragged Bailey in for her fitting.)

And, if she were perfectly honest, she felt beautiful wearing it. Beautiful… and vulnerable. Just wearing something so incredibly impractical made her feel somehow less capable of doing stuff. Like getting her own glass of champagne. Or changing a tire. She frowned. It was as if the very fact of wearing swooshing fabric made her *need* a man at some weird visceral level.

Bailey left Liz and her father behind and turned the corner to the covered portico outside the conservatory. There stood Ian.

She sucked in a breath at the sight of him and cool air hit her lungs. He turned. She shivered.

He wore a slate gray tux with a deep plum tie and pocket square and he had an ivory boutonniere with pine green ivy accents. And, yes, Liz had detailed what the men would be wearing, too. Now that Bailey saw it all in living color, she couldn't help but admire how incredibly *lickable* he looked. The crisp white shirt complimented his dark hair and green eyes and suddenly she was right back in the cabin with him, naked and nervous, and her gut filled with an unsettling mixture of hope and need because now that they'd done the deed, she knew how good he was.

She knew, suddenly, with a sensation that felt like the drop in a roller coaster, that she'd done more than fall into bed with this man.

Oh, sweet raspberry pie. *So this is what falling in love felt like.*

Her hand moved involuntarily to cover her gut which felt as if the earth had dropped out from under her. He turned and caught her gaze.

He didn't smile.

If she thought her chest hurt before, it was nothing compared to the raw ache of watching his expression go from frowning into the distance to shock. He stepped toward her across the slate pavers of the courtyard and reached a hand out to her hair. She barely felt his fingertips play with the ends before he dropped his hand again.

"Bailey, you look—"

"Ridiculous. I know," she said. She backed behind some topiary thing bedecked in twinkly lights, her heart pounding sluggishly in her chest.

"I was going to say, ethereal," he breathed.

Her tongue darted out to her Petal Dew painted lips. Where did they come up with these color names? "I do?" she said.

He nodded, and then a smile slowly tilted the corners of his mouth as his eyes raked down her body and lingered—yes, they did, ladies and gentlemen!—on her cleavage for a couple moments longer than necessary. "Who knew you were hiding all this underneath those flannel shirts?"

"This isn't nearly as warm."

His eyes crinkled. "Seems to me we stayed plenty warm last night even without flannel."

"*Shh!* How can you bring that up now?" But now that he *had* brought it up, it's all she was thinking about. Oh, who was she kidding? She'd never stopped thinking about it.

"I'm sorry. Am I supposed to wait until the reception to hit on the maid of honor? Will I get in trouble with the etiquette police?"

"Stop kidding. You know what's expected. This is your brother's wedding."

He winked. "Got it. After the 'I-do's' you snag a bottle of champagne, and I'll scope out coat closets."

"We are not—!"

But then he leaned forward and kissed her full on the mouth—the briefest of moments—but it lit a fire that burned all the way to her toes. He pulled back and smiled. Bliss swept through her.

The string quartet began something lovely Bailey couldn't remember the name of, and he bowed with what appeared the faintest hint of regret.

"I believe that's my cue to get in there," he murmured.

"I guess you'd better go then." She dropped her gaze to where her hand rested lightly on his chest. Like it belonged there.

Who would have thunk she'd fall in love with a sexy geek?

She couldn't help but return his smile.

"Ian? *There* you are!"

They turned as one to the soft admonishment. Helen swept forward, a vision of loveliness in a satin gown of deep forest green. Her dark hair swirled gorgeously around her shoulders and down her back, unhindered by pounds of hairspray.

"It took me longer than I expected to change after setting up the cake. So sorry to make you wait."

Bailey watched as Helen held out an expectant elbow to Ian… and he *took it!*

His eyes were all apology as he stepped away from Bailey, Helen dangling like a goddess off his sleeve. "Right. Marcia said you needed me to escort you in."

Helen reached out one of her freakishly long arms to rest perfectly manicured blush-pink fingertips on Bailey's arm. "I'm sorry about the change in plans, Bailey. We discussed it at the rehearsal last night, but it seems no one told you. Liz wants you to go in right after little Clara. I hope you aren't upset."

Bailey forced a smile to her lips and clutched her bouquet tighter. "Sure. Why would that upset me?" She made a dismissive noise with her lips that no doubt sounded like a twelve-year-old boy.

Helen patted Ian's arm and smiled warmly up at him. "We should go."

He nodded and didn't look back as he walked away with Miss Alabama at his side.

Liz and her father entered the portico behind her, and Bailey swallowed the emotion threatening to overwhelm her. "Kick butt in there," she said over the tears blurring her vision.

Liz nodded a watery smile. "Thanks."

The music changed again, and the sound of soft laughter and *oohs* and *ahhs* filtered out of the conservatory as Clara toddled her way down the aisle.

Bailey stepped around the corner and over the threshold into a fairy realm. The conservatory was a long, large room along the back of the inn with arched, multi-paned windows all around. Liz had covered the ceiling in tiny white twinkling lights woven with sheer ivory ribbons, and the columns that ran the length of the room were decorated with more lights, ribbon and pale blue and purple flowers. An ivory carpet, as in *actual* carpet, formed the aisle to where the groom and his best man stood. They stood in front of a large, fieldstone fireplace elaborately decorated with more ribbons and flowers and dozens of ivory candles burning in tall, clear glass jars.

Bailey had never seen anything so gorgeous. Not even the royal wedding for which she'd gotten up at four a.m. to watch live on TV—not that she'd admit that to anyone—could compare.

She held her breath, her ballet flats gliding soundlessly over the carpet (because she'd been petrified of wearing heels) and caught Ian looking at her.

He watched her, his expression unreadable. Then he glanced away as she took her position across from him. She blew out a breath and looked toward the entrance to the conservatory, the music swelling.

It should have looked ridiculous—like Sci-Fi princess hair at the Winter Carnival Snow Belle Pageant. But somehow, Liz's pale lavender gown, the subtle purple highlights in her hair, and her somewhat untamed bouquet of ivory flowers with soft lavender and green accents and trailing ribbons didn't seem silly or childish at all. Liz walked down the aisle, beaming. She hugged her father one last time then turned toward Carter. The look in Carter's eyes was one Bailey would never forget for as long as she lived.

Wonder.

Carter looked at Liz as if he'd never seen anything so extraordinary, as if he, too, counted himself one of the luckiest people alive.

Liz turned and handed Bailey her bouquet, and Bailey fought the tears that sprang to the back of her lids, because after she'd seen that look in Carter's eyes, she'd glanced over at Ian hoping she'd see the same.

But he was looking at Helen—*smiling*—like a man in love.

IAN SWALLOWED THE unsettled feeling that had knotted his gut ever since Helen had swept into the entryway in a radiant display of southern charm. He *should* feel something for her. By all accounts, she was stunning. Warm and open and lovely. He did *enjoy* being around her. She was… pleasant in a reassuring, fresh-baked cookies sort of way, but maybe that's because she was always smiling and smelled like cinnamon and sugar like a hot Mrs. Claus.

He frowned. Did he want a woman who smelled like cookies?

He glanced at Liz as she appeared at the end of the aisle with her father, looking radiant and happy as a bride should.

Carter sucked in an audible breath. Ian knew the feeling, because it's exactly what he'd felt when he'd caught sight of Bailey in the entryway looking like a fairy sprite in her magical realm.

Hell, he didn't even know where phrases like 'fairy sprite' sprang from, but as he'd looked at her, it was as if a moon beam had landed on Earth and sprung to life—that's how dumbstruck he'd been. And he'd said something dumb, like how ethereal she looked, which a woman like Bailey would probably take as an insult, and as he thought this, he realized he was smiling, because that's what he loved about the woman. There wasn't a reasonable, predictable bone in her body.

He glanced at Helen again.

No, he didn't want a woman that smelled like cookies.

He wanted a woman that smelled like snow and fiercely defended cheesecake.

He couldn't help grinning to himself as he thought about what Bailey would think of *that* characterization, and he glanced back toward her, but she was looking at the floor, her throat working as if she were fighting tears.

Who would have thought Bailey was the sentimental sort?

The ceremony flew by. More tears. Laughter. Joy. The officiant pronounced the happy couple husband and wife, and his little brother swept his bride into a deep, lusty kiss that had everyone cheering.

The newlyweds beamed as they walked back down the aisle to the front lobby where they would form a receiving line and have hors d'oeuvres and champagne.

Ian extended his elbow to Bailey. She grabbed it but refused to make eye contact. He leaned toward her. "Crying? You're not getting all soft-hearted on me, are you?"

She did look at him then, her eyes glistening despite the rigid line of her chin. "Not at all."

His own smile faltered as he watched her battle tears. He nudged that stubborn chin with his knuckles. "Buck up. It's a happy occasion."

"Don't touch me," she said.

He nodded to a second cousin as they walked by and leaned toward her ear. "Did I do something wrong?"

"Just... don't talk to me. I'll make a scene if you talk to me."

He chuckled and she shot him a dirty look. "It's okay to be vulnerable, you know. People expect women to get weepy at weddings."

"I'm not crying. I'm *angry.*"

"Angry? At me?"

She gave him that look again then tugged her elbow from his hand. "No. At myself."

"I don't understand."

"Never mind. It's Carter and Liz's happy day. Just… let it go. Please."

She was right, it was Carter and Liz's happy day. But he had no intention of letting it go.

After shaking a million hands and nodding at distant relations he hadn't seen since his parents' funeral, the photographer swept the wedding party away for pictures while everyone else enjoyed hors d'oeuvres and cocktails. Ian did his best to smile for the camera while wondering what could have possibly happened between the time he and Bailey had kissed outside the conservatory and the end of the ceremony.

It didn't help that Helen was waiting for him when he rejoined the rest of the wedding guests for the reception. She didn't know anyone, so it seemed rude to let her fend for herself.

The DJ announced Mr. and Mrs. McIntyre, and Carter and Liz took to the dance floor as Journey played *Open Arms.* It was a dated, hokey song, but apparently it had some special meaning to his new sister-in-law.

Ian watched his brother hold his new wife as she beamed back up at him, and something shifted in his chest like a key turning a lock. He glanced at Helen, but his gaze naturally moved toward Bailey. She hid in the corner by a topiary. Her arms lay crossed over her chest, she held her chin high and something about her expression made fierce protectiveness surge up inside him. She looked defiant and… alone.

He mumbled an excuse to Helen and then worked his way through the crowd toward Bailey. She tried to escape through a rear exit, but he anticipated this and cut her off at the pass.

"Nice try, but you'll be up to your pretty little ankles in snow if you go that way."

She stomped her slippered foot and faced him, arms still crossed. "What do you want?"

"I want to know what's got you so upset. Is this about last night?"

"No. It's… nothing. Stop chasing me."

He crossed his own arms. "I'm not chasing you. I'm trying to—"

"*Psst!* Bailey! I need you in the kitchen. *Now.* Oh, hi Ian."

Sandi stood just around the corner dressed in an apron with giant dark splotches smeared down the front.

"Ohmigod! Mom! What happened to you? What's that *smell?*"

"Your father had an accident with the balsamic vinaigrette. There's no time to explain, I need you to come help me finish plating the salads. Daniel is in no state to do anything." Ian followed as Sandi all but dragged Bailey toward the kitchen.

"What's wrong with him now?"

Ian shot Bailey a quelling look at her long-suffering tone.

"Don't look at me like that," she said. "It's a valid question."

They swung the kitchen door open to chaos. Bailey's father sat on the floor in a pool of more foul smelling salad dressing, moaning as the inn's kitchen staff scurried around. "Oh, dear sweet Bailey! Don't you look the sight!"

"So do you Daniel."

"Was it a lovely wedding? I do so love a good wedding. And funerals. Funerals are always such an occasion. Oh, don't mind me, my sweet. Just step around this old bag o' bones. There's a girl."

"Mr. Adams, let me help you to a chair," Ian offered as Bailey continued to look at her father as if he were a large bug she'd just found stuck to her shoe.

"Oh, thank you, my boy. Thank you. You're a good lad."

Bailey's hands went to her hips. "Oh, quit the blarney, Daniel. You're not actually Irish."

Daniel puffed his chest. "I most certainly am and don't you ever forget we share the same proud blood!"

Daniel shook his fist enthusiastically, nearly causing Ian to lose his footing in the puddle of vinegar dressing beneath them. Sandi found a kitchen stool for Daniel to prop himself against. He moaned again and clutched his side.

"Oh, 'tis a poor time o' year to die," he muttered.

"Oh, stop whining. Nobody's dying," Bailey sniffed. "You!" She motioned to one of the inn's staff. "Is there a mop around here so we can clean this up?" The teenager produced a mop, and Bailey lifted it toward a nearby sink.

"Oh, sweet mercy!" said a voice from the doorway. "Honey, don't put a floor mop in the prep sink or the health department will shut this place down!" Helen swept in on a wave of southern charm and pulled an apron from a hook by the door. She had it knotted behind her before she was three steps into the room.

"Young man—yes you, sweetie—could you take this mop from this woman who's clearly not dressed for cleaning floors and make this slip hazard a thing of my memory? Thank you, hon. You're a darling. What are we working on? Salad course? Who is working on mixing a new batch of vinaigrette?"

Daniel sat up a little straighter in his chair. "You are a vision my dear. What is your name?"

"Miss Helen, sir." She bustled over with a kitchen towel and wiped off Daniel's cheek. "You poor thing. You let these good people take care of you and don't you worry. I'll handle the rest." She sniffed the air around him delicately. "*Mmm.* Balsamic vinegar, a bit of Dijon and," she tilted her head a smidge, "maple syrup?"

"Oh, you're a right quick lass," marveled Daniel. "Ayuh. And just a hint of tarragon."

"And this is going on?"

"The mixed green salads."

"Pear or granny smith apples?"

"Granny smith."

"Excellent."

She turned away and clapped her hands briskly. "Someone find me a hair net, please? We have work to do!"

Sandi swiped at the dressing on Daniel's arm as he grimaced and clutched his side again.

"Oh, it's bad this time," he breathed, sweat beading up on his forehead. "It's real bad this time."

"Hush," Sandi cooed. "We'll take care of you."

"Should I call an ambulance?" Ian asked.

Bailey waved away his concern. "No. It's probably just another kidney stone. Mom can drive him."

"*Just* a kidney stone?" Daniel wheezed. "It feels like a…" he gasped and looked about ready to pass out, "grapefruit trying to…" he gasped again and moaned loudly, "… get out. Besides… I have to supervise… dinner."

Sandi looked at Bailey disapprovingly. "I'll take care of him. Let's at least find a place for him to lie down. Where's your room?"

"My room? Why—?" She glanced up at Ian and cut herself short. "Down the hall on the right. The Flower Fairy room. It's unlocked."

"If I don't see you again," Daniel gasped as he leaned heavily against Sandi's shoulder. "Know that I loved you… and you'll always be… my lucky charm."

Bailey didn't reply as Sandi helped him out the door. She turned and watched Helen command the kitchen staff, sending them on their way with trays filled with neatly dressed salads. She stepped out of the kitchen and walked in the opposite direction.

"Where are you going?" asked Ian. "The reception is this way."

"I need some air."

He blew out a breath and caught up with her. "Bailey, I wish you'd tell me what's going on."

"I'm an idiot. That's what's going on."

"I'm not following you."

She pressed her lips together and shook her head. "Look, if you want Helen—and who wouldn't?—you can have her."

He shook his head. "I don't want Helen."

"Right."

"No, seriously. Bailey, I..." He dropped his voice to a whisper and tugged her into an alcove by a bay window. "I didn't choose her. I swear."

"Then why is she *here?* Why is she, right now, saving the day?"

"Because Marcia is convinced I'm making a mistake."

"Are you?"

"Not when I do this," he said.

And then he kissed her.

CHAPTER TWENTY-TWO

SHE FELT RAW. Raw and *hungry*. And when he pressed his palm to her cheek and pulled her toward him she went to him like a moth to a bug light. Except she was smart enough to know she'd only end up singed in the end. Not that that stopped her.

Bailey allowed herself to flirt with danger for a few delicious moments as his lips played softly over hers, and then she pushed at his chest with her palms.

"*This* is the mistake," she whispered. "What happened last night wasn't two people starting a relationship, it was two people falling into bed because we were hungry and tired and cold."

"And annoyed and a little turned on."

"Don't make light of it, I'm being serious. Last night has all the hallmarks of a one-night-stand, and, frankly, it's a successful pattern for me. So let's not rock the boat and pretend it's anything more, okay?"

She mustn't ever pretend it could be anything more.

His thumb brushed across her cheek distractingly. "Why don't you like your father?"

"Excuse me?"

"You heard me."

"We're not talking about him. We're talking about us."

"Something tells me it's all tied up together. The poor guy is doubled over in pain like he's been kicked in the nuts, and you looked about ready to spit on him for good measure."

"It wasn't that bad."

He raised one eyebrow. "You were dismissive and rude."

Bailey rolled her eyes. "Look. I know he's in pain. Or thinks he is, but the guy has been down this road so many times they've built rest areas for him. Every time I turn around he thinks he's dying from something. Usually it's just reflux. Or a kidney stone. There was the one time they thought it might be appendicitis… but he'd pulled a muscle or something.

The man has self-diagnosed Lyme disease, Chronic Fatigue Syndrome and Pseudo Gout... not even real gout! So don't tell me I'm unsympathetic. If someone is in real pain, I'll be there for them, but don't send me some sperm donor who was never there for me and tell me I'm not considerate of his feelings!"

Ian tilted his head sympathetically. "Where was he?"

"Who?"

"Your dad. You said he was never there for you. Where was he?"

"With his other family. The man has more kids that he can keep track of."

"That must have been hard growing up without a dad around."

She shrugged. "No different than you."

His lips compressed thoughtfully. "No. I think I had it easier. I *knew* my dad loved me. And I know my uncle does, too. But you didn't, did you?"

"Don't get all psycho-analytical on me."

"You don't know what healthy love looks like, so you push men away or only get into relationships with losers you know you'll never fall for. That way you don't run the risk of falling in love and getting hurt because that's all you've ever known."

She didn't reply. The truth was not pretty served up like she was some pathetic loser on a talk show.

"I'm right aren't I?"

A single traitorous tear slipped out and slid toward his hand.

"It kills me that you don't trust me," he whispered.

"It's not that."

"Then why are you pushing me away? I feel like you're breaking up with me."

She hiccupped in shock. "Were we ever together?"

His hand dropped abruptly. "I guess not. My mistake."

"Ian, wait."

"Why? I've clearly misread things. I guess I thought all the time we've been spending together, the talks... last night. Hell, call me a girl for saying it, but I got the impression I meant something to you."

"You did! You *do!* Aargh! I know I'm messing this up. *Please don't go.* I've never done this before!"

"Done what?"

She shuddered. "Told someone I'm falling in love with them."

He went still. "Say what?"

"*Shit*," she whispered.

His lips formed a soft smile. "I'm pretty sure that wasn't it. I'm pretty sure you just said you were falling for me."

She forced herself to meet his eyes. "What if I did?"

His gaze went all warm and gentle on her. "It'd make me one very relieved guy, because I truly did think you were breaking up with me."

"Why would I do that?"

He chuckled and pressed a single kiss to her forehead which was just so damned *sweet,* a burst of something light and pure and, oh, so giddy lit up inside of her. "You are something else, Bailey Adams. Something I'm glad I've found."

She swallowed over the lump in her throat. "Really?"

He nodded and then bent to rest his forehead against hers. "Really."

And then his lips curved, and she angled closer and showed him what she still couldn't bring herself to repeat.

Finally, she pulled back. "I'm so happy," she breathed.

His fingers caressed her cheek. "I'm so glad we're not breaking up."

"No. Definitely not."

"Good." He kissed her once more. "Let's get back to the reception."

He made as if to tug her out of the alcove, but she resisted. "Wait. We can't. Not together. Marcia will shish kabob us if she finds out we're together."

Ian sighed and hugged Bailey tight. "You're right. Which means we'll just have to keep a lid on us until my commitment to the show is over. But then…"

She held her breath. *Then?* "What?"

"We can breathe easy."

"Right. That's what I thought you meant."

CHAPTER TWENTY-THREE

IAN HADN'T SEEN Bailey for a little while. Apparently her father had gone to the hospital after all, Jack had come from Lucky's to finish serving dinner, and Bailey had spent the better part of the reception pretending she wasn't making big fat adorable googly eyes at him every time she thought no one was looking.

Last he'd seen her she'd been playing a game of musical chairs with the youngest guests in one of the sitting rooms while the adults waltzed to Michael Buble and drank champagne under the twinkly lights.

The crowd had thinned once Liz and Carter said their goodbyes and disappeared for the night. They'd be leaving in the morning for their honeymoon.

A sense of peace washed over him as he asked the bartender for a cola. He had to hand it to Marcia. It hadn't turned into a fiasco after all. Nick had encouraged the guests to record little tributes to the happy couple throughout the evening as a video photo album, and Helen had been gracious enough to help out in the kitchen until Jack arrived.

He accepted the cool glass and leaned against the bar. At the far corner of the room, he saw a dark figure staring out the window. He frowned and walked over.

"Quite an evening, eh?" he said, taking a seat at her table.

She started and turned and that's when he noticed the worried tissue in her palm. "Hey. What's the matter?" he asked.

Helen shook her head, her wide eyes bright with unshed tears. "Nothing. I'm just being silly."

"Aw, come here." He wrapped her in a hug and patted her shoulder. "No one wants to see a beautiful woman cry."

She sniffed and hiccoughed a laugh. "Then I'm safe."

"Hey. Come on. What's going on? Is it the wedding?"

She shook her head. "No. It was beautiful. Your brother and his wife seem very happy. It was lovely. Everyone was very gracious."

"Then what?"

"You'll think I'm being ridiculous." She breathed out a slow, shuddering breath. "It's just… when I went in to help with dinner…"

He laid his hand on hers. "I'm so sorry about that. You shouldn't have felt the need to fill in when you were a guest, but I'm grateful you did."

She put her other hand on his. "That's just it. I *wanted* to do it. I love running a kitchen. Ian, it's what I *do*."

"I know. You're the queen of cupcakes. Obviously you make more than cupcakes…"

"No, you're right. I make cupcakes. Frilly little girlie desserts that people *ooh* and *ahh* over in the bakery windows. I enjoy that, don't get me wrong, but…"

"But?"

"I want to *feed* people, Ian. Cupcakes are… dessert. And when I was young and enjoying the novelty of it, the timing was right and then my dad set up my first shop… Well. You know the rest. So here I am." She gestured toward herself. "The Alabama Cupcake Queen."

"I'm not following you."

She blew her nose and sniffed, and Ian handed her another tissue. Thank goodness Liz had insisted they place them strategically around the venue. "I'm saying I enjoyed being in the kitchen helping with dinner. It reminded me that there's more to me than just… being dessert."

He frowned. "You didn't have to come out if you didn't want to."

She shook her head. "Jack came." Her lips pressed together and she raised her chin. "He made it very clear my help wasn't needed anymore."

Her chin began to wobble again, and Ian pulled her into another hug. Oh, for Pete's sake. Did weddings make all women weepy? "He didn't mean anything by it. He probably thought you wanted to rejoin the reception."

"I know."

"Then why all the tears?"

She looked up at him through her lashes. "Because here I am again and… what am I even *doing* here? I like Sugar Falls. I do. And I think I could be happy here, but nobody wants me here. Jack doesn't want me in his kitchen. *You* don't want me…"

"Hey, not true. Of course you're wanted. I've missed you. And your cupcakes. Sorry to admit that. I have."

"It's okay. I make killer cupcakes."

"You do."

She laughed a bit which eased the ache in Ian's heart. He liked Helen. More than liked. She had an easy, nurturing manner that made a person feel at peace, and it wasn't until she'd arrived in Sugar Falls that he'd been sure he'd made the right choice.

"I'll admit I was mad at Marcia for dragging you here, because I didn't want to lead you on when I was still struggling to figure things out, but it's helped me clarify some things. I'm glad she did."

"Me, too."

"I'm sorry about how I left things between us, but I didn't want to make a mistake we'd both regret. That wouldn't have been fair to either one of us. You understand."

"I do." She smiled a quiet, knowing smile and rested a cool hand on his cheek. "You're a good man, Ian McIntyre. I'm glad I met you."

"Same here."

She stood and squared her shoulders. "I suppose I should head to bed now."

"Yeah." Ian stood, too, hesitating for a moment, realizing that this was a turning point for them. He reached up and brushed a lingering tear from beneath her eye.

"Thanks for listening," she said.

He pulled her close and gave her another hug, grateful he'd been given the gift of meeting such a remarkable woman, so much like his mother. He turned and pressed a kiss to her cheek before pulling away. "Thanks for being so understanding. You're one in a million, Helen."

"I'd settle for being someone's number one."

CHAPTER TWENTY-FOUR

———————————

BAILEY HUGGED THE SIDE of the road as another car whizzed by. The wind kicked up, sending fine, biting pellets of snow at her face. Zack lumbered ahead of her like the oblivious, lovable Bernese he was. She tugged her hood tighter around her face and tried to look at the bright side. A.) If the weather turned and she had to shelter out here, she could totally use Zack as a furry yurt, and B.) she still had an income, such as it was. She'd been filling in more at Lucky's, which she hated with a purple passion, but at least the pay was decent.

Cleaning jobs were hit or miss.

Then there was Ian.

She let out a different sort of sigh, one that drifted frighteningly close to besotted teenager in lovesick mode. Maybe her career prospects stank like a rusted out catalytic converter, but at least she had Ian.

For now.

She kicked a clump of ice and watched it skitter across the pavement.

Two weeks. It had been two whole weeks since she'd ripped her heart out of her own chest and handed it, still beating, to a man she couldn't even call her boyfriend. Not publicly, at any rate. Since the wedding, Marcia had kept Ian under strict lock-down. He'd managed to send only a handful of e-mails under the guise of working on a Treasure Trakker update, but even then, he hadn't mentioned her wedding day confession even once.

They'd talked about the update he was working on, how fast Chewy was growing and how incompetent the radiologists at the health center were who wanted Sandi to come in for a repeat mammogram, because the first was 'inconclusive.' They shared geeky Sci-Fi jokes and funny puppy video links, hinted at wanting to sneak away to the cabin together and generally kept things light and easy.

Part of her was grateful—what more was there to say?—but part of her worried that as gracious as he'd been, he was relieved to have an excuse to put some emotional distance between them.

Of course, now that Daniel had passed his kidney stone, he was over the moon at the success of his *Happily Ever After* viewing parties which Bailey found about as enjoyable as a weekly root canal. Who wants to see their off-screen secret boyfriend playing tonsil hockey with other women?

The truth was, it was hard not to feel like she was in a limbo between what might be (she and Ian!) and what definitely wasn't (she and her own garage.) She wanted to be hopeful, she really did. That fragile-as-a-butterfly's-wing sense of wonder blooming inside her wanted to believe that once the hoopla and excitement of the show died down and she and Ian were free to explore what they had together, that it would work out for them. They'd be the match no one ever saw coming.

And yet... there was that darker part of her—the pragmatic, trailer-park, knee-deep-in-reality part of her—that knew, deep down, girls like Bailey and guys like Ian didn't end up together in real life.

The pragmatic part of her couldn't forget how, at the wedding, while she poured her heart out on the floor in front of him like so much vomited emotion, what did he do? Kiss her *on the forehead.* Which had to be code for: you're sweet. Delusional and out of your league. But sweet.

She blew out a cloud of frustration and watched it swirl away in the wind.

Her cell phone rang. She pulled it from her pocket and nearly fumbled it into the snow bank as Zack bumped against her leg. For some reason he found phone calls exciting. "Hello?"

"Bailey, I hope you're sitting, because I've got news... Your garage is back on the market!"

"Who is this?"

A heavy sigh. "Valerie. Who did you think it was?"

"A prank caller. Val, I know you don't like me, but this isn't even remotely funny."

"I'm not kidding. The deal fell through."

Bailey skidded to a stop. Zack turned his head questioningly. "What? Why? Are you serious?"

"The inspection uncovered something about hazardous waste and disposal costs. Anyway, you know what this means, don't you?"

"You let me bid too high the first time?"

"It *means* you get another shot at it. And, yes, they've lowered the asking price."

She couldn't help herself. Excitement shivered through her along with the cold. "How much reduced? By fifty percent?" That would make it a no-brainer. What garage didn't have a bit of hazardous waste?

"Not that much, but I'd say there's definite room for negotiation."

Bailey held the phone to her ear and willed herself to breathe as Valerie told her the new asking price.

"Are you still there? Bailey?"

"I'm here."

"I suggest you jump on this if you can. Let me know."

"Yeah, sure. I'll need to run the numbers again. And Valerie? Thanks."

She hung up and slid her phone back in her pocket. Holy smokes. *It wasn't over.* Her skin prickled with excitement. *She still had a chance!*

"Come on, Zack. We're jogging home today!"

She pulled the dog around and ran him home, wiped him down, fed him his treat and set him in his crate for when the Titweillers came home then roared out of the driveway toward downtown. She'd take one more trip to Sugar Falls Savings Bank. Maybe, just maybe, she could pull this off after all.

An hour later she stood outside the bank and looked across at the empty garage with the 'for sale' sign taped to the overhead door.

Five thousand dollars. She was still five grand too short. And that was without accounting for whatever hazardous waste disposal the inspection had apparently uncovered.

The sense of longing was so deep she could feel it echo inside her. Valerie had hinted the owners were getting antsy to sell and move to warmer climes. Now was her chance. If not her, someone else would swoop in and grab it. It was prime real estate smack near downtown. Within walking distance to Lucky's and the convenience store where the creepy old guy gave her free mocha lattes from the machine every Thursday.

But how would she ever get her hands on five grand?

CHAPTER TWENTY-FIVE

THREE WEEKS LATER, Liz and Carter were still frolicking down south (the lucky bastards), Valerie had finally popped an 11-pound alien out of her belly, and Bailey was enduring the unthinkable yet again: waiting tables at a Lucky's *Happily Ever After* viewing party while friends and neighbors watched Ian's 'journey of love' on the big-screen TV Daniel had bought just for that purpose.

Excited chatter filled the pub along with the clinking of glasses and the scraping of chairs on the floor. The place was stuffed to the gills with people eager to see one of their own on national TV, and every week the crowd grew larger.

Bailey poured herself a tonic and lime from the tap and tried to appear nonchalant as she slid around to stand in the shadows by the outside wall. It felt a bit surreal to see the man she'd admitted she had feelings for (okay, *loved*) cavorting week after week with other women on a giant TV for all to see. Okay, and yes, she was just a teensy bit jealous. (Who was she kidding? She bled green at this point.)

She had to remind herself that these were women he dated in the past, like former girlfriends. Although you generally didn't have to see your boyfriend frolicking around with said former girlfriends at sexy slumber parties. Or group yoga. Or getting down and dirty organizing mud bowl charity events with women who had apparently gifted all their actual clothing to orphans and were forced to run around in scraps of fabric that would make actual bikinis blush. But, whatever.

You'd think she'd be immune to it after weeks of watching and texting Ian during the show. (And, yes, sometimes sexting, but nothing raunchy, because, let's face it, that was kind of icky when she was standing in the bar with her mother's friends whooping as Ian took his shirt off—again—on national TV.)

For the past couple of weeks, they'd managed to sneak out to Ian's cabin for a private rendezvous in the middle of the day. Ian would pretend he was grocery shopping, would walk into the local store with his bags, ditch them in the rear with Wanda's niece, Rebecca, and climb into Bailey's car only to reverse the process a couple of hours later.

You'd think the paparazzi that followed him would wonder why it took the man two hours to buy a package of paper towels and a pound of ground beef, but they didn't seem to catch on.

Bailey sucked on her straw and watched the screen.

Last week Ian had said goodbye to Leah, and Cheryl had voluntarily left after remembering she was actually in love with her ex-fiancé from home. Which left Mary Beth and Helen. Or, as Bailey liked to refer to them: Bimbo #1 and Bimbo #2.

Mary Beth was a physical therapist specializing in pediatric patients suffering from traumatic injuries which made her on par with Mother Theresa in the eyes of the viewers. It didn't hurt that she was from Kentucky, had lost a brother or uncle or fiancé in Iraq to an IED and organized a youth choir of former patients that had sung on the National Mall for Memorial Day.

Plus she was 'saving the ultimate gift' for her future husband. Bailey wanted to gag. If she hadn't already bagged Ian, she might've resented the woman. Now she just felt sorry for her, because Ian was...

Kissing her on national TV?

Bailey choked on her tonic and tried not to hyperventilate as she watched *herself*... and Ian... and *herself*...

Oh God!

... *kissing* in his media room on TV! There was a voiceover, and if the blood roaring in her ears like a tsunami would quiet down already, she might be able to hear.

"...Does this quiet hometown boy harbor a secret that will jeopardize everything? Stay tuned..."

"Whoa! Isn't that Bailey Adams?" someone yelled out. Damn that Hank.

"What's she doing on TV?"

Patrons rubber-necked in their seats to scan the pub as Bailey stared in horror at the sight of her groping Ian's butt. *Ack!* She stumbled backward, knocking into the small suit of armor with the green plaid sash by the cash register.

"There! She's hiding in the corner!" Owen. Damned voice like a megaphone.

"I'm not hiding," she muttered.

Someone laughed and pointed at the screen like they were watching bad porn, and her face flamed. Nothing could be more embarrassing. She prayed for it to end.

And then it did. The groping video of her with Ian was replaced with an image of Sugar Falls as seen from a moving vehicle. Marcia's voiceover filled the pub. "Love is always a journey. For many, it is a journey that takes them far away from what is familiar. My love challenges are designed to break people out of their comfort zone, to help them see one another with clarity and honesty."

The camera followed the familiar path up Blackberry Hill, the leaves still holding a hint of autumn color, the sky a bright, painfully brilliant blue. "For others, however, love is a journey that begins at home. When there is unfinished business, sometimes love can only blossom if we return to that which is holding us back."

The camera cut to Bailey hauling cleaning supplies up the front walk of Ian's home, the vacuum cord dragging on the walkway behind her like the train of Cinderella's bedraggled, post-ball gown. Oh, lovely. That was not a flattering angle. Or outfit. TV Bailey stooped to grab her dragging cord, her ass filling the screen. The crowd inside the pub erupted in laughter. What the hell? Why were they even showing this?

"Ian traveled far to find love," Marcia's voice continued, "but will a past relationship get in the way of moving forward? Tune in next week as we…"

The crowd cheered and jeered loudly as the show ended, dozens of patrons voicing their take on this unexpected twist.

Bailey's stomach roiled. She caught Wanda's questioning look over the bar, shook her head, ditched her glass by the cash register and fled.

ALL WAS DARK AT THE house when Bailey got home. Her mom was having a girls' night out.

Bailey let the door slam behind her and shoved her coat at the hook on the wall. It missed and slid to the floor. She didn't bother to pick it up.

Why? Why would they show that clip of her and Ian kissing? There was nothing between them. At least there had been nothing between them *then*, before the show when they'd pretended to be all over each other to freak Marcia out. How dare Marcia use that footage against them? This was obviously a ratings ploy, but what did it mean for Ian? Was Marcia trying to head-off any tabloid chatter about Ian and Bailey? Or was she just trying to embarrass Bailey so much she hoped Bailey would go away for good? Would Ian want to call a stop to their cabin sneak-aways?

Erg! She stepped into the kitchen and opened the lower cabinet. It was a Kahlua night. Or... fine. It was a peppermint schnapps night. Whatever. Bailey took down a plastic cup and poured a half inch into the bottom.

"Bailey?"

Bailey jumped at the sound of Sandi's voice from the darkened living room. Only then did she notice the TV was on, its light flickering even though no sound came out.

"Why are you sitting in the dark?" Bailey asked. "I thought you were having a girls' night with Connie and Becka."

Her mom pointed the remote at the TV and pressed a button. "I didn't feel like it."

Bailey took down another plastic cup and poured a half inch for her mother. Something told her it wouldn't be refused. She kicked off her shoes on the way to the living room.

"What are you watching? Not *Happily Ever After*, I hope."

"Oh. No. It's nothing." Sandi shifted from her seat on the floor. She accepted the plastic cup and took a long sip.

Bailey perched on the edge of the couch. A pile of tissues lay crumpled on the carpet next to her mother. Schnapps burned a trail of unease down her throat. "Mom? What's going on?"

Sandi didn't answer right away, just twirled the liquid in the bottom of her plastic cup, staring at it. "I had the follow-up 3D mammogram today. They did an ultrasound." She took another swig of schnapps. "They want to do a needle biopsy now."

Bailey set her cup down. "They found something."

Sandi nodded. "It's a... mass... here." She pointed to her left breast. "One point three centimeters."

"One point three centimeters?" Bailey repeated. A centimeter never sounded so large before. "When is the biopsy?"

Sandi blew out a breath. "A week from next Monday. They said the pathology report is usually back in a few days. I should hear back no later than a week."

Bailey nodded as if the action of moving her head up and down would somehow make this all seem more real. *A mass. Biopsy.* The words swirled around in her head like ugly images she couldn't unthink. "So then you'll know. In a couple weeks, you'll know."

"Yeah."

Bailey slid down to the carpet next to her mother and reached an arm around her shoulders. "I'm sorry, Mom. I'm sure it'll be okay." She wasn't sure of anything. Suddenly the whole mess with Ian and the show and the loan didn't matter anymore. This was her *mom*, the only parent she'd ever really known. The only one she'd ever been close to. "It'll be okay," she repeated, but even as she said the words, she could feel herself choking up.

"I hope so." Sandi hugged Bailey back, the scents of Pantene and Jean Nate enveloping Bailey like nothing had changed. Even though everything had.

"I'll take you. We'll be all right," Bailey said.

Sandi shook her head. "I know you don't do well in hospitals, honey. I'll have Wanda take me."

"I want to support you, Mom."

Sandi turned and rested her hand on Bailey's cheek. "You are, sweetie. You are."

Bailey took a slug of schnapps and coughed as it hit the back of her throat. She grabbed the remote. There was no sense wallowing when they didn't have any news. They both needed distraction. "Here. Let's finish watching your movie." She clicked 'play' as Sandi tried to grab the remote from her.

"You don't want to—"

Bailey stared at the screen, struggling to process what she was seeing. "What? Why are you watching this? Where did this even come from?"

Twelve year-old Bailey walked across the screen, her white dress rippling around her skinny legs, pointy chin held high, hair done up in tight twin buns.

"I found it in the back of my closet."

"I asked you to burn it."

Sandi turned to her, aghast. "Why would I do that? I love this video!"

"I look stupid," Bailey harrumphed.

"You looked beautiful."

"I looked like a fool. Didn't you hear that snicker-cough as someone tried to cover their laughter?"

"First of all, Old Man Richards always had that phlegm problem. Second of all, you didn't make a fool of yourself. You were brave."

Bailey snorted. "I ran away. I didn't even stay long enough for the interviews."

"I know," Sandi said wistfully. "I wish you would have. You had a real shot at winning."

"No I didn't." She pressed the 'stop' button and dropped the remote onto the coffee table with a clatter.

"Of course you did! You had a certain quality about you. A self-possession. You weren't afraid to take risks. I was so proud of you."

Bailey shifted in her seat. "Please don't say that. There was nothing to be proud of."

"Are you kidding? You had a vision and you weren't afraid to stand in front of the whole world and show them how unique you were. You were defining femininity in your own way."

"I wasn't defining femininity. I was making fun of it."

Sandi shook her head. "I don't understand."

Bailey set her empty plastic cup down in front of her. "Let's not talk about this now."

Sandi frowned. "No. I want to know what you mean."

Bailey fidgeted under her mom's gaze. "I was making fun of it, okay? All of it. I thought the pageant was dumb."

Sandi's face fell. "You...? I sewed that dress myself."

"I know."

"I spent days on it."

Bailey hung her head. "I know."

The silence was like a weight on her heart.

"Why didn't you say something?" Sandi whispered. "Why did you go through with it?"

"Because I didn't want to disappoint you."

Sandi refused to meet her eyes as she began picking up the used tissues off the carpet. She stood. "Well, you have."

"Mom, wait..."

"Bailey, not tonight. For once... for now... this isn't about you."

CHAPTER TWENTY-SIX

BAILEY HUNG HER VEST on the hook in the employee break room—which was little more than an oversized closet that smelled like Jack's gym bag—and changed out of her boots. Bone-deep fatigue pulled at her shoulders, or maybe that was just the residual effect of Zack's pulling on his leash.

She pulled an apron from a hook and tied it on. Lord, waitressing sucked. It didn't help that she had been battling a flu-like bug for the last week and any comfort she might've taken with Ian over the situation with her mom had been cancelled in the name of public health and safety.

Plus, she hadn't seen Chewy in days.

She sniffled, squirted hand sanitizer into her palm and headed off to do battle, er, serve people.

Jack hollered at her as she walked through the kitchen. "Hey, sicky, don't be giving my customers the flu. You sure you're better?"

"I'm sure. Thanks for the sympathy."

"Anytime, sis."

Bailey's heart did a little wobble every time he used the familial term. They were half-siblings and lived in different towns until they were adults, so the only time she'd ever seen him was when his mom brought him to the pub or one of Daniel's many "death watches."

There was something truly sick about a group of people that continued to enable a hypochondriac with their over-the-top sympathy and noodle casseroles. But Jack was okay. And he'd forgiven her for The Incident all those years ago when he'd been left bleeding all over his mom's kitchen floor like a stuck pig, a sewing needle sticking out the side of his nose, and Bailey prostrate on the floor having failed at her one and only attempt at a home nose piercing.

Bailey paused. Wanda looked like she could handle the crowd out front a few more minutes. "Hey, Jack?"

"Ayuh." He didn't look up, expertly and efficiently chopping the shaved steak on the grill, steam rising as he tossed in some sliced onions.

"Never mind. I should get to work."

"Spill it. What's up, Tryp?"

Bailey blew out a sigh. She love-hated that he called her that. It was short for 'trypanophobia' or 'fear of needles' which was highly embarrassing, but, she supposed she owed him that for not having better aim. Now they had a common fear of needles and blood, and that was a stronger bond than DNA.

"Mom… Sandi… is going for a biopsy Monday morning. I thought you'd want to know."

He frowned and pulled the fries out of the deep fryer to drain. "What kind of biopsy?"

"You know." Bailey pointed to her chest.

"Shit." He plated the fries and shaved steak and slathered on some pub cheese sauce. It was a heart attack on a plate, but one of Bailey's favorites. "Does Wanda know? She'll want to know."

"She's driving Sandi to the appointment."

He half-smiled and passed the plate through the warming shelves to her. "That's probably wise. Now eat. You're going to have a long shift tonight. You know how busy Trivia Night gets."

"These are for me?"

He nodded. "I heard that rattle-trap of yours pull in. You should fix that exhaust leak."

"Tell me about it. I hit a pothole the other day, and it made it ten times worse."

She picked one of the super-hot gooey fries from the plate and bit into it despite the fact that it sizzled on her tongue. Comfort food. It was so damn nice of Jack it made her chest feel tight. She didn't deserve it.

"Hey, Tryp?"

"Yeah?"

"Thanks for helping out around here. Daniel really isn't doing well."

She didn't even roll her eyes. Much. "I know. Besides, I owe you."

He grinned and took an order from Wanda. "Don't you ever."

Bailey finished her plate o' cholesterol, chased it down with a tonic and lime and washed up again before heading out to wait tables.

Since the first disastrous night, Sandi had taken back the reigns for Trivia Night which was fine with Bailey. It was probably good for her mom to stay busy anyway. It would keep her mind off worrying about other things.

Certainly 'other things' worried Bailey enough for both of them.

The front door jangled again as Bailey finished taking Table 3's drink order, and she got a brief glimpse of tousled dark hair and a flash of green eyes that had her smiling to herself in instant recognition. She didn't even need to *see* him to know he was in the room. She could feel it.

She passed the drink order across the bar to be filled and went to the register to cash out a customer. "Hi, Ian."

"Hey, Bailey." He ducked his head to avoid being clocked by the customer's scarf as she whipped it onto her neck. He grinned conspiratorially at Bailey. "Feeling better?" he asked.

She nodded and took the woman's credit card for swiping. The woman turned to see who Bailey was talking to and her eyes grew wide with recognition. "You're that bachelor on that show!"

Bailey rolled her eyes behind the woman's back.

"Yep. That's me."

The woman leaned close to Ian, resting her red-lacquered nails on his chest. "I really like that sweet baker. I hope you pick her. She has such class." The woman turned and gave Bailey the hairy eyeball while she signed her receipt. Old hag.

After the woman left, Ian shook out of his coat and eyed the pub for an empty seat. It wasn't *Happily Ever After Viewing Party Night* busy, thank the Lord, but it was Trivia Night busy, and the place was filling up quickly. "I'll go see if I can snag a spot by Hank and Owen."

Bailey watched him make his way through the pub, patrons stopping him to clap him on the back or shake his hand. He was a regular celebrity in their midst.

And she was as besotted as the rest of them.

She delivered the drink order, got extra napkins for the couple with the toddler, grabbed the appetizer for Table 5 and groaned when the door jangled yet again. The area by the register was crowded with patrons—most trying to get in. The crush made her claustrophobic and cranky. And then Marcia arrived.

Bailey swiped at the sticky juice the toddler had shaken onto her apron and went to welcome the newest arrivals. "We're full up. There's room at the bar or you can wait for a table, but it probably won't clear now until after Trivia is over."

Marcia stepped away from the couple and the toddler as they moved en masse out the door. Bailey waved goodbye and prayed for a good tip.

"Seat me in your section," Marcia said. "But while I'm waiting, bring me a diet cola, no ice, twist of lemon. And a straw."

"I'm sorry we can't serve patrons who aren't seated." Because she'd just made that rule.

Marcia sighed. "Fine. We'll wait until you clean the kid goo off that table and take that one."

Bailey was about to protest that there was a party in front of them, but then realized they were waiting for a booth and wouldn't fit at the table. "I'll be just a minute."

Marcia didn't reply, having already turned away to murmur something in Nick's ear. Those two were an odd couple if ever there was one.

Bailey swept the carnage left from the toddler off the table, pocketed the tip—thank you very much—and swept the largest chunks of food from the floor with a napkin before bussing the dirty dishes. Blech.

She took a dessert order, cleared the appetizer plates from Table 2, assured Table 3 their entrees would be up soon, and picked up Marcia's uppity, special, no-ice cola from the bar. A hand snaked out and grabbed her wrist.

Bailey shuffled her sneakers back toward the attached arm, happy tingles shooting over her skin. "Marcia's here," she warned out of the side of her mouth.

"That's why I'm playing it cool." Ian spoke into his beer as he watched whatever sports event was on the big screen in the corner. "I've missed you," he said.

Bailey sighed and sank against his hand as it rubbed small circles on her lower back. "Me, too. *Erg.* I've gotta go. Marcia's waiting."

"Spit in her soda for me," he said with a smile as he took a sip from his bottle.

"You know I only do that to yours."

His eyes crinkled. "Made you smile."

She pulled away with regret, delivered Marcia's soda and took their order. Marcia took a sip and her eyes unerringly traced the path from where Bailey had just come to rest on Ian's back. She looked at Bailey.

"You aren't nearly as clever as you seem to think. Don't think I don't know what's been going on. No man needs that many paper towels."

Bailey swallowed and waved dismissively at Jack as he motioned toward the order for Table 3 waiting on the warming shelves. "I don't know what you mean," she lied. "Excuse me, I need to get another table's order."

Bailey turned and retraced her path to the door to the kitchen. Marcia followed. "A word with you?" she said. "In private?"

"I'm working, Marcia. It'll have to wait."

"Not when you're jeopardizing Ian's contract."

Bailey bit her lip, caught Wanda's eye, and motioned to the waiting order. "Table 3?" she said. Wanda grabbed the food for her.

"Okay, Marcia. Three minutes. That's all I can spare. It's Trivia Night, and it's a zoo if you haven't noticed."

She led the way to the employee break room. Marcia shut the door.

"Back off."

"Excuse me?" said Bailey.

"Honey, you need to keep your eye on the prize. That man is distracting you from what really matters."

"What prize?"

"A little bird told me you might be looking for some extra funds."

Damn it. Where were all these talkative birds in the dead of winter? She wanted to know. "Maybe. What's it to you?"

"Don't be difficult. I'd like to help. I'm in the business of making dreams come true, or haven't you heard?"

"Sure you are. You're like Cruella de Vil working for the Humane Society."

"Funny."

"And you can take your offers, whatever they might be, and stuff them. You've tried to make a fool of me. Why did you even have to put me on that show? Now I'm a laughingstock in my own hometown."

Marcia shrugged. "Viewers are curious about you."

"Because you put me on national TV!" Bailey hissed.

"Bafflingly enough, you're quite popular on social media. I think people are intrigued by the whole hometown girl thing. But I don't see it working out.

"Oh, sure, you have your little secret meetings," Marcia continued. "I'm sure it's all impossibly exciting the 'us against the world' thing you've got going on. But you're not what Ian is looking for. He wants a beauty queen, mother figure. Hell, all men like a woman who cooks. What man wants a mechanic? No one, that's who. It's emasculating."

"Screw you. I don't have to listen to this."

Marcia stopped her with a hand on the arm. "But, it doesn't matter what I think. Or Ian. Or even you. The fact is, we're not enemies here. We're both a little desperate. And you have the power to do something for me, and I have the power to do something for you."

"I'm not desperate."

"Listen. Here's the deal. Last season I got stuck opposite that damned singing show, *Encore!*, and its killing my ratings. I need something big this season to draw in viewers—apparently a happily-ever-after isn't enough for them anymore—and *you* are that draw."

Bailey opened her mouth to object, but Marcia forged on. "All I'm asking for is your cooperation. I want you at the Fur-ever Yours Vaccination Day we're holding to kick-off the Winter Carnival. Let the fans believe you're holding a torch for Ian. Let them fall in love with you a little. And then, later, let them see you get heartbroken. Cry into the camera—viewers love nothing more than ugly crying. And I'll see to it that that garage you want so badly is yours."

"What if I don't end up heartbroken?"

Marcia tilted her head in sympathy. "Oh, honey, that's the spirit."

"You are such a fraud."

"Wrong. I'm one of the most honest people you've ever met. Sometimes the truth sucks. But you and I, we're pragmatic. We know the deal going in so we aren't going to get hurt. Right? We won't *let* ourselves get hurt."

Bailey didn't respond. It hit too close to home. "I have to get back to work," she said.

"Fine. Just… think about it."

"No. You're asking me to gut myself like a deer for your ratings. I won't do it. I'll get that garage, but not because I've sold my soul to the devil."

"I'm not the devil, Bailey."

"Sure you're not."

Bailey's hands shook as she picked up the drink order for Table 4 and rushed to catch up with all her customers. Damn that Marcia! Who the hell did she think she was, playing puppet-master over the world? As if Bailey would ever 'make a deal' about her real life.

She and Ian had as much of a shot of working as anyone.

She glanced over at Ian. A group of college girls were crowded around him taking selfies. Bailey's stomach roiled.

She wasn't jealous. This wasn't jealousy at all.

It was fear.

CHAPTER TWENTY-SEVEN

BAILEY TURNED HER CAR into the seldom-used logging road and cut the engine. Her palms felt sweaty on the steering wheel even though it was below freezing. She took a breath, got out, and grabbed her duffle bag from the back seat. Marcia's offer nagged at her conscience.

It wasn't as if she'd agreed. She'd refused Marcia's calls, deleted her texts and otherwise made it plain she couldn't be bought.

But none of that stopped the nagging doubt that maybe, just maybe, she was making a mistake. What if Ian *did* dump her at the end of the show? Then she'd be left with nothing. Nothing but a broken heart.

She swallowed hard.

Sneaking around in the cold and the dark made it feel that what they were doing was somehow wrong. All she wanted was some time alone with Ian and a little reassurance what they had was real.

Because, watching that godawful show week after week ate at her like she'd swallowed a tape worm.

This week had been the worst. They'd shown Ian on his challenge dates with the two bimbos, and seeing him laugh and smile and hold hands with those all-American cover models made her sick. Helen looked like Jennifer Garner with those girl-next-door dimples and that mile-wide smile.

She hated Helen's smile.

She hated not knowing if Marcia was right.

And she hated that she was creeping through the woods in the half light for what amounted to little more than a hook-up.

She pulled up her collar against the cold and started the short hike up through the woods to the cabin. The light was fading, but she liked it that way. It was less likely anyone would see her. Now that the show had started airing, the paparazzi and fans around Ian had been as thick as black flies in May. She and Ian had been forced to become more secretive.

She pushed aside the low-hanging branches of a white pine and crunched over the hard, crusted layer of snow on the ground, trying not to think about Marcia or Helen or swarming insects.

He didn't even know she was going to be here tonight. He'd texted with an invite about an hour ago. Grace had reported some suspicious activity around the cabin, and he was coming up to check it out, he'd said. (Hint. Hint.) She'd texted back: *I've gotta work. :(*

Ian's cabin came into view, and Bailey heaved a sigh of relief that she hadn't gotten lost. She blew on her fingers, hefted the duffle higher on her shoulder and hiked to the door.

Her heartbeat sounded like thunder in her ears as she pulled the key he'd given her out of her pocket. She felt nervous as all get-out every time she came here. Nervous and unsettled. But that was ridiculous. Grace was probably imagining things when she was here with her girlfriends over the weekend. Bailey saw nothing out of place. Probably just some snowmobilers or mischievous raccoons.

The sound of a car down on the main road carried through the cold air, and she hurried to make her fingers work. The door opened.

There. She was in. She quickly closed the door behind her, her nerves singing along her spine. She felt like the Pink Panther breaking into the Louvre instead of a girlfriend preparing to surprise her boyfriend.

She opened the woodstove, popped in a little fire-starter thingy and lit it. There. In about an hour she should be ready to take her coat off. Just in time for Ian to show up.

She sat on the bed and pulled off her boots and socks. Then she lay down, tucking her legs under the comforter. After a few minutes, she got up, opened the root cellar, retrieved a soda and sat down again. She'd learned that secret rendezvous involved a lot of waiting around.

She drank the soda and lay back feeling enormously weary. She closed her eyes.

Less than ten minutes later, the door sprang open.

"Bailey?"

"*Ian!*" Bailey jumped to her feet, the empty soda can clattering to the floor. "Surprise!"

He blinked, staring at her, one hand on the doorknob another holding a chunk of firewood.

"I thought you were an intruder," he said, his eyes sliding down to stare quizzically at her bare feet.

"Nope. No intruder. Just me coming for a… a visit." Oh, Burnt Toast! She had *drool* on her cheek! She swiped at her face with the sleeve of her coat then remembered what she had under it. She whipped her coat off and let it fall to the floor.

His eyes went wide. "Wow. You look…"

Cold? Yes. As in *freezing*. She was sure that's what he was going to say, because underneath her long coat she wore nothing but a matching set of ice blue hipsters and push-up bra… and enough goosebumps to host an Olympic mogul competition. She glanced down. Man, though, did this bra ever make the girls look good.

"…amazing," he finished.

"Th-thank you." She fought not to let her teeth chatter and took a step closer to the woodstove.

"What are you doing here? I thought you had to work tonight?"

"I switched shifts with Wanda."

"I'm relieved it's you. I saw smoke and thought I had squatters in here."

"Nope. Just me," she said. She sidled up to him. *Um, hello?* Why was he not snuggling up to the half-naked woman here?

He frowned and closed the door. He held up a finger. "Hang on. I have to make a phone call."

"Now? Can't it wait?" She went on tiptoe and pressed a kiss to his lips.

He smiled against her mouth. "You're making it hard to think."

"That's the idea." She wrapped herself around him—partly for warmth and partly because she figured that's how women seduced men—by pressing their half-naked bodies against them. She snaked her arms around his neck.

He laughed and tossed the chunk of wood on the floor. "All right. All right. Just give me two seconds, and—"

A light flashed through the window. Then again. And then someone pounded at the door. Bailey screamed and dove to the floor. She slithered under her coat.

Ian flung the door wide. "Jeff? What the hell? You scared Bailey half to death."

"Hey, I'm not the one that called in to report squatters at my cabin."

"Sorry for the false alarm. I saw smoke, but it was just Bailey."

"I see that now." A beam of light flashed across her face as Jeff aimed his flashlight into the cabin. "Hi, Bails."

"Hey, Jeff."

"You guys might want to close the curtains. I heard something in the woods over there. Might have been a deer. Might have been paparazzi. If you're okay here, I'll check it out."

"Thanks," Ian said. "And Jeff?"

"Yeah?"

"Could you, ah, *not* come back?"

Jeff's stern face cracked a momentary smile. "Sure thing. Have fun, you two."

"Bye," Bailey murmured. Her face burned with humiliation. She yanked the new down comforter from the bed—God bless her thoughtful boyfriend—and burrowed under its billowy softness.

Ian closed the door. She heard him pull the shade into place. "You're safe now."

She stood, the comforter poofing around her. She couldn't look him in the eye. Heck, she couldn't look *Jeff* in the eye now, either. And if what Jeff suspected was true, she probably wouldn't be able to go in public ever again.

"This was a mistake," she said. "I should go."

"I wish you'd stay."

"Stay? What if he's right?" She sank to the bed like a giant marshmallow. "What if the paparazzi *were* out there?"

"Well, I imagine Marcia will hear about it soon enough..."

Bailey felt the blood leave her face. Marcia? *Ack!* Marcia would be furious if evidence of her and Ian's relationship hit the tabloids.

Not that her standing in a cabin in her skivvies constituted *proof* of relationship status. Still. "Oh God, Ian, I'm so sorry." She couldn't breathe all of a sudden, the comforter suffocating her. She pushed it away from her face.

"Forget it. I wouldn't be surprised if half the paparazzi were hired by Marcia anyway. You know how she likes to stir the pot. Don't worry about it."

"I don't know how you can be so calm about this." He chuckled, which only grated on her nerves. "I fail to see the humor here," she said.

He sat on the bed next to her. "You're beautiful when you're flustered, you know that?" He lifted the hair from her neck and leaned toward her.

She swatted at the hand sliding up her nape. "Cut it out. I'm trying to talk to you."

He grinned, the kind of grin that made his eyes crinkle. "I thought we established how I do my best thinking."

She shook her head. "What am I doing here? What are *we* doing here? This isn't a relationship. This is a booty call. All we do is come up here for sex."

"Says the woman wearing nothing but a trench coat and underwear. Not that I'm complaining. This look totally works for me."

"Of course it does. You're the man of the hour. Women fall at your feet. *Literally!* Don't think I didn't see that woman hurl herself in front of you the other day. It's embarrassing."

He chuckled again. She smacked him in the shoulder. "Hey!" he said.

"It's not funny! Every woman in America thinks you're some ultimate catch. How do you think that makes me feel?"

"Lucky?" She narrowed her eyes at him. He ran the hand that had been on her nape through his hair. "Okay. Maybe not lucky. Honestly, I don't know. You tell me."

"Nervous."

"What have you got to be nervous about? I'm here with you."

"Are you? Or have I just thrown myself at your feet more effectively than anyone else?"

"You're beautiful, Bailey. Different. That's why I'm with you. Where's this even coming from?"

"What if Marcia's right? What if what we have is made more exciting because we're not supposed to be doing this? What if you want me because I have a smokin' hot body and that's it?"

"There's more to it than that."

"Is there? Because your eyes have fallen into my cleavage, and I'm about to throw them a ladder to climb out."

"It's a wonder of physics, that bra."

"Ian, I don't want our relationship defined by sex. I want more."

He sighed and met her eyes. "Sweetheart, I didn't ask you to show up here in your skivvies. I just asked you to spend time with me. If anyone is defining our relationship by sex, it's you."

She pulled the comforter higher over her chest. "My apologies for trying to be sexy," she said.

"Sexy isn't about what you wear. It's about how you wear it."

"What's that supposed to mean?"

"It's about confidence. Sexy isn't looking for someone else to validate you."

Her skin went cold. "What?"

He ran a hand through his hair. "I'm sorry. That sounded harsh. I didn't mean that."

"No. I think that's exactly what you meant." She stood and grabbed her coat from the floor, struggling to turn the sleeves right-side out as the comforter puddled around her. "My mistake for looking for some reciprocity and 'validation' from my… What do I even call you?"

He gripped her arm. "Come on. I don't even know why we're fighting here. Can you just breathe for a minute and talk to me?"

Her breath came in shallow little bursts. "Breathe? *Breathe?*"

"And talk to me. What's gotten into you?"

"I don't know where I stand, that's what's gotten into me!"

"Where you stand? Listen, nothing has changed between us…"

"Exactly. *Nothing has changed.* Nothing, Ian. I poured my guts out to you at the wedding, and what have I gotten since? Nothing! You've never said anything except how beautiful I am and how we should make up superhero powers for the next Treasure Trakker game and how Chewy learned how to sit on command. It's been *weeks*, and we're still stuck in the same place as the first night."

She sniffed, angry at her own weakness. "I watch you day after day as women *hurl* themselves at you, and it has finally dawned on me that *I'm no different.* I'm exactly like them, hoping that the great and wonderful Ian McIntyre will pick *me.* Meanwhile I wait on pins and needles, hoping you don't wake up when this is all over and realize Marcia was right. There is no more *us* when there is no more *us against the world."* She sniffed again. "Well, no more. I'm done waiting."

"I thought we agreed to keep things cool until after the show aired? You said—"

"I take it back." She shoved her arms into the sleeves of her coat and pulled it around her.

"What?"

"What I said at the wedding. I take it back. Forget I ever said anything."

A muscle in his jaw twitched. "It's hard to forget someone told you they love you."

Her eyes felt hot as she fumbled with the ties to her coat. "Could have fooled me."

He reached for her. "Bailey, come on."

"Don't touch me! Don't try to pretend this, this *thing* between us is okay. It's not. It's messed up, Ian. We sneak around like criminals. We lie to our families. I don't know what it is, but it's not a relationship."

"It's all I can give you right now."

She shook her head. "No. It's not. It's all you *will* give me."

His lips compressed with impatience. "That's not fair. These are hardly normal circumstances."

"*Exactly*. These aren't normal circumstances. This is me watching you, week after week, kissing one woman after another even though I told you something I've never told anyone else. Even though I don't even know if I should call you my boyfriend. Or not, because I can't tell anyone about us!"

She made a sound of choked frustration. "It's seeing you more on TV than I do in person. It's watching you with Helen and never quite understanding why you two didn't work out, because she's as nice and beautiful in person as she is on that goddamned TV..." She shook her head. "I thought I could handle it, but I can't."

He didn't say anything. He didn't tell her not to worry about it. He didn't tell her Helen was in the past. Her voice was a whisper. "I mean. She's still *here*, in Sugar Falls. I have to listen to people talk about how great she is, how perfect you'd be together...*to my face.*"

"You know I have no control over that. The show hasn't ended..."

"Or maybe you and she haven't ended."

His features hardened. "Don't do this. What we have is separate from all that."

"Is it? Because it doesn't feel separate. It feels all mixed up. *I* feel all mixed up.

"You know what I hate the most?" she said. "It's the fact that I've become this person I don't even recognize. You've made me need something I was just fine living without before. You've made me *feel.* And it hurts. It hurts, Ian. *Here.*" She thumped her own chest with her fist, her vision blurry. "And I hate you for that," she whispered.

He stared at her, his chest rising and falling. Silent.

"Aren't you going to say anything?" she asked.

"I don't know what you want me to say. Your feelings are your feelings." His lips formed a grim line.

She shivered, the floor rough on her bare feet. "I want you to tell me what you're thinking."

"Truth?"

"Truth."

"The truth is: I don't hate you. Far from it. And the truth is, I never pictured myself with someone like you."

She stumbled back as if physically slapped. "I see."

He ran a hand through his hair. "Would you let me finish? You wanted the truth, well there it is. The truth is I went from sitting in my apartment and eating Chinese food every Saturday night to walking around a house I don't recognize with a TV producer breathing down my neck, stepping over dog toys and *you* in my life.

"Which is fine. It's *good*. I love Chewy, and—"

"You love your dog? That's what I get?"

He looked at her, his eyes sparking. "I know you're asking me to clarify things between us, but that's not entirely up to me. This is a two-way street. If *you're* not sure about what we have, I can't make it happen on my own."

He blew out a long breath. "Falling in love shouldn't be this hard."

And there it was. The truth.

And the worst part was, she couldn't refute any of it. He was only speaking what she'd known in her gut all along. She and Ian didn't make sense.

She yanked the tie to her coat tight. "If I'm so wrong for you, maybe you *should* give Helen another chance."

He shook his head regretfully. "I didn't say it wasn't worth the effort. I just can't give you reassurance you aren't prepared to accept."

"You haven't tried."

"I've jumped through enough hoops." He blew out a long breath and grabbed his coat. "When you're ready to trust me, let me know."

She stared at him, his coat in hand, and then he said the one thing that felt like an icicle through her heart.

"I'll see you 'round, Bailey."

CHAPTER TWENTY-EIGHT

"YOU'RE TRYING TOO HARD."

Helen glanced up from the lemonade she'd been poking at with a straw. She probably shouldn't have come early to wait for Marcia, but she'd been bored sitting at the hotel. Bored and *thinking*. "I beg your pardon?"

"I said you're trying too hard. That's your problem."

Helen stopped fiddling with her straw and stared at the man who had the gall to armchair quarterback her life. Aside from the wedding where he'd dismissed her from the hotel kitchen without so much as a thank you and told her she should go dance at the ball and leave the cooking to him, he'd never spoken a word to her.

Jack Adams swiped his hands clean on a bar towel as he watched her through the pass-through then tucked the towel into his apron. A mop of dirty blonde hair fell over his eyes, and Helen took that moment to assemble a neutral expression. She was certainly not going to let some rough around the edges diner cook make her feel inferior. Even if there was something about him that made her blood heat like August in Alabama.

"I didn't realize I had a problem."

Which was laughable, because just moments ago she'd been wallowing in her own self-doubt. She was alone and rejected in an unfamiliar town. It was the dead of winter, and everyone skied and skated and snowshoed—had entire *carnivals* to celebrate winter activities— while it was all she could do to get her southern blood to pump through her veins at these temperatures.

Now he chuckled, which was annoying and oddly sexy. Nobody laughed *at* her. Nobody.

He ducked back into the kitchen and appeared a moment later at the end of the counter, a white ceramic bowl cradled in one hand.

Helen girded herself for the fact that he was coming near. He moved easily, assuredly, as if he owned the place. Which, she supposed, he probably nearly did. Then he slid the bowl under her nose so the scents of beef and vegetables and hearty herbs tickled her nose. She knew this stew. She'd had Ivy order it sent to her hotel room more than once.

Jack's lips quirked up at the corner. "Eat something. You look hungry."

She grabbed her spoon and watched it disappear into the thick broth even though his cocky demeanor rankled. She didn't want to feel warm fuzzies toward this man who had summarily sent her on her way as if she'd somehow ruin roasted vegetables and carving meats. She'd been handling things just fine the night of the wedding, thank you very much. She didn't need his orders or his advice. She was *so tired* of being told what to do.

She stirred the spoon around in her stew without eating.

"Refill?" he asked, slanting impossibly blue eyes toward her near-empty lemonade.

"Please."

He pulled the cup away, and she barely avoided contact. She shivered anyway then scolded herself for being weak.

He set a fresh glass of lemonade in front of her and passed over a new straw.

She made a point of using the old one.

"When a guy is interested, it doesn't matter whether you make it easy for him. He'll still be interested. If he's not interested, still doesn't matter."

"I'm sorry. Did I ask you for… anything?" She took a bite of stew just to prove she wasn't affected by his nearness.

It tasted rich and complex with a hint of burgundy and basil. Comfort food. She resented how good it tasted even as she ate another spoonful.

He shook his head and leaned back against the counter, his lean frame relaxed and oh, so, confident. "Just trying to be of help."

"I didn't realize I needed any."

His lips hitched up at the corner again. "What I can't figure out is why you even care. I mean, Ian's a decent guy, but why would a woman like you need to try so hard?"

She pushed the stew away. "A woman like me? What's that supposed to mean?"

"Don't get in a tizzy. I'm only saying you're a sexy, talented, good-looking woman. Why chase after a guy who's not into you?"

She shot to her feet, burning humiliation fighting with heat of another sort. "I am not chasing after anyone," she said primly.

"Honey, you've chased him all the way from Alabama to East Kobunk, New Hampshire." There was that chuckle again.

She swished her hair off her face. "For your information, I have a contract with the show. They *asked* me to come. Not that it's any of your business."

He shrugged which was almost worse than him saying something.

Who was this man to say anything at all? What business was it of his?

"Ian and I have a special relationship. You wouldn't understand."

But instead of mocking her again, his eyes went bright with sympathy... which was somehow worse. "You know there's something going on with my sister, right?"

She swallowed and looked away, wishing he'd go back to being rude and intrusive. Yes, she knew there was something going on. She had eyes, didn't she? She blew out a breath and forced herself to look back into those hypnotic baby blues. "I know that everything happens for a reason, and the right woman will win his heart in the end."

The pitying look turned hard, and he pushed abruptly off the counter. "Don't say I didn't warn you."

"Bless your heart for trying," she muttered.

He glanced back over his shoulder, the smirk back in place. "Don't cuss me out, Miss Alabama. And don't think I don't know you just did."

With that, the door to the kitchen swung shut behind him, and she swiveled around, ready to skip lunch even though this infuriating man's beef stew was the only thing that warmed her in this frigid climate. She glanced at her watch and wished Marcia had chosen somewhere— anywhere—else to meet. Why did she have to make it so... public?

"Helen! Sweetheart! So sorry we're late." Marcia swung her ridiculously oversized turquoise bag onto the counter and leaned in for a hug then pulled back just as abruptly. Helen knew the hugs were for her benefit. Marcia seemed to think all southerners were huggers. "I have news." She mimed a need for coffee to one of the wait staff. "You and Ian will be hosting a pet vaccination clinic on Valentine's Day! We're calling it 'Fur-ever Yours Valentine's Vaccination Day.' Don't you love it?"

Marcia waved at her as if it didn't matter what she thought. "I know. It's tomorrow. But we're going all out with local promo, and all you need to do is show up looking fresh and cheerful. The rest will take care of itself. The vet down there has offered her services, so you and Ian will just be responsible for schmoozing with folks as they wait in line."

"Of course." Helen nodded in agreement like the trained monkey she'd become. She was the owner and manager of a highly successful bakery chain, and yet she'd been reduced to nodding in agreement to everything Marcia dreamed up. Plus, she could *feel* Jack smirking at her from behind the pass-through. She turned, any appetite she might have had gone, especially knowing Jack had been right.

"I'm not hungry for lunch after all. I think I'd like to head back to the hotel," she announced.

"Oh, sure. Rest up. Tomorrow will be a busy day, and I want my southern belle looking fresh. Ivy, arrange for something refreshing for Helen. I don't know, a mud wrap or mani/pedi. But natural, no red nails or crap like that. She needs to look wholesome."

Ivy waited to roll her eyes until Marcia had turned away again. She walked with Helen to the door. "You wanna stop at the corner and get cheesecake?" Ivy asked under her breath.

Helen smiled and looped her arm with Ivy's. Bless her heart, she was a love. "That sounds perfect, yes."

MARCIA SLID INTO a booth, emptied a packet of artificial sweetener into her coffee and stirred it deliberately. She set the spoon on the table and glanced across at Nick. "I'm worried."

God bless the man, he didn't even ask what she was worried about, just nodded in that slow, thoughtful way of his.

"We're down to the wire, and I'm reduced to putting on puppy parades. I'm screwed," she said.

Nick raised one eyebrow and cocked his head.

"Fine. A slight understatement. Royally effed is more like it. What the hell is going on with Ian and that Bailey chick? Can you explain this to me? Man to man, so to speak? Because I'm not getting it."

Nick inhaled deep and long and took a sip of his black coffee. He set it down again, cupping his hands around it. She loved watching his movements, so meditative and considered. Not like 'Ed the Ex' who was about as meditative as a Mardi Gras parade. Nick took another sip. "I think you know who is meant for each other and who isn't, but you're fighting it, because you're scared to trust your gut."

He looked up and met her gaze, and something brittle snapped inside her. She felt a rush of emotion, sweet and hopeful, and the longer she held his gaze, the more that soft and vulnerable feeling poured into all the hard, empty places inside.

"I'm not sure what you mean." Which was a lie, because she knew, *knew*, what he meant, and she couldn't look away from the truth anymore, couldn't deny that he was right.

Dang it all, the man was *always* right.

She felt her lips lift at the corners in a sappy, watery smile. She loved the feeling and dreaded it all at the same time, because if Marcia Powers didn't have her edge, what did she have?

"Yes, you do. Let go and let it happen," he urged. He held her gaze and smiled, slow and sure, as if the line between employee and interested male no longer existed.

She scoffed, grasping for something familiar to hold onto as her world shifted like tectonic plates finding a new equilibrium. She drank her coffee with a shaking hand. "You sound like one of your meditation mantras now. If I had control of this disaster of a season, I might be able to let go of it, but it's a damned runaway train, and if we can't stop it, you and I, my friend, are strapped to the same tracks, and there won't be anything I can do to save you."

He stretched out his long arm and touched her cheek, the softest caress. She soaked it in like a drop of rain in a California drought. Then he smiled again.

"Can't think of a better way to go than lying next to you."

Her throat closed up then, clogged full of something she hadn't known she kept inside even as it welled up at his words. Her vision blurred. "I'm afraid to let go," she whispered, hating the way her voice hitched and so grateful she could finally *feel* again. It had been so long since she'd allowed that. *Too long.*

"Don't worry. You got this."

She dabbed at her eyes with the rough fabric napkin, grateful she was facing toward the street and away from the other patrons. "Aren't you supposed to say *you've* got this? Isn't that the alpha male thing to do?"

"Nah," he said. "I have enough faith in you for both of us. I'm saving my strength for the hot sex."

She flashed him another watery smile and let out a long, steadying breath as a zap of awareness shivered through her. The sex would be hot, she could feel it. "I've been pushing on the end of a string, haven't I?"

He nodded.

"I need a new tack." She frowned, thinking, then looked up. "Dang. I need to talk to that woman."

"Who?"

She waved her hand in the air as a thousand thoughts bombarded her at once. "The hair lady. The lady who does the hair. *Aargh!* Cinderella's mom! She's the key. Right now. I can't *believe* I didn't think of it sooner."

She scootched out of the booth and slung her bag over her shoulder. "I'm not in the mood for pub food right now. Can you pay for this and meet me at Meg's Super Styles? Oh, and bring a slice of cheesecake from that place on the corner. I don't give a damn anymore how big my ass is getting."

He looked up at her, completely placid, as if she leapt up and started shouting orders all the time. Which, she did. "Aren't you forgetting something?" he asked.

She paused, perplexed, then dropped her bag on the floor and leaned over to press her lips to his. But he grabbed her face and held her, kissing her back, his lips firm and oh-so-*yes,* until she sank to the seat next to him, her body going soft against his. Finally, his lips formed a grin against her own, and he eased back.

She exhaled, speechless.

"You want strawberries on that cheesecake?" he asked.

CHAPTER TWENTY-NINE

"OH, GOD BLESS YOU sweetie, yes, put that right over there." Wanda tied her apron behind her. "I want to get these prepped before Sandi, Skye and Darla get here. We've got a lot to do to get ready for the Winter Carnival."

Bailey dropped the bag of potatoes on the prep counter. She tried to act normal. She tried to pretend she hadn't gone home last night and cried big ugly tears into her pillow while cursing a world in which women would be attracted to men who would only, inevitably, let them down.

She'd woken feeling drained and defeated, her eyes puffy and aching.

Just like her heart.

She hated that she'd been reduced to *this*.

After spending her life pitying and looking down upon the women who'd fallen all over themselves trying to win her father's love, she was horrified to discover… she was just like them.

Now it was Friday, Winter Carnival kick-off weekend, and Daniel was sick—again!

Wanda shook out the potatoes into the sink to wash them, all brisk efficiency.

"It's a damn good thing Daniel has you and Jack to run this place when he disappears." Here she was—miserable—and who was holed up in bed moaning about their fate?

Wanda glanced over at Bailey with a frown. "Now don't go being hard on your daddy. He probably caught this flu from you."

"It's been going around. It could have come from anywhere."

"True. So it's not his fault he's feeling poorly. Your father's a good man. Now go grab me another bag of potatoes, hon."

Bailey snorted. She couldn't help it. She could taste the bitterness on her tongue. "I can't believe you defend him like this time and again. If it's not one thing it's another, and then we're all left to circle the wagons while he lolls around in bed." She made a swirling motion with her hand.

Wanda's fists came to rest on her hips. "Is that how you see it?"

"Pretty much."

Wanda shook her head and got back to spraying down the potatoes. "We 'circle the wagons' as you put it because Daniel is *family*. You should count yourself lucky you've got family that will support you when you're down and out."

"Right. Got five thousand dollars you could spare?"

Wanda's face softened. "Oh, honey, you know I wish I did."

"I wouldn't take it from you anyway."

"That's because you're too proud for your own good."

"That's because I know you need it as much as me."

Wanda waved the sprayer at her. "Now don't you feel sorry for me, young lady, I'm in a good place. A damn good place, and I thank your daddy and my lucky stars every day for it."

"No offense. But Daniel is the last person you should be thanking. What has he ever done for you? You, my mom, everyone is always running to help him when all he's done is left you all high and dry. This is an unhealthy pattern. It's messed up."

Wanda turned off the sprayer. "That's where you're dead wrong. After my louse of an ex blew himself up, I was in a bad way. No skills. No money. Baby on the way. Daniel *saved me*. For the first time, I could be proud of myself instead of scared. I love your daddy. He's the best thing that ever happened to me."

"He knocked you up and left you!"

"He gave me my precious Skye and gave me purpose. I love Danny to pieces."

"You divorced him within the year. I think that says it all."

"Don't you see? Your daddy has a gift, honey. He made me feel *needed* for the first time ever. But then, I didn't need him anymore." She smiled and shrugged as if that made any sense whatsoever, her eyes drifting past the bar to Phil who was sitting in Wanda's section again drinking his afternoon coffee and making moony eyes at her. Young, slightly lanky Phil with the too-long hair and the puppy dog eyes.

"Why don't you go out with Phil?" Bailey asked. "He's getting a bit poochy from eating so many of Skye's desserts while he waits around for you to notice him. He'd be devoted to you."

Wanda's cheeks turned pink. "Phil doesn't want a crusty old woman like me."

"You're barely forty, Wanda. I hardly call that 'crusty'."

"I'm nearly twice his age. That kid is barely old enough to buy alcohol." Her eyes grew soft. "Doesn't mean I don't appreciate the attention. And that smokin' backside of his. Dang," she said softly. "That's inspiration not to skip Zumba class right there. *Ooh*. Talk about hunky-dunky men. Look who just walked in."

Bailey held her breath.

The bell over the door jangled as Ian stepped over the threshold. He shook the dusting of light snow off his shoulders and held the door for Skye as she carried one of her bakery boxes in.

Bailey stilled like a deer caught in the headlights. This was the downside of having a boyfriend no one could know about. No one could know when you broke up, either.

"Am I late?" Skye asked.

Bailey shook her head and pasted a fake smile on her face. "Still waiting for my mom and Darla. Don't know who else can make it."

"I'll bring this out back."

Bailey straightened the menus by the cash register as Skye walked away and avoided looking up. "What are you doing here?" she finally said.

Ian glanced around. "We need to talk."

"Sorry. We're having a family meeting. Daniel's sick, and we need to plan for Winter Carnival stuff."

"Sign says you're open. Should I just take a seat?"

He made his way to a corner booth and took a seat. Bailey trailed behind him. She huffed out a breath. What the hell was he doing here? Twisting the knife in the wound? "Do you want to hear the specials?"

"No. I'm not here to eat. You've been ignoring my calls."

"There's nothing left to say."

He pulled something out of his coat and slid it toward her on the table. "I beg to differ."

Bailey glanced at the weekly tabloid on the table. The blood rushed from her head. "*Oh, shitake mushrooms.*"

"My thoughts exactly."

She sank onto the bench seat opposite him and slid away from view of the street. "Has Marcia seen this?"

"Who do you think gave it to me?"

Bailey stared down at the grainy photos of her in her underwear hanging off of Ian. Her stomach roiled. The caption read *Sweet Scandals! Sugar Falls' Ian McIntyre Caught in Love Shack with Hometown Hottie!*

"At least they think I'm a hottie," she said, heat flooding her face. "Marcia must be furious."

"I think apoplectic might accurately describe it."

"You should have told her she doesn't have anything to worry about. I'm out of the picture."

"Not… exactly."

"Don't be cruel. You and I are… done."

He ran a hand through his hair, and for a moment she had the urge to reach up and straighten it. Then she realized that wasn't her place anymore. If it ever was. "That's why I'm here. I thought you'd want to hear it from me."

"Hear what?"

"Marcia still wants you at that Fur-Ever Vaccination thing tomorrow."

"Why?"

"I'm guessing because, now that this is out, she figures she'll roll with it and let everyone believe you're still in the picture."

"But I'm not."

He caught her eye for one heart-stopping moment, as if he wanted to say something, as if it hurt him to hear those three words as much as it hurt her to say them. Then he looked away. "I'll see if I can talk her out of it."

He stood, regret and a day's worth of stubble clouding his features. "For what it's worth, I hope we can still be friends after this is all over."

She pressed her lips together, emotion clogging her throat. "Yeah. I don't think that's gonna happen."

His eyes met hers—weary, apologetic—and for one brief moment, she thought he might lean down and kiss her, as if he'd return the heart he'd ripped out of her chest the night before and all would be right.

But then he walked out, her heart still in his hand.

CHAPTER THIRTY

SHE HADN'T SLEPT all night.

Instead, Bailey had stared at the popcorn ceiling of her cubicle of a bedroom as bags the size of Texas formed under her eyes.

There was no way out of this.

Her gut heaved as she sat up in bed. There was only one other person she knew who understood the humiliation of tabloid notoriety.

She called Liz.

"Hello?"

"Liz, it's Bailey."

"Bailey!" A pause. "How are you?"

Bailey sighed. She could tell from the tone of her voice Liz had seen the tabloid. No doubt Ian had filled his little brother in on all the gory, humiliating details. "Let's see: I've been dumped, my lily-white New England skin is blinding people at check-out counters across the nation, Marcia has reamed me out like a deluxe valve job, and I don't think I can show my face in public *ever again*. How's Florida?"

"It's not that bad."

Bailey knew Liz wasn't referring to the weather.

"Not that bad? I'm a laughingstock! Creepy men feel a renewed permission to leer at me. Mothers pull their children closer. And Frankie Sullivan asked me to autograph my ass!" (For the record, she had flatly refused and told him to wash his mouth out with soap for even daring to ask her.) "What am I going to do? Marcia wants to parade me around that stupid vaccination clinic today like some lovesick moron who can't take the hint." She proceeded to fill Liz in on the events at the cabin and Ian's visit to the pub the day before.

"I don't think you have a choice," said Liz. "You need to go. You have to face this. I know how humiliating it is to have your underwear show up in print—okay, I wasn't wearing mine at the time—but if you slink away now, everyone will think Helen is the one for Ian, and that's not true."

"You told me you didn't see us together."

"No. I said I hadn't pictured you as being ready for a commitment. I was wrong."

"Look where that's gotten me."

"Hey, if Ian didn't have some feelings for you, he wouldn't have bothered to tell you about the vaccination clinic. So be brave. Show him and Marcia and everybody else that you aren't a joke."

"How?"

"I don't know. I'm sure you'll figure it out." There was another pause. "There's one more thing. Valerie mentioned... that garage you've been wanting has sold."

"That deal fell through—"

"They paid cash this time. Just in the last few days. I'm sorry."

Bailey mumbled her goodbyes and tossed her phone on the bed.

Perfect. To be honest, she'd half expected this to happen. The universe seemed to be in the mood to kick her while she was down.

Now she had nothing left to lose.

She blew out a breath. It was a surprisingly freeing thought knowing she'd hit rock bottom. Suddenly she didn't give a flying cow-patty what anyone thought anymore, and she realized she had no intention of slinking off like a coward.

If the world expected her to give up while everyone fell all over the super-sized feet of Miss Helen, they had another thing coming.

And the world *loved* Helen. Who wouldn't? She was everything Bailey was not. Charming. Sweet. Nurturing. Beautiful.

Bailey crawled out of bed and stepped into a hot shower. After a while, she shut the water off and rested her head against the shower wall. She couldn't do anything about the garage, but she could do something about how people saw her. She could hold her head high today.

But how? How could she not look like some pathetic loser crashing Ian and Helen's charity pet vaccination event if she didn't even have a pet of her own?

Wait. That was it!

Bailey thrust the shower curtain aside and reached for a towel. In a couple of hours she'd either stand around like a fifth wheel or show the world she was just as capable of winning Ian's heart as Helen.

FORTY-FIVE MINUTES LATER, Bailey knocked on Mr. Henderson's door. The sound echoed in the cool air. Bright February sun blinded her as it reflected off the metal siding of his trailer. She waited. She knocked again.

Finally, she heard movement inside and the door squeaked open. "What?"

"Hi, Mr. Henderson. Bailey Adams here. From across the street?"

"Yuh."

Oh cripeys. The man was wearing a bathrobe and those hideous old-man slippers and looked for all the world like a serial killer eating a Pop-tart, his face all pale and bloated. But he was Bailey's only hope. "Um, I was actually checking in with you to see if you'd like me to take Fluffy to a vaccination clinic they're having today downtown."

He stared at her with watery eyes for a moment, and she wasn't sure if he understood, then he muttered, "No money," and swung the door closed.

"Wait! It's free! No cost!"

The door opened a crack. Mr. Henderson shrugged in the shadows. "Knock yourself out."

"Great. No problem. Do you, um, have a pet carrier by chance?"

"No."

Okaaaaaay. She glanced around his feet and into the shadows of his living room. It was ten in the morning, and the man had all the curtains drawn and no lights on. "Do you, ah, know where Fluffy might be?"

"Nope." He shut the door.

"Okay. All right. Good talking to you."

Bailey rubbed her hands together for warmth and looked around. She needed a carrier. She glanced at Mr. Henderson's recyclable bins overflowing with beer cans and a freakish number of laundry soap jugs. But no cardboard boxes other than pizza boxes. She frowned and stalked back across the street to her own trailer and looked around for something, anything, that might hold a cat.

Okay, one might not recommend a gym duffle as a cat carrier, but it had a ventilation panel on one end, so she figured it would serve in a pinch. She slung it over her shoulder, grabbed a pouch of tuna from the cupboard and went in search of Fluffy.

An hour later, her fingers were stiff with cold, and she had dirty, wet splotches on both knees from kneeling on the ground to check under all the cars in and around the trailer park.

Then she spotted him.

Bailey held her breath and slowly ripped off the top of the tuna pouch for fear a sudden movement would scare the cat away.

Fluffy's tail twitched, and he looked ready to bolt for one heart-stopping moment, but then he lifted his back leg and licked his private parts in the universal cat language for, "whatever."

Bailey pulled a bit of tuna out of the bag and let it drop on the ground in front of her. She waited.

Fluffy ignored her.

"Here, kitty," she whispered, tossing another bit of tuna out. "Here kitty, kitty, kitty…"

He stopped licking his nether regions long enough to twitch his nose in the air.

"That's right. Tuna! You like that? Come and get some."

She inched closer and he stood up and eyed her warily.

"*Shh*. Don't worry. I just want to give you a treat. It's okay."

He flattened his ears and backed up a step.

"Now don't get mad. Eat the tuna." She tossed a bit toward him. It landed with a plop in the snowy dirt in front of him. He eyed it distrustfully. "It's yummy. Try it."

She inched the bag off her shoulder and eased it to the ground. Fluffy took a tentative step forward and sniffed. Dear Lord, at this rate, the clinic would be over by the time she got there. She tossed another hunk toward him.

There! That did it! Fluffy stepped forward and ate the bit of tuna then looked up.

"You like that, did you? Here." Throwing caution to the wind, Bailey shook the rest of the package onto the ground and watched in triumph as Fluffy started eating it.

Then, sucking in a breath and holding the duffle wide, she threw it over the unsuspecting cat.

Now, the truth is, she hadn't entirely planned how—once she had trapped the hissing, fighting, clawing cat under a duffle with the zipper open—she planned to turn it over, keep the cat inside and zip it up. But, once she'd gotten this far, there wasn't a chance in hell she was going to let a slightly disgruntled cat get the best of her.

She slid her hand around to find the edge of the opening and with one swift (albeit ill-advised) move, flipped the duffle and held the flap over the cat.

Fluffy screeched and became like an octopus with claws, digging at Bailey's skin as she grabbed the zipper with shaking hands and tugged, trying to pull the flap closed even as Fluffy slithered out and raked her cheek before she shoved him back like a painful whack-a-mole game.

Bailey sat in the slush, panting, her cheek on fire and thin lines of blood welling up on her hands and forearms. Beside her, the duffle meowed and wiggled like a being possessed.

A wave of nausea swept over her at the sight of her arms, but she swallowed it with sheer force of will. She would. Not. Faint. She swiped the claw marks on her jeans and they beaded up again, sending bile gurgling up her throat.

Oh God. She had to get Band-Aids.

Moments later she stared at the medicine chest in her bathroom. Who didn't have Band-Aids?

Searching around, she found an alternative that'd have to do. She fixed herself up as best as possible, set the duffle in the back of the car, and headed to town.

She could do this.

She could show Ian and Marcia and the world she was just as philanthropic and junk like that as Helen.

By the time she'd reached downtown, Fluffy had settled down to a constant low keening sound and the occasional body slam against the side of the duffle. Bailey pulled into a parking spot a couple of buildings away from the common and nodded to a woman walking her cat on a leash.

Show off.

Bailey wrestled the duffle bag out of the backseat and slammed the door shut. She trudged through the slush on the sidewalk to stand in line with the other pet owners and craned her neck for a glimpse of Ian.

A news van, a radio station truck and probably at least a hundred people and assorted animals crowded around the town common as pet owners and *Happily Ever After* fans pushed to get closer to either free vet care or a peek at the handsome reality TV couple.

Bailey's breath left her like a leaking balloon as she caught sight of Ian crouched next to an adorable mutt: the world's most photogenic dog and the ridiculously photogenic man above him. She sighed when Helen stepped into view, all long limbs and wide, southern smile as she charmed some besotted teenage boy and his Pit Bull mix at the registration table.

Ian glanced up, caught her staring at him and frowned. He leaned in to say something to someone next to him, and then he was walking toward her, the crowd moving like a parting sea to see where he was going.

"Bailey? What are you doing here? I thought I told you'd I'd get you out of this." He frowned down at the duffle bag at her side. It moaned.

"What happened to your face? And why are you wearing masking tape all over your hands?"

The woman in front of her turned around and scowled with disgust then tugged her precious little white cat's leash a bit closer before picking it up and petting its docile little fluff-head.

"Nothing. Nevermind. What's with the twenty questions? I'm here to do a little public service of my own." She patted the duffle gingerly. It poked back at her.

Ian reached toward the bag. "What have you got in there?"

"I wouldn't touch that if I were you," Bailey said pulling it sharply away and earning a loud snarl of protest in return. "He's not exactly thrilled with the idea of the whole vet thing."

"He?"

"My cat. I mean, my neighbor's cat. Mr. Henderson's not able to get out, poor thing." (On account of the alcoholism and bathrobe fetish.) "So I offered to take his beloved kitty here for his, um, shots."

"You," Ian said incredulously. "*You* offered to take him for his shots? Did you bring your fainting couch?"

"Ha. Ha."

"I'm serious. Bailey, you don't belong here. I don't even know why you'd come. You hate needles, and this is like a needle festival."

His dismissal washed over her along with a wave of light headed-ness each time he spoke the word 'needle.' "I want to help."

"By passing out on someone's pet Chihuahua?"

"There are mostly large breeds here," she said lamely. She stared at him. He swam in front of her eyes a moment before she wrenched her eyes back into focus.

"Oh, for Pete sake," he growled. He grabbed her arm and all but dragged her through the crowd. She hated that her arm sang with happiness to be near him again. "Hey, Marcia, look what the cat dragged in."

Marcia glared at her, a fake smile glued to her ultra-white teeth. "Bailey! What are you doing here? Ian said you weren't coming."

Bailey raised the duffle. "Just helping out my furry friend here."

Ian leaned over and whispered something to the vet on the other side of the metal table. "Okay. In you go." He gestured for Bailey to enter the travel trailer they'd set up as a portable vaccination station. "We have to get this animal back to its owner. He's housebound, apparently," he said to the others waiting in line.

Bailey shimmied past those in line, earning a few forced smiles and a handful of dirty looks. Way to win the public over. She preceded Ian up the metal steps into the trailer. He shut the door.

"Doctor Killion you remember Bailey, I'm sure." Ian was all solicitous introductions.

Doctor Killion's eyes went wide. "Oh. Yes." She frowned and turned to Ian for some explanation of why this mad, fainting woman would be back again. Ian just smiled across at Bailey.

"Go ahead," he said.

"Right." Bailey lifted the duffle onto the table "My neighbor's kitty. Poor thing never gets any proper care. Half the time it's eating out of the garbage cans."

Ian rolled his eyes so far back Bailey was sure the vet would think *he* was about to faint.

"So, you've no idea what his vaccination history is?" the vet inquired.

"No. I'm sure it's nothing. Poor thing."

"All right," the doc said standing back. "Let's have a look. You can take him out now and place him on the examining table."

Bailey looked at the bag and back up again. "Um." Ian and the doc looked at her expectantly. "Okay. Sure."

Bailey reached a hand out to the duffle and yanked the zipper back in one swift motion. Out shot the cat… straight at Ian's chest.

"*Aargh!*" he yelled. A ball of gray fur ricocheted off his torso and skidded across the metal table toward the doctor. She shrieked—a surprisingly girlie sound for such a masculine woman—and dove to the side, Fluffy careening into a rolling cart of vaccine and other important looking supplies. The cart tipped sideways, little bottles of vaccine rolling along the floor, tripping Bailey as she struggled to remain upright. Fluffy climbed back up the side of Ian, red dots of blood welling up on the skin of his arm and neck. He grabbed the cat by the scruff and demanded Bailey open the goddamned duffle.

But all she could see were bright red lines seeping through the material on his chest and along his sleeve. Twin dots of blood beading up on his neck like he'd been struck by a kitty vampire.

Her vision grew hazy and she clawed at the door handle behind her needing to escape before everything closed in again.

And then she was shoved against the wall of the trailer as Ian lunged to shut the door, but it was too late. Fluffy bolted to freedom.

Funny thing about a frenzied cat dashing through a crowd of leashed dogs. Things can get chaotic pretty quickly.

Bailey stumbled down the steps, gasping for breath and clear vision as Ian bolted through the crowd after Mr. Henderson's cat, dogs barking excitedly. And then one dog broke free and dashed after Ian, its leash dragging, and Bailey's vision came back with a jolt.

"Chewy! *Ian!* Chewy's loose!"

Ivy came dashing forward. "I'm sorry! She saw Ian and yanked right out of my hand!"

Bailey pushed through the crowd, desperately looking for Ian, the dog, and the escaped cat. Ian came back into view from around one of the enormous snow sculptures and stopped, panting, looking around.

He and Bailey spotted Chewy and Fluffy at the same time. The pair were heading toward the main intersection in town.

The same one that had killed Meg's husband and Old Man Richards two years ago.

Her heart thumping so hard it hurt, Bailey ran with all her strength toward the intersection, screaming Chewy's name. But she was so far away. Too far away. Panic shot through her.

And then a blur of movement sped into view. Helen—dashing like a gazelle across the common, leaping over low railings and veering through parked cars and around moving vehicles like a quarterback in the Super Bowl going for a touchdown.

Cars skidded to a stop as Helen ran through traffic calling Chewy's name. She was nearly upon them now.

But the teen in the clunker with the bass beat booming didn't hear or see the commotion. He careened toward the intersection, speakers thumping, oblivious to the woman ducking down to grab a small dog.

The collective gasp of onlookers meshed sickeningly with the sound of tires skidding on pavement as Helen dove like an avenging angel, and tumbled horridly across the pavement with Chewy in her arms.

For a few moments there was no sound. No one dared move or speak, and then they heard the faint but unmistakable sound of Helen as she called out, "I've got her! She's okay!"

Bailey watched, her vision blurring for a different reason now as Ian rushed ahead and knelt beside Helen, gingerly holding her as Frankie got out of his car, the music still thumping as he grabbed Chewy's leash. Then Ian turned, his face ashen, as he called for an ambulance. Then they were all lost in a sea of bodies, the crowd surging forward to help and thank and congratulate the woman who'd risked everything to save a dog.

How in hell could Bailey ever compete with *that.*

BAILEY SWALLOWED a few times as the wave of barking dogs and excited gawkers forgot about the free vaccinations and moved en masse toward the sounds of a siren and the excitement of heroic rescue.

"Bailey. May I speak with you a moment?"

Bailey turned and blinked. It took a moment to register who was speaking to her. *Marcia.* "In a minute. I need to… see Chewy."

"Ian's dog?"

Yes, that's right. Not her dog. Not their dog. *Ian's* dog. "I'll just be a minute."

Murmurs of 'compound fracture' and 'dislocated shoulder' whispered through the crowd like wind through summer leaves.

"She looks like she's in good hands, and it seems they have other things to worry about." Marcia wiggled her eyebrows at Nick and motioned for him to go film the events at the accident scene for future at-home consumption. "Why don't you let them breathe for a moment?" Marcia set a staying hand on Bailey's arm. Bailey shrugged it off.

"What do you want, Marcia? I know I'm not your favorite person."

Marcia didn't seem put-off by Bailey's words. "You misunderstand me then."

"Do I?"

Something that might have been a smile passed over Marcia's face. "Yes. I don't have personal feelings toward you. Any feelings I have are based on what the viewers are telling me."

"And what are they telling you?"

"That they're confused."

"Excuse me?" Bailey watched the vet walking back through the crowd with some metal stick-leash around poor little Fluffy's neck. He hissed at Bailey as he passed by toward the travel trailer. She took an involuntary step back.

"I'll be honest with you, Bailey. The viewers see the sparks flying between you and Ian, and then they see Helen…" She motioned toward the intersection where even now an ambulance awaited with flashing lights and the crowd cheered as the paramedics helped Helen onto a stretcher. "I mean, look at her! She's beautiful, generous, successful…" Marcia turned. "Look at you. You dress in flannel and pigtails and swear like a four year-old."

"I'll take that as a compliment."

"Whatever. My point is, viewers don't know what to do with you, and that puts me in an awkward position."

"I don't see how."

"Don't you? I've characterized you as a thing of the past. But when the photos of that ridiculous episode with you two prancing around in the dark came out, what choice did I have but to keep you in the storyline? It's clear you haven't gone away, and the viewers want more dirt now than ever. That tabloid spread only whet their appetites. So, I'm going to need you to shoot a mini interview. A profile piece to help the viewers get a bit more background on you before the finale."

"You're just trying to build me up so you can cut me off at the knees. I won't do it."

"Actually, your contract says you will."

"Then pay me for it."

"We already did."

"Bite me." Bailey started walking away.

"Actually, I have a proposition that might make this all a bit more palatable."

Bailey paused. Turned. "I can't imagine what would."

"You do the interview so we have our little montage on the mysterious Bailey for the viewers, then keep your distance until after the finale. If you do, I'll make sure you get your down payment so you can buy your little garage."

"Haven't you heard? It's sold. You're too late."

"Not if I'm the new owner."

Bailey froze. "Say that again?"

"You heard me." Marcia admired her manicure a moment before gracing Bailey with an evil, self-satisfied smile. Okay, maybe it wasn't *evil,* but it wasn't *nice.* "I bought that little dump outright. Cash sale. Ridiculously overpriced, but I figure my cheating ex-husband deserves to have his alimony wasted."

"Why would you do that?"

"I should think it's obvious. I'm saving my show." Marcia sighed as if having to explain to a kid how day and night work. "I'll see that you get your dream garage if you disappear from Ian's life—and Chewy's—until after the finale."

"What about after the finale?"

"The public has a very short attention span. After the finale doesn't matter."

"It will if you don't get your happily-ever-after."

Marcia sighed and a look that might have passed for sympathy crossed her face. "What you think you have with Ian isn't real, honey."

"What do you know about it?"

"I've seen it. It's my job. You two thought you were pulling one over on me, and then things went a little further than you planned. Am I right?"

"Does it matter?"

Marcia shrugged, her cream-colored shawl impossibly expensive looking. Soft. *Clean.* Bailey's jeans stuck to her knees and her masking tape bandages itched. "When things went further than you expected, it made it all very exciting. Once you two are in the real world without the film crews and the paparazzi and the world's eyes on you, that excitement will fade, and you'll realize the two of you don't have anything in common except for an unhealthy obsession with Sci-Fi films.

"I know. I know it *feels* real, but it's the illicit nature of your relationship that gives you that little thrill every time you see him. It's not Ian."

"I'm pretty sure it is Ian."

Marcia shook her head sadly. "I know you think of me as the devil woman—as if I'm some puppet-master who likes to call the shots—but that couldn't be further from the truth. I want people to be happy."

"Because you're so happy?"

"Because I've been so *un*happy. I know you won't be truly happy until you can be your own boss. You're an independent woman. I admire that. But know this: Ian won't be truly happy until he has a partner to share his life with. He doesn't need a playmate, Bailey. He needs a partner. *A wife.* Look at them! They look like those pictures that come in photo frames." Marcia turned toward the happy little family: Helen, Ian and a face-licking Chewy. "Are you going to stand here and tell me that emotion in Ian's eyes isn't real? Ian lost his family tragically. Don't stand in the way of him making a new one."

Bailey took a shuddering breath.

"Well? Do we have a deal?"

Bailey glanced over at Helen and Ian and Chewy again. Who was she kidding? They *did* make the picture perfect family. What she and Ian had… maybe Marcia was right. Maybe the excitement and the illicit nature of it all had made it seem more than it was.

A garage of her own, though, was something she could count on. Something she could be certain wouldn't have a change of heart and decide it needed to go off and find a new wife to knock up and family to move in with. It wasn't going to forget and give her pierced earrings for graduation.

It wouldn't break her heart.

She turned away from Chewy's happy yelps as the dog licked the glamorous and heroic Helen all over her face in front of cell phone cameras and TV crews. Helen grimaced beautifully and waved to the crowd before being wheeled into the waiting ambulance.

"Come on," Marcia said. "What will it be? It's all or nothing. You either take what you want or walk away empty-handed. There's no middle ground here."

Bailey turned her back as the ambulance sounded its siren and pulled away… with Ian and Helen inside. "I'm in."

CHAPTER THIRTY-ONE

———————————

BAILEY PULLED INTO the gravel lot behind the garage and cut the engine. So. This was it. Her future.

She got out and slammed the car door. The sun was high in the sky, bright and a bit blinding as it reflected off the nearby snowbanks.

It should feel bigger than this, she thought. Knowing it was nearly hers now, standing here, staring at the brick exterior, holding the key to the back door in her hand… it should feel *momentous* somehow. And yet…

She couldn't put her finger on it. She couldn't quite figure out why she wasn't feeling proud that she'd made it this far. She'd gone to Marcia that morning, and they'd worked out a deal. Strangely Marcia hadn't appeared as happy about it as Bailey had expected her to be.

Bailey shrugged and slid the key into the lock. The door swung open, the familiar scents of old tires, motor oil and axle grease like coming home. She looked around.

Nice. She could put the coffee maker in that corner, by her office. And to the left, she'd set up a waiting area for customers. It had a view of Lucky's across the way and if you looked just right, you could see a sliver of the bandstand on the common and the fountain beyond that.

Then there was the shop space. Two full bays. *An in-floor lift.*

She'd install good, bright lighting of course, but otherwise it was good to go. She'd be in business. At long last.

She thought about advertising and who her first customers might be. Skye, Darla, Jack and Wanda would talk her up for sure. Maybe she could talk to her mom about running a special for women getting their hair done over at Meg's to attract the female demographic: Oil Change & Blow Out Deal.

Sure, it'd take some time to get a full set of tools, especially for some of the specialty jobs, but Liz had helped her figure out what she'd need to set up with the basics and then use a portion of cash flow for re-investment in the business.

She blew out a breath. Soon she'd be busy setting up accounts with parts suppliers, working out an accounting system, and setting up advertising but Liz had that all mapped out already, so it was merely a matter of implementing the plan. It wasn't as if she were new to the game. She'd done much of the same things over at Willard's. Now, though, she would do it for herself.

It'd take at least a week of elbow grease to clean the place out. Decades of grime, some used tires, and assorted debris had been left behind, but she could recycle and toss most of it. The empty gasoline containers and oil drums would have to be disposed of carefully. Some things were still potentially hazardous or explosive, but it wasn't like she was a smoker, so there really wasn't any danger.

Then it would be hers.

The knock on the door startled her out of her reverie. "I'm sorry. We're not op—" But then the words died on her tongue. She worked the front lock with fumbling fingers. "Ian!"

He nodded and entered without a word, looked around. "So, this is it," he said.

Her heart thudded hard in her chest. "Yeah."

His lips pulled up on one side, not quite a smile.

"It's good to see you," she said. "How's Helen?"

"Fine. I mean, not fine, obviously, but she'll be okay. She's pretty tough."

"Yeah."

He blew out a breath as if working up the courage to get an unpleasant task over with. "I was just heading to the pub thinking you might be working so I could deliver something. Then I saw you here." He fished in his chest pocket.

"You were looking for me?"

"Here."

"What's—?" She looked at the slip of paper he held toward her, confusion warring with hope inside her, but then she realized what it was. "A check?"

"Consider it the rest of what I owe you for training Chewy."

"We both know you owe me nothing."

"Don't be so proud. I'm sure you've barely scraped together a down payment for this place. You'll still need tools and a basic parts inventory to get off the ground."

"That's not the point. This is insulting. I feel like a prostitute. Or a charity case."

He didn't reply, just held it toward her, his expression unreadable.

She glanced at the check, then did a double-take. Her eyes flew to his face. "Who keeps fifty grand sitting around in a checking account?"

"I had it transferred from my brokerage account this morning."

"Of course you did."

She felt dirty. Dirty and guilty. And *angry*. Damn him for reducing what was between them to *this*.

"You wanted the money. I'm giving it to you. Take it." His voice was hard as he held the check toward her. It felt like a dare. Like she'd reach for it and the check would morph into a rancor and chew off her hand.

She took a step back. "*No*. Whatever you think of me. I'm not like that."

He let out a heavy sigh. "Look, I know about Marcia's deal. I know she's got you over a barrel. Just take it and tell her to screw herself."

"No."

"Why the hell not? I'm giving you the chance to walk away from her, to save yourself further humiliation."

She stepped back. "Because I want more. I *deserve* more than this."

He choked, his hand falling to his side. "You think you deserve *more?*"

She knew he was thinking about the money and that hurt most of all. But it wasn't about the money. She deserved a man that wanted her in his life no matter how hard it was. She deserved a man who would fight for her—not write a check just to soothe his conscience so he could walk into the sunset unburdened.

Tears burned the backs of her eyes. She'd die before she spelled it out to him. "Yes, I do."

He shook his head. "Wow. I've seriously misjudged you."

"Yes, you have."

He turned his back on her, his hand closing over the knob of the door to leave, and then he stopped. "You always implied that I expected special treatment because of who I am: the millionaire bachelor. Not true. If anyone does, it's you. You think life owes you for a raw deal. Well, welcome to the club, sweetheart, because I don't feel as if I've gotten the best deal, either. Consider this check your PB&J and suck it up. You and I are done."

Then he let the check drop from his fingers and slammed the door behind him.

THERE WERE NO TEARS after that.

Bailey drove home, the brilliant February sun mocking the black void inside her. Just when the world seemed ready to embrace longer days and brighter skies, the fates ripped the floor out from under her and plunged her back into the abyss she thought she'd crawled out of.

Maybe she deserved it. But she didn't think so.

She didn't deserve to be kicked to the curb and misjudged.

She didn't deserve to have her heart broken by a man who she wanted to hate and rail against more than anything. But she couldn't.

Because… *she still loved him.*

The tabloid sat on the coffee table in front of her—mocking any hopes of a happily-ever-after with Ian.

"Are you going to torture yourself with that forever?"

Sandi came up behind the couch and rested her hands on Bailey's shoulders.

"Just a day or two, then I'll get over it." Bailey closed her eyes. While she'd been off dreaming about her future at the garage, Wanda had driven her mom for her biopsy.

Now they were both in limbo, waiting for a future to unfold that may or may not hold further heartache.

Sandi sighed and came around to settle onto the couch beside Bailey. "Come here, you. I think we both need a hug." She wrapped Bailey in a comforting cloud of Jean Nate, and they sat like that, each lost in their own thoughts.

"I'm sorry, Mom," Bailey mumbled into her mother's shoulder, all the grief and regret and worry she'd been tamping down inside suddenly bubbling up and over. "I'm *so* sorry…"

Her mom made soothing noises and rubbed circles on Bailey's back with her palm which only made Bailey's breath hitch on a sob. "For what, honey? You've got nothing to apologize to me for."

Bailey pulled away. "I *do*. I've hurt you, Mom. I've been sarcastic and moody and dismissive of your hard work and everything you've done for me. It started with the pageant, and I guess it never really stopped." She sucked in a breath, "The truth is, I *wanted* to win that stupid pageant, but when I got out there, I got scared. I got scared, Ma—" And then the tears came, tumbling out in ugly hiccoughing sobs. "I wanted to be b-brave. I did! But I didn't fit in. I'm so sorry I let you down."

Her mother gripped her shoulders. "Now, listen here! You *never* let me down. Yes, I admit, I poured everything I could into that dress and preparing you for that day. And a part of me knew you didn't want to do it, but I knew you had a shot. A *real* shot to show that Allison Franklin and her snooty daughter what *real* girls with spunk and spirit and class can do.

"Every year she came into the salon and had me do their hair *to match* and went on and on about that God-damned pageant..." Sandi's voice choked with emotion. "I was so *sick* of listening to her talk about her wonderful, talented, artistic—*gah!*—Melanie, and I was thrilled to finally get the chance to show you off. *You*, Bailey!

"Because I believed in you, and I knew you wouldn't glide out there like some twelve year-old with... with *thirteen* years of ballet lessons behind her, because they'd somehow managed to start dance lessons in utero. No, you'd march out like *you* in all your confident glory, and your idea seemed so perfect and clever and..." She stopped to search for a tissue and blew her nose noisily. "But..."

"I wasn't brave."

"You were! You *are*. Look at you? You go after what you want no matter what anyone says."

"And no matter who it hurts."

Sandi's eyes grew soft. "Even when you hurt yourself. Yes."

"I don't know what to do, Mom." She shook her head, swiping at her eyes and nose with her shirt sleeve. "Every time I go into that shop I'll be thinking about what it cost me to get it."

"Maybe it's not too late."

Bailey looked up. "I wish it weren't, but I've already run off the stage."

CHAPTER THIRTY-TWO

"LYDIA, GET THE DOOR."

Ian stood in the hallway, rooted to the spot like a deer frozen in the middle of the road. He knew what was coming. He could hear them moving up the front path like a swarm of locusts descending on him. *The ladies had come for another visit.* Chewy yapped excitedly at the front door.

Sighing, he tugged the knot of his robe tighter and went to open the door. Presumably someone had their hands full.

Grace tumbled over the threshold first. "*Oh!* Oh, hello, baby! Aren't you a little pumpkin?" Grace dropped to her knees just inside the foyer to pet Chewy who promptly threw herself on her puppy back the better to trip the other women pushing through into his entryway.

"Grace, get that dog out from under foot. Claire will trip, and Kate will have our hides if we break the surprise." Grams shrugged out of her coat and hung it on the newel post. She glanced at Ian. "You're not dressed? Are you ill?"

"I'm not ill," he said dodging her cold hand as she attempted to hold it against his forehead.

"Where's the step?" Claire said from behind a large cardboard box.

"Oh, do take care!" Lydia fretted.

"Was this the only box you could find? I'll break my neck." Claire inched her way over the threshold. "Am I in?"

June, another friend of Grams' tugged the door closed behind them. "You're in. Here. Let's bring it into the living room and set up."

"Set up?" Ian said. "What's going on?"

Grace put Chewy down and wrapped Ian in a quick hug. "Oh, don't be grouchy, big brother. You know they're only here to cheer you up."

"Then why are you here?"

"Because, I wanted to tell you in person that whatever is about to happen was *not my idea.*"

"Now you're making me nervous."

"It's okay. They mean well. Just roll with it, and I'll get them out as soon as I can. I know you want your privacy."

"Think of it as a second housewarming party," Grams said from the kitchen. He heard clanging sounds and water running. "Where do you keep your tea? Oh, never mind. Found it."

Grace glanced at his robe. "You might as well get dressed."

He retreated to his room, Chewy yapping on the other side of the closed door, and jerked his arms out of the sleeves of his robe. *Fine.* He'd make nice for twenty minutes and then politely but firmly ask them all to leave.

He yanked the door open after tugging on random clothes and returned to the living room. "So, what's in the box?"

"A surprise!" Lydia nearly shouted, her bright blue gloves fluttering excitedly in front of her.

"Kate discovered something while helping me put away the Christmas decorations in the attic and thought you should have it," Grams said as she uncovered a tray of blueberry muffins. She held it up to him.

"No, thanks," he said.

June, Kate's grandmother, set down a brown paper bag. "She thought it made sense for you to keep these here with the house."

The ladies looked at each other. "Oh, I can't stand it!" Lydia said. "Claire, show him what's in the box!"

Claire opened the box and pulled out…

"A slide projector?" Ian frowned.

June pulled out a couple of square boxes from the bag. "And slides. These were taken by your grandparents, Ian, when your parents first moved in here. Well, into the first house. When Kate found these she knew you would want to have them."

Lydia clasped her hands. "It's like it's all come full circle."

"I've never even seen these," Ian said. "They must be ancient."

Grams took a bite of muffin. "You don't remember, do you? Your grandfather McIntyre was quite the shutterbug, but he was old school technology all the way. We all tried to convince him to try a video camera, but he was stubborn. I got these from your Great Aunt after your grandparents passed on. I forgot I even had them."

Ian stared at the boxes, the projector, the expectant faces of his grandmother and her friends… and then met Grace's strained smile.

His cell phone beeped and he pulled it out of his pocket. A text from Grace appeared on the screen.

Sorry! Told them not 2. Kate is ready to pretend a labor emergency if u need 2 bolt. Just say the word. Luv u!

Ian forced a smile. "Wow. This is…"

"Oh, no!" Grace said, clutching her phone. "Grams, we have to go. It's Kate."

Ian frowned and tried to gesture to Grace that he didn't need rescuing. He could handle this.

But Grace's face had gone white, and he knew she wasn't a good actress.

"Grace? What's going on?" he asked.

"Kate's having contractions. For real. Jim is taking her to the E.R. to get things checked out. I need to go watch Liam and Lily."

"Oh, no," Lydia whispered. "It's too early for that. Isn't it?"

June looked shaky. Kate was her granddaughter, after all. "She's not quite thirty-two weeks. Let's get to the hospital and see what's going on. Time enough to worry then."

Claire marched back to the foyer and started handing out coats. "I'll drive. Enjoy your surprise, Ian."

He nodded woodenly. "I'll be over as soon as I take care of Chewy."

Grams set her hand on his arm. "Might as well stay put until we know more. If you leave now, your caravan of fans will follow, and Kate and Jim don't need that circus right now."

He nodded, an odd tightness in his throat constricting his words. "Sure. Have someone call me."

"We will."

Then they were gone as if someone had popped the celebratory mood like a balloon and the air had all whooshed out around him in a five-minute whirlwind. He looked down at Chewy. She whimpered and cocked her head and he picked her up like the well-trained owner he was.

He carried her into the living room.

Claire had set the projector on the coffee table. A slide carousel sat next to it. Ian plugged in the projector, set the carousel in place and turned the lights off. He pressed the on switch and turned around.

And felt like he'd been sucker punched.

His mom smiled at the camera, she was dressed as Wonder Woman, Dad was dressed as Superman. He and Carter were Ninja Turtles, and Grace was dressed as a Cabbage Patch Kid with a hat hand-crocheted by their mom and a large cardboard box around her decorated to look like packaging.

For some reason he couldn't remember that Halloween. It was funny, because inconsequential things would come to him easily (the chipped tile in the bathroom, the way his dad always winked over mom's shoulder at them when they got fidgety in church) but then days like this, when they were all together, seemed just out of reach, as if those times never existed.

His mom posed, impossibly beautiful and happy, gesturing to the plaque by the front door that read *home is where the heart is*. He remembered the plaque, at least. It had gold, yellow and white flowers around the words. His mom had been at the dining room table for days hand-painting it after watching some crafting show on TV. She was always doing little projects like that. She'd been quite proud of it. Once when they were older and he and Carter had gotten into a scuffle in the front yard—he couldn't even remember why now—she'd hauled them apart and pointed to the plaque by the front door. *Some day you, your brother and Gracie will be the only family you have. You'd better learn to get along.*

She was dead before the end of the year.

He'd punched Carter. He remembered the Halloween picture now. Carter had made some under-the-breath jibe at Ian as they'd stood there for the picture, and Ian had punched him. Or pushed him. The details were fuzzy. His dad had threatened them with Kryptonite. Ian had denied doing anything even though Carter had stumbled forward. Mom told them she'd use her Lasso of Truth on them both.

Then Grace had thrown up all over her knitted Cabbage Patch braids mom had spent a week crocheting because she'd gotten into the candy stash, and he and Ian were sent inside for laughing about it.

He stared at the silent image, the memories flooding back. As if he were a kid again, he felt a bubble of unconscious laughter gurgle in his throat. Then it emerged as a croaking noise. Then another. And before he could control it, horrible, ugly noises that weren't laughter after all bubbled up from inside him. Ugly, awful convulsions he didn't know what to do with.

Sobbing. He was sobbing, and it *hurt* and then Chewy was licking his face. He realized there were tears, and he slid to the floor, his dog in his arms. He stroked her head and let her slobber over him and cried for the family that was never, ever coming home.

Then he cried for the home he could never, ever rebuild. No matter how hard he tried. No matter how much money he made. No matter how much everyone tried to help him forget.

Because… *he remembered.*

He remembered.

He stared at the image and cried until there was nothing else inside him but the raw, empty place grief had carved there… until the light faded in the sky... until Chewy had fallen asleep, too tired to lick his tears away... until he'd had enough and reached over to unplug the projector so that the memories would fade. And he could go back to forgetting.

He forced himself to think of the future. The dog. Jim's twins. The show. Bailey.

No, not Bailey—*Helen.*

But try as he might, there was no forgetting. Instead, memories came flooding back from his childhood, from the show, from midnight lightsaber battles with Bailey to the image of Helen's serene smile as she lay on Main Street, Chewy cradled in her arms...

He swiped a hand down over his face.

There was no denying the woman was amazing. Truly.

And choosing her should be easy.

But it wasn't.

Marcia was right. She'd handed him his future on a silver platter tied up with a neat little bow, and he'd made a mess of it all. The worst part was how he was hurting people in the process. Women who had put their emotions out there and their lives on hold, waiting for him to figure out what in hell he wanted out of life.

He hadn't anticipated, though, how much building the house would change him—how nostalgic it would make him for a life that had ended twenty years ago... how much it would make him remember particular flashes of the tragedy. One minute you were happy and expecting and alive and the next you were surrounded by emergency sirens.

He imagined it that way. He'd been at a sleepover the night his parents died. All the kids had been. All the grief and tragedy and anguish... The smell of the fire and the heat of the flames... The urgency of emergency crews... all of it had only ever been in his imagination.

And the worst part was he remembered how much fun he'd had. While his parents were dying, desperately trying to reach one another, he'd been eating popcorn, telling ghost stories and making shadow puppets on Derrick's bedroom wall with his flashlight. He'd been living while they'd been dying.

Chewy whimpered at his feet, and he picked her up, her round puppy belly warm in his arms. She licked his face. Then he realized she was licking new tears he couldn't hold back.

He buried his face in her fur, his breath shuddering out.

What do you do when life turns upside down? What was there to do? There was nothing to do now but wait.

"Let's go watch a movie, Chewy," he finally said.

"I JUST TALKED TO GRAMS," Grace said on the other end of the phone. "Kate and the babies are fine, but there's a slight amniotic fluid leak. Kate's got an IV, and they're keeping her on bed rest for now."

A weight lifted from his chest even though Chewy lay across it snoring softly. "Thank God. Thanks for calling."

"No prob. And I may be calling you to spell me with babysitting duties seeing as Liz and Carter aren't back yet."

"Be happy to."

"Okay. I've gotta go. I have a Candy Land date with Liam."

"Have fun."

They said their goodbyes. Ian gave Chewy one last hug and then scootched out from under her off the new leather recliner. He grinned crookedly. He'd never forget that night sitting here with Bailey in the old bean bag chairs. He wondered if she would forget. Had she already?

He climbed the stairs to the kitchen for a drink and caught sight of the framed picture of his mom and dad that Kate had given him.

He walked toward it. Maybe it was the awful way things had ended with Bailey or the anxiety in the air over Kate and the babies, but suddenly he felt overwhelmed by the memories. The loss. The gaping, family-sized hole in his heart that had never been filled. And he was overcome with the overpowering need to hold someone. *To be held.*

The grief counselor Aunt Joan had sent him to after the fire had told him it could take years to fully grasp what had happened and how it affected him—that he might never be able to put it into words, and that was okay.

At age eight, he thought it was a goofy thing to say. At age thirty-four, he knew it was total bullshit. He could entirely grasp what had happened, he knew exactly how it affected him, and he had more words about the tragedy than he had people to listen.

He looked again at the photo. At his beautiful mother and smiling father. He thought of Helen—beauty-queen pretty like his mother had been. Sweet, capable and perfect for him in so many ways. He thought about what it would be like to tell Helen, to share with her this awful aching emptiness that threatened to consume him.

When he thought about confiding in her, he knew she would hold him and wrap him in compassion...

And suddenly, he knew what he had to do.

He had to quit screwing around pretending he didn't know what he wanted out of life. He *knew.* He knew with the clarity of a starry mid-winter night sky. He knew with the force of frigid January air in his lungs.

He chuckled a bit to himself, a low laughter that had everything to do with irony and nothing to do with humor.

He'd always thought that change was hard—gut-wrenching and traumatic—like having your parents wrenched from your eight year-old life. But now he realized that although change is hard, choices can be harder. Making a choice means accepting the outcome of that choice, whether you could foresee it or not.

Still, *he chose Bailey*.

He thought about Bailey fainting in his arms. Chewy's ridiculous, sparkly leash. The night of the rehearsal dinner when he and Bailey faced each other in the cabin, naked in more ways than one. He'd made the choice then to reveal things he'd held inside for too long. And she'd listened to him. Challenged him. Held him. *Loved him.*

For once it wasn't about what a woman could give him, but about what he could be for her. How he felt when he was with her—and what he did not feel. Not lost. Not orphaned. Not alone.

He wanted to hold and protect her even though she'd resist him every step of the way.

He was wrong. Falling in love shouldn't be easy.

It should be transforming. It should pull you out of where you're hiding and shake your world upside down.

It should slap you aside the head and tell you to wake up.

It should kick you in the shin.

He had no idea if after everything that had happened between them whether Bailey would give him another chance. But, for the first time in a long, long while, he wasn't making a choice out of fear but out of hope. Hope for the life and happiness his parents had. He couldn't be afraid of the fires to come. He couldn't live his life worrying he might lose it all.

That wasn't living.

That was dying.

Marcia was right. When you're challenged, when you're faced with the question of whether to push forward together or part ways, the choice becomes clear.

It becomes beautifully, crystal clear.

He picked up the phone before he lost his nerve. Or, more, before something else threatened to intervene, because now that he knew his path, a sweet serenity seeped through him. He heard Marcia's voice and it was quickly replaced with excited anticipation. He was doing this. He was really and truly doing this.

For the first and last time.

"Marcia, it's Ian." He looked back at the picture. So many people would say he was making a mistake, but he knew he wasn't. "I've... You were right. I should have trusted the process more. I'm... I'm ready to propose."

Silence met him for the first time in any conversation with Marcia. "Well, shitake mushrooms. You have me speechless."

He sucked in a shaky breath, emotion hard in his chest. *Shitake mushrooms.* It's exactly what Bailey would have said. He blew out a long, steadying breath. As much as this was going to disappointment some people, one woman really, he knew it was time to commit to a path. "I'm ready."

"You damned well better be." Static came over the line as if Marcia were juggling some things on the other end. "Okay, we're shaking things up. I'm not letting you squirrel your way out of this one. We'll do the finale live. If you're committing to this woman, you're doing it on live TV, do you hear me? *Ack!* This gives me only two days to pull this crapfest together, so don't screw me over, Ian. My ass is on the line. You're absolutely sure?"

"I am. I promise. I don't want to mess this up either."

Not this time.

CHAPTER THIRTY-THREE

BAILEY STOOD AT THE front window of Lucky's, every preparation she saw being made causing her heart to squeeze a little tighter. There were box trucks full of supplies and dozens of crew members running around—a perfectly efficient chaos of construction and food prep and traffic control as the *Happily Ever After* crews prepared for the finale.

So this is how Marie Antoinette felt looking out her window.

Marcia had called back her troops from wherever she stored her evil minions, and there'd been a flurry of activity over the last 48 hours, transforming the everyday common in the center of town into a magical wonderland of twinkling lights and silver sparkles and starry ice and snow sculptures.

The air of excitement and tight-lipped activity could only mean one thing: Ian was going to propose.

She'd seen it before, of course, in prior seasons of the show. Everyone knew the bachelor narrowed it down to two final women and then they made a big to-do of him dumping one woman and leaving her broken-hearted and sobbing ugly mascara-streaked tears at the camera. Then he proposed to the other.

No. None of it was a surprise.

And yet… even though she *knew* it was coming, was prepared for the inevitable 'final end' of this thing she had had with Ian which, let's be honest, had lasted a whole lot longer than any other relationship she'd ever had, it gutted her in a way she hadn't anticipated.

She'd expected to feel at least a trifle satisfied that she'd predicted the outcome. She wasn't taken by surprise this time.

And yet she was.

She hated, *hated,* to admit that she'd held out a small ember of hope that she and Ian would be different. They'd break the rules about couples like them. A girl from the trailer park and a hot, tech millionaire. They'd show everyone.

Marcia's assistant, Ivy, said they didn't want Bailey until nearly nine o'clock. Frankly, she was still in disbelief she had any role in the show at all. She'd protested an appearance on the finale seeing as everyone in Sugar Falls must know she and Ian had broken it off, but Marcia had simply waved her contract in her face.

Bailey wondered how long it would take for Ian to dump the proverbial 'hometown girl' on live TV. Five minutes? Would they drag it out to ten?

She fought hot, angry tears as they threatened the back of her eyes and tightened her fists at her sides. She *wanted* to be angry at Ian for leading her on, even though he hadn't. She *wanted* to rail at Marcia for making her fall for him, even though she hadn't.

She wanted to hate Helen.

But she didn't.

Helen had done nothing wrong. The woman couldn't help that she was beautiful and kind and talented and in love with Ian. She couldn't help that she was the perfect match and Bailey wasn't.

Aargh! It sucked. All of it sucked and *hurt* and the worst part was that there was some, small traitorous part of her that was almost *happy* for Ian. He would finally get what he wanted. Despite the misery it cost her, she wanted him to be happy.

Even if it wasn't with her.

She swiped her eyes because a few of those tears had managed to spill over and turned away from the window. She only had to make it through tonight now. After tonight, it would all be over.

"Bailey, can you prep the cutlery? Skye is over to the bakery getting more desserts. I have a feeling we'll be hopping tonight like water in hot oil." Wanda swept by on her way to restocking condiments for the tables.

"Sure. No problem." *Rolling utensils in napkins is what I live for.*

Wanda glanced up as she unscrewed a row of salt shaker tops. "Any word yet on your mom?"

"What?" Bailey swept another knife and fork into its napkin jelly roll. *One down. Two hundred to go.* "Um, no. Not yet."

"I know you're worried, hon. We all are. Whatever happens, we're here for you."

"I know." Bailey swallowed hard and looked up. "Thanks."

Wanda started pouring salt, little white grains dancing on the tray around the shakers. "If you need to knock off early this afternoon, I can cover for you. I know you said you were fine helping, but—"

"They don't want me until later. I'm okay." Apparently they didn't need to unduly prepare her for sacrificing herself on national TV. She wondered whether they'd even have Ian talk to her at all. Maybe they'd go straight to his proposal to Helen? Ivy said they'd never done a live finale before, so who knew what would happen? Ivy had asked Bailey to be at hair and makeup by seven. The show started at nine. She wondered what one should wear to a break-up.

Why even bother dressing up at all? It would serve Marcia right if she showed up in a flannel shirt and jeans. Then there'd be no surprise about who Ian chose in the end.

Or…

Bailey's hands stilled.

Or maybe she could leave on her own terms.

"On second thought, Wanda. I think I will take you up on that offer."

Wanda smiled encouragingly. "Sure thing, hon."

BAILEY BURST THROUGH the door, short of breath, not bothering to hang her coat on the hook as she threw it toward the couch on her way by. "Mom? You home? Mom?"

Bailey pushed open her mother's bedroom door. Sandi sat on the edge of the bed, silent, the phone on the comforter beside her.

"Mom?"

Sandi raised her eyes. They were bright with unshed tears.

Bailey took a halting step forward, but then she understood, and the earth fell away beneath her feet and she stumbled to her knees. She fumbled to grasp her mother's hand. "You've heard."

Sandi nodded. "Yes," she managed.

"Then…?"

Her mother swallowed, a ghost of some unreadable emotion passing across her expression before her face crumpled, fear and grief crushing Bailey at the same time her mother's arms came around her.

"Oh, mom…" So this was it. This is what it was going to be like when she learned her mother had cancer. Oh God. She'd prepared for this. Each day she'd schooled herself to grieve in advance so she could be strong when the time came, and already, she could feel herself growing numb, the ice seeping in to harden her heart for what she must face.

What they both must face.

"It's benign," her mother whispered. "Honey, it's benign."

And then the ice crumbled before it had a chance to fully form, melting into tears of relief instead of tears of grief which only served to make Bailey cry harder. *"Oh, mom."* And they hugged and cried and laughed and cried some more until her mother set her aside and grabbed the tissue box from the dressing table and their hands collided as they yanked out tissues by the fistful.

Bailey blew her nose noisily, the joy of relief mixing with the dread of certain heartache to come. Somehow, though, it calmed her to cry now. It emptied the vulnerable places inside so she could face with dignity what was still to come. She wouldn't cry on live TV. She wouldn't give Marcia that.

No. She'd do this *her* way.

It seemed ironic that her mother's news had given her back her heart in time for it to be broken again.

But she wouldn't run away. Not this time.

She squared her shoulders and took a shaky, steadying breath.

"Mom. I've got a favor to ask of you…"

CHAPTER THIRTY-FOUR

IT DIDN'T TAKE LONG for the good news of Sandi's test results to ripple through the crowd at Lucky's. No one had talked about it in the weeks leading up to the biopsy results, and yet everyone seemed to wear a smile of relief tonight that only added to the anticipation of *Happily Ever After*'s finale.

Bailey's gut felt like she'd eaten bad seafood.

Without the responsibility of working a shift, she had far too much time on her hands. Customers camped out at tables without expectation of moving for the duration. The show had erected a giant movie screen at the far end of the common so the crowds could watch from outside, but it was a cold night, and draft beers were only three dollars. Daniel was back, manning the taps and grinning like a fool despite the fact that his daughter would be publicly humiliated in a couple short hours for the entertainment of TV viewers nationwide.

She wished Liz and Carter were back from their honeymoon. It was hard not having her BFF here. Not that Liz would understand. She still believed fairytales came true.

Bailey snorted and glanced at the neon ad-sign clock above the bar. It would soon be time to report for hair and makeup. She wondered where Helen was. And Ian. Both of them were, no doubt, sequestered somewhere before the big reveal. She'd witnessed an escort of clustered handlers come in a short time ago and hustle someone that looked a lot like Ian into the opera house.

No. She was on her own. She stepped out the back door of Lucky's to go sit in her car to wait. Without warning, a slim figure hidden beneath a low baseball cap and cloaked in a parka ducked between cars. Bailey sat upright.

What in hell—*Helen?*

Bailey gawked at the poor disguise—hell, she'd recognize those ungainly long limbs anywhere—as Helen snuck toward the neighboring opera house. Wait a minute. Was she sneaking in to see Ian? Before the show? Was that even allowed? And, more importantly, why?

IAN PACED IN THE SMALL backstage room of the opera house, too restless to sit. So many things could go wrong tonight.

He ran a hand through his hair and blew out a steadying breath. He could do this. At the end of the night all the anxiety and preparations would be worth it. And the woman he had to finally and publicly let go would understand why his heart was with another.

He heard the door snick open behind him and turned, ready to send whomever it was packing, but the words died on his tongue. "Helen?"

"Can I come in?"

She pushed in and leaned back against the closed door as if uncertain of her welcome.

"What are you doing here?"

She grimaced and pushed away from the door, worrying the ball cap in her hand. "What I have to say is something I don't want to say for all the world before I say it to you. This deserves to be said in private."

She stepped forward, a muscle in her cheek working. "I… I want to tell you that I'm so grateful to have had the chance to come on the show, because it's opened my eyes to something I've been blind to for a very long time."

She smiled then, a tentative tilt to her lips. Dread settled in Ian's gut.

"Helen, you don't have to…"

"No. I want to say this. I know it's kind of a given at this point, but you've been so, so sweet throughout this process, and I forgive you for that moment back in Antigua when you didn't propose. I understand now. I know how hard it is to open yourself up to love."

"I never, ever wanted to hurt you. Either of you."

"You haven't. I mean, at the time it hurt, but every relationship has to go through a challenge or two, right? That's what Marcia always says. It makes us more certain of what we want."

"Yes, it does."

"All along," she said, "I've been trying so hard. You've no idea how hard… to make up for the loss of my mother. To be everything to everyone. And I want you to be the first to know… I'm quitting. I'm selling my business. I'm so sick of making sweets. I'm not even allowed to eat them, or I'll get fat. I'm so tired of the good ol' boys who talk down to me and want to marry me only to keep me barefoot and pregnant. I want to eat *beef stew* and bangers and mash, whatever they are, and drink coffee even though it stains my teeth. And I don't ever want to settle for being the runner up."

He stared at her, her eyes bright with unshed tears, not certain he understood where this was all going.

She held his gaze. "And because I know you need to hear this before you go out on live TV, I want you to know that I've *never* been more certain…"

"You don't have to—" Oh God. Had he misread her?

"…that I don't love you."

Ian stilled.

She smiled. "*Phew!* That was harder than I thought it would be, but it feels so *good* to get it out there."

"You don't love me? Are you sure?"

She shook her head, relief written all over her features. "No. No, I don't." She cupped his cheek with her good hand. "I'm sorry."

He pulled her into a hug, careful not to squash her injured arm. "Thank God."

CHAPTER THIRTY-FIVE

MARCIA SIGHED A HAPPY SIGH. The finale was always a bit bittersweet for her. Of course, it was gut-wrenching to the viewers who watched the runner up reduced to tears and heartbreak. Tonight they'd double the heartbreak, but the reward in the end… She'd be lying if she didn't admit it gave her a bit of a high to think about it.

Tonight they would knock the ratings out of the park.

She glanced over to where Nick was fussing with a piece of equipment, directing the lighting crew in last minute prep. The big proposal in the end wasn't the only trick she had up her sleeve tonight.

She saw Ivy come in the side door of the opera house and give her a thumbs-up. She nodded. Yes, tonight would be *perfect.*

After a last-minute check in hair and makeup, Marcia strode confidently to where she'd be narrating the finale. They had an outdoor dais set up, like a snowy cupid's cloud, and it made her feel a little hokey and powerful stepping up onto it. Nick winked at her.

She waited for her countdown, then her cue…

Then she smiled warmly at the camera, a rush of adrenaline shooting through her. She welcomed the viewers. She was live. On national TV. Anything could happen. And it would all go according to plan.

The big screen came to life and the audience turned in their white beribboned chairs to view it. Damn if it didn't look just like a wedding.

Marcia stood back to watch their reaction as the pre-recorded segments played out before them. Their perplexed glances as they realized Bailey wasn't one of the final two on that beach in Antigua, that it was Mary Beth and Helen. The excited chatter during commercial break and then the gasps of surprise as they watched Ian tell each of the women… "I'm sorry. I just don't see myself rushing into a burning building for you."

More gasps and a few boo's rippled through the crowd and then Marcia stepped into place again as the screen cut to her on her cupid's cloud.

"You might think that's the end of our love story, but I'm here to reassure you we still have more to come. You see, one of our final two women wasn't ready to take no for an answer." A brief clip of Helen carrying cupcakes up Ian's front steps flashed on screen and then cut to Bailey opening the door. "Yes, this *may be* the most dramatic season finale ever." She chuckled for the camera, her image smiling back at her from the large screen. "But first, let's take a look at Ian's journey so far. You won't want to miss a single moment as we count down to the dramatic conclusion of this season of *Happily Ever After!*"

They cut to commercial and Marcia unclipped her microphone and stepped over to Nick. "Come with me."

"What? Where?"

"Just come with me. Don't worry. Ivy will get me when it's time. We've got a commercial break and a twenty-minute montage of Ian's journey before I need to be back. And there's something I want to do. Tonight. *Please.*"

That got his attention. She seldom said please.

It was surprisingly easy to fade into the shadows and sneak down behind the buildings. Ivy held the door and Marcia grinned as Nick frowned. It was fun to throw him off balance for a change, her rock.

She gripped his hand and pulled him in, her nose wrinkling. Okay, maybe it wasn't the most romantic spot on earth, but it was the only place she could guarantee would be empty.

The smell of old motor oil and decades of dirt surrounded them. Nick frowned. "What's going on?"

"I have something to say, and I wanted to say it tonight before I lost my nerve."

"Go ahead."

Her hands shook. She liked how his felt warm and steady as he held them. "You've known me a long time, even when I was still married to Ed." She sucked in a breath. "And you've stuck by me, even when I'm at my worst which, I know, is often."

His lips tilted a bit.

"You've watched me pour blood, sweat and tears into this job and you, more than anyone, know how much it means to me to get it right. But for the first time," her breath hitched a bit, but she kept going, "for the first time, I didn't see a match coming, and that shook my confidence. But you, you never wavered. Through everything, you never wavered. I love that about you. I love you," she finished on a whisper, her heart on her sleeve, waiting for his reaction.

She wasn't disappointed. His usually taciturn face lit from within. "Damn, woman. It's about time you admitted that." And he grabbed her face and pulled her in and she didn't give a hoot about whether they'd have to redo her lipstick before she went live again. It was worth it to have Nick upsetting all her plans. Oh, how she loved this man.

She pulled back, breathing fast, her pulse thundering now. "I'm not done. We don't have much time, but… wait here."

"As you wish," he grinned.

She slipped out of his grasp and through the closed door behind her and turned. *Yes!* Ivy had worked her magic. The old back room had been transformed. Where before there'd been big empty barrels and crates, Ivy had tacked up white sheeting and spread the room with candles in jars just like that Liz had done at the wedding.

Marcia didn't care if it wasn't how things were done. She'd done the thing where she let the man take charge in the past, and that'd left her heartbroken. From now on, she was taking charge of her love life.

And that started with the proposal.

She grabbed the lighter Ivy had left and quickly lit all the candles. Okay, it took a few minutes, but when she was done, it looked gorgeous. Breathtaking.

She hurried back out, closing the door behind her.

Nick waited by the entrance.

She smiled and reached out to grasp his hand… and was thrown to the floor when the room exploded behind her, hurtling the door she'd just passed through at her back.

CHAPTER THIRTY-SIX

BAILEY HAD BEEN WATCHING the large screen on the common from inside Meg's salon when the explosion occurred. A brilliant flash of orange and then shock waves of pressure slammed her eardrums like a sonic boom.

She'd been watching the video montage of Ian's history. Old pictures of his mom as a Mrs. New Hampshire pageant contestant. A segment from when Treasure Trakker won some video game award of the year. Then they'd moved on to vignettes of him from the show.

She watched Mary Beth cry and then smile as she reunited with her pediatric patients and a doctor that looked like he had his eye on her. She watched Helen's stricken face when Ian sent her home. Her dad welcomed her with a wordless hug, then Helen visited her mother's grave and set a cupcake on top as sappy, sentimental music played in the background. Gag. That must have been Marcia's idea.

Clearly, it was a set-up for how happy they planned to make Helen in the end.

There was no footage of crazy, obsessed, 'can't-get-over-him' hometown Bailey.

That was her last thought before all hell broke loose. At first she thought it was a terrorist attack. Then she realized where the flash of light and thunderous noise had originated and knew there was a much more likely explanation.

Bailey burst out the front door of the salon and looked kitty-corner down the street to her garage. In flames.

She didn't think as she hiked up her white skirts and dashed toward the wreckage. Broken glass and twisted pieces of unrecognizable building littered the road as smoke and airborne debris choked her.

Or maybe those were tears. She was watching her dream literally go up in flames.

Rescue crews and others rushed from the town common toward the site, shouting at one another to 'move it' and 'get back' and then she noticed the two bodies, one crouched over the other on the sidewalk in the midst of the debris still raining down.

"You need to move!" she shouted, stumbling toward them, bits of hot ash falling around them like the scene of an action movie. But it didn't feel thrilling. It felt terrifying.

"Is anyone else in there?" Bailey gasped, and then she tripped on the damned dress and fell to the ground near them. "Nick? *Marcia?*"

Nick shook his head and looked at her, eyes bright and a bit manic. *Shock.* "Just us. It was just us," he said. "No one else was around."

Bailey tugged at them to stand up. "We need to get out of here."

Nick nodded, swept Marcia into his arms, and they stumbled toward the common through the crush of people who were already surging toward the accident. Ivy waved and pushed toward them, camera crew and staff trailing behind her like ducklings caught in a hurricane.

When Ivy reached them, she gasped and barked to one of the crew members. "Marcia's hurt! We need an ambulance!" Ivy turned back to Nick. "How bad is she hurt?"

"Nothing a good long soak in a hot tub won't fix." Marcia pulled her face away from Nick's flannel shirt. She looked dazed. Dirty. A red smear of blood crossed her temple. One high heel was broken, twisted and dangling. And, impossibly, improbably, she *smiled.*

She pushed her normally sleek hair out of her face. "Ivy. I hope to God you're getting this on camera."

Ivy motioned to the cameraman behind her to keep filming and then Marcia's battered visage blinked to life on the large screen at the end of the common. Ivy's voice shook. "We go live in twenty…"

Bailey turned to Nick. "Nick? Are you okay?" He was still ashen, but he seemed to be gaining equilibrium. He helped Marcia balance on her one good heel.

"He's fine. We're both fine. Just a bit stunned. He'll be fine." Marcia straightened her no-longer white jacket and allowed a handler to smooth her hair a bit… but not too much.

Nick tucked his chin down. "Speak for yourself, woman. You nearly blew us up back there!"

"You were *in* there?" Bailey asked.

"How was I to know there'd be explosive stuff in there?" Marcia asked.

"They were in the fire!" someone remarked excitedly from behind the camera crew.

Marcia turned to those pressing near to get a better view. "He saved me," she said pointing to Nick and squeezing one of his biceps.

"Marcia was nearly killed!" someone else gasped.

A crowd began to form around them despite emergency crews racing by.

Ivy leaned forward. *"And live in three... two...!"*

Marcia squared her shoulders. "Welcome back, America! *Phew!* Well, we've had a bit of excitement here during the break, but we're all fine and Sugar Falls' finest are on the job, so no reason to worry. I'm here to tell you that the flames behind me are *nothing* compared to the relationships heating up on this season of *Happily Ever After.* I know I've said it before, but this may be the *most* dramatic season *ever.* We've watched Ian's journey from his tragic past to his professional triumph, and now, tonight, we'll get to see—"

"Excuse me, ma'am. There's still an explosive risk here. I'm going to have to ask you and everyone else to step back for your own safety." Jeff Dayton made sweeping motions with his arms toward them as firefighting crews pushed forward to fight the blaze. A siren sounded as a pumper truck pulled out from the fire station around the corner.

Marcia smoothed her hair back so the camera could get a good look at her forehead gash. "We're live, officer."

Jeff frowned at the camera and then turned back to her. "Only if you move out of harm's way, ma'am."

Marcia scootched en masse with cameramen and spectators to a spot further away and smiled for the at-home audience. "Yes, well I've already survived that fire thanks to this man right here," she said for Jeff's benefit. She turned to Nick. "The man I love."

"He saved you?" someone asked.

"Yes, that's right. We had candles and there was an explosion and this man carried me to safety."

She leaned conspiratorially toward the camera. "Yes, ladies, it was as hot and romantic as it sounds. Sadly, I never did get a chance to ask him—"

Nick put a finger on Marcia's lips and winked at the camera. "I'll take it from here if you don't mind," he said. Marcia went silent as he grasped her hands in his. "Marcia, my love, you've made dozens of happily-ever-afters for others. Now it's time you had your own."

He brought her hands up to kiss her knuckles much to the swooning delight of the crowd. "I love you, and I'd walk through flames every day of my life if it meant I got to spend it holding you." More swoons and *aww*'s as sirens sounded in the background. The crowd on the common stared raptly at the big screen. Then Nick knelt on the slush-covered sidewalk and the crowd gasped and squealed with anticipation. "Marcia? Will you do me the honor of becoming my wife?"

Marcia's face crumpled as she hiccoughed out a 'yes' and then the crowd roared with applause across the common. The happy couple kissed, and when she had her breath back, Marcia thanked the viewers and apologized for the need to cut for commercial.

As the large screen went to a placeholder image for the break, Marcia cast a warm gaze across the street toward the opera house. Bailey followed her gaze. Ian and Helen stood together, Ian's arm protectively around Helen's shoulder.

Ivy's cell phone rang. She wordlessly handed it to Marcia who frowned and asked who it was.

"Your boss."

"Shit." Marcia took the phone. "Christian!"

Marcia nodded. "Yes, sir… I understand… Absolutely… Okay." She passed the phone back to Ivy without saying goodbye.

"I take it he saw the proposal," Nick deadpanned.

"He did. He says he's shocked."

"He's not the only one," Ivy muttered.

Marcia shook her head as if stunned. "He says social media is going crazy. 'Best season ever,' they're saying." She looked at Nick. "He says it was fantastic, and he's pushing for a bonus for us. He wants us to do it all again next season."

Nick pulled her into a hug. "That's fantastic!"

Marcia pulled back from him, ashen. "Fantastic? How do I recreate *this?*" She gestured to the chaos around them.

"I see what you mean. We might not have a budget for explosives."

"Nick, I didn't make this happily-ever-after. It happened despite me! *To* me!"

Nick gripped her shoulders. "Not true. You always say if two people are meant to be together, they'll overcome any challenge you throw at them. I'd say we did that tonight."

She frowned, thinking. "I do say that, don't I? I am *awesome!*"

"That you are," Nick grinned. "That you are."

Bailey stepped back and stumbled on the hem of her dress. She fell against Marcia, of all people.

Marcia put out a hand, choking on her laughter. "What in God's name are you wearing? Is that a Halloween costume? Who in wardrobe is punking me?"

Bailey's face flamed.

And then she saw—through the smoke and chaos and fire hoses snaking down Main Street—Ian holding hands with Helen. He leaned in to listen to something she said, and then pulled away, *smiling.* Who smiled during such a disaster? A man in love, that's who.

Bailey's gut twisted as he reached out and pulled Helen toward him, enfolding her in his arms like a treasure. And if that weren't enough, he leaned down and *kissed her!*

For some reason, Bailey couldn't look away. She forced herself to watch what she'd lost. Maybe she deserved to be heartbroken and humiliated. Maybe she deserved to feel this way for letting pride and doubt get in the way. But whether or not she deserved it, she didn't intend to wait around for Ian to tell the world it was over between them, and he was engaged to Helen. Nothing could be more obvious.

She backed away from Marcia and Nick and the rest of them, Ian's massive check like a stone in her pocket. She didn't feel the need to tear it up in his face anymore. She could mail it, thank you very much.

And she'd watch his happily-ever-after on television like everyone else.

CHAPTER THIRTY-SEVEN

WHEN IAN HAD FIRST heard the blast, his heart had climbed his throat. He'd rushed to the street only to see Bailey's beloved garage engulfed in flames.

Then, further down, he'd seen the small white-robed form dash through the wreckage like some other-worldly being. She stumbled and fell, and a colorful curse sliced the air. He'd been one heartbeat away from racing toward her when the trio had pulled themselves up and moved toward the common and away from him. Safe.

Then emergency crews were there, and Ian had pitched in to help evacuate people out the rear entrance of the opera house, and by the time he was back on Main Street, he'd come across Helen.

They watched the proposal together, and then Helen had wished him good luck. He'd thanked her, kissed her on the cheek, ready to go find his woman.

But she'd disappeared.

"Where'd she go?" Ian burst through the gawkers lingering near the cordoned off area around emergency crews. "Where's Bailey?"

Marcia waved a hand. "She was right here. Can't miss her. She's dressed in the most ridic—"

Her white princess gown.

Marcia yanked off her broken heel and put the shoe part back on her foot. "Somebody had better find her. I've got a live finale to finish here."

Shit!

He'd blown it.

He'd *known* the finale would look like some run-up to his proposing to Helen. Marcia told him it would. She said it would make the crowd go wild with excitement when they realized who he was really proposing to.

But now Bailey's dream had just gone up in flames and, worse, she thought he was proposing to someone else.

Where would she be? Where would she go to lick her wounds?
Then he knew.

 "I know where she probably is," Ian said. "Follow me."

CHAPTER THIRTY-EIGHT

BAILEY WAS GLAD SHE couldn't see the big movie screen from the back steps of Lucky's. She didn't want to see the charred remains of her beloved garage on the nightly news. If Liz were back from the last stop of her honeymoon, visiting her parents in Florida, she'd probably make a joke about how things tended to blow up around them. But she wasn't.

Bailey was on her own.

She struggled to open the back door of Lucky's as if it would open by sheer force of will, but the restaurant was empty, evacuated because of the accident. She sank onto the metal landing and hugged her knees.

A part of her felt like crying, but the space inside that made the tears didn't have the energy to put toward it. Crying meant she still held out hope for something that would never be.

And she had no hope left.

She'd risked it all. And she was left with nothing.

Okay. So Ian wanted Helen after all. Helen probably wouldn't move here, because she had that chain of cupcake bakeries down south. So when they inevitably had sex, because—hello?—Helen was drop-dead gorgeous, at least their adorable babies wouldn't be running around the streets of Sugar Falls advertising for years what Bailey had lost because she'd been more concerned about getting her hands on that garage than making it work with Ian.

As if a garage would keep her warm at night or make her laugh or tell her, when she was old and shriveled, that she was still 'hot.' And at the end of her days, would it be enough to have rotated thousands of tires over the years?

Aargh. She'd end up as pathetic as Sully—hoping someone else would carry through on the potential she'd never acted upon.

She shivered and swept a hand over the smudged, wrinkled fabric of her dress. Why had she even worn it? What had she been trying to prove?

"That I was brave," she said aloud. She'd wanted to show everyone she was brave enough to be herself not just in front of the judges of that long-ago pageant but in front of the world—or at least the viewing public of *Happily Ever After.*

She'd wanted to prove that it didn't matter to her what anyone else thought.

Yet, here she was, alone, hiding in a back alley. She tried to run a hand through her hair and realized she still had the ridiculous twin buns in place. Ugh.

She wasn't brave. She was a coward.

She was a woman who fainted at the sight of blood, ran away from her troubles and hid from the world when things got tough.

Enough already. It was time she stopped feeling sorry for herself.

It was time she figured out that it wasn't all about her.

Not even this time.

She stood up and smoothed out the dress.

She stepped off the last step, and lights flashed across her vision. A group of people appeared at the corner of the building. More lights blinded her.

"Bailey, wait."

She froze, her hand tight on the railing. "Marcia, go away."

"No." Marcia hobbled toward her on uneven shoes, Nick following with his camera. "Not until you get your happily-ever-after."

Bailey sighed. "That's not in the cards for me this time, and we both know it. But that's okay. I'm okay with that." She turned to walk away.

Marcia caught up to her and stopped her with a hand on her arm. "Honey, no one's 'okay' with that. Not even you."

Bailey stood perfectly still, willing herself to be strong, to be brave, but then the truth spilled out, the tears falling soundlessly onto Marcia's hand.

"I can't talk to you," she whispered.

"Can you talk to me?"

Ian.

Bailey raised her eyes and peered through the glare of the camera lights. A murmur went through the small crowd, and then Ian stepped into view. "Hey," he said.

"Hey." She bit her lip as Marcia stepped back.

"I'm sorry," he said. "About your garage and… everything." His arm stretched to encompass the whole of regret that stretched between them before he let it fall to his side again.

Bailey shrugged. "Me, too."

He stepped closer and reached toward her, brushing the pad of his thumb across her cheek. She closed her eyes and absorbed the warmth and concern emanating from that lone point of contact. A cool wind whipped her white dress around her legs.

What a mess. What a horrible, miserable, unforgivable mess.

She could hear the noise from Main Street, could smell the smoke and ash drifting through the night air, could feel silent eyes upon them, but somehow she didn't care. She had some things to say. She could hold her head high if she came clean. It was now or never.

All or nothing.

"I'm sorry, too," she said, forcing herself to look at him. "I'm sorry… I made it so hard to love me."

He shook his head and reached out to grasp her hand. She clutched it as if she were in danger of falling off a cliff, because each truth pushed her closer to the edge. "You didn't—" he said.

She cut him off. "And I'm sorry I made you doubt we could make it work between us, and that I ever let you think, for even a moment, that it was only about the money."

She sucked in a breath, the cold air sharp in her lungs. "But I'm not sorry I fell in love with you. Because falling in love with you made me stronger. It made me see that I've been running away ever since that day I stood in front of the Snow Belle Pageant judges and chickened out.

"I ran into that shop class in high school and turned my back on everything I thought made me weak."

She blew out a hard breath. "But I'm done running. I'm done putting up a good front. I'm a geek at heart. A geek and a romantic… and I secretly love shiny things…" her voice broke. "And I not so secretly love you and wish you and Helen every happiness, and I will always, ever, be grateful for what we had."

He stood, his body rigid, and then his lips curved, beautifully, sadly and she sucked in another hard breath even though her lungs felt as if they might shatter inside her. Her heartbeat thudded in her ears, and then he stepped closer still and wrapped his arms around her. She cried into his shirt, regret soaking it with tears.

"Oh, Bailey. Sweetheart," he soothed. "*Shh…*" He pulled away to look her in the eye. "Honey, Helen and I aren't together."

"You're not?"

"No. You and I are together."

"But I thought—"

"I know. I know what you thought. It's not true."

"But Marcia said you wanted a beauty queen, someone like your mother…"

"Nah. I want someone like my mother as my mother. I'd prefer someone like you as my wi—"

"Stop!" Marcia jumped from behind the cameras. "Not *another* word! I've worked too damn hard for this payoff."

"Wait. What?" Bailey asked, spinning back to Ian. "What were you just saying?"

"Ian!" Grace burst forward from the crowd. "Thank God I've found you. Jim called… Kate…" She caught her breath. "There are complications, and they're talking c-section. He needs someone to watch the kids. I can't find anyone in this mess… My car is parked down by the high school…"

Ian turned apologetic eyes to Bailey even as he grasped her hand and squeezed. "Marcia, I'm going to need a car."

Marcia's mouth gaped open. "What? *Now?* You can't leave now!"

"And we're live in two minutes!" Ivy warned.

"*No!*" Marcia shrieked. "No one is going anywhere! Ivy! Run this clip as-is when we get back from break, then cut to another commercial." She swiped a clump of hair out of her face and glared at Ian and Bailey as if she could pin them in place with her eyes. "That gives me just enough time to keep these two from ruining everything."

She waggled a fierce finger in their faces. "Now listen up! You will *not* steal this moment from me, do you hear? Not *another* word until you are on that common and the cameras are rolling! Babies can damn well *wait!*"

Marcia limped away, barking orders to her swarming assemblage, but Ian tugged Bailey's hand and held her back.

She leaned toward him and whispered, "Did you… did you just propose to me?"

He swore under his breath and ran a hand over his face. "No. Forget that. That was a mistake."

Her heart crashed to her toes. Of course. It was a slip of the tongue. Would she ever learn?

But then he was beside her, gripping her hand tight, his left knee on the ground, looking up at her. "*This* is a proposal," he whispered.

She froze, the air sucked from her lungs, disbelief making her lightheaded.

"It's not the way I planned it," he said. "But I'll be honest. I don't want to share this moment with the world. I want it to be ours and ours alone. I want you to be mine, Bailey Adams. For the rest of our lives. I love you and…"

"Yes!" she cried pulling him up so she could kiss him properly. "*Mmf!* Yes!"

He laughed and dodged her lips. "I haven't even asked you yet."

She smacked him on the arm. "Then hurry up. You heard Ivy. We go live in two minutes."

He smiled. "Don't rush me, woman. I only plan to do this once."

He swallowed and brushed the hair from her temple. His hand shook. Somehow that made it feel real. Her heart beat slow and heavy in her chest. "I've missed you," he said.

"I've missed you, too."

His fingers stroked her cheek again. "It's funny how I always thought I'd know the perfect woman for me by whether I could picture myself running back into a burning building for her."

She held her breath. "Can you?"

"No. Every time I try to imagine it, all I see is you under that damned car, feeling like my heart has stopped, and it'll never start again until I can hold you and feel your heart beating against mine."

His gaze held hers, bright and fierce. "It's not about the fire at all. It's about wanting a person in your life so badly you feel you can do anything, and you'd risk it all for fear you will be left without them, left with nothing. You make me feel that way, Bailey."

She smiled, warmth whispering through her.

"Will you marry me?" he asked.

"*Yes.*" She pulled his face to hers again and kissed him soundly, thoroughly, happiness flashing through her like gleaming sabers in the dark.

CHAPTER THIRTY-NINE

—————————————

Twenty-six years.

Twenty-six years he'd spent looking behind him, reacting, retreating into his own world instead of looking forward and reaching out. All that was about to change.

Bailey had no idea their adventure together had just begun.

She scowled, an elegant brow expressing her emotion. He loved that eyebrow. Loved what it did to him when she turned that look at him. She insisted he account for himself. He grasped her chilled fingers in his hand and tugged her toward the corner of the building. The crowd cheered.

She balked. "You already proposed. It's over. Why do we have to go out there?"

"Because it's not over."

"I—"

He smiled. He couldn't help it. "Trust me, will you? I promise no one will laugh this time."

She nodded and let him lead her out toward the common. A murmur swept through the crowd. The fairy-lights on the bandstand lit back up, then the lights around the common, and the lights in the trees. And then, just as he'd planned it, he heard the distinct flash—*humm*—then another, and another as a rainbow-colored honor guard flashed to life in the hands of dozens of volunteers.

Bailey stared at the spectacle, eyes wide, and for a moment he worried it was too much, but then she laughed and turned to him and squeezed his hand and started running through the glowing archway.

He heard familiar voices wishing them well along the way. His cousin, Rachel. His aunt and uncle. Jeff Dayton. Meg from the hair salon and her four-year-old daughter. And then they slowed to a walk, the crowd eerily quiet as they got closer to the bandstand, emotion tight and hot inside him. There was Grace, "The doctor isn't there yet, so we've got a few minutes," she said. Carter and Liz. "Just got back," said Carter.

Wanda, Phil, Daniel and Sandi—all with tears in their eyes. And then Claire, June, Lydia and Grams. Finally, Helen holding Chewy… *smiling*.

He and Bailey reached the bandstand, and he helped her up the steps as a hundred toy sabers went silent, and then he forgot how to breathe as one of Marcia's crew clipped a microphone to his shirt.

"Well," he finally said, "I bet you're all wondering why I've gathered you here tonight."

A ripple of laughter went through the crowd, but he only had eyes for Bailey. "I love you, Bailey." *Aww*, they said. "And I always wondered what happened at the end, when the Death Star exploded and they all finished rejoicing," he continued. "But now I know. They lived their happily-ever-afters. Those that remained didn't let the tragedies of the past stop them from dreaming about a future.

"And I'm dreaming about my future now—*with you*. And it doesn't have anything to do with a big house on the hill which, by the way, I'm seriously thinking of selling to my cousin. And it doesn't have anything to do with whatever might remain downtown where that garage you planned to open once stood. Our future is right here. It's whatever we choose to make it, and I don't know what that is yet or where, but I can tell you that you're in it. Whatever the future holds, we're in it together."

She nodded and went on tiptoe to kiss him and he forgot his train of thought as her warm sweet lips pressed to his. "I like that." She squeezed his hands. "No, I *love* that. I love *you*."

She glanced nervously at the crowd and continued. "I thought I knew what was ahead for me, but now it's gone, and I realize… it's okay. I'm okay. Losing something big kind of opens up the possibilities for something better.

"I've done some things I'm not too proud of. I've been selfish and stubborn, but finding yourself alone in a back alley in a princess costume gets you thinking." Laughter rippled over the common. "I've saved for a long time to achieve my dream, and now that it's gone up in smoke…" she looked out at the crowd, at the sea of faces there and back at him. "Now, I think I'd like to use that money to make someone else's dreams come true, to help people right here in Sugar Falls who are just starting out get grants and small business loans. People like my mom, who always wanted to own her own salon. Or Frankie Sullivan, who's headed to college now but when he gets back to town, should see me, because that kid… that kid has potential."

She smiled and pulled something from within her dress and held it up to the crowd. "And I'm not alone. Ian McIntyre has agreed to donate fifty thousand dollars to the cause, and I have his check right here!" She waved his dog training check and grinned, and his heart swelled. Oh, yes, life with Bailey would be an adventure. *Treasure Trakker: Life with Bailey Adams.*

Chewy ran up the steps, Helen stumbling up behind her.

"And I will also contribute to the fund," Helen added. "Because I believe in following your heart and happily-ever-afters."

The crowd erupted in cheers, whistles and roaring applause, and he laughed and held Bailey tight to his side, and it didn't even bother him when someone's cell phone rang. For the first time in a long time he was in the thick of it. He was living life right along with everyone else here in Sugar Falls. He wasn't alone.

He was with family.

Grace stepped forward, and he leaned down to hear her. "Uh, Ian? We should get going. They're wheeling Kate into surgery *now*."

Grams fidgeted at the foot of the bandstand and her toy sword flashed on and off. Carter coughed. Liz looked uncertain. Helen raised her eyebrows.

He straightened back up and smiled at his fiancée. "I love you, Sweetheart, but are you thinking what I'm thinking?"

She nodded and shrugged. "Babies wait for no one."

And she grabbed his hand and they dashed down the steps, asking Jeff for a police escort to the hospital as the crowd cheered and laughed around them.

CHAPTER FORTY

THE COFFEE WAS COLD and tasted awful, but she drank it anyway, because her fiancé had walked across the entire hospital to bring it to her. But it wasn't her fault. She couldn't move.

Her future niece was asleep in her arms.

Bailey looked down at Lily's tousled head as it lolled to one side, her sweet, toddler legs dangling off the side of the neighboring chair as she snored softly. She'd been overtired, over-excited and overly-loud when they'd arrived at the hospital, but Jim had to be with Kate in the delivery room, so Grace had taken Liam for a walk and Bailey had offered to entertain the big sister to-be.

She'd read a magazine to Lily which only made her howl for her mommy, so Bailey decided the situation required drastic measures. After twenty minutes of mock dueling and an orderly asking them to quiet down, Lily had thrown her arms around Bailey's neck with a happy sigh and fallen asleep.

Turns out Bailey was good with kids. Who knew?

Ian eased into the seat next to her and stroked a hand over Lily's tangled hair. "Out cold, she is."

"Master, am I," whispered Bailey back at him. They kissed, sweet, pure happiness flowing through her. "Love you, I do," she said.

"Just so we're clear, I will not have sex with you when you do the voice. That's just creepy."

"Even if I wear my fancy undies?"

He seemed to ponder this. "Try this, we might," he said, wiggling his eyebrows. She chuckled and shifted a bit to ease the ache in her arm and back. Okay, yes, they were geeks.

"I expect a ring, you know. Something big and in-your-face. Something to blind Ellen Lambert when I go in to visit my little twin niece and nephew in the pediatric ward."

"Will this do?"

He pulled a box out of his pocket and popped it open. Bailey recognized it as one from that famous jeweler that sponsored the show. She blinked. "Yeah. That'll do. I thought it took you a while to get coffee."

"Almost forgot it, to be honest."

She held out her hand as if it were the most natural thing in the world for a man to slide a ginormous, glittery rock onto her finger. She held it up. "I still have those buns in my hair, don't I?"

"*Mm-hmm*," he said. He grinned. "Trust me when I tell you, they're kind of sexy. Oh! Almost forgot!" He pulled a pink gift-shop bag out of his other pocket and held it out. "I picked something up for the twins."

Bailey pulled two tiny T-shirts out of the bag. She read, *"The Love is Strong with This One."* She looked at Ian and laughed.

"Admit it," he said. "You love that I'm such a geek."

"No," she said, going in for another kiss. "I love *everything* about you."

He leaned back, a satisfied smile on his face, his arm an easy weight across her shoulders. "You know, I'm thinking we should go as Han and Princess Leia for Halloween this year."

"I'm surprised you don't want to be Luke."

"*Meh.* Luke is just an orphan. I'd rather be Han." He winked at her, green eyes dancing. "Han gets the girl."

Dear Reader,

I hope you enjoyed Ian and Bailey's uncommon love story. I have to admit, I'm a total reality dating show junkie, and it was such fun to imagine how the drama and tears and missteps I see on TV might lead to a forever love off-screen.

If you enjoyed *All or Nothing* you won't want to miss the final chapter in the 'Betting on Romance' series with *Deal Me In,* Jeff and Grace's story.

But I'm not leaving Sugar Falls yet. I have all-new adventures planned for Daniel's 'lucky charms' so look for Jack and Helen to kick off the 'Lucky Charm' spin-off series in *The Runaway Cupcake Queen.*

Also, be sure to sign up for my mailing list at www.cheriallan.com to receive invites to exclusive contests and info on new releases!

Sweet regards from Sugar Falls!

~ Cheri

Be sure to start where it all began, with Jim and Kate, in Book One of the 'Betting on Romance' series:

LUCK OF THE DRAW

If only life had a refresh button...

Kate Mitchell never planned to be a 31-year-old widowed single mom, but when her soon-to-be-EX husband up and dies, her dreams of finishing college and starting over are thrown in the air like a game of 52 pick-up. When she's given a leave of absence from work and told to "quit or recommit," Kate retreats to idyllic Sugar Falls, New Hampshire, to figure out whether she can discover her passion and pay the bills. Cue the fresh air, summer sunshine and one sexy local contractor.

Tall, dark, and handy…

Volunteer fireman and all-around hunky guy in a toolbelt, Jim Pearson has sworn off complicated women with messy baggage. They cling to his nice-guy stability and skills with a power saw just long enough to straighten out their lives and move on… but then he meets the cute single mom staying at Grams' lake house for the summer.

While a sizzling attraction draws them together, Jim's distrust of complicated women and Kate's incredibly complicated life threaten to pull them apart. But forces beyond their control—match-making grandmothers, the lazy backdrop of summer, and their own reckoning with the past—conspire to make them risk it all... and bet on love.

Our match-making grandmothers are at it again, *Stacking the Deck* against Liz and Carter in Book Two of the 'Betting On Romance' series:

STACKING THE DECK

Who said coming home is easy?

Liz Beacon has life all planned out—prioritized, color-coded *and* cross-referenced. She long ago traded in the geeky high school nickname, teenage pounds and dysfunctional family for a fab career, killer abs and a man every woman would envy. Okay, so her sex life is non-existent and her almost-fiancé is technically a coworker. Life, if not perfect, is still on track. But then, Liz is called home to Sugar Falls, NH, to prepare her childhood home for sale. She's spent ten years denying her insecurities and hokey lawn-ornament roots. There's nothing she'd rather do less than face all she happily left behind, including her embarrassingly one-sided high school crush.

Carter McIntyre has sailed through life on his winsome smile… and by the skin of his teeth. A college drop-out with ADHD, he's learned it's safer to play the carefree charmer than step up and take over his uncle's landscaping business. But then his class valedictorian returns to Sugar Falls and hires him for some home improvements. Now Carter's wondering if it's too late— to grow up, take a chance and win over the only girl who ever believed in him…

Is the game of love worth the price?
Book Four of the 'Betting On Romance' series:

DEAL ME IN

Grace McIntyre never planned to lose her virginity in a seedy motel to the hottie with the eagle tattoo, but she *knew* he was The One--until a heart-wrenching goodbye proved he wasn't.

Despite three tours of duty and one heroic mountain-top rescue, Army veteran Jeff Dayton no longer dreams of a career in search-and-rescue. Two years ago, his politically-ambitious sister needed help spiffing up the family image to win a seat in the state senate, so Jeff returned home to Sugar Falls, New Hampshire, to walk the straight-and-narrow and take a job as a small-town cop. Now his tattoos are covered, his rock-n-roll father is under wraps, and Jeff *should be* bored out of his mind... but he never figured on reconnecting with his free-spirited high school sweetheart, Grace McIntyre.

Grace and Jeff have managed to dance around their rocky past since he's come back to Sugar Falls, but when they're both assigned to the town's Harvest Festival planning committee, their attraction sparks to life, igniting both old passions and burning regrets. New revelations help them see each other in a new light, but it takes a small-town festival calamity—complete with a llama petting zoo, a female empowerment "demonstration," and Jeff's rocker dad on the main stage—to force these two to let go of the past and find the strength to forgive. Because half the fun of the game of love is winning... and the other half is deciding to play.

About the Author

Cheri writes kissing books about love and other shenanigans from her charming fixer-upper in rural New Hampshire. She is often distracted by social media, reality television, and a menagerie of cats and dogs. If you find her whizzing down the slopes at the nearby mountain with her family or inadvertently killing perennials in her garden, bring her coffee. She will gratefully provide the conversation and chocolate.

Cheri loves to hear from readers!
E-mail her at cheri@cheriallan.com.
Friend her at facebook.com/cheriallanauthor.
Or, visit her website and blog at www.cheriallan.com.

If you enjoyed this book, please consider telling other readers by writing and sharing a review. (It's ridiculously helpful and makes an author happy!)

Look for the conclusion of the 'Betting on Romance' series with *Deal Me In* because—after all—every woman deserves to get lucky.